Carol Ericson is a bestsel̶l̶e̶r̶ ̶o̶f̶ more than forty books. Sh̶e̶ ̶h̶a̶s̶ true-crime stories, a love o̶f̶ ̶f̶i̶l̶m̶ ̶n̶o̶i̶r̶ ̶a̶n̶d̶ ̶a̶ ̶w̶e̶a̶k̶n̶e̶s̶s̶ for reality TV, all of which fuel her imagination to create her own tales of murder, mayhem and mystery. To find out more about Carol and her current projects, please visit her website at authorcarolericson.com 'where romance flirts with danger.'

A *USA Today* bestselling author of over one hundred novels in twenty languages, **Tara Taylor Quinn** has sold more than seven million copies. Known for her intense emotional fiction, Tara's novels have received critical acclaim in the UK and most recently from Harvard. She is the recipient of the Readers' Choice Award and has appeared often on TV, including *CBS Sunday Morning*. For TTQ offers, news and contests, visit tarataylorquinn.com

Discover more at millsandboon.co.uk

CRIME LAB COLD CASE

CAROL ERICSON

COLTON'S SECRET WEAPON

TARA TAYLOR QUINN

MILLS & BOON

First Published in Great Britain 2025
by Mills & Boon, an imprint of HarperCollins*Publishers* Ltd
1 London Bridge Street, London, SE1 9GF

www.harpercollins.co.uk

HarperCollins*Publishers*
Macken House, 39/40 Mayor Street Upper,
Dublin 1, D01 C9W8, Ireland

Crime Lab Cold Case © 2025 Carol Ericson
Colton's Secret Weapon © 2025 Harlequin Enterprises ULC

Special thanks and acknowledgment are given to Tara Taylor Quinn for her contribution to *The Coltons of Alaska* series.

ISBN: 978-0-263-39724-6

0825

This book contains FSC™ certified paper and other controlled sources to ensure responsible forest management.

For more information visit: www.harpercollins.co.uk/green

Printed and Bound in the UK using 100% Renewable Electricity at CPI Group (UK) Ltd, Croydon, CR0 4YY

CRIME LAB COLD CASE

CAROL ERICSON

Chapter One

Natalie bolted upright, her heart pounding in her chest, her T-shirt soaked with sweat. Her wide eyes darted around the darkened bedroom, searching for an anchor, but the relentless green of the forest closed in on her. Her legs bicycled under the sheets, running from her dream, running from him.

Trapped in the tangled bedcovers, she thrust out her arms, clawing through the branches, scrabbling for an escape. Her hand hit a hard object, knocking it to the ground... the floor, where it shattered.

Her gaze shifted toward a glimmer of light that peeked through a crack in the blinds. Windows. A streetlight. Her bedroom.

Closing her eyes, she fell back against her pillow. The dream had come at her like a sledgehammer, annihilating the fragile facade she'd pieced together for the past fourteen years to cover her trauma.

Maybe it was about time she dismantled that facade and faced her fears.

LATER THAT MORNING, Natalie parked her suitcase in the lobby of the FBI office where she worked in Quantico.

When Francesca, sitting at the front desk, stopped speaking into her headset, Natalie pointed at her bag. "Okay if I leave this here while I run upstairs and collect a few things?"

Francesca nodded. "You're traveling today?"

"Long flight to the West Coast." Natalie wrinkled her nose and patted the carry-on strapped across her body. "I just need to pick up some files before I leave."

"Go ahead. I'll…" Francesca answered a call and pointed at her eyes with two fingers, then aimed those fingers at Natalie's suitcase.

Natalie left her to it and hustled up the stairs to the records office. She dropped into a chair in front of one of the computers and logged in with her smart card. There was no way around leaving a trail. If anyone bothered to check, she could excuse her interest in these two missing-persons cold cases as being related to her assignment with the Marysville forensics lab. They *were* related.

She searched the database for the two cases and didn't even have to review them—she knew them by heart. She printed out both and grabbed two file folders from the supply cabinet.

The door to the office swung open with a bang, and she clutched the folders to her chest and spun around.

Special Agent Jefferson barreled into the room, and Natalie sidled in front of the printer, now spitting out pages of the first report. "Were you looking for me?"

Jefferson ran a hand over his bald head, as if he'd just broken into a sweat instead of her. "Agent Brunetti, didn't we give you a final briefing yesterday?"

Natalie swallowed and held up the folder before plucking a stack of papers from the printer and stuffing them inside. "Just dropped by to pick up a few more cases. I'm ready to go, sir. My flight leaves in a few hours."

Jefferson shook back the sleeve of his expensive navy suit and glanced at his even more expensive watch. "Better get going. Dulles is no picnic in the afternoon."

"I brought my bags to the office. I'm leaving for the airport straight from here." She slid the second set of papers into the other folder and crammed both folders into the bag at her feet. Then she yanked the bag up by the strap and hitched it over her shoulder.

"You're ambitious. I'll give you that, Brunetti." Stepping back, Jefferson narrowed his eyes. "Aren't you from that area? Seattle or something?"

She dipped her chin. "My family lived there for a while."

"It's good you have some familiarity with the location." He leveled a finger at her. "You're not going to be welcome there. You're an outsider, digging into their business, examining what they did wrong, telling them how to improve."

Natalie held up one hand in a stop sign. "I'll be diplomatic. We all want the same thing…to solve those cold cases."

"We do want to solve the cold cases, and the King County Sheriff's Department can get back to that business after we do ours—find out why and how so much evidence in that forensics lab in Marysville got corrupted or lost. The lab supervisor, Michael Wilder, should be happy to help. He wasn't in charge when the evidence got compromised. As far as we can tell, he's been running a tight ship."

"Has he, though?" Natalie tilted her head and readjusted the bag's strap on her shoulder. "The lab had evidence from the Kitsap Killer case just a few months ago and didn't run a basic test for a sex identifier, which would've solved that case earlier."

"That wasn't Wilder's call. The sample was sent to Seattle."

"His lab was responsible for the case."

Holding up a finger, Jefferson said, "Diplomacy, remember?"

"Got it. Now I'd better order my car for the airport, or I'm going to undiplomatically miss my flight." She made a move for the door, and Agent Jefferson shifted his stout frame out of her way.

She waved her hand in the air as she walked down the corridor, feeling his eyes boring into her back. She squared her shoulders and straightened her spine.

She had a feeling Jefferson had objected to sending her out to Seattle to look into the anomalies at the forensics lab in Marysville, but she did good work. Nobody could dispute that—even though she had some personality issues.

But she had a job to do and an ulterior motive for doing it, and she didn't really care what the lab rats in Marysville thought about her...especially Michael Wilder.

MICHAEL PUSHED HIS laptop away and massaged his throbbing temples. He'd been working all week to prep his lab's files for the FBI oversight inspection. He'd cleaned up a mess when he took over as manager for the forensics lab in Marysville, but all his hard work over the past few years hadn't even scratched the surface of the mishandling of evidence that had occurred ten to fifteen years ago.

He smacked his hand on his desk, sending the pens and pencils in the holder into a frenzy. Rubbing the spot on the blotter he'd just hit, he lifted his head and peered at the cubicles outside his office window. Had anyone witnessed his flare of temper?

After the year he'd had, his bosses with the Washington State Patrol had mandated therapy for him. He hated talking to a shrink as much as he hated getting ready for some nosy FBI agent poking around his lab, but he had to admit the anger-management exercises Dr. Russell had been drilling into him seemed to be working. Until now.

As he dug his fists into his eyes, someone knocked on the open door. Michael blinked as he focused on Nicole Meloan's curly mop, as she stuck her head inside his office. Nicole ran Evidence Receiving, and she'd been putting in as many extra hours as he'd been. "Are you still here, Nicole?"

"I could ask you the same thing, but I have a feeling I know why we're both here after hours." Nicole pursed her lips, her usually pleasant face contorting into a frown.

She looked as mad as he felt, but he had to set an example. Michael took a deep breath through his nose and let it out slowly through his lips—another one of his coping mechanisms. "I appreciate your getting everything in order in the evidence room. It won't be so bad. A lot of what Agent Brunetti will be looking at is evidence compromised before our time. That'll keep him too busy to snoop around our current evidence and practices."

Nicole screwed up one side of her mouth. "I hope so. I have a process in my area."

"Don't we all." Michael twirled a finger in the air. "You should get out of here."

"On my way." She tucked a wild lock of hair behind one ear. "D-do you need anything? Are you alright? Is Ivy okay?"

Michael refrained from rolling his eyes. His staff meant well, but damn. Was it ever going to stop? His lips stretched into a smile. "I'm good, Nicole. My sister, Molly, is still here, and Ivy's thrilled. You go ahead. I'll see you bright and early tomorrow when we have our meeting with Agent Brunetti. Don't worry. We'll show him how we get things done around here."

"We sure will." She wiggled her fingers in the air as she turned.

Michael slumped in his chair. Did it look like he wasn't doing okay? He'd worked hard to get back to okay. Did everyone else just see right through him?

Closing his eyes, he massaged the back of his neck for one minute, then packed up his laptop and grabbed his jacket from the hook by the door. He'd already missed dinner and the bedtime rituals, so he might as well make it an even later night.

As he left the lab itself, he made sure the self-locking door closed behind him. The forensics lab had a lobby area with a security guard manning the front desk.

The soles of Michael's shoes plodded across the vinyl flooring that extended from the lab to the lobby, causing Miles to glance up. When he saw Michael, he saluted. "Working late again, chief?"

"Story of my life, Miles." Michael rapped on the desk as he walked by. "You got the good shift again, huh?"

Holding up a textbook, Miles said, "Nice and quiet for studying...but I never said that."

"My lips are sealed, but when you're done with school and I need a nurse, I'm counting on you for special treatment."

"You got it, man."

Michael pushed through the glass doors and inhaled the fresh, pine-scented air. He hadn't left the building all day, and the moist droplets that clung to his face and hair refreshed him. He wouldn't tell Dr. Russell he'd been cooped up all day. Getting plenty of fresh air came under the heading of anger management. Once this Nat Brunetti person did his thing at the lab and left, Michael planned on getting back to normal hours...until the next crisis.

The beep of his remote echoed in the nearly empty parking lot, despite the mist that seemed to mute every other sound. Before sliding behind the wheel of his truck, he placed his bag on the passenger seat.

He dropped onto the driver's seat and cranked the engine. He clutched the steering wheel as the truck idled. He didn't have to do this. These nighttime visits to the scene of the crime didn't help matters. That lonely stretch of trail didn't have any answers for him. The scant evidence the killer left behind had already been bagged and tagged a long time ago—and he hadn't been allowed to see any of it.

Grunting, he threw his truck into gear and stepped on the accelerator. He wanted to get this out of his system before the meeting with the FBI tomorrow. He needed the fresh air, anyway. Dr. Russell would approve...sort of.

Michael wheeled out of the parking lot of the lab and hit the road. The truck practically drove itself toward the forest of the national park. He drove past the turnoff for the camping area and continued into the heart of the woods.

If not aware of the trail head tucked behind some boxwood bushes, it could be missed, especially at night with no cars parked along the road. But he knew all about it.

Michael pulled his truck onto the soft shoulder as much as possible and cut the engine. He slid from the truck and eased the door closed. Flicking on his flashlight, he parted the bushes to reach the trailhead.

To this day, he couldn't figure out what Raine was doing on this trail. She'd never hiked a day in her life. He stepped carefully onto the moist ground, which was scattered with leaves, his work shoes no replacement for a pair of hiking boots.

His flashlight illuminated the trail in front of him, and he followed it to the first bend. A soft moan reached out to him across the still air, and he tripped to a stop as he saw a figure crouched in the darkness.

Adrenaline pumped through his body, and he lunged forward, one hand outstretched. "Raine!"

The person on the ground jumped to her feet, her face a white oval in the darkness, eyes glittering like a deer caught in the beam from his flashlight.

"Stop!" She thrust her arms in front of her, as if to ward him off. "I won't let you kill me like you killed her."

Chapter Two

Natalie squinted into the light, which was blinding her, her mouth dry, her fight-or-flight instinct on high alert. The large figure loomed in front of her, his arm extended as if to grab her.

He couldn't be the man from her past, but his presence in the woods at night, alone, signaled danger. She shoved one hand into a pocket, curling her fingers around the cold metal of her weapon.

Then she spun away like a startled fox, and crashed through the bushes back toward the campsite, where she'd left her car. The man yelled behind her, which made her propel her legs to pump harder through the underbrush, snapping twigs and crushing dry leaves beneath the soles of her sneakers.

If he tried to follow her, she'd shoot first and ask questions later. To hell with her career. She'd vowed never to be a victim again, and she'd kept that promise to herself…and to Katie. When she reached the edge of the empty campsite, she doubled over, wedging her hands on her knees. Her heavy breathing and pulse pounding in her ears blocked the noises from the forest.

When she caught her breath, she straightened up and

tilted her head, her ears attuned to any sounds of footsteps or running. A few birds twittered, scolding her for upsetting their nighttime peace, and some animals rustled in the underbrush, but no human sounds reached her.

On shaky legs, she made it to her rental car in the campsite's parking area. She peeked into the back seat and checked her tires before dropping behind the wheel and drilling the ignition button with her knuckle to start the engine.

The stranger who'd accosted her back on the trail would hear her car if he was still in the area. He'd know she'd gotten away, foiled whatever plans he had for her. He should've been worried about the plans she'd had for *him*.

She removed her Glock from her jacket pocket and placed it on the console. She swung out of the parking lot, her tires spewing gravel, squealing and fishtailing as they hit the asphalt.

Her breathing didn't return to normal until she saw the lights of Marysville ahead. A few sets of headlights crawled along the mostly empty streets where a couple of fast-food joints glowed with a warm welcome for late-night noshers. Her stomach growled, but the last thing she needed was greasy food before turning in. The food on the plane was bad enough.

She pulled into the guest parking lot of the hotel, pocketed her weapon and slid from her rental car. She stomped her feet before entering the lobby, dislodging some dirt and debris from her shoes.

Crossing the lobby to the elevator, she waved at the front-desk clerk.

His eyes widened, as he lifted his hand. "Are you okay, Ms....?"

"Brunetti." She slowed her pace. "I'm fine. Why do you ask?"

"It's just…" His face flushed, as he seemed incapable of completing a sentence. He patted the top of his head.

She reached up to her hair, which had come loose from her ponytail, and felt leaves and a small twig among the strands. As she combed her fingers through her rat's nest, she smiled at the clerk. "Just doing a little exploring in the woods. Might've gotten carried away."

The young man hunched forward on the counter, looked both ways and cupped a hand at the side of his mouth. "You might want to be careful in the woods at night. A woman was murdered there several months ago, and the cops haven't caught the killer."

A shiver ran up her back, despite this being old news to her. "I'll be careful. Thanks for the warning."

She made a beeline for the elevator without turning around and stabbed the button several times. When she got to her room, she studied her reflection in the full-length mirror. She rubbed a smudge of dirt from her cheek and picked a few more twigs from her hair. Then she shrugged out of her dirty jacket, fell on top of the bed and toed off her sneakers, still caked with mud.

Had she almost just shot a man in the woods for shining a flashlight in her face? She'd been somewhere else when he'd come upon her, but an excuse like that wouldn't fly with the local police. It also wouldn't help her find out what happened to Katie fourteen years ago.

And she had every intention of putting that mystery to bed—even if it cost her her job…and her sanity.

THE FOLLOWING MORNING, Michael made it to the lab with a lot less confidence—and a lot less sleep—than he'd intended. He'd been prepared to attack this meeting with Special Agent Brunetti with all systems humming, and he'd barely made it out of the house today with matching socks.

The encounter with the woman in the woods last night had rattled him. The rumors of his guilt were still circulating, and now, someone had caught him returning to the scene of the crime. What had he been thinking going back there? Would she report him to the police? He hadn't done anything wrong, except for thinking she was his wife, Raine, for one crazy minute.

He must've done something, though. Lunged at her. Reached for her. Blinded her with the flashlight. He'd scared her, and she'd taken off like a scared rabbit. All she'd left behind was the scent of roses.

He'd wanted to explain, soothe her fears, but going after her would've made everything worse. He'd taken off soon after he heard her car start up. At least she hadn't called the police on him—not that he knew of, anyway.

Nicole appeared in his office doorway. "Are you ready for the meeting?"

"As ready as I'll ever be. Are you and the other department heads prepared?" He stuffed the file he'd been blindly staring at into his bag and pushed back from his chair.

"I think so. I mean, most of us weren't even at the lab when the...discrepancies occurred. Not sure what the FBI expects from us now." Nicole stepped away from the door as he approached.

"They expect cooperation and for us to open our files to them. I think we can all do that. It's not like any of our jobs are on the line over this corruption." He turned and locked his office door behind him. With the FBI in the house, now was the time to follow security procedures to the letter.

Nicole tucked an errant curl behind her ear as she took the lead to the conference room. "Everyone keeps saying corruption. Maybe it was just mismanagement. Maybe they weren't that good at their jobs."

"Could be." Michael shrugged. "It's not up to us to figure that out. We'll leave it up to Special Agent Brunetti to make the conclusions after his investigation."

The department heads had already gathered in the conference room, and Michael scanned the faces for the FBI agent. He grabbed one of the chairs at the head of the table, his back to the door, and connected his laptop to the projector. As he brought up the presentation on his computer, the mumbling in the room ceased, and he glanced over his shoulder at an attractive woman poised at the door, her brown hair pulled back from her face, accentuating a pair of high cheekbones and intelligent, brownish-gold eyes.

His gaze took in her olive-green suit and smart laptop case slung over one shoulder, and the truth smacked him in the face. Special Agent Nat Brunetti was a female—all woman, as a matter of fact.

He schooled the surprise from his face. He couldn't be accused of sexism. If he hadn't seen the first name of the special agent, he wouldn't have made any assumptions about her gender.

Standing up, he extended his hand. "Special Agent Brunetti, I'm Dr. Michael Wilder. Welcome to our lab. We look forward to assisting you."

Her full lips twitched, but she took his hand in a firm grip. "Good to meet you, Dr. Wilder. Thanks for the welcome, and you can call me Natalie or Nat."

"Please, call me Michael." He flung his arm to the side. "We'll go around the room, and everyone can introduce themselves to you and say a few words about their department. Only Dr. Volosin from the DNA lab is missing, as he's at a conference out of town. His assistant manager, Dr. Rachelle Butler, is representing the lab today."

Most of his staff had friendly words and smiles for Agent Brunetti, but the welcome wagon hit a rut when it came to Lou Gray, who oversaw vehicle evidence. Lou scowled at Natalie from beneath a pair of bushy eyebrows. "Are you Fibbies trying to disrupt our work here? Point the finger for mistakes made years ago?"

Natalie placed her fingertips on the table and leaned forward. "I assure you, Lou, that's not my job. If mistakes were made, and it looks as if they were, we want to make sure they don't happen again—here or at any other forensics lab. This isn't a search-and-destroy mission."

Lou nodded, but he didn't seem entirely convinced. He'd been working at this lab at the time of the anomalies, so he was probably feeling more threatened than most.

The rest of the introductions went more quickly and less prickly, and the meeting went even faster than Michael had anticipated. Natalie—he refused to call her Nat now—didn't ask a lot of questions, but the ones she did come up with were pertinent and precise. She also managed to put everyone at ease and establish an air of camaraderie in the room, notwithstanding Lou's hesitancy.

He could do this. They all could. They were on the same team and wanted the same thing. The FBI had sent one of their best and brightest.

Natalie deferred to Michael to wrap up the meeting, and as his team filed out, they all said a few words to Natalie, asked a few questions. His grumpy staff had sprouted halos in the past hour, all on their best behavior. Even Lou managed a smile on his way out. This audit would be a breeze.

As Natalie chatted with the last of the department heads, Michael closed out his presentation and disconnected his laptop from the projector. When he and Natalie were alone, he tapped on the conference table. "You can set up shop in this room during the audit. Lots of room to spread out with an available projector for presentations, if needed. Or I can get an office, if you prefer."

She took a turn around the room, brushing past him. "Are you sure you don't need this meeting space? I would prefer it, but not if I'm inconveniencing your lab. I'm already putting them out."

He caught a whiff of Natalie's perfume when she swept past him, and he tilted his head. Had Raine worn that scent? Did his sister? He cleared his throat. "Putting them out? After that meeting, I think you have them wrapped around your finger."

"I may have to tiptoe around Lou." Crossing her arms, she wedged her hip against the table. "Otherwise, I had strict orders from my boss to fit in and make this as painless as possible for all of you. We know these anomalies aren't the fault of you or your staff."

"Ah, so it's all an act?" He hitched his bag over his shoulder.

"Does it really matter? I'm here to do a job, and I'll do whatever it takes to get it done properly." Her fingers curled into the silky material of her pale yellow blouse. She'd shrugged off her jacket a few minutes into the meeting, which hadn't taken away from her professionalism at all.

And she was a professional, although he was no longer convinced about her sincerity.

He turned toward the door. "It doesn't matter to me. As long as you don't ruffle feathers while you're here, you'll have the complete cooperation of my staff."

She made a move behind him. "I didn't mean to offend

you. Your department heads are wonderful and seem like a competent group. I know we won't have any issues at all."

As he reached the door, the smell of her perfume wafted over him again, and he inhaled the scent of roses. He stopped short and spun around. "You."

Her eyes widened, and she rose from the desk slowly. "What?"

Reaching behind him, he pushed the door to the conference room closed with a snap. A muscle ticked in his jaw as he saw her eyes dart over his shoulder at the closed door, her frame stiffening.

She asked, "What are you doing?"

"It was you in the woods last night on the Devil's Edge Trail. It was you who accused me of murdering my wife."

Chapter Three

Natalie froze. Her gaze shifted to the window that looked out onto the lab, its blinds firmly drawn. She licked her dry lips as she gave her attention to the man in front of her. His height. His frame. His deep voice. The stranger from the trail.

"I—I…" She covered her mouth with her hand. How could she explain to him that she hadn't been accusing him of murdering his wife? How could she explain that for one frantic minute in a haze from the past, she thought he was the man who'd chased her and Katie through the woods, snatching Katie and taking her away forever?

He folded his arms across his broad chest and settled his back against the door. A vein throbbed in his forehead. "Are you going to tell me that you weren't on the Devil's Edge Trail last night around ten o'clock and that you didn't tell me that you weren't going to let me kill you like I'd killed her?"

Her cheeks flamed with heat. Is that what she'd said? She bit down on her lower lip and tasted blood. Her tongue darted to the droplet and licked it off. "I was there, but I didn't know that was you out on the trail. I couldn't see your face. The light was in my eyes. And I-I don't remember what I said. You frightened me, and I yelled out, but I certainly don't remember saying those words. Why would I? I didn't even know that was you out there, and even if I did, I wouldn't be accusing you of murdering your wife."

He blinked. His black, sooty lashes sweeping over his startling blue eyes for a second. He rubbed his jaw and took a deep breath. The vein stopped pulsing. "You yelled *something* at me."

She gave him a jerky nod. "Yes. Yes, I did. I'm sorry. You startled me. I yelled something, but I don't remember what. I certainly didn't accuse you of murder. Look, I know what happened to your wife and I'm sorry, but I read you were cleared. You wouldn't be running this lab if you hadn't been."

The volcano that seemed to have been building in his body dissipated without an explosion. He ran a hand through his inky black hair and shook his head. "I apologize. I must've misinterpreted what you said. I saw a woman in front of me, afraid, and yeah, that's what I imagined you said."

Natalie's shoulders dropped. He believed her. He'd put it down to his own fevered imagination…instead of hers. "That's ridiculous that we met that way. What are the odds? Talk about your bad first impressions."

His rather stern mouth quirked into a lopsided grin, and her heart skipped a beat. "I've been on edge, and I was an idiot aiming that flashlight in your face in the dark. Anyone would be startled."

"My own actions weren't exactly measured." She flicked her hair off her shoulder. "Why don't we get back on even footing here and go out to lunch? My treat, or at least the FBI's."

"Sounds good. Let me make some meeting notes first, and you can get set up in here." He opened the door and paused. "Contact Felicia, our admin assistant, if you need anything in the way of office supplies or printers or software log-ins. She'll set you up."

"I'll do that. Thanks." She lifted her hand and waved, as much to send him off as to clear the remaining tension from the conference room. Despite her ridiculous explanation and his ready acceptance of it, strands of that tension still vibrated in the air.

She clicked the door closed behind him and sank into a chair at the conference table. She folded her arms on top of the cool mahogany and buried her face in the crook of her elbow. How could she have been so careless? So... emotional?

She didn't want anyone to recognize her as the teen who'd been with Katie Fellows when she'd disappeared—least of all, Michael Wilder, her contact at the lab. He had to believe she was here to audit the historical evidence of his lab, which was bad enough. But she'd just about pulled it off with that meeting—all jovial camaraderie, all "let's work together as a team," all "no blame here."

They'd bought it. Ate it up. Even Wilder. She raised her head from her arms and tightened her ponytail. That name suited him, with his dark good looks and barely suppressed fury.

Had he become furious enough with his wife—almost ex-wife—to off her? He had been cleared, people had seen him elsewhere at the time, but people lied all the time to protect others.

She moved to the end of the table and plopped down in the chair she'd been previously occupying. She flipped open her laptop and opened a new document. Might as well get a list of supplies and items going for Felicia.

Her head snapped up, and she narrowed her eyes at the

blinds covering the conference-room windows. How had Michael identified her as the woman from Devil's Edge Trail? She doubted he could've seen her any clearer than she'd seen him with that beam of light in her face.

She drummed her thumbs against the edge of her keyboard. She'd have to watch herself around him. The man might have a hair-trigger temper, but a keen intelligence added fire to those blue eyes…and she'd felt the heat all the way down to her toes.

MICHAEL FINISHED THE last of his notes on the meeting this morning and drained the dregs of his coffee. He'd cut way back on caffeine and tended to nurse his one cup of coffee until the cold, bitter last sip.

He saved his file with a tap and leaned back in his chair, massaging his temples. Maybe he needed to cut back even more after this morning's embarrassing outburst.

He'd just accused the FBI agent assigned to investigate his lab of calling him a killer—in the woods, in the middle of the night.

Steepling his fingers, he rested his chin on the apex. What the hell was Special Agent Natalie Brunetti doing on Devil's Edge Trail at ten o'clock at night? She'd never clarified her presence there and he'd been too flustered and ready to accept her explanation to ask.

Why didn't she mention the encounter this morning? If it was true that she hadn't recognized him, why wouldn't she talk about a frightening meeting with a strange man in the woods? Unless she didn't want anyone to know she'd been on that trail, presumably her first day in town.

Did the FBI have some ulterior motive in sending Brunetti out here? Were they trying to pin Raine's murder on him, after all? FBI agent arrives in Marysville and goes out to the scene of his wife's homicide her first night in town. What are the odds?

Maybe she did recognize him. Maybe she was expecting him. Maybe she was hoping to rattle him.

His head jerked up at the sharp rap on his door. Natalie's fake smile didn't even reach her whiskey-colored eyes. He pasted one on to rival hers. "Lunchtime already?"

"I know. We must've both been working hard for the time to pass so quickly." She clasped her hands loosely in front of her. "Are you ready for lunch? I can come back later."

"I'm starving." He pushed back from his desk, his chair banging the wall behind him, and Natalie jumped. She had that look again from the woods, as if she was ready to bolt. "Do you mind walking? There are quite a few lunch spots near the lab, and 'd like to stretch my legs."

"That sounds perfect, as long as it doesn't rain."

"Around these parts, that's always a gamble." He reached for the compact umbrella he kept in his desk drawer. "You always need to be prepared for rain."

"Don't I know it. I mean, so I've heard, but that's why it's so lush and green. It's a good trade-off, don't you think?" She stepped away from the door as he grabbed his jacket.

He was thinking a lot of things, none of which he was about to share with her. "I like it, but then I grew up in the desert. Give me another twenty years here, and I might grow to hate it."

Natalie's eyes widened but she nodded, as if she knew exactly what he meant.

As they walked through the lobby, Michael jerked his thumb toward the security guard behind the desk. "Do you want to borrow an umbrella, just in case? Might be better than the two of us trying to squeeze beneath this one."

The thought of sharing an umbrella with him seemed

to seal the deal for her. "That's probably a good idea. I'll have to buy one while I'm out here and remember to keep it with me."

Michael detoured to the security station. "Sam, do you have an umbrella our guest can borrow?"

"Sure do." Sam gestured toward Natalie, while nudging a wire basket filled with multicolored umbrellas with the toe of his shoe. "Take your pick, ma'am."

"Thanks, Sam." Natalie hunched over the selection and picked a dark green compact umbrella. "This one should work."

Michael glanced at the large tote bag as she tucked the umbrella inside. Was this supposed to be a working lunch? He planned to get a little work in, but probably not the kind she intended.

As he ushered her out the front door, he glanced at the gray sky, still too light for rain. "Sandwiches for lunch okay, or do you prefer something more substantial?"

"Sandwiches will work, as long as I can get a Diet Coke." She rubbed her forehead with her knuckles. "I'm just beginning to feel a little jet lag. I think I'm going to need some caffeine to get through the afternoon."

"They have about a million types of soda at this place. You know those self-serve machines with every conceivable choice. Sorry, this is not a high-end joint."

"Do I look like I need high-end?" She tapped her chest, her silk blouse just visible beneath the expensive-looking dark green jacket that matched the umbrella she selected, a Burberry raincoat over top. He'd recognize those buttons anywhere.

He shrugged. "I've been out to DC before. You Fibbies do things a little differently back there."

"I assure you. We do eat sandwiches at places with self-serve soda machines." She tipped her head back and sniffed the air like a native. "What do you think? Rain?"

"I think we're safe today, but all bets are off tonight." He steered her toward the entrance to the Fantastic Café, its blue-and-white awning over the door faded from too many rainstorms.

The restaurant buzzed with activity, and he put his lips close to her ear, that rose scent tickling his nose. "I see a waitress clearing off a table by the window. I'll grab that while you get in line to order."

"Sure." She shuffled to the back of the line, the color on her cheeks heightened.

Had he gotten too close? Too familiar? If he hoped to get any information out of Natalie, he'd have to find the right balance with her. She was skittish and falsely friendly at the same time.

He reached the table just as Wendy scooped up her tip. "Can I stake a claim to this table, Wendy?"

"It's all yours, Michael. Any of the gang with you?" She stood on her tiptoes and surveyed the line at the counter.

"Nope. Someone from another agency doing some work at the lab."

"Drop your coat, and I'll make sure nobody sits here…or steals your coat." She patted his arm. "How's Ivy?"

"She's good, thanks. My sister is still here." Some people in town had eyed him with suspicion this past year, but never Wendy. She had his back.

As Wendy walked away, he shed his coat and placed it on one of the chairs at the table. Then he joined Natalie one place away from the counter.

Pointing at the menu posted behind the registers, he asked, "See anything you like?"

"Do you recommend the tuna melts? I haven't had one of those in a hot minute."

"Everything's good here. I'm having the turkey club and homemade potato chips, which are way better than the fries."

"Sold." When it was Natalie's turn, she placed their order and held up the plastic number the cashier gave her. "You can put this on the table. I'll get our drinks."

"Root beer for me. Just the plain stuff, no vanilla or cherry or whatever else they have." He held out his hand. "Do you want me to take your bag back to the table?"

She clamped her arm against the bag, pinning it to her body. "That's okay. I'm used to lugging it around."

He watched her thread her way through the line still queuing up at the counter before turning toward the table. She had an edginess to her. He knew a lot of cops who displayed wariness. He figured the FBI must be the same.

He set the number on the edge of the table and sat on the chair next to his coat. As he pulled some napkins from the dispenser, Natalie returned with their sodas.

"You weren't kidding about that soda machine. There were flavors I never even heard of." She put his paper cup in front of him, along with a straw. "Plain old root beer."

"And how about you?" He tapped the side of her cup with his straw. "Did you take a walk on the wild side?"

"Plain old Diet Coke for me, but I might do a refill with the Zesty Blood Orange flavor." She hung her bag on the back of the chair next to her and sat in the one across from him.

They spent the next few minutes poking straws into their drinks, grabbing napkins and chatting about the weather, but Michael had no intention of wasting this lunch on small talk. He needed answers from Special Agent Brunetti.

Once their food arrived and he gave her time to eat, he held up a potato chip. "Was I right?"

"So good. Everything is."

"You know—" he wiped his hands on a napkin and balled it up in his fist "—we had that heated moment in the conference room when I accused you of accusing me, but I never did get around to asking you why you were in the forest at night in the first place. On that trail."

Natalie swallowed her bite of food, covered the bottom half of her face with a napkin and then took a sip of her drink, each movement measured and precise.

Michael could see the wheels turning in her head.

She repeated, "On that trail."

"It's called the Devil's Edge Trail. If you keep following it deeper into the woods, it ends with a drop-off into a canyon. Really dangerous at night if you don't know the terrain. Why were you there?" He took a big bite of his sandwich, as if her answer was only of mild interest.

She rolled her eyes to the ceiling and snapped her fingers. "That's why it looked so different from the picture. I was on the wrong trail. I was trying to find the Bright Star Trail."

He decided to employ her delay tactics, and took his time patting his mouth with a napkin and sipping his root beer. "Bright Star is the opposite direction. Why would you be taking that trail...or any trail at that time of night?"

A potato chip snapped in her fingers, and she dropped the pieces onto her plate. "One of the cold cases—Lizzy Johnson. Hikers discovered her body on Bright Star. After flying all day, I got restless and decided to check out one of the scenes."

At night? He left the words unsaid and shrugged. "Yeah, opposite direction from that campsite."

A smile twisted her lips, and her dark eyes drilled into

him. "I guess I could ask you the same thing. What were you doing on Devil's Edge Trail at night?"

Unlike her, he didn't feel any need to lie. She already knew his wife had been murdered and that he had been the prime suspect for a while. He pushed away his plate and folded his arms on the table. "I often go to Devil's Edge at night, although not as often as I used to."

Her nostrils flared, as if she was sensing danger, but she pursued it. "That specific trail? Why do you go there at night?"

"That's where my wife was murdered."

Chapter Four

Natalie couldn't breathe for a second. Michael's wife was murdered in the same place where Katie disappeared? How had she not known this?

Why was he visiting the scene of his wife's murder? If he was innocent? She became aware a few seconds too late that her mouth was hanging open.

"I-I'm sorry. I didn't know that." She cleared her throat. "Do you mind if I ask you why you go there? Isn't it upsetting?"

Spreading his hands, he said, "I'm not sure I can answer that question. I think at the beginning I went hoping to find some overlooked clue."

She could relate to that. She was hoping to find some overlooked clue in Katie's disappearance…fourteen years later. She found herself nodding.

Seemingly encouraged, he continued. "I wanted answers, not just to clear myself, but for my daughter."

Second whammy in one lunch. Michael had a daughter? "I didn't realize you had a daughter. Her mother's death must've been traumatic for her…and you."

"It's been—" he shook his cup, rattling the ice "—confusing for her. She's young. Just turned two. But it's not the first time she's been without her mother."

He pressed his lips together, clamping down on any more confidences.

Their conversation had taken a detour she hadn't expected. Had Michael, or anyone else, made the connection between Raine Wilder's homicide and the disappearance of Katie Fellows fourteen years ago? Not that she actually believed the same person was responsible. Too much time had passed, and the victims had different profiles—one was an older, married woman with a child, and the other was a carefree teenager.

Plenty of wooded trails and dark forests and deep canyons surrounded Marysville, and crime scenes dotted these areas. It wouldn't be unusual for different killers to zero in on the same spots for their evil deeds.

She sniffed and dabbed her nose with a napkin.

"Sorry. I didn't mean to put a damper on lunch. I haven't been great company in a long time." He jabbed a finger at her cup. "Do you want that refill now?"

"Please." She gave the cup to him, her fingertips brushing his hand.

"Zesty Blood Orange?"

She shook her head. "No. Just the regular Diet Coke. I kinda lost my curiosity."

Ten minutes later, they walked into the lobby of the lab. Natalie held up the umbrella. "Didn't open it once."

Sam peeked out the window. "You'd better hold on to it. Once the wind kicks up, it'll bring the rain clouds with it."

Pointing to the ceiling, Michael said, "You can smell it already."

Natalie asked, "Are you sure about the umbrella?"

"That one's been around for a while. If someone comes looking for it, I'll send them your way." Sam winked.

"Thanks, Sam." She followed Michael up the stairs, and they stopped at the top, where their paths diverged.

"I forgot to ask if you got everything you needed today. You good in the conference room?"

"It's perfect. Room to spread out. I'm going to need it, as I'll probably be dragging some boxes up from the evidence room."

"That conference room will afford you plenty of space for that." He turned slightly, running a hand through his hair. "Thanks for lunch and sorry it got so heavy."

"I think that's unavoidable in our line of work and thanks for the recommendation. Lunch was delicious, and I feel like I can fight off this jet lag for another three hours." She shook her cup, still half-filled with soda, at him.

"We're all at your disposal. Let any of us know if there's anything else you need."

She held up her finger. "There is something. I need access to the lab's personnel records—hard copies or online—for the past fifteen years or so. I need to compile a database of the lab employees who were here during those years when the evidence went wonky."

"That's one way of putting it. We don't have those records here, but I can call Seattle for you and request them. I'm guessing they're all online, so it would be a matter of giving you access to the personnel program. I don't even have that. Human Resources for the Washington State Patrol would be responsible. But I know the HR manager. I'll give her a call."

"Thanks, Michael."

He strode off to the left to catch up with one of his lab managers, and Natalie turned right toward the conference room. She stumbled to a stop when she reached the door, which was open a crack. She thought she'd closed it firmly, but then probably not everyone knew she'd set up shop here. Maybe Felicia could print her a temporary sign she could tape to the door.

An empty coat-tree sat in the corner, and Natalie hung up her raincoat and newfound umbrella. She dropped her oversize bag at her feet.

As she flipped open her laptop, she reached for the mouse on her right. Her fingers skimmed across the empty mouse-pad, and she turned her head to find the mouse off the pad and out of reach.

She screwed up her mouth on one side. She preferred using a mouse to the touchpad on the laptop and always brought it and the mousepad with her when she traveled. She'd left it on the mousepad. Had someone been in the conference room to clean up?

Her gaze shifted to the credenza against the wall, and she blew out a breath. Someone had cleared out the pitcher of water, the coffee pot, the tray of muffins and cups that had been there during the meeting. Felicia, or whoever had cleaned up, probably dusted a few crumbs from the table, too, and repositioned her mouse.

As she reached for her mouse, Dr. Butler tapped on the door. "Sorry to interrupt you. Just wanted to tell you that if you want to interview me before Dr. Volosin comes back later in the week, I can provide you with anything you need."

"Thank you. Dr. Volosin isn't returning until the end of the week?"

"That's right. He's helping with a case down in Portland right now." Dr. Butler glanced over her shoulder. "You might find me a little easier to work with than him, anyway."

Raising her eyebrows, Natalie asked, "Another Lou Gray?"

Dr. Butler flicked back her long, beaded braids. "Dr. Volosin has also been at this forensics lab for a long time, like Lou, so they were both here during the cold-case time periods."

"Got it." That's exactly why Natalie wanted to speak to Dr. Volosin instead of the amenable Dr. Butler. The more outwardly contentious the interview, the greater possibility of getting to the truth.

As Dr. Butler turned to leave, she paused in the doorjamb. "I'm glad you're here, Agent Brunetti. Michael knows his stuff, but he can't always be everywhere at once."

Dr. Butler closed the door behind her before Natalie had a chance to ask her what she meant. She made a mental note to definitely talk to Dr. Butler before her boss returned.

Natalie returned her attention to her computer and accessed the file she'd started before lunch. She'd created a database of the cold cases she'd been sent to investigate and had set one up for her own personal investigation, as well.

The shadow database mimicked the official one. She'd investigate the evidence for both sets in the same way, using the same methods. She didn't know why her department had left off those two cases, including Katie's, but it hadn't been her place to suggest which cold cases she'd investigate and which ones she wouldn't. She didn't want to draw attention to her interest in those cases.

The fact that Michael's wife had met her demise in the same location that Katie disappeared had shocked her. She'd made a habit over the years of searching for Devil's Edge Trail in relation to homicides to keep tabs on any other crimes in the vicinity. She'd missed Raine Wilder's murder.

She and Michael had been in that location last night for their own ghoulish reasons. Of course, he'd been willing to reveal his motive, while she'd kept silent. Nobody needed to know her ulterior motives for being here. Nobody needed to know her connection to this area.

She'd studied a few of the faces in the cafe at lunch. Of course, she remembered the restaurant from her teen years here. She'd even remembered the homemade potato chips. Sometimes she and her friends, including Katie, would pop into Fantastic Cafe on their way home from school just to pick up an order of chips. They'd hold the little brown bags with the grease spots leaking through the waxy paper cupped in one hand, while plucking out chips and popping them into their mouths. The best part was licking the salt off her fingers. She'd needed all her concentration at lunch today not to do the same. Lost in the memory, a smile tugged at her lips.

The two other girls in their clique, Bella and Megyn, had avoided her after the incident. Had she reminded them of their shared loss of Katie Or had they just figured she was bad news and toxic company? It had been her idea, after all, to go into the woods at night.

Bella and Megyn hadn't joined them that fateful night after what had happened on their previous outing into the woods. Natalie shivered. That should've been a warning to all of them, but she and Katie liked to push the envelope.

Her email notification pinged and she clicked on the new message. She scanned the email from the Washington State Patrol HR department. Michael must've gotten right on her request for the personnel records. The email included a link to their employee records and a temporary username and password for Natalie.

As she clicked on the link, an alarm sounded in the building. She half rose from her chair and peered through the blinds. People began emerging from offices and work areas, heading toward the stairs.

She jumped up when someone knocked on the conference-room door. Before she had a chance to answer it, Michael poked his head inside the room.

He said, "It's a fire drill. I'm sure it's just a test, but we have monitors, and they'll report any infractions of the rules. That means everyone out of the building."

"I guess I could use a break, anyway." She started to gather her files and reach for her bag, but Michael put his hands up.

"We're meant to leave everything behind. Just grab your coat. Security will be watching the front door while we're out in the parking lot."

Natalie snatched her coat from the tree and followed Michael out the door, joining the stream of people descending the stairs. As she stuffed her arms in her coat, she said, "I hope the rain hasn't started. I also left my umbrella behind."

"We're good for now." They surged through the open front doors with the rest of the lab employees, and Michael put a hand on her back. "We have to gather all the way across the parking lot, even if it's a drill."

"I work for the government, too. This is nothing new to me." They joined the others under some trees, on the other side of the parking lot. "Thanks for contacting HR so quickly. They already sent me a link to the personnel database and a log-in."

"We have strict instructions to play nice with the FBI— any outside agency, really. There are too many cold cases on the books that show a lack of cooperation between agencies. In a lot of instances, that lack of cooperation is why they're cold cases."

Natalie said, "It's good to hear departments like yours are putting emphasis on working with outside agencies. I'll be sending good reports back to my supervisor."

He lifted one eyebrow. "Can the FBI claim the same?"

"What does that mean?" A gust of wind kicked up, bringing the scent of rain with it, and she glanced at the clouds scudding across the sky.

"Come on. The FBI is notorious for playing its cards close to the vest. The Feds expect everyone else to turn over all their stuff, but they keep a lot of information to themselves."

She put a finger to her lips.

It wasn't the FBI that was keeping secrets from Michael, but her secrets wouldn't matter to him—except the one where her friend disappeared from the same trail where his wife was murdered.

A horn blared from the building, and people began shuffling across the parking lot. She cranked her head back and forth, scanning the area. "That's it? The fire engines didn't even show up."

"Could've been a planned exercise. We also have active-shooter drills and shelter in place. I'm not sure what warrants a visit from the fire department, but I don't think the powers that be want to keep us out here any longer." He held out a hand, palm down. "I just felt a big, fat raindrop."

"Perfect timing." Natalie hugged her coat around her frame.

By the time they entered the lobby, the skies had opened, and water spattered the windows. Most people who worked on the second floor avoided the elevator, so Natalie climbed the stairs with the other lab workers, nodding at a few familiar faces from the meeting earlier in the day.

When she reached the conference room, she shoved open the door and removed her coat. After hanging it up, she took her place in front of her laptop and returned to the email with the log-in information for the employee database.

She cross-checked the database with the dates of her cold cases with the missing or corrupted evidence, including Katie and Alma's cases, which were similar Several of the same people had worked all the cases, which didn't surprise her. A few of those employees still held positions at the lab.

The crimes were clustered in a ten-year span. Ten years at the same forensics lab didn't jump out at her as unusual at all. Lab rats had to put in the time to be considered specialists in their fields. Being designated a specialist came with its own perks and bragging rights.

She noticed a few people packing up and leaving the office. She'd decided to keep the blinds open on the windows of the conference room. She didn't want anyone to think she was hiding anything from them…even though she was. Appearances sweetened the path to acceptance.

She saved her files and chugged some tepid water from her glass this morning. She'd accomplished a lot today, not the least of which was getting to know Michael Wilder a little better. He'd opened up to her more than she'd expected.

Part of being transparent was not working alone after hours, so she logged off her computer and started packing. She reached down for the bag at her feet and opened it to slide in the laptop.

When she glanced inside, her heart stopped. Her two files, Katie's and Alma's, were gone. She dragged the bag to the table and spread it open, ridiculously checking corners that couldn't possibly accommodate two file folders.

She slumped in her chair. Someone in this office had stolen those files…and they'd orchestrated a fake fire drill to do it.

Chapter Five

Michael picked up his cell phone and tapped his sister's name. Pathetic that he had to call to tell her he'd be home in time for dinner tonight...for a change.

Molly answered on the first ring. "Don't tell me you're gonna be late again. I actually cooked dinner. You know, like I chopped some onions, peppers and garlic, and turned on the stove and everything."

"Sounds like spaghetti sauce."

"Duh, it's the only thing I know how to cook, except eggs—not that I'm above having eggs for dinner."

Michael smiled into the phone. When his mother had suggested Molly come out and help with Ivy, he thought she was joking. His sister didn't have a single housekeeping bone in her body, but it turned out Mom was right. Ivy didn't need housekeeping or home-cooked meals or orderly toy bins. She needed attention and love and fun, and Molly could supply all those things in spades.

Michael coughed. "I'm calling to let you know I'll be home by six. I was going to take you two out for pizza tonight, but if you went through the trouble of cooking, I'm going to make it worth your while."

"You might wanna keep that pizza on standby, just in case things in the kitchen go south. See you at six."

When Molly ended the call, Michael cupped the phone between his hands and took a deep breath. Maybe it was time to turn the page, move on. Verbally explaining to Natalie today why he was visiting the location of his wife's murder made him realize how fruitless it was…and how ridiculous it all sounded—about as ridiculous as Natalie's explanation about taking the wrong trail.

She presented herself as a thorough professional. No way would she mix up those two trails. So what was she doing on Devil's Edge at night?

A knock at his door refocused his attention, and he glanced up to see the very person from his thoughts, as if he'd conjured her. "Wrapping it up? Hope you had a productive first day."

Leaning against his doorjamb, she said, "I did. Got a lot of work done. That fire drill was kind of annoying and broke my concentration, but I guess these types of systems need to be tested. Was it a test?"

"What?" He slipped his phone into his pocket and logged off his computer.

"The fire drill. Was that a planned test, or…?" She shifted the bag on her shoulder, grasping the strap with both hands.

"I don't have a clue. The alarm sounds, and I head outside." He shrugged. "Do you want to lodge a complaint or something?"

"Maybe."

He glanced up from shoving his laptop into his bag. She'd sounded serious about that, but she had a smile on her face. Or was that a grimace? "If you're serious about it, I suppose you can contact the building manager, but I don't think it would do any good. You know these government agencies. We play by the rules."

"Oh, I understand if it was a test, but not if it was a prank. That's unacceptable."

"A prank?" He blinked. "You mean, like someone pulled the alarm for laughs? I hope you haven't gotten the impression that I foster an environment here that would encourage that."

"No, no. I guess not. Maybe an accident." She smoothed her hair back with one hand. "I guess I'm just annoyed that it broke my concentration, but I did create a couple of databases that are going to be very useful. Did you realize that a few of your current lab employees were around during the time that evidence was…mishandled?"

"Yeah, I'm aware." He pushed back from his desk and stood up. He told Molly he'd be home on time tonight, and he'd stick to that. "I don't have to tell you to tread carefully there. Nobody wants to be grilled like a criminal."

"We just want to find out what happened to the evidence and make some progress toward solving these cold cases. Everyone… The families deserve answers and justice, if possible."

"Justice is always possible." He flicked off his office light, and Natalie stepped back into the hallway. "If you need some recommendations for dinner tonight, I'd be happy to text you a list of places."

"I'm okay. I might just wander around the downtown area and see what looks good. My hotel is walking distance."

"Good idea. You'll find something."

They walked outside together, and Natalie hesitated before she turned in the opposite direction in the parking lot. Should he have invited her to dinner? *Bad idea.* He didn't want to mix business with pleasure. Because he had to admit, he found the company of Special Agent Natalie Brunetti pleasurable.

By the time he got home, the smell of garlic saturated the air, and his mouth watered. He came up behind his sister in the kitchen and tapped her on the shoulder.

She jumped. "You scared me."

"You didn't hear me come through the door?" He skirted her and dipped a spoon into the bubbling tomato sauce, blew the steam away and slurped up the sauce. "Mmm, good."

"Maybe you should get a watchdog to warn me." She jerked her head over her shoulder and clapped a hand over her mouth. "I'm sorry."

He dropped the spoon on the counter. "Is Ivy still napping?"

"She was a little cranky. I put her down for a nap, so she'd be bright-eyed and bushy-tailed for Dada." Molly aimed her knife at a loaf of sourdough bread on a baking sheet. "Can you finish the garlic bread? I already mixed up the garlic butter and sliced the loaf. You just need to spread some butter on both sides."

"This really is a homemade dinner. You could've bought some frozen garlic bread." He stepped to the sink to wash his hands.

"I thought you needed a celebration. The FBI audit started today, right? Your prep should be over. No more long nights at the office."

"It did, and it is." He scooped a knife in the butter and slathered it on the first piece of bread. "The prep is over, but I'm not sure my work is completely done. The agent the FBI sent out seems to be a stickler. I have a feeling she'll be asking us to jump and fetch."

"*She?*" Molly wiggled her eyebrows up and down. "Is she hot?"

Michael wrinkled his nose. "If you like kind-of-uptight, stand-offish, holier-than-thou women. Then she's your type."

"Not my type." Molly threw open a cupboard door, which smacked against another cupboard. "But that might be a nice change for you."

He opened his mouth to protest but snapped it shut as he caught sight of Molly's stormy face. Molly's ex-girlfriend had been just that type, a corporate lawyer who'd supported Molly as she struggled with selling her art. Molly's haphazard lifestyle had finally lost its charm for Gracie, and they broke up last year.

Holding up the baking sheet with the bread, he asked, "Ready for the oven?"

"About fifteen minutes should do it. I already preheated the oven." She took two plates and two bowls from the cupboard. "You wanna set the table?"

He slid the baking sheet onto the rack in the hot oven, and as he took the dishes from her, he heard Ivy cry out from her room. His hands tightened on the plates. Ever since her mother left, Ivy had been having a tough time waking up from sleep.

Michael almost believed that Ivy dreamed of her mother and at the moment she woke up, she remembered all over again that she was gone. Not that Raine had been a great mom to Ivy. Raine had abandoned her daughter once before when she left him. Then she'd decided in the middle of the divorce proceedings that she really did want her daughter. That's why he'd been suspect number one in her murder—they'd been fighting over custody of Ivy. No way in hell would he have allowed Ivy to live with Raine. Now, he didn't have to worry about that.

As Molly turned, Michael put a hand on her arm. "If you don't mind setting the table. I'll get her."

"Of course. She'll be thrilled to see you home for dinner. I'm just the babysitter."

Michael rubbed his sister's back. "You are her rock right now...and I think she has more fun with you."

"Nobody has ever called me a rock before—not even you." She sniffed and dabbed her nose with the back of her hand.

He moved his hand up to her neck and gave it a quick squeeze. "Mom told me you were the one to watch Ivy, so she has faith in you, as well."

That first cry was Ivy's last, so Michael poked his head in her darkened room to make sure she was awake. She still slept in a crib. He'd been ready to move her to a toddler bed, had bought the bed and everything, but when Raine was murdered, and Ivy's development seemed to regress, he'd shoved the box into the garage. Same with the little plastic potty. He'd rather deal with diapers and have a successful run at potty training later than force the issue now.

He drank in the sight of his little girl standing in her crib, holding on to the railing and swaying back and forth to a mumbled tune. His heart swelled as he watched her, and ached a little, too. How would he be able to give her everything she needed? How would he be able to raise a daughter on his own? It had been hard enough trying to raise her with a mother like Raine—who'd been absent, self-obsessed, narcissistic—but at least Raine had loved Ivy, and Ivy had loved her mother.

A sigh escaped his lips, and Ivy jerked toward him. A smile engulfed her pixie face, and she raised her arms as she said in a singsong voice, "Daddy."

She'd recently switched back to calling him *Daddy*. *Dada* had been her baby name for him, and she'd regressed to that months ago, but now *daddy* was creeping back into her vocabulary. That had to be a good sign, right? Hell, he'd take it.

He strode across the room and scooped her up, his hands firmly under her arms. He swung her around until her legs flew in the air behind her and her giggles turned into shrieks of laughter. Then he cuddled her close and kissed her forehead, both cheeks, her chin and her nose.

She patted his face and then repeated the same set of kisses, landing the final one on his nose. Their ritual melted his heart every time.

"Auntie Molly cooked us dinner. Spaghetti." He tucked her under one arm and spun around to the changing table, which she'd outgrown. "But first we'll get another pull-up."

Her lower lip jutted forward. "Unnywear, Daddy."

"That's right, underwear." Molly had started reintroducing the language for potty training, and Ivy seemed receptive. Maybe they'd have another go at it.

Once he had a clean pull-up in place for Ivy, he took her to the sink, and she climbed up on her step stool to wash her hands.

As she rubbed her hands under the faucet, he asked, "What happened when you went on the swings at the park today? What kinds of pictures did you paint with Auntie Molly?"

Raine's disappearance had caused Ivy's language to lag, and Michael had consulted with his psychologist friend for tips on getting her to talk more. He tried to follow through on her suggestion to ask Ivy specific questions instead of open-ended ones. It seemed to work.

Tonight, Ivy babbled on about flying on the swing, and how Molly had twisted up the chains and then released them until Ivy spun around. She was still talking about the dog she painted when they made it to the kitchen just as Molly was taking the bread out of the oven.

When Molly closed the oven door, Michael set Ivy on the floor. "Get your plate and cup from Auntie Molly and set your place at the table."

Ivy scampered to Molly and took the brightly colored plastic, partitioned plate and cup from her. On the way to the table, she poked at a picture hanging on the fridge. "Here, Daddy. Peaches."

Michael's chest tightened as he glanced at the scribbles on the page, barely making out a pair of ears, a nose and four stick legs. Ivy still remembered the dog. "That's a nice picture of Peaches, sweetie."

"Mama take Peaches." Ivy put her plate and cup on the table and climbed into her booster seat.

Their dog, Peaches, had disappeared at the same time as Raine. The babysitter had reported that Raine had taken Peaches for a walk after visiting Ivy. He'd thought it cruel of her at the time to take the dog and not return her, but when those hikers discovered Raine's body on the trail, Peaches was nowhere to be found. He hadn't seen the dog since.

Raine had been visiting Ivy that night while he'd been at work. Natasha, Ivy's babysitter, had called him as soon as Raine showed up at the house, but he didn't think there would be any harm in Raine visiting her daughter for a few hours. When she left with Peaches, Raine had told Natasha she was taking her for a walk and would bring her back before Michael got home.

Natasha had freaked out when Raine turned up dead. He never did figure out if Natasha believed him guilty of the murder, but she couldn't work in the house anymore. So Ivy lost her mother, her babysitter and the dog all at once.

Ivy had talked about the dog when she first disappeared but hadn't mentioned Peaches in a while. He didn't know if this was a good sign or more regression. He'd ask the shrink.

Ivy's chatter at the dinner table *was* a good sign, though. And as Molly and Ivy had a spaghetti-slurping contest, he laughed so hard, things almost felt normal again.

When he tried to help his sister clean up the kitchen, she shooed him away to play with Ivy. By the time he'd colored some mermaids, built a castle with blocks, knocked it down and read a few stories, Ivy was ready for bed.

After tucking her in, he tapped on Molly's door. "You still awake?"

"C'mon in. I'm just sprucing up my profile for this dating app."

He groaned as he pushed open the door. "I don't get how you think those dating sites work."

"They work." She glanced up from her phone. "You should try it sometime. I'll help you with a profile, if you think you have any pictures where you're not scowling or brooding."

"No, thanks." Did Natalie think he was a scowler and a brooder. "Hey, I just wanted to thank you again for looking after Ivy. She seems…better."

"She's a little firecracker. I think she's starting to spark again."

He chewed his bottom lip. "Did she draw a picture of Peaches on her own, or did you ask her to do it?"

She shook her head, and her black bangs fell over her eyes. "I didn't mention Peaches, and when she drew the dog, she didn't tell me that was Peaches. In the kitchen was the first time I heard the name from her."

"Maybe it just occurred to her when she saw the picture on the fridge. Just triggered the memory of the dog."

"They never found the dog's leash or collar or…anything?" Molly tossed her phone on the bed and folded her hands in her lap.

"You mean like a dead dog in the woods?" He scratched his chin. He didn't want to tell his sister the number of times he'd been out on that trail calling Peaches's name. "Nothing, not even bones that might be hers."

Hunching her shoulders, she said, "Peaches could be a witness to murder."

"It's not like she could point out anyone in a lineup."

"Dogs are pretty smart." She tapped her head with her finger.

"You didn't know Peaches." He smacked the doorjamb. "I'm going to do some work. Thanks for dinner and cleaning up—and be careful on those dating apps."

She waved her hand in the air. "Bye. Mind your own business."

He closed her door and sank into his recliner, pulling his computer onto his lap. He flipped it open and drummed his thumbs on the keyboard. He didn't know exactly what he was looking for, or even how to start, but something in Natalie Brunetti's demeanor had set off alarm bells in his brain…and he didn't mean the way his body reacted to her. That feeling originated somewhere far south of his brain.

Sometimes her smile looked fake to him. It could just come down to an auditor trying to get on the right side of the objects of her investigation. Then there was the whole bizarre reaction to the fire drill this afternoon. She'd been digging for something. And what the hell had she been doing on Devil's Edge Trail last night? It's not a trail any stranger would just stumble on.

He launched a search engine and entered her name. A few Natalie Brunettis popped up, and he clicked on their social-media profiles. None was for his Natalie, but then, FBI agents didn't typically splash their lives in pictures across the internet.

He dug a little deeper. Maybe she'd received some awards from the FBI. Maybe she'd been a featured speaker at a conference. Maybe she'd worked a big case that had grabbed headlines. His Natalie remained elusive.

Michael balanced the laptop on the arm of the chair and went back into the kitchen. Molly had left a plate in the sink, so he rinsed off the breadcrumbs and opened the dishwasher. He rolled his eyes at the helter-skelter way his sister had loaded the dishwasher, but he'd never complain about her haphazard ways again. She was helping him bring his little girl back.

Molly had left a half a bottle of red wine on the counter, its cork shoved in the top. He'd asked his sister to avoid drinking alcohol around Ivy, and he followed his own rule. His daughter had seen enough of that in her short life.

But with Ivy sound asleep, Molly must've grabbed the opportunity to down a couple of glasses, by the looks of it, and he'd do the same. He snagged a wineglass from the top shelf of the cupboard and poured himself a healthy quantity.

He took a sip and carried the glass back to the living room. Seated once again with the computer in his lap, he ran over that first meeting with Natalie in the woods. Had he really imagined she'd said those words to him? Called him a killer?

Something about that trail had drawn Natalie into the woods after dark, and he knew it hadn't been one of the cold cases. He'd reviewed those cases before she arrived. Devil's Edge hadn't been host to one of those crime scenes… just his wife's.

His fingers hovered over the keyboard, and then he attacked it, searching for Devil's Edge Trail in Marysville, Washington. He physically shuddered when the first item on the page recounted Raine's murder. He skimmed past several more articles about her homicide until he reached the more benign links discussing the route of the trail and its flora and fauna.

Frustrated, he took a big gulp of wine. Was Natalie out here trying to tie him to his wife's murder? Why would she waste her time? He'd been officially cleared.

He set down his glass on the end table beside him and rubbed his hands together. He flexed his fingers and came at his search from a slightly different angle. This time he searched for crimes and Devil's Edge Trail.

Of course, he had to slog through Raine's murder again, but on the next screen he stopped scrolling at a headline that mentioned the disappearance of a teen from Devil's Edge fourteen years earlier. Unlike Raine, this girl's body had never been found, and law enforcement at the time had eventually dismissed the girl, Katie Fellows, as a runaway, despite her friend's insistence that the two of them had been stalked through the woods by a strange man.

He did another search, for Katie Fellows this time, and clicked on an article that had been published at the time of her disappearance. As he read through the article, which contained a few pictures of the girls, he stumbled across the name of Katie's friend—Nat Cooper. *Nat.*

He tapped one of the photos of the accompanying article and enlarged it with his fingers, zeroing in on the face of Nat Cooper, her curly dark hair and big eyes giving him a jolt.

He fell back against the recliner and took another slug of wine. Nat Brunetti hadn't taken a wrong turn last night. She hadn't been trying to catch him in the act.

Nat Brunetti had her own reasons for returning to Marysville…and she didn't want anyone to know about them.

Chapter Six

Dishes clattered next to her, as the busboy cleared the table and collected the tip. Natalie hunched over her coffee and massaged her temple. The nightmare had hit her hard last night, and her head throbbed this morning. Instead of settling her terrors from fourteen years ago, her proximity to the scene of the crime had stoked them.

And now, someone had her files. There must be cameras in the building. If she asked security to identify the person sneaking into the conference room during the fire drill, she'd have her suspect, but then she'd have to explain what those files contained...and why.

The security guard may not know or care about the files, but it would get back to Michael, and he seemed to run that lab like a tight ship.

If Special Agent Jefferson found out about her ties to this area and her private investigation into a cold case, he'd yank her off this detail in a hot minute. She had no doubt that if Michael found out, he'd report her to Jefferson. Michael seemed cooperative, but who wanted the FBI snooping around their forensics lab?

She might've even suspected Michael of stealing the files to get some dirt on her, and he *had* insisted that she leave everything behind in the conference room, but she'd been with him for the duration of the fire drill and evacuation. He could've had someone do his dirty work while he distracted her. His employees seemed loyal to him. They'd even supported him while suspicion hung over his head about his wife's homicide.

He'd had an alibi for the time his wife disappeared, too. At work. Didn't mean he hadn't hired someone for that evil deed, either. The man had just enough smoldering anger beneath his dark, moody good looks to be a suspect.

The time on her cell phone told her to get to the lab for another day of scanning through databases, files and case records amid sidelong suspicious glances—hers not theirs. She'd be holding her breath all day waiting for that shoe to drop, that phone call from Jefferson ordering her back to DC. Because why else would anyone be interested in her files?

How did this person even know she'd had anything to hide? Hadn't she come across as professional? Cooperative? One of the boys? Someone must've seen beneath her demeanor to the desperation and deceit. The only person she'd spent any time with had been Michael.

It started with Michael.

Fifteen minutes later, she pulled into the parking lot of the lab, checked in with security with her temporary badge and jogged upstairs to her temporary office. Then she made a beeline for Michael's office.

She hovered at his open doorway before he noticed her, and she studied his face in profile as he worked at his computer. He wore his black hair swept back from his high forehead, and his hawkish nose gave him the appearance of a Roman emperor. Oh, yeah. He could command just about anyone to do anything…except his wife. And her.

It took her a second to realize he'd detected her presence and was now staring back at her, those blue eyes startlingly out of place for a Roman emperor.

Feeling her cheeks warm, she tilted up her chin. "Good morning. I wanted to ask if I can have a key to the conference room. It does have a lock on it, but I'd like a way to get back inside. I'll be bringing the case files up there today and would be nice to secure them."

He swung around to face her and steepled his fingers. "Of course. I'll get one of the guards to check on that for you. Did you have a nice evening? Jet leg?"

"Not too much. I had some food delivered to my hotel from a diner down the street and got to bed early." She left out the part where her nightmare kept her tossing and turning all night. She must have bags under her eyes if he thought she had jet lag. Should've applied more concealer.

"I'm sorry. I should've invited you to dinner on your first night...second night here. In fact, everyone in the lab should take a turn having you over for a meal." He'd crossed his arms over his chest and was watching her from half-lidded eyes in a position that hardly screamed out a welcome. Was he being sarcastic?

Her lips tightened for a second. "You're joking, right? Nobody needs to wine and dine me."

"This is Marysville, not the Beltway. We don't wine and dine. I'm talking about a home-cooked meal. My sister actually made dinner last night, and it wasn't half bad."

"Y-your sister? You live with your sister?" She didn't expect that.

"She's been out here for the past six months, helping me with my daughter." With his arms still crossed, his fingers bunched into the sleeves of his button-down shirt, crumpling the fabric.

"You're lucky to have her help."

He gave a brief nod. "Do you have any children, Nat?"

His narrowed eyes and hard jaw turned the question into an interrogation, and she shifted from one foot to the other. And when had he started calling her *Nat*? She'd gone by her old nickname until about four years ago, but she did still sign most of her FBI correspondence as *Nat*, as she'd joined the Bureau as Nat Brunetti—and it made people think she was a man. Michael must've seen that correspondence.

She cleared her throat. "No, I don't have any children."

"Married?"

"No." Was he asking for personal reasons?

"Ever been married?"

"As a matter of fact, I *was* married, briefly." She turned away from his office. She didn't feel like telling Michael about her short, disastrous marriage that she ruined. "I can talk to security about the key to the conference room, if that's okay with you."

"Absolutely." He swung back to his computer screen. "If there's a problem, have them call me."

She went back downstairs and approached Sam behind the security desk. "Hi, Sam. I'm Natalie Brunetti. I borrowed the umbrella yesterday."

"Sure, I remember. You can keep it."

"Thanks, but I came down here to ask if you have a key to the conference room upstairs. It's my temporary office while I'm here, and I'd be more comfortable if I could lock it." She jerked her thumb toward the ceiling, as if Sam needed a reminder which direction was upstairs.

"I have that key. Let me check in the back. You can wait here."

"Thanks." She leaned against the counter while trying to frame her next request to Sam in her mind.

A few minutes later, he emerged from the office behind the counter jingling a set of keys on a silver ring. "I have two keys for that office. I'll keep one here, and you can take the other."

"Perfect."

He removed one key from the ring and dropped it into her open palm. "Just make sure you return it when you leave."

"I'll put it on my list." She dipped her hand into her purse to retrieve the key fob for her rental car. As she slid the conference room key onto the ring, she asked, "Does the lab have a lot of fire drills like the one yesterday?"

"Not like the one yesterday." He swung the ring containing the other key around his finger.

She caught her breath. "No? How was yesterday's different?"

"It wasn't planned. Took us all by surprise. I thought for a minute there might've been a real fire."

"So it was a…prank?"

The key stopped twirling, and his dark eyebrows jumped toward his bald pate. "A prank? I hope not. I think it may have been a mistake or the alarm got tripped somehow. The fire department is having a look today."

"I suppose you wouldn't bother to check camera footage to see who pulled the alarm." She held her breath, trying to crack a smile.

He shrugged. "That wouldn't do us much good, anyway. Some alarms are out of the camera view. It's not worth investigating."

For you, maybe.

"I hope it's the last one. It interrupted my work." She held up the keychain with her new silver key dangling from it. "Thanks again for the key."

"Yes, ma'am."

She gave him a broad smile before going upstairs. Ugh, he'd called her *ma'am*. He must think her an uptight witch, and she was still none the wiser about who pulled that alarm yesterday to gain access to her so-called office.

When she got back to the conference room, she closed the door behind her and parked herself in front of her laptop. She supposed she could log in to the FBI database and print those two files out again, sending them to a printer in this office, but there would be a trail, and she didn't want to push her luck.

She might not get the opportunity, anyway. If someone at this lab stole those files to get her pulled from this audit, she'd probably hear about it soon enough. And then she'd have to come clean to Jefferson, and even his supervisor, that she was Nat Cooper and investigating a cold case that had involved her.

She worked under a cloud of apprehension for another hour before shooting off an email to Nicole Meloan in the evidence room. It was time to take possession of the case files. Most of these cases were cold, but not all. She wasn't here to solve old cases…except her own. She was here to comb through evidence that had been mishandled over the years, mishandled to the point that it had come to the FBI's attention.

A few seconds after she hit Send on that email, the conference room phone rang. "Natalie Brunetti."

"Hi, Natalie. This is Nicole. Just thought it would be easier to call then send emails back and forth. I believe we have all the case files here that the FBI ordered a few months ago for your audit. If you're missing anything, let me know. I'll contact the King County Sheriff's Department, as they handled all those cases and sent over the material."

"You're an angel. I'll be right down. Do I need a dolly?"

"Everything's already loaded for you on a dolly. You don't even need to come down to fetch it. Jacob, our part-time facilities guy, is here, so I'll have him deliver the boxes to the conference room."

Natalie had already jumped up from her chair in anticipation of collecting the files. At Nicole's words, she dropped back into her seat, disappointment washing over her. She'd wanted to get those files herself. She'd wanted to take a look at the evidence room.

She took a deep breath. She still had the right and the obligation to inspect the evidence-receiving room. "That's perfect. Thank you so much, Nicole. I suppose I can arrange a look at the evidence room another time."

Silence.

"Of course. Give me a heads-up, and I'll show you around."

"I'll give you a heads-up, but I'd rather have a look on my own. I'll be doing the same in all the labs, and I apologize in advance for the intrusion, but that's kind of what an audit is all about."

"I know that. Don't worry about it. Just let me know when you're ready for your inspection."

"Thanks, Nicole." *Another pissed-off customer.*

If she couldn't go down to the evidence room to grab the files herself, she could at least help Jacob unload. She opened the conference-room door and kicked the doorstop into place.

Five minutes later, a young man with long, dirty blond hair came out of the elevator pushing a dolly stacked with boxes in front of him. Natalie almost salivated at the sight of the boxes. This is what she did, or had been doing for the past few years—inspecting case evidence, looking for anomalies, contradictions, gaps.

By the time Jacob reached the conference room, Natalie was rubbing her hands together. "You must be Jacob. I'm Natalie."

He gave her a shy grin and pointed to the open door. "In here?"

"Yes, please." She swept a hand along one wall. "I made some room here."

Jacob parked the dolly and hoisted the first box from the top of the stack, making it look easy, but she knew how heavy those boxes could be. "Do you want them in any particular order?"

Rapping on the second box with her knuckles, she said, "By case number. See the number in the upper-right corner of the box? Try to match those up. That'll order them by date, too."

"Should be easy. That's how Ms. Meloan had me load them. She's kinda particular."

Natalie released a sigh. She couldn't imagine anything going awry under Nicole's watchful eye…or Michael's, for that matter. This lab had put its troubles behind it when Michael took over, although Dr. Butler seemed to have some doubts.

"It's a good thing she is kinda particular. Makes our job easier." She reached for the next box.

"No, no. Leave it." Jacob settled the first box on the floor and walked back to the dolly. "I'll get all of them. Some are pretty heavy, and you don't know which ones until you try to lift them."

"Okay, I'll do the directing."

As Jacob lifted each box, she checked the case number on the side and pointed to a spot on the floor. The kid didn't even break a sweat.

When he finished, he rested his arm on the dolly's handle. "Better you than me."

"I know." She placed her hands on her hips and surveyed the stack of boxes. "Looks like a lot of work."

"Yeah, it's not just that." He scratched the blond stubble on his chin. "It's what's in those boxes—pictures and stuff with blood on it. Yeah, no thanks."

Tilting her head, she said, "You *are* working in a forensics lab. You'll have to get used to it if you're going to pursue a career in forensic science."

"Me?" He thumped his skinny chest. "I'm no science major. I'm majoring in journalism. I'll write about these cases, not investigate them."

"If you're on a crime beat, the blood and gore may be unavoidable."

"I plan to avoid crime. Politics, a different kind of blood and gore."

Natalie perched on the edge of the table. "So this is just a part-time job for you, not an internship."

"Yeah, my dad got me the job. He's a deputy with King County." He pointed at the boxes. "You'll probably see his name in there a few times—Reynolds."

Natalie's stomach dropped. Reynolds was the name of one of the cops that worked on Katie's case. In fact, Reynolds interviewed her when she'd reported what happened in the woods. She nodded. "I'll keep an eye out for it. Thanks, Jacob."

She held the door as he wheeled the dolly back into the hallway, and then closed it behind him with a decisive click. It was bound to happen. Marysville was a small town. People might know her. They wouldn't know her married name, Brunetti, but there were probably a few of her high-school classmates that might remember her. She twirled a curl around her finger. Maybe she should wear her hair straightened, and dye it blond, although she doubted Deputy Reynolds would recognize her. Maybe nobody would. She'd been a Goth girl with heavy, black eyeliner, burgundy lipstick, wearing all black and chunky Doc Martens. Her parents saved her from dying her hair black at the time by refusing to allow it.

Huffing out a breath, she snapped on a pair of gloves and grabbed a notepad and a pen. Crouching in front of the first box, she tipped off the lid. She lifted several items from the box and spread them out on the conference-room table. Then she pulled up a chair and got to work.

In this first case, the cops had found the murder weapon, a knife, but something had gone wrong during the chain of custody and any fingerprints from the knife had become inaccessible and unreadable. Understanding where the chain of custody had broken down posed difficulties. There were failures at many levels.

She took notes on the case and created a file for fingerprints. If all the cases featured print errors, this might go faster, but she had a feeling the cops would've picked up on that immediately.

The next case she grabbed was one of the closed cases, but only because the Creekside Killer, a notorious serial killer in the area, had confessed to it. The investigation still contained anomalies in the finger printing.

So many law-enforcement agencies had lined up to speak to Avery Plank, the Creekside Killer, hopeful they could close out some of their cold cases with a confession from him. Plank did not disappoint. Unfortunately for those cops, a psychopathic serial killer couldn't be trusted. Who knew?

Plank had confessed to one homicide near Kitsap College, and as it had turned out, he was lying. The real killer was only too happy to have Plank take the credit for his crime. There could be more of those right here.

Natalie gave an involuntary shiver. Had the Creekside Killer been stalking her and Katie that night? They'd already been scaring themselves silly in the woods with witchcraft rituals designed to speak to the dead. Turned out they had more to fear from the living than the dead.

The next box contained some bagged evidence—probably the bloody clothes Jacob Reynolds had mentioned earlier. She opened the paper bag carefully and pinched a plastic bag between two fingers, pulling it out. It swung from her fingers as she held it up to the light.

A woman's top, but no blood. It must've contained DNA or hair on it. She dropped the plastic bag onto the table and reached into the other one again. She felt like a kid reaching into a candy jar for a treat, except that the treats were ghastly reminders of long-ago murders.

Natalie plucked up another plastic baggie, a smaller one, and cupped it in her hand. The shiny object inside caught the overhead light and she gasped.

She recognized the necklace…because it was hers.

Chapter Seven

Michael knocked on the conference-room door. After a few seconds of silence, he peered through the slats of the blinds pulled down over the window. He expected to see Natalie on the phone or hunched over her computer. Instead, she was staring at an object in her hand, her mouth slightly agape.

He tapped on the window, and she jerked her head up, her eyes round in her pale face. "C-come in. It's open."

Poking his head in the door, he said, "I hope I'm not disturbing you. I'm heading out for lunch and wanted to invite you to make up for sending you out on your own for dinner last night."

"I could use a break." As she dropped a plastic bag into an evidence bag, she tipped her head toward the boxes lining one wall. "Got started on the deep dive today."

His glance swept the desk in front of her. The paper evidence bag sat on one side of her laptop and a grubby box sat on the other side, its lid on the floor.

She folded down the top of the evidence bag and dropped it into the box. Bending over, she swept up the lid and secured it on the box. Then she jumped to her feet, and began peeling off her blue gloves. "In fact, I'm starving. Same place as yesterday?"

"If you like, but there's a Thai place you should try before you leave." His gaze darted toward the box containing that paper evidence bag. What had she been looking at, and why had she been so anxious to put it away before he entered the room? Maybe she'd just found some incriminating evidence that implicated the lab and everyone in it.

While she fussed with her coat and purse, he cocked his head to the side and memorized the case number and name—Conchas. No regulation that said the investigated couldn't investigate the investigator.

She spun around, her stylish raincoat hanging over one arm, and her expensive leather purse strapped across her body. "Walking or driving?"

"This one's a drive but not too far."

They stepped out of the conference room, and she turned to lock it up with a silver key hanging from a keychain. She tucked the keychain in a side pocket of her purse and patted it. "Got the key from Sam this morning."

"That's a good idea, especially since you now have the case files and boxes from the sheriff's department in here."

"I was going to pick them up, but Nicole had already arranged for Jacob to deliver them to my office, and they were all in order by date already. I never did get a look at the evidence-receiving room, though."

"Nicole is organized. I'm sure she'd be happy to give you a tour of evidence receiving anytime you like."

"Yeah, that's the thing." They stopped in the lobby, where Natalie hung her coat around her shoulders. "She offered, but I told her I didn't want a tour. I'd like to go through the evidence room on my own. I'll be recording my visit, too. I may have ruffled Nicole's feathers."

"Don't worry about it." He held the front door open for her. "She'll get over it. They all will."

"Are you trying to tell me everyone is not as gung ho about this audit as they're pretending to be?"

"Think about it. Someone comes into your place of work where you spend countless hours trying to get it right, and that person pokes into everything and tries to prove you've been doing it all wrong."

"Except it's not you, is it? Your predecessors made the mistakes. The FBI is just trying to find out how it happened so that it doesn't happen again here or at any lab."

"We know that, but it doesn't stop anyone from feeling accused and maybe unsettled." When they reached his car, he opened the door for her and went around to the driver's side.

When he slid behind the wheel, she said, "I hope I'm not making anyone feel that way."

"It's not you. It's the situation. You've impressed everyone, so if Nicole has a problem, let me know."

"She absolutely did not have a problem. Just a little hesitation, which I totally understand."

"Good. Feel free to access any areas of the lab you need." As he started the car and pulled onto the street, Michael glanced at Natalie, who was staring out the window. He hoped that his openness would encourage her to be upfront with him. He'd checked out the online case file for the Katie Fellows disappearance. The case was still open, but the lead detective had put it down as a runaway.

What did the case mean to Natalie today? If it were just a coincidence, she should've mentioned that she'd gone to high school in the area and had been with a friend when that friend had gone missing. Why the secrecy?

The FBI conducts a background investigation when hiring agents, so surely, this must've come up in her past. Of course, departments didn't look at a background every time they gave an assignment, so the Bureau probably hadn't realized her connection to this area when they gave her the gig…and she hadn't told them.

He pointed to the restaurant's red-and-gold awning as he rolled past, looking for a parking spot on the street. "That's it."

Once settled at the table, menus in hand, water in front of them, Michael asked, "Did you get a lot of work done this morning? It looked like you were engrossed when I peeked in the window."

"Engrossed?" She took a gulp of her water. "Yeah, there's a lot to cover. Going over fingerprint mishaps now."

The waitress saved Natalie from any more of Michael's questions, but he had no intention of giving up on this. If she wouldn't tell him what had her so spooked about that file, he'd needle her until she did. Didn't he have a right to know who was going through his lab with a fine-tooth comb and why?

Michael took a sip of his spicy Thai iced tea and stirred the ice with his straw, clinking it against the glass. "I saw you had the Conchas file. Cold case murder of a young woman about fifteen years ago, right?"

"Thirteen. It was thirteen years ago." She picked up her glass quickly, and some of her drink sloshed over the rim, creating a puddle on the table. She dabbed it with a napkin.

"I guess law enforcement couldn't get Avery Plank to confess to that one." He caught a bead of moisture trailing down the side of his glass. "Although I'm sure they tried."

"Plank turned out to be a boon to departments with unsolved murders everywhere, didn't he?" Natalie planted her elbows on the table. "Do you think he was toying with law enforcement by confessing to crimes he didn't commit and leaving them to wonder about crimes he *did* commit?"

Like Katie Fellows?

"Instead of trying to take credit for everything, he was messing with their heads and playing coy about murders he was responsible for." He rubbed his knuckles across his chin. "I wouldn't put it past him. He likes to play games. In the end, detectives have to look at the proof and not just take his word for it. They got burned before with that cold case out at Kitsap College."

"Terrible, how that turned out." Natalie moved her water and tea glasses out of the way, as the waitress delivered their plates of spicy basil fried rice.

"Does the Conchas case have fingerprint issues."

She glanced up from her plate. "I—I really didn't get a chance to delve into the case, yet. After lunch."

Michael gave up for now, and changed the subject to why she chose the FBI and how she liked it so far, although he was sure her choice of career had something to do with what she experienced as a teen. She managed to skirt her motivation for joining the Bureau with trite statements about looking for justice and doing the right thing. Who didn't want those things? Not everyone went in for law enforcement.

As they finished up their lunch, Nicole came sailing into the restaurant and waved when she saw them.

Michael murmured under his breath, "Here's your chance to set Nicole straight on when you're going to invade her space."

Natalie tossed her napkin at him and waved back at Nicole.

Nicole made a detour to their table on her way to the counter. "Work lunch?"

"Always. If I'd known you were coming here, I would've invited you along." Then he wouldn't have had the chance to grill Natalie about the Conchas case—not that he'd gotten anything useful from her.

"Last-minute decision." She waved a piece of paper in the air. "I took a lunch order at the office. Not everyone can afford the luxury of a sit-down lunch outside the office."

"Ouch." Michael clapped a hand over his heart.

"I'm joking. You deserve a break, boss. You know, he's had a rough six months." Nicole patted his shoulder. "But you shouldn't be the only one tasked with making sure our visitor is wined and dined. Natalie, I'd like to invite you to my house for dinner tonight—nothing special, probably takeout and a bottle of wine."

"I don't want to put you out, Nicole. I really don't need wining and dining. I think Michael felt guilty last night, but you all are going to get sick of me at work. You don't need to see me in your homes, too, intruding on your family time."

Nicole's eyes shimmered as she held up one hand. "Well, I live alone, so I'd welcome the company. We don't even have to talk shop."

"If you're certain. I'd love to come over." She pushed away her almost-empty plate. "Just no Chinese."

"I'll surprise you, unless there's something you can't stand." Nicole pressed her fingers to her lips.

"Surprise me." Natalie plucked the check from the edge of the table. "And you're right about it being a luxury to eat out. I need to get back to work."

"We all do." Michael made a grab for the check, but Natalie snatched it away.

"If the staff is going to be inviting me home for dinner, the FBI can cover a few lunches."

They left Nicole waiting for her take-out order, and Michael drove back to the lab. As they parted at the stairs, Natalie turned toward him. "I think Nicole invited me to make up for her hesitancy when I told her I needed to have a look at the evidence-receiving room."

"I think you just caught her off guard earlier. She's not much of a cook, though, so I don't know that you're getting such a good deal."

"You're a terrible boss." She flicked her hair and sauntered back to her office.

She didn't know the half of it.

As soon as he pulled up the chair to his desk and logged in to his computer, he did a search for the Conchas case. He skimmed through the awful details.

Sierra Conchas was a young woman, barely twenty years old, who disappeared on her way home from her part-time job at a gas station's convenience store. Cops discovered her broken-down vehicle on the road that followed the woods. Signs of a scuffle outside the car but no other tire tracks in the vicinity.

Hikers found the body in a ravine days later, partially clothed, bloody, a torn T-shirt beside her. Stab wounds. Michael brought up photos of the crime-scene evidence, which had been processed through this lab at the time.

No knife was found. No DNA. Fiber from a black beanie or maybe a ski mask, but no DNA on that, either. The blood on Sierra's shirt belonged to her. No rape, so no bodily fluids left behind. Torn fingernails, as if she put up a fight, but no skin cells beneath the nails.

Damn. Not much to go on here. Also, not the MO of the Creekside Killer, who usually strangled his victims and left them beside water. But what had Natalie found so interesting about this case? It didn't mimic Katie's case in any way, except for the setting. And to face facts, in the Pacific Northwest, most murder victims were dumped in the forests, down ravines, off trails, in the water.

He clicked through the pictures on his computer and stopped at a baggie containing jewelry, or at least a silver pendant shaped in a circle with four knots through it.

He skipped back and forth through the file to discover that the pendant was around Sierra's neck, but Sierra's mother had never seen it before. He checked the date of Sierra's death against the date of Katie's disappearance. Sierra had been murdered about seven months after Katie disappeared.

Could the pendant have belonged to Katie? Had her parents reported any jewelry along with the clothing she was wearing when she went missing? Maybe Natalie thought the two cases were linked?

He jumped when his phone rang. He'd become as absorbed in the case as Natalie had been.

When he glanced as his display, knots tightened in his gut. A call from Detective Ibarra, the detective investigating his wife's murder, usually brought bad news.

He closed his eyes as he answered. "Wilder here."

"Michael, it's Gil Ibarra. I know you probably don't want to hear from me."

"That's not true, Vince. I want to hear from you when you call to tell me you've found the person who killed Raine. Is that what you're calling about?"

"Afraid not, Michael." Ibarra took a breath, and Michael's shoulders tensed. "Full toxicology report finally came back on Raine's autopsy."

"Thought you had that already."

"Preliminary toxicology. She had a lot of substances in her system."

"I'm aware." Michael's hand gripped the arm of his chair. "What did you find this time around?"

"You said your wife, er, Raine had been on antidepressants, and we found a bottle of Lexapro in her purse—ten-milligram pills. Do you know if this was her regular dosage?"

Michael pinched the bridge of his nose. "I'm not sure what she took or how much. She hid that from me, so it wouldn't come up in the custody dispute."

"The medical examiner said the usual dose is ten milligrams, and those are the pills Raine had." Ibarra made a clicking noise with his tongue. "But Raine had a lot more than that in her system, probably five times that amount."

"What are you saying? Raine took an overdose of her meds? You can't be suggesting suicide now, right? She was strangled with some cloth tie, or did you get that wrong, too?" Michael's heart was raging in his chest.

"She was strangled, so not suicide, but if someone was able to ply her with an overdose of meds before taking her out to that trail before killing her, we're not looking at a stranger here. No, Raine's killer knew her. Knew her very well."

Chapter Eight

After studying the pendant more closely, Natalie was convinced it was hers. How did her pendant from that night wind up around Sierra Conchas's neck when she was murdered? The person who killed Katie must be the same person who killed Sierra. This had to be the answer.

She'd given her witch's knot to Katie that night to ward off the evil spirits of the forest, or some such nonsense. Katie had been wearing that pendant when she'd disappeared. It had never been found. Natalie hadn't even thought about it at the time, and Katie's mother wouldn't have reported it as something her daughter was wearing because she didn't know Natalie had given it to Katie.

Natalie's family had moved out of the area before she graduated from high school and before Sierra's murder. Had Sierra's mother told the police that the necklace didn't belong to her daughter. Did the police ever wonder where it had come from?

She knew being close to the scene of Katie's disappearance and looking at other cases would yield clues. This had to be the first of many. Katie's killer had taken her pendant and left it on another victim. Was that part of his

MO? Had he taken items from his victims and given them to other victims?

Sierra's killer had stabbed her, but the police never found any blood in the area where Katie went missing. They hadn't found Katie at all. Where had he taken her? What had he done with her?

When they took off running in opposite directions that night, she'd run toward the campsite area, even though it had been empty. But Katie had foolishly barreled toward Devil's Edge itself, toward the steep drop-off into the craggy rocks. The sheriff's department had searched the rocks, though. They hadn't found anything.

Natalie thought she'd heard a car's engine that night. Had their pursuer somehow gotten Katie in his car and taken her away. Her breathing became shallow, and her fingertips started going numb.

She made her mind a blank and took deep breaths through her nose from her stomach until they filled her chest, and then released them slowly through her mouth. She'd never taken meds for her anxiety, but a behavioral therapist had taught her to control the onset of a panic attack through modulated breathing. It worked most of the time.

Water helped, too. She pushed away from the desk and locked the conference room door behind her. A lot of good that lock had done her this morning with Michael spying on her through the blinds, but she'd look even more suspicious if she closed those blinds and tried to keep everyone out. She decided to stop at his office on the way down to the breakroom just to keep the lines of communication open.

She slowed down when she approached his closed office door. He usually left his door wide open for his staff. She tapped on it.

He answered in a muffled voice. "Come in."

She eased open the door, and he turned from where he was standing at the window, hands in his pockets. His stormy scowl softened a tad when he saw her.

"Do you need something?"

She didn't, but he obviously did. She stepped into his office and shut the door behind her. "Are you okay?"

"Yeah. What do you mean?" He tried a smile, but it didn't work.

She placed a hand flat on her belly. "It's not your daughter. Is Ivy alright?"

"Ivy's fine." He ran a hand through his black hair. "I guess it's no use pretending to an FBI agent. Have a seat."

She perched on the edge of a chair facing his desk, as he took his own advice and dropped to his swivel chair.

"I just had some interesting news about my wife's murder." He swiped a hand across his mouth. "They found elevated levels of her antidepressant medication in her system."

"What does that mean? Not suicide?"

"No, she was definitely strangled with a garrote, but the detective is implying that someone drugged her first. Someone she knew. How could a stranger be able to slip her meds?"

Natalie bit her bottom lip. "What about at a bar? Had she been drinking at a bar? Someone could've slipped her something and then followed her to the woods."

He folded his hands in front of him, his knuckles white. "The day Raine died she'd been at my house to visit Ivy. The babysitter, Natasha, had been home at the time. When Raine left my house, she took our dog for a walk. Natasha wasn't sure, so she called me at work, and I told her it was fine. Raine never returned."

"And the dog?" Natalie tucked her hands beneath her thighs as her knees bounced up and down.

"Peaches never returned. Never found her leash. The point is—" he flattened his hands on his desk, his thumbs touching "—Raine didn't go anywhere else. She took the dog out for a walk and ended up dead on Devil's Edge Trail. I always figured this was a crime of opportunity. She'd gone to the trail for a walk, someone with bad intentions saw her and killed her. Now…"

"Now it looks like someone drugged her first." She scooted her chair closer to his desk and leaned forward. "Maybe Raine took the meds herself. Maybe she did plan to kill herself."

"And someone finished the job for her? Far-fetched."

She drummed her fingers on his desk. "She could've had a pact with someone. What if she wanted to die, anyway, and figured she'd stick it to you on her way out by having someone kill her to pin the blame on you."

"Whoa." He held up his hands and crossed one finger over the other. "Raine had issues, but even she wouldn't go that far. You've got quite the imagination."

"It's happened before, hasn't it? I've seen a few cases where people didn't want their families to lose out on their life-insurance money with a suicide, so they staged a murder." She swallowed. "Why did the cops zero in on you at first? Was it just because you were the husband, and the two of you were in a custody dispute?"

"That and I didn't have a clear alibi. After Natasha told me Raine had taken Peaches for a walk, I didn't feel like running into Raine when I got home. So, I left work a little early and drove to the woods to take a walk." He spread his hands. "Cell-phone service is spotty on some of those trails and the cops couldn't track my phone continuously."

"Definitely a problem." She twirled a finger in the air. "Does this new information put you back on their radar?"

"It doesn't help, but a witness saw me coming out of the woods and getting into my car at about the same time as Raine's murder. Saved me."

"Thank God for that. I guess Peaches couldn't do much to protect Raine?"

He put his hands about eighteen inches apart. "She was… is a little pug."

The knock on the door startled Natalie, and she pulled back from Michael's desk. His tale had her spellbound.

He leaned back in his chair. "Come in."

Nicole popped her head inside the office. "Oh, good, both of you. I have the food all ordered for delivery, Natalie. Seven o'clock? I'll email you my address."

"Seven is fine, Nicole. Thanks."

Nicole nodded her curly head. "And, Michael, is it okay if I take off a little early today? I don't have any more deliveries scheduled, and I have a few errands to run."

"I hope not on my account." Natalie stood and smoothed her slacks.

"That's all taken care of. I have a few personal matters."

"Sure, no problem." Michael stood and stretched, and Natalie had the satisfaction of noticing that the storm clouds had cleared from his brow.

Nicole remained in the doorway, so Natalie scooted past her. "I'll look out for your email, Nicole. Thanks, again."

For the rest of the afternoon, Raine's homicide occupied Natalie's thoughts, replacing the mystery of how the pendant got around Sierra's neck.

Michael had been through the ringer these past six months. She'd remembered how the cops had suspected Katie's boyfriend, Zane, in her disappearance, and it had wreaked havoc on his life. He had to transfer schools—just like she'd moved away.

She couldn't imagine what Michael had been through, trying to take care of his daughter while law enforcement had him as their prime suspect in his wife's murder.

By the time she wrapped up her work, quiet had settled on the second floor of the lab, and she had an hour to go back to her hotel, change, pick up a bottle of wine and make it to Nicole's place.

She glanced down the hallway toward Michael's office, the door firmly closed. He hadn't stopped by on his way out to say good night. Had their discussion this afternoon unsettled him?

When she'd seen him in distress at his window, she couldn't help herself. Something about a strong man showing his vulnerable side plucked all her strings. Her ex-husband had never shown her that side. Joe didn't have any demons at all, and at first, she thought that's what she needed in a partner. She'd had enough for the two of them, and Joe just couldn't handle her tormented side.

She didn't blame him. They'd parted as friends. But she didn't want a friend as a spouse. She wanted someone who understood her down to the core. Someone with his own darkness to wrestle. Michael had that darkness.

Snorting, she locked her office door. She'd just met a potential wife killer, and she had him pegged as her next spouse.

An hour later, bottle of pinot noir on the seat beside her, Natalie followed her GPS to Nicole's house. She did a double take when she passed the turnoff to the campsite near the Devil's Edge Trail.

The location of Nicole's home defied Natalie's expectations of a modern condo in the heart of the city. Older homes tended to hug the forest line, unless some developer had come in to rip down an outdated house and put up an expensive cabin with glass walls and wooden decks with hot tubs.

As she pulled in front of Nicole's house, she saw immediately that no fancy developer had touched this place. Nicole had definitely made some improvements to the original, though. A neat, wooden fence ringed the property. Tidy flower boxes adorned the windows, and fall blooms added a touch of color to the freshly painted clapboard front. Beige pavers with flecks of gold created a path to the front door beneath the towering pines. Even the trees had been trimmed into manageable accents to the house without overpowering it.

Nicole opened the door before Natalie had a chance to knock. "Welcome. I'm glad you found me out here."

"What a lovely spot." Natalie held up the bottle of wine. "Hope you like red."

"Perfect." Nicole studied the label. "It'll go with the Indian food I ordered. I hope you like Indian. I didn't get anything too spicy."

"The spicier the better."

Crooking her finger, Nicole said, "Follow me to the kitchen. You can pour while I plate the food. The delivery guy just left."

Natalie squeezed into the tiny kitchen behind Nicole. Her host apparently hadn't had the time, inclination or money to spruce up the inside of her place as much as the outside. The old-fashioned kitchen sported the original linoleum in a faded gold, with the dated appliances lined up against both walls.

At least the food smelled good. The pungent aroma of curry hung in the air, with an undercurrent of warm, sweet cardamom, which gave the kitchen a homey feel.

Nicole reached into a cupboard and took out two wine-glasses. "Fill 'em up."

As Nicole dumped the food from the cartons into glass serving dishes, Natalie filled each small wineglass almost to the halfway point. She had to drive back to her hotel, and she and her rental car were still getting acquainted.

"Should I put the raita in a dish?" Nicole held up a small Styrofoam cup of the yogurt accompaniment to their spicy food.

"Nah. Let's live dangerously and spoon it out from the take-out container. In fact, we could've done that with all the food and saved you some dishes."

Nicole shook her head. "It's bad enough that I can't cook. I can at least present someone else's food in a pleasing way."

They carried the dishes to the table, where Nicole had set two places with World Market-type colorful plates and placemats. They sat across from each other and toasted.

As they clinked glasses, Nicole said, "To a speedy and satisfactory audit."

"I will definitely drink to that—and to one that doesn't ruffle anyone's feathers."

"About that—" Nicole gave her a glance from the corner of her eye "—you just took me by surprise today when you suggested you wanted a look at the evidence-receiving room on your own. It's my little fiefdom, and I'm protective over it. Of course, I understand why you need to survey it, just like you will for any other area of the lab."

"And I understand your balking at the idea. I'd be the same if someone wanted to look over my files."

Nicole raised her glass again. "So here's to understanding all around."

As they ate and chatted about the lab, Natalie's gaze wandered over Nicole's shoulder to take in the pictures on the sideboard. She zeroed in on one with Nicole in a wedding dress, standing next to a smiling man in a tux. She had to hand it to Nicole. Natalie didn't have any of her ex on display, wedding or otherwise.

Nicole twisted her head around. "Ah, my wedding picture."

"Sorry. Didn't mean to be nosy." Natalie ripped off a corner from the naan on her plate. "I'm divorced, too, but I boxed up my wedding photos."

Nicole swirled her wine before taking a sip. "I'm not divorced. I'm a widow."

Natalie put down her fork and reached across the table to squeeze Nicole's hand. "I'm so sorry. What happened?"

"Suicide."

Natalie squeezed harder. "That's awful, Nicole."

Nicole sniffed and dabbed her nose with a napkin. "He was a cop. Had a lot of those typical cop problems."

Feeling as if she'd been intrusive enough for one night, Natalie went back to her food and waited for Nicole to continue...if she wanted.

She didn't.

"Anyway, do you like the food? I love Indian, and we have just two restaurants in town. This is the better one. The other is more for quick takeout."

"It's delicious. Great choice."

After that bombshell, conversation lagged between the two of them. Questions swarmed in Natalie's head, but Nicole had shut down any more discussion about her deceased husband.

She helped Nicole in the kitchen and when they finished, Nicole offered her coffee and homemade cookies.

"It's funny. I don't like to cook, but I do like to bake, and I think I'm pretty good at it."

"I'm sure you are, but honestly, I can't eat another bite of food. Maybe you should bring the cookies to the lab tomorrow and put them out in the lunchroom."

"I've done that before." Nicole placed two plastic containers in a bag and pushed it toward Natalie. "If you're not going to have a cookie, take some of this leftover food. You can bring it for lunch tomorrow...unless you and Michael are going to make your lunch dates a habit."

Natalie glanced sharply at Nicole, but she'd ducked into the fridge to put away more food.

Is that what the lab thought? She and Michael were on lunch dates while the rest of them worried about what she'd find in the audit that might implicate them in wrongdoing?

She picked up the bag. "That is a good idea. Then I can use more of my per diem for dinner instead of spending it on *work* lunches."

Nicole held up the bottle of wine. "You're going to leave this with me to finish off, aren't you?"

"Better you than me. I gotta drive home." Natalie made a move toward the door. "Thanks again, Nicole. Dinner was great, but I hope everyone is not taking Michael seriously and inviting the orphan home for dinner."

"They probably will." Nicole winked. "We all want to stay on your good side."

"This doesn't hurt." Natalie raised the plastic bag of food and swung it in the air with her fingertips.

Nicole walked her out to her car, and Natalie lifted her face to the mist that had rolled in and clung to the needles of the pines. "Smells good out here."

"It's lovely. That's why I won't move."

"Don't blame you." Why should Nicole move? Had this been her husband's house? Had he ended his life here?

Natalie climbed into the car and placed the bag of food on the passenger side. "Thanks again."

She reversed out of Nicole's driveway and bumped along the access road back to the highway. Her fingers scrabbled around the steering wheel and column to find the high beams. She didn't want to hit any unsuspecting animals crossing the road. She worried less about people and cars, as not too many populated the highway or forest at this time of night—not typically.

When she hit the first curve in the road, she had to pump the brakes. She should be used to hopping into rental cars and adapting given the amount of traveling she did for the Bureau, but every car seemed different.

A red light blinked on the dashboard, and she dropped her gaze to read it. Some weird-shaped icon blinked back at her. How the hell was she supposed to read that? Couldn't be the gas. The rental company had given her a car with a full tank, and she'd hardly driven anywhere since she arrived in Marysville.

The road dipped and the car picked up speed. At least it was still running. She tapped the brakes, and the car seemed to whoosh forward. At the bottom of the incline, the road snaked to the right. Heading into the turn faster than she wanted, Natalie eased on the brakes. The sponginess of the pressure made her press harder. The car shuddered but didn't slow down.

She gripped the steering wheel and turned it slightly to navigate the turn, while pressing the brake pedal. She made the turn okay, but the brakes were not responding to her pressure.

Another incline and the car went faster. She didn't want to stomp on the brakes and put the car into a tailspin. She tried tapping, but all she got for her efforts was a clunking sound from the engine.

As she came out of the descent, another curve awaited her. This time she applied full pressure to the brakes, but her foot almost when through the floorboard. As she fumbled for the button for the emergency brake, an animal darted into the road, its gleaming eyes pinned to the oncoming car.

With the brake pedal on the floor and one of her knuckles jabbing the emergency brake, she jerked the wheel to avoid the animal, and the car lurched once and then started zooming down a hill, straight for a tree.

Chapter Nine

Michael kicked a tree stump with the toe of his hiking boot. He'd promised himself not to come out to this spot again. What good did it do? There were no answers among the trees. No clues left on the trail.

If the cops got wind of his nighttime sojourns out here, he'd probably make it back to the top of their suspect list. The news from Detective Ibarra today had tilted him off course, had crushed his theory about a stranger homicide.

Raine had been hanging out with some shady characters, but murder? The cops had already checked out her boyfriend, and he'd had a better alibi than Michael.

Maybe Natalie had been right. Maybe Nicole took additional pills on her own. She'd had no self-restraint. She could've reasoned the more pills the better. Some stranger had taken advantage of her disorientation and killed her. There had been no sexual assault, but her clothes had been ripped. She could've fought off her attacker's sexual battery, and he'd struck back and killed her.

He tipped back his head and yelled to the night sky, "Enough!"

As he turned to leave, a sickening thud echoed through

the forest. That was no animal, unless some critter had recently acquired a metal coat.

He jogged down the path, back to his car, which was parked just off the road. He got in and turned on his headlights, then eased forward, sweeping the empty highway. Looking in his rearview mirror, he saw smoke rising from the forest on the other side of the road.

He threw his car in Reverse and backed up several feet. Then he pulled it off the road and jumped out. His nostrils twitched at the smell of burning rubber. As he got closer to the smoke, his flashlight picked out skid marks on the road leading into the forest.

He ran into the underbrush, where a car had just forged a new trail. He followed the broken branches and flattened bushes into the woods, and his adrenaline ramped up even more when he spotted a car, its front end crumped against a tree.

Smoke continued to pour from the damaged vehicle, and the smell of gasoline permeated the air. He scrambled toward the car and peered through the driver's-side window.

His heart slammed against his chest as Natalie pushed against the airbag, which was pinning her to the seat. He tried the door handle, but the lock was engaged, so he pounded on the window.

Natalie turned her pale face toward him, and several seconds later, he heard the locks click. He yanked open the door and pulled her out of the car and away from the airbag.

He shouted, even though she was right next to him. "We need to get away from the car. I smell gasoline."

"My purse." She reached around him.

"I'll get it. Move." He ducked into the car and grabbed her purse and a plastic bag from the floor of the front seat.

He stumbled back and joined her several feet away. "Let's

keep moving toward the road and call nine-one-one. Are you alright? Can you walk?"

"I'm okay." She dabbed her fingers against an abrasion on her forehead.

When she swayed on her feet, he swept her up in his arms and carried her back toward the highway. As he tromped down the trail her car had blazed through earlier, her head fell on his shoulder, the curly tendrils of her hair tickling his chin. The ease with which she fit into his arms, and against his chest, didn't surprise him. He knew, from at least this afternoon, when she'd sensed his turmoil, that wrapping his arms around her would feel right.

A crackling noise behind them spurred on Michael's footsteps, and he didn't put Natalie down until he reached the asphalt.

Clinging to his shirt, she craned her head around. "The car's on fire. Oh, my God. You saved my life. I couldn't get out from under that airbag. I thought those things were supposed to protect you."

"I think you were just panicked. You would've eventually shimmied out from under it." He slipped his phone from the pocket of his jeans and tapped it for 911.

"Don't downplay your heroism. If you hadn't come along when you did, I'd probably still be stuck in that car, which is now burning." She tilted her head back and sniffed the smoky air.

Michael spoke into the phone to the 911 operator, asking for an ambulance.

When he hung up, Natalie said, "I don't need an ambulance. I'm okay." She examined her forearms. "I think I'm going to have some bruises from the airbag, but I never lost consciousness, and I'm not injured anywhere."

"Never hurts to get checked out, and you should be grateful the airbag went off, or you might have gone through the windshield into that tree. What the hell happened, anyway? I assume you were coming home from Nicole's place."

"I was." Hugging her purse to her chest, she said, "The brakes on the car went out. It was kind of a perfect storm. I was coming out of an incline and a curve, and an animal ran into the road. I swerved to avoid it and crashed through the tree line. Luckily, I met bushes and underbrush first before running into the first tree. I think the car was slowing down by the time I hit the tree."

"Brake failure? On a new rental car?"

"I'm no mechanic." She held up her arms, which were already turning blue with bruising. "But I pressed on the brake pedal, eased it on and finally stomped on it. At first it was spongy; then my foot went right to the floor. Maybe it's a good thing I saw that animal and pulled off in a relatively safe area. It's almost as if..."

"As if what?" He plucked a leaf from her hair, his fingers lingering over a soft curl.

"This place, this area." She bit her bottom lip. "It's where..."

"It's near Devil's Edge." Where Raine was murdered and where Natalie's friend had disappeared. Did she think the animal was infused with Katie's spirit and had saved her?

He opened his mouth, but an approaching siren saved him from spilling the beans and admitting he'd spied on her. Too bad she couldn't trust him enough to tell him. He'd trusted her, and it had been a while since he felt he could trust a woman.

"Is that why you were nearby?" She placed a hand on his arm. "You went back?"

"I did, but I'm done with it. I'll let the sheriff's department do its job and find the answers that are evading me."

"I'm glad you did go back. If you hadn't, I might not be standing here beside you."

He put an arm around her and pulled her close, whispering in her hair. "And that would've been a tragedy."

He didn't get to gauge her response, and maybe she didn't even hear him because the emergency vehicles pulled up, bathing both of them in red lights, assaulting their ears with wailing sirens.

An hour later, the fire department had doused the car fire, and an EMT had checked out Natalie's vitals and injuries. She'd escaped what could've been a disaster pretty much unscathed.

He'd had to explain to the cops that he'd been out for a drive, but nobody seemed to think it odd that his drive had taken him past the exact spot where his wife had been murdered.

Natalie had called the rental-car company to give them the bad news, but they'd been more concerned about the faulty brakes and a possible lawsuit than blaming Natalie. They'd promised her a new car delivered to her hotel first thing in the morning.

As the emergency personnel wrapped up and cleaned up, Michael took Natalie's arm. "You're sure you're okay?"

"Clean bill of health from the EMTs." She dusted her hands together and winced.

"You're gonna have some wicked bruises on your arms and probably your chest from that airbag."

She pressed her fingers against her chest. "Feeling it already."

"I'm driving you back to your hotel. Do you have everything?"

She held up her purse and the plastic bag. "Got my purse and my leftover Indian food from Nicole's dinner."

"You mean I risked my life going back into that car for Indian food?"

She winked. "You obviously have never had the biriyani from Taj Majal."

"I have, actually. It all makes sense now." He yelled over to a deputy. "Are you done with us? I'm taking Natalie to her hotel."

The deputy waved back. "All good."

Michael opened the door for her and had to help her inside as she stiffly lowered herself to the passenger seat.

When he got behind the wheel, he said, "I hope you have some ibuprofen in your room. You're going to be sore."

"Going to be?" She rubbed the back of her neck. "It's already kicking in."

When they arrived at her hotel, Michael hurried to the passenger side of the car to help her out. He snagged her purse and bag of food from the floor, then wrapped his arm around her waist.

As they walked through the sliding doors of her hotel, she extricated herself from his hold. "Thanks, Michael. I can manage from here."

"No way. I'm not getting on the bad side of the FBI by neglecting one of its agents. I'll see you up to your room and get you settled."

"You don't have to get home?"

"Ivy was sleeping when I left, and my sister was ensconced in her bedroom perusing dating apps on her phone."

Natalie wrinkled her nose. "Brave girl."

She didn't object again when he placed a hand on the small of her back and steered her toward the elevators.

As they rode up to the third floor, he said, "I don't expect to see you at the lab tomorrow. You should rest."

"That's the last thing I need to do. If I lie down for hours, my body is going to be too stiff to move. The EMT told me to stretch and move around." She tapped her keycard against her door, and it clicked open.

"Don't know how much stretching and moving around you're going to do at the office." He bent over and opened the tiny fridge. "You want the food in here or did your near-death experience make you hungry?"

"You can put it away, but if there's a small bottle of wine in the minibar, I'll take it."

He studied the minibar. "You want something stronger?"

"No, but help yourself."

He plucked a bottle of chardonnay from the fridge and twisted off the cap. "Only the finest. Is there a glass somewhere?"

She bounced on the edge of the bed and held out her hand, wiggling her fingers. "I'll drink it from the bottle."

He handed it to her, and she placed it to her lips and took a long draw from the bottle.

Cupping the bottle between her hands, she said, "That was scary. I've never even been in a fender bender before."

"I'm glad you're okay. Maybe I was meant to be in that spot one last time." He sat in the desk chair and hunched forward, his elbows on his knees. "How was your dinner with Nicole, otherwise?"

"It was good. Food was delicious, and the conversation flowed. She knows a lot about crime." She picked at the label on the bottle. "Nicole told me about her husband. That's awful. Did it happen here or before she moved here?"

"It happened here, just around the time I started at the lab. I'm surprised she told you about it. She usually doesn't talk about her husband's death."

"I'm afraid I asked her. I saw the wedding picture and assumed she was divorced like me. Just used it as a conversation starter, and it had the opposite effect." She took another sip from the bottle. "She said he was a cop. Was it a depression thing?"

"He was a cop. You met Jacob Reynolds, our part-time gofer. His dad, Max Reynolds, was Frank Meloan's partner."

Natalie put a hand to her throat. "Wow, so many connections in this town."

Michael knew exactly what Natalie was thinking, as Max Reynolds had been assigned to Katie Fellows's case. It felt weird having this deception between them. Why wouldn't she just tell him? Did she think he'd report her to the FBI to get her off the audit and out of their hair? She must.

He stood suddenly and stretched. "I'd better get going. Nobody is going to raise their eyebrows if you don't show up."

"I'll be fine." She scooted off the edge of the bed and put the bottle of wine on the credenza. "If my neck gets any worse, I'll take a trip to urgent care. Otherwise, the rental-car company is delivering another car tomorrow morning, and I'll be there."

"You could sue the company, you know. How do brakes fail on a newish rental car?"

"I suppose they'll have to do some accident investigation first to make sure I wasn't at fault. You know the cops had me blow into a breathalyzer. Good thing I had just one glass of wine at Nicole's and plenty of food."

As she stood in front of him, he could smell the fruity aroma from the chardonnay on her breath. Good thing she hadn't downed a mini bottle before getting in the car.

He placed one hand on her shoulder. "I'm just glad it wasn't more serious for you."

Her eyelashes fluttered, and her lips parted.

Was he going to do this? How could he with secrets between them? He'd had enough deception from Raine throughout their marriage. He'd vowed never to accept that poison again…no matter how tempting the fruit.

Obviously not hampered by the same principles, Natalie decided for him. She stood on her tiptoes and leaned forward to place a gentle kiss on his lips. "Th-that's a thank-you. Or maybe that's the wine."

He'd stood frozen just in case it was the wine, but she kissed him again, pressing her soft lips against his and winding one arm around his neck.

He kissed her back this time but kept his hands to himself, sort of a half-assed compromise between his ethics and his lust.

She drew back, placing her hands on his chest. "Bad idea? I thought, you know, we had something."

"We *could* have something." He shoved his hands in his pockets. "But I already had a relationship built on distrust, and I'm not going there again. It almost cost me my freedom."

Her fingers curled against his chest. "Distrust? Is it because I'm doing an audit of your lab? It's my job, Michael. It's not personal."

"Oh, I think it's very personal, Nat… Nat Cooper."

Chapter Ten

Natalie's hands dropped from Michael's chest, and she took a step back from him and all the promise that had been in his eyes a minute earlier. "What do you know? Does everyone know?"

Folding his arms, he perched on the edge of the desk behind him. "Why don't you just tell me?"

"You know my maiden name, so you must know about my connection to this area." She fell onto the bed and crossed her arms behind her head. "You must know about Katie Fellows…and that I was with her the night she disappeared."

"No thanks to you. I had to sleuth around to find out—not because I wanted dirt on you. I want to know you—the real Natalie." He swung the chair around and straddled it, crossing his arms over the back and resting his chin on them. "Tell me what happened and tell me why you're hiding it."

He wanted to know the real Natalie? If he did, he'd probably run away, like Joe had.

"The why is easy. If the Bureau knew about my history here, they never would've sent me to look into the lab. I need to look into the lab. I think the muddling of evidence here is the reason Katie's case got short shrift."

"And maybe the fact that her body was never found."
He licked his lips. "Is the first part harder to talk about?"

"Not really. I've been over it in my head a million times.
I've talked about it and analyzed it from every direction
with my therapist." She lifted her head. "Don't."

"Therapy is good. You need it for...trauma?"

"It happened fourteen years ago, when I was a teenager.
You'd think I'd be over it by now, but I can't shake the memory of it. Maybe, and I know this sounds bad, but maybe if
Katie's body had been found and someone had been tried
and convicted of her murder, I could move on."

"Doesn't sound bad. It makes sense. That's why you're
here. So you can move on. Maybe you can start that process by telling me what happened that night."

She scooched up to the top of the bed and plumped some
pillows against the headboard. Might as well get comfortable. "It was all my fault. I was into Wiccan stuff and all
that nonsense. I was the new kid my junior year of high
school. I was a Goth girl at a school that didn't have Goth,
so Katie glommed on to me from the start. I piqued her curiosity, I guess. Anyway, we kind of formed a clique with
another girl, Bella Owens."

"Is she still in town?"

"She's in Seattle, but her family still lives here. They
wouldn't be too pleased to see me show up on their door-
step." She drew her knees to her chest and wrapped her
arms around her legs. "Bella couldn't make it that night,
but Katie and I snuck out to the woods to conjure spirits."

"Let me guess, at midnight?"

"Not quite, but late enough that it was pitch-black. We
had our little offering on the floor of the forest, and then we
started hearing noises from the trees. Once we figured out
the noises were human, not animal, that's when we made

a run for it." She leaned her chin on her knees. "I figured she'd run toward the campsite area, like me, but she took off toward the drop-off at the end of Devil's Edge."

Michael asked, "Did you call the police?"

"Not right away. I made my way home and texted Katie the rest of the night, but she never answered. I didn't get a wink of sleep and when Katie's mom called our house that morning to ask if Katie was with me, I went into a panic. I told my parents what happened, and they marched me down to the sheriff's station in town—right into Deputy Reynolds's office."

"Did you see anyone that night? Hear a voice? A smell? Anything?"

"The voice was distorted, just like out of a horror movie. That's what sent us fleeing through the woods. Didn't see or smell anything but woods and pine." She scooped the bedspread in her hands, curling her fingers into the material. "And I didn't tell them the entire truth."

"You left out the Wiccan ritual."

"I didn't want everyone blaming me more than they already did. Katie was a good girl before I showed up. I led her down a dark trail—one that literally got her killed." A tear leaked from the corner of her eye, and she brushed it away.

Michael sprung from his chair and sat on the side of the bed, next to her. He took her hand and rubbed his thumb in a circle on her palm. "You were a dumb kid. You both were. My friends and I could've died a half a dozen times with the stunts we pulled in high school—and that really would've been our faults. But what happened to Katie isn't your fault or hers—just the deviant who snatched her."

"I have to uncover what happened to Katie, Michael. It's the only way I can live with this. There had to have been more and better evidence collected from the woods. The forensic lab's mishandling of that evidence allowed a murder to walk."

"Wait, wait." He lunged for his jacket, which was hanging on the back of a chair, and plunged his hand in the pocket, withdrawing his phone. He swiped across the display. He held out his phone. "Wiccan pendant."

She stared at the picture of her necklace on Michael's phone. "How did you even figure that out?"

"I saw you looking at something in a baggie when I showed up for lunch today, and I noted the case you had spread out before you. Didn't take me long when I researched that case to figure out this was what you were looking at. Is it yours? Is that what freaked you out?"

"It's mine. I gave it to Katie that night when we started hearing sounds from the woods. It was supposed to ward off evil spirits, but I guess I should've given her something to ward off evil humans."

"Your pendant that Katie had when she disappeared ended up around another murder victim's throat. Unless a random killer came across this pendant in the woods, picked it up and decided to use it in his next murder, the person who abducted and probably killed Katie is the same person who killed Sierra Conchas."

"Exactly. And Sierra Conchas *is* one of my assigned cold cases."

Michael got it, and with no judgment aimed at her. For the first time in a while, Natalie felt a lightness in her chest, the ability to take a full breath and release it. Why had she waited to tell him the truth?

She twirled a lock of hair around her finger. "I guess with all this knowledge, you could torpedo my audit here. But they'd probably just send someone else in my place."

"Is that what you think I'd do?"

"You weren't happy about my arrival." She leveled a finger at him. "Admit it. Lou Gray is not the only one at the lab who resented my presence. He just didn't hide it the way most of you did. If I'd told you all this at the start, you would've had me on the first plane back to DC."

"Maybe. Is that why you—" he slid off the bed and pocketed his phone "—showed some interest in me?"

She stifled a laugh. "I'm not that devious. I showed interest in you because I like the way that one lock of black hair keeps falling into your face. I like the way your blue eyes light up your otherwise scowling complexion when something excites you. I like the way your lips curve up every time you mention your daughter. And I like the way you look at me."

"What way is that?" His eyes smoldered and his nostrils flared.

"Just like that."

He hesitated before stuffing his arms in the sleeves of his jacket. "I'm not going to report you to the FBI. I'm not going to interfere with your investigation into the lab. And I might even be able to help you."

She scrambled off the bed. "Really? You'd do that?"

"I know what it means to have questions, to want justice." He cupped her face with one hand. "And I know what it is to feel guilt, even when everyone tells you it's unwarranted."

"Thank you, Michael. I don't want to get you into any trouble at the lab."

"What trouble? The lab collected and analyzed evidence for some cold cases, and two of them now seem linked through that witch's-knot necklace. Sierra Conchas's case is on your radar, and now the Katie Fellows case is, too."

"But nobody knows about that pendant—nobody but us."

"Maybe we should keep it that way for now." He kissed her swiftly on the lips, as if any longer contact would ignite an inferno, and made a beeline for the door. "If you feel worse tomorrow, go straight to urgent care."

When the door closed behind him, Natalie raised her fingers to her mouth and pressed them against her lips, imprinting his kiss there for the rest of the night ahead.

Who knew being honest had its perks?

She downed the last sip in the little wine bottle and tossed it in the trash. As she turned toward the bathroom to get ready for bed, a knock on the door stopped her.

A rush of warm, stickiness flooded her body. Had Michael changed his mind? She launched herself at the door and pulled it open. "I'm glad you…"

Her words trailed off as she stared at a man in blue scrubs, his blond hair tousled, as if he'd just spent all night in surgery. Her brain fogged over. Had the EMTs sent someone back here to check on her? Had they discovered something off in her vitals?

"Y-yes?"

"It is you. I wasn't sure when I saw you at Thai Boat, but face-to-face, yeah. Nat Cooper."

Natalie stepped back, hiding halfway behind the door, blood roaring in her ears. "I don't know what you're talking about. That's not my name."

"C'mon, Nat." The man clawed through his hair with his fingers, making it stand on end even more. "It's me. Zane. Zane Tolbert."

Natalie clapped a hand over her mouth. Of course, it was Zane. Hair had turned a dirty blond, but he still had a smattering of freckles across his nose, and he hadn't added an ounce of fat on his tall, lanky frame. Katie'd had the biggest crush on Zane, and they'd just started getting exclusive when she disappeared.

She hissed through her fingers. "What are you doing here?"

"I wanted until that guy left, Michael Wilder. Honestly, if he'd spent much more time in here with you alone, I was going to charge in here to save you." He whispered. "He probably murdered his wife."

"He did *not* murder his wife." She grabbed Zane's arm and pulled him into the room. "What do you want, Zane? I hope you haven't told anyone I'm here. I'm, uh, here on official business."

His eyes popped open. "I heard in town that you were some kind of cop here to look into Wilder at the lab. But if that's not it, is the official business Katie's disappearance?"

"N-no, not really. I'm with the FBI, and I'm looking into some cold cases—not Katie's and not Raine Wilder's homicide." She pointed to the chair Michael had recently vacated, and she sat on the edge of the bed. "Is this a social call, or what?"

"Look, I understand why you wanna keep a low profile here. You were persona non grata when you and your family left. A lot of people blamed you for Katie's disappearance."

One of Natalie's eyes twitched. Not more than she blamed herself.

"Not me. I never did. You didn't make Katie do anything she didn't want to do." He scooped his hair from his eyes. "Do you have a beer or something? I just got off a twelve-hour shift, and I'm beat."

"In there." She aimed a toe at the minifridge. "Are you a doctor?"

He crouched in front of the minibar and pulled out a can of beer. "I'm a nurse."

"Why did you follow me? What do you want, Zane?"

"I never got to talk to you after Katie went missing. The cops even thought I may have had something to do with it, but I know who did it."

"You do?" Twisting her fingers in her lap, Natalie swallowed.

He dropped his chin to his chest. "I think it was a cop."

Chapter Eleven

Natalie rubbed her arms. If the thought hadn't occurred to her more than once, she would've laughed in Zane's face. "How do you know that? Do you have proof?"

He took a gulp of beer from the can. "I don't have proof. How could I have proof? I was a kid, just like you. But it was weird, right? I mean, you'd told them what happened in the forest, and they looked at her like a runaway. We knew Katie. She was not runaway material. The cops were so quick to jump on it. Then there was the evidence. Where did it all go? They combed the forest and found jack? That's hard to believe."

Evidence. It always came back to the evidence. "Stuff like that happens all the time, Zane. In my line of work, I see it all the time. Mistakes happen. What else makes you think it was the cops? That's a heavy accusation."

"It was that Reynolds guy."

"What?" The spot on her forehead where the airbag had hit her began throbbing. "Deputy Max Reynolds?"

"Yeah, I can't stand that guy, even today, but back then he was always leering at Katie. She told me about it once."

"She never told me that." Natalie dragged a pillow into her lap and hugged it to her chest.

"Yeah, well." Zane grinned, and Natalie remembered why Katie'd had such a crush on this guy. "She told me she didn't want to tell you because she was afraid you'd say something to Reynolds and get in trouble. She said you were always so protective of her."

"She said that?" Natalie's nose tingled, and she rubbed the tip of it. "I guess so. I wish she would've told me about Reynolds, though. I think she did mention one time that she thought he was cute, but a lot of the girls felt the same way. But the rest? That's creepy."

"Anyway, when I saw you, and then someone told me you were some kind of cop here on an investigation, I knew I had to talk to you just in case you can use it." As he rose from the chair, he crushed the empty can in one hand. "Whoa! What happened to you? Your arms are all bruised."

"Had a run-in with an airbag." She squared her sore shoulders. "Look, I'd appreciate it if you didn't tell anyone my identity. Sounds like small-town gossip really gets around."

"It does." He ran a finger over the seam of his lips. "I won't say a word…as long as you let me know if you find out anything about Katie's disappearance. I'm not gonna lie. That really messed me up for a while, you know?"

"I know." She patted his arm. "Good to see you, Zane. You like nursing? Everything going well?"

"Nursing's great, and my girlfriend and I are expecting a baby in about five months. We're having a girl, and I gotta tell you, it makes me nervous around here."

"Congratulations. You'll be a great dad." She ushered him out of the hotel room without ever agreeing to keep him posted on Katie's case. He'd have to find out just like everyone else—and now, more than ever, she had every intention of solving that mystery.

THE NEXT MORNING, the rental-car company called her while she was finishing her makeup. They fell all over themselves apologizing for the brake failure and had delivered a new car to the hotel, along with the key to the conference room, which she'd left on the car's keychain. She hadn't even thought about that key last night—not that their thoughtfulness absolved the company from their total failure in providing a sufficient car. The hotel desk had the keys, and the car was gratis. That would make the FBI happy.

Natalie tossed her phone on the bed and plucked a pair of low-heeled boots out of the closet, skipping her high heels for today. Her back and neck didn't need any more stress.

She downed a couple of ibuprofen along with her breakfast in the hotel restaurant. Then she stopped by the front desk to pick up her keys to the new rental.

Her drive to the lab took longer than usual, as she kept tapping the brakes. The other drivers on the road were probably happy to see her make a turn and get out of their way.

On the way to her office, she stopped at the lunchroom to stash her leftover Indian food, which she'd have for lunch at her desk today. Next to the coffee machine, a plate of chocolate-chip cookies beckoned.

She lifted a mug from the tree, poured herself a cup of coffee, added lots of cream and dropped two cookies onto a paper plate. Nicole must've brought these in today.

As she turned with her coffee and plate in hand, she almost bumped into Dr. Butler. "Oops. Excuse me. Nearly dumped my coffee on your nice white lab coat."

"My fault." Dr. Butler pointed to the plate of cookies. "I heard Nicole brought in her famous chocolate-chip cookies, and I couldn't get here fast enough."

Natalie slurped some of her coffee to reduce the level.

"I should have some free time this afternoon, Dr. Butler. Is today a good time to visit the DNA lab?"

"Call me Rachelle and today would be great. I think Dr. Volosin is coming back tomorrow, a little earlier than I expected." Rachelle made a face.

"Send me an email, Rachelle." Natalie raised her cup to the doctor and went to her office.

When she reached the door of the conference room, she stood in front of it with her coffee cup in one hand, plate of cookies in the other and her bag hanging over her shoulder.

She was about to stoop down to place the cookies on the floor, when Jacob Reynolds came up the stairs.

"I'll hold that for you." He tucked some files under his arm and held out his hand for the plate.

"Thanks, Jacob." Natalie handed him the plate and dug her keys out of her bag. She unlocked the door and bumped it open with her hip. "You can put those down on the desk and take one for yourself. I really don't need two."

"Thanks." He swiped a cookie from the plate and took a bite that demolished half of it. With crumbs stuck to his chin, he asked, "Are there more in the lunchroom?"

"There are, but I think they're going fast." She tapped her own chin, but he didn't understand her meaning. "I meant to ask you, Jacob. Is your dad still on the job? You mentioned he was a deputy for King County."

Fourteen years ago, Jacob Reynolds would've been about six years old. What was a married man with a young child doing leering after a teenager? Maybe Zane had just been jealous. Reynolds could've just smiled at Katie at the fast-food place where she worked to send a teenage boy over the edge with despair. But Zane had told her specifically that Katie had been bothered by the cop's attention.

Was Katie right at the time? If Katie had told her about Reynolds, she probably would've gone off on the guy. She'd had no fear in those days...but those days were long gone.

Jacob finished chewing the second half of the cookie and swallowed it in a big gulp. "Yeah, my dad's still a cop. He helps out with homicides, but he's still on patrol. That's how he got me a job here. He knows a lot of people at the lab. His partner was married to Nicole Meloan. He..."

"I heard what happened. Must've upset your father."

"Yeah, Dad...well, cops don't show too much emotion. He kept saying that Frankie never acted depressed around him. I think he felt kinda guilty that he didn't see it."

Join the club.

"I see you found the cookies," Nicole said, as she stepped into the office and brushed her fingers against her chin.

Jacob got the hint this time and rubbed the crumbs from his chin as his face turned a bright red.

Natalie's own face had warmed at the thought of Nicole catching her gossiping with the part-time gofer about her personal affairs. "I wanted to make sure I nabbed one this morning after missing out last night. Thanks again for dinner, Nicole."

"Yeah, but now I feel bad after hearing what happened to you last night."

Jacob took the opportunity to duck out of Natalie's office with a quick wave.

Natalie touched the abrasion on her forehead. "Nothing to feel bad about. The brakes could've gone out on that car at any time."

"I know, but it happened way out of town on my godforsaken little patch of land, and you went right into the forest. I can't believe you're at the office today."

"The airbag saved me, just a few bruises."

"Let me know if you need anything."

Natalie picked up the cookie. "I think I'm covered."

If Nicole had heard or been upset that Natalie had been discussing her husband with Jacob, she hadn't shown it. But now, Nicole would think her an office busybody if Natalie asked her about Max Reynolds. She must've known her husband's partner fairly well, although Frank must've been younger than Max.

Teens' perception of adult age was notoriously bad, but Natalie figured Deputy Reynolds was in his early thirties at the time of Katie's disappearance. She'd thought he was kind of cute, but old, at the time.

As she logged in to her laptop, she bit into the cookie and closed her eyes. People around here were not joking. This cookie was heaven.

The sugar and the second cup of coffee gave her a boost of energy, and she managed to complete the work on her databases outlining the evidence in all the cold cases, and any irregularities in that evidence.

The work this morning gave her the impetus to call her boss. She had to tell Jefferson about the car, anyway.

A few minutes later as she ended the phone call, Michael tapped on her open door. "I knew you'd show up. How are you feeling?"

She stretched her arms above her, linking her fingers. "A little stiff, but otherwise, okay. Just talked to my supervisor, and he's happy with my work so far."

"Your official work. Anything on the unofficial?" He'd lowered his voice, but her office door was still open.

"Had a surprise visitor last night after you left." She put a finger to her lips. "Don't want to discuss it here, though."

"Lunch?"

"I brought in leftover Indian from last night at Nicole's." She dabbed at a cookie crumb on her plate and sucked it off her finger. "Do you think it's a good idea for us to lunch together every day?"

He sat on the edge of the desk and quirked his eyebrows up and down. "I think it's a great idea."

"Other people in the office might notice and resent it." She shoved back from the desk and massaged her neck.

"Why would they? I think they'd be happy that we're getting along because it means the lab audit is going well, and nobody is going to get blamed or lose their jobs. It's not like a competition where you're going to investigate one area and not another. I'm the head of the lab, and if I go up in flames, they all go up in flames. That's my take."

"My take is that I don't want it to appear I'm schmoozing with the boss while investigating the lab."

"Schmoozing. Is that what we're doing? I kinda like the sound of that." He smacked the desk. "I'm going to order out and join you in here for a working lunch. Is that a good compromise? Then you can tell me all about your midnight visitor."

"Knock yourself out. It's your lab."

"I'll be back with my lunch in about thirty minutes."

"I'll be here."

When Michael left the office, Natalie pulled her access card out of her laptop and shoved it into the plastic holder hanging from the lanyard around her neck. She hadn't told Michael about the missing files, either, or the other case that had caught her eye.

If she told him about the files, she'd have to admit that she believed someone in his office was trying to sabotage her work. She'd have to confess that she'd even thought he'd done it.

Sighing, she stood up, grabbing the paper plate and coffee cup from this morning. The spasm in her back had her clenching her teeth. Time for more painkillers.

She returned to the lunchroom, washed out her coffee mug and put it on the sink to dry. Only two cookies remained from this morning, and she eyed them as she retrieved her lunch from the fridge. As she heated her foot in the microwave, she got a couple of Diet Cokes from the vending machine in case Michael forgot to order a drink with his lunch.

The microwave beeped, and she gingerly removed the plastic container with her fingertips. She threw another glance at the cookies and said, "Ah, hell."

She'd given her second cookie to Jacob, so this was just a replacement. She dropped one cookie on top of the plastic lid and hauled everything back to the conference room. She tucked the drinks under one arm, as she wrangled the key out of her pocket and into the door lock.

She didn't want to start eating without Michael, and her food needed to cool off, anyway, so she logged back in to her computer and brought up the ghost database on Katie's case.

There had been a cigarette butt found on Devil's Edge Trail the morning after Katie's disappearance, but no DNA on it. How could DNA be missing from a cigarette butt? There were also a few cigarette butts near Sierra's abandoned car—again, no DNA detected.

Odd. Usually, crime-scene investigators salivated when they found something like a cigarette butt near a body or crime scene. Even if the DNA didn't yield a match in CODIS, they still had someone's DNA.

She threaded a pen through her fingers and dropped it

when Michael showed up at her door with a bag of food and two drinks in cups.

He held up the cups. "Didn't know if you had anything to drink."

She bent over to pick up the pen and tapped it against the two cans of soda. "Great minds think alike."

"Ah, but I got you the Zesty Blood Orange Diet Coke this time." He shoved the drink toward her. "If you can handle it today."

"I don't know. Indian food and Zesty Blood Orange Diet Coke." She popped the lid from her plastic container. "Sounds disgusting."

He inhaled through his nose. "That smells good. Beats my turkey on rye."

She stirred through the chicken and rice in her dish. "Nicole packed a lot in here. I'm happy to share."

"I'm good with my sandwich." He walked his swivel chair backward toward the door and closed it. "Can we talk and eat?"

"I think I can manage." She spread a piece of paper towel on her lap and got to it. "After you left last night, I mean right after, Katie's old boyfriend, Zane Tolbert, knocked on my hotel door."

Unfolding the waxy yellow paper from his sandwich, he asked, "She had a boyfriend?"

"Beginning stages." She waved her fork in the air. "Anyway, he recognized me at the Thai restaurant yesterday. I was afraid someone might see that little emo girl beneath the facade. Honestly, I'm still that little emo girl, so it's no surprise he ID'd me."

"He followed you to your hotel? That's not good."

"Zane didn't really go into how he found me at the hotel. It could've been word of mouth, local gossip." She poked at a piece of chicken. "Rumor has it that I may even be here looking into you."

Michael dropped his sandwich. "You're kidding. Jeez, people still think I did it."

"I set him straight on that, but I did admit that I might be doing a little investigating of my own into Katie's disappearance, and that's when he dropped his bombshell."

"He killed her." Michael took a big bite of his sandwich.

"No, but he thinks the cops might've had something to do with her disappearance or at least the cover-up. He said that Deputy Max Reynolds was inappropriately interested in Katie at the time, and Katie noticed. She complained to Zane about it."

"Did she ever mention it to you?"

"No. Zane said she was afraid to tell me because she thought I'd march up to Reynolds and make a scene." Her lips quivered at the corners, halfway between a smile and a grimace.

Michael walked his fingers to hers and brushed her skin, so subtle nobody would've noticed even if they were sitting at the table with them. His touch caused a little shiver to ripple across her flesh.

"I can look into Reynolds. I have a lot of connections at the sheriff's department, which pretty much saved me from going crazy when I was suspect numero uno over there."

"That would be great—as long as you're low-key."

He turned his thumbs toward his chest. "I'm the epitome of low-key."

Toying with the straw in her cup, she said, "There's something else I need to tell you."

He held up his sandwich. "Should I take this bite, or am I gonna choke on it?"

"Oh, take the bite. It's not that shocking." She took a sip

of her Diet Coke,. "I had a file with Katie's case and another one with a possibly related case…and somebody stole them from this office during the fire drill the other day."

Michael swallowed his bite of sandwich and then thumped his chest with his fist. "You're kidding."

"I'm not." She shoved away the soda and cracked open the can of the other one. "That's why I was acting all unhinged about the fire drill. I think somebody set that off on purpose to get into my office and look around. They found the files and took them."

"I don't know why you just didn't tell me that in the first place." He studied her face and then slowly brushed the crumbs from his fingers. "Oh. You suspected me."

"Maybe for a brief moment." She held out her thumb and forefinger. "I didn't want to start off on the wrong foot—accusing your staff—and I'm not exactly supposed to have those files, anyway."

"I could be someone just wanted to sabotage your work, not necessarily that those files meant anything to them."

"Just? Isn't it bad enough that someone wants to sabotage my work? And why would they want to do that?"

"You know why. We've been through this already. Some people in the lab are annoyed that the FBI wants to interfere in our work."

"If the work is sloppy…" She spread her hands. "Besides, these are cold cases. We're not auditing anything recent."

"We have some old-time employees at this lab. Dr. Volosin, Lou Gray, Nicole was an intern and Felicia's been here longer than any of them, I think." He held up his hand and ticked off a finger with each name. "Some see it as an affront to their professionalism. You're FBI. You must've run into this dozens of times with dozens of departments."

"True, but nobody ever stole a file from me before, and these are files I shouldn't have in the first place. Kind of hard to report the theft."

"What's the second case? You said you took two files, Katie's and who else's?"

"Another abduction from a trail—Alma Nguyen. Even though the cops found Alma's body, the circumstances mimicked Katie's case, so it caught my eye." She glanced at the time on her laptop. "I need to wrap it up. I'm supposed to meet with Rachelle in the DNA lab this afternoon."

"Rachelle?" Michael crumpled the sandwich paper in a ball and flicked it into the plastic bag. "She went home sick."

"That's too bad. I guess I have some free time."

Her cell phone rang, and she glanced at the display. "It's the rental-car company. I hope they're not calling for more information. I told them everything I remembered."

She tapped her phone to answer. "Hello?"

"Natalie, this is Axis Rental Car Company. Do you have a minute?"

She rolled her eyes at Michael, who was busy cleaning up the trash from their lunch. "Sure. What do you need?"

"We had our mechanics do a preliminary examination of the car today. It's a good thing it didn't burn up or explode."

"That's for sure."

The woman on the phone cleared her throat. "But we do have a problem."

"A problem?"

"We won't be taking responsibility for the failure of the brakes, Natalie."

"User error? I swear I didn't stomp on them or lock them up. They just stopped working."

"N-not user error."

Natalie waited, but the pause grew uncomfortably long. "Well, that's good. What was it, then?"

"Both brake lines were cut, Natalie. Someone tampered with those brakes—on purpose."

Chapter Twelve

Something was not right on the phone. Michael kept trying to catch Natalie's eye, but she avoided his gaze and gripped the edge of the table as if afraid she'd fall over.

"I—I don't know how that would happen. I didn't do it... Yes, yes. I understand. I'll let them know."

She ended the call and sat still, the phone resting on her shoulder.

"What was that all about? What did the rental-car company say? They're trying to blame you for the accident?"

Her eyes finally focused on his face as she peeled the phone from her ear. "They said the brake lines were cut—on purpose. Somebody tampered with the car."

"What?" He dropped the plastic bag in the trash. "How does that even happen?"

Natalie jumped up suddenly. "I almost died in that crash. Do you think someone did it on purpose? Do you think someone's trying to harm me? First, the stolen files and now, the brakes."

"Wait a minute. Stolen files to hijacked brakes is a big leap. One is mischief. The other could've been deadly." He sat on the desk and folded his arms. She couldn't think that someone in this lab wanted her gone so badly they'd tampered with the brakes of her rental. "The rental-car company has had the car, a heavily damaged car, back barely one day, and they're making these claims? Sounds like they're prepping for a lawsuit coming their way. You had the car at Nicole's. Do you really think someone crept out to your car while you and Nicole were eating and cut the lines?"

"I don't know." She sucked in her bottom lip. "It could've been done before, right? Someone could've nicked the lines a little earlier in the day, at my hotel, or…here."

He downed the rest of his Diet Coke and crushed the can. "C'mon. What would be the reason behind it? Someone doesn't wanna look bad at work, so they mark you for death."

Hunching forward, she planted her hands on the table. "They had no way of knowing if or when those brakes would go out, so, no. I don't believe I've been *marked for death*, as you so elegantly put it. But what if someone just wanted to scare me off. Send me back to DC with my tail between my legs."

"Anyone who's talked to you for five minutes know that's not going to work. Look, no attorney is going to take the rental-car company's word for the failure of the brakes after they had one of their own mechanics take a cursory look… and you shouldn't, either." He brushed some crumbs from the table into his hand and tipped them in to the trash. "Is it going to scare you off?"

She tossed her hair back over her shoulder. "Of course not, but I'm going to be looking at people through a different set of eyes."

"That's a good policy, anyway." He stopped at the door and twisted his head over his shoulder. "I can check under your hood, if you like."

She raised her eyebrows. "That sounds like an improper proposal."

"I wish." He snorted as he left the office, closing the door behind him.

Michael chewed on the inside of his cheek all the way back to his office. He'd brushed off Natalie's concerns because he didn't want to worry her, but if someone in his lab was trying to run off the FBI agent, they had a real problem.

Lou Gray's name came to mind immediately. He didn't want to remind Natalie that Lou oversaw all evidence related to vehicles—evidence collection, car-crash investigations, tire tracks…and brake lines. If anyone knew how to nick a brake line for the slow release of fluid, it would be Lou.

When Michael got back to his desk, he made a call to Lou at the garage. Lou's assistant told him Lou was in the middle of overseeing the search of a drug dealer's car, knee-deep in panels, flooring and cushions.

The guy was a total professional. He had *curmudgeon* written all over him, but Michael had a hard time imagining Lou sneaking around after Natalie and tampering with her rental car. Lou would know better than anyone that that kind of tampering could be spotted in a second.

Rubbing his chin, Michael logged in to his computer and looked up Alma Nguyen's case. Alma's body was found about five months after Sierra's. Didn't share much in common with Sierra, except age, gender and approximate location of the body. Sierra had been in a car on her way home from work. Alma had been with friends in the woods, much like Katie.

Sierra had been stabbed. Alma had been shot. Just on method alone, the police were hesitant about linking the crimes, except neither crime scene yielded much evidence… or that evidence had gone missing.

As he scrolled through the file, he realized that he knew Alma's mother. Penny Nguyen worked as an accountant in town. He'd never used her services, but she'd been recommended to him on a few occasions.

He read through her interview with a tight throat, his gaze shifting to the picture of Ivy hugging Peaches. He blinked and continued reading the screen. Mrs. Nguyen had mentioned Alma's jewelry—one piece missing, replaced by a bracelet she'd never seen before.

Michael clicked through the file to find pictures of the evidence. He double-clicked the personal-items file and skipped past Alma's bloodstained clothing. Besides the clothing, items found on the body included a hair clip, a cross on a chain and gold hoop earrings. The list didn't contain a bracelet.

He flicked back to the crime-scene photo of Alma's body crumpled on the trail. He zeroed in on her hands and wrists. One sleeve of her jacket, rolled up, revealed a bare arm. The other sleeve hit the top of her hand.

He zoomed in further on her right wrist and his heart stuttered. A glint of something metal peeked out from the sleeve. It did look like a piece of jewelry.

He returned to the evidence list and went through every item again—no bracelet listed. Why had Mrs. Nguyen mentioned a bracelet and one can be seen on the photo of the body, but the evidence list didn't include it?

He logged out of his computer and grabbed his jacket. He had a sudden need for tax advice.

NATALIE JERKED UP her head at the sound of the knock. She squinted through the blinds over the conference-room window and gestured for Michael to enter.

"Are you still looking for something to do this afternoon?" His eyes were bright with excitement, which caused an answering flare in her chest.

"What did you have in mind?"

He stepped inside the room and closed the door. Tucking his hand behind him, he leaned against the door. "You mentioned the Alma Nguyen case, so I looked it up in the database."

"Okay." She dropped her pen and swiveled her chair to face him.

"In the statements, Alma's mother, Penny Nguyen, mentioned something about jewelry. Said her daughter's bracelet was missing, and that she was wearing another, unfamiliar bracelet."

Natalie's pulse ticked up a few notches. "Jewelry again. What did you discover about the bracelets?"

Parking on the edge of the desk, he said, "There was no bracelet in the list of Alma's personal items, but I looked at the pictures of her body from the crime-scene photos, and I can detect something metal around her wrist."

"Wait." She waved a hand in the air as if to clear her own confusion. "How did Alma's mother know about a bracelet if one wasn't found with the body and listed as evidence?"

"I'm not sure, but I'm about to go on a field trip and find out. Do you want to come with me to talk to Penny Nguyen? She still lives in the area." He dragged a hand through his hair. "I thought it would better if you came with me, just in case..."

"Just in case she's one of the people who believe you murdered your wife." Natalie's heart gave a painful thud.

"Exactly. If Zane Tolbert believes that, there must be others. I don't want to terrify the woman."

"I'll come with you, but first..." Natalie clicked on some

files, opening the case for Sierra Conchas. "Sierra was murdered before Alma, right?"

"About five months before. Different MO. Someone shot Alma." Michael shook his head, as if trying to erase the crime-scene photo from his brain.

"Katie disappeared seven months before Sierra's homicide, lost a pendant that wound up around Sierra's neck. Was Sierra missing any jewelry?" She snapped her fingers in the air several times. "What if the MO of this guy is to take a piece of jewelry from one victim and leave it on his next? It could tie all these girls together. That's what I've been trying to find—a link between Katie's disappearance and other murders in the area."

She found the page she was looking for and leaned in to scan the personal items list. Michael hovered over her shoulder for a second pair of eyes.

He read off the list out loud. "A number of stud earrings along her ear down to the lobe, several bangles on her arm, some of which fell off in the struggle, and the witches'-knot pendant, which we know didn't belong to her. Did anyone report that Sierra was missing anything at the time of her death."

"I didn't see that anywhere, but it's not hard to imagine that her killer took one of those bangles without anyone noticing and slipped it over Alma's hand." She tapped her fingers on the desk. "But if that happened, where is it? Why isn't it listed in the evidence of Alma's personal effects?"

"That's what I'm hoping Mrs. Nguyen can tell us." Michael wagged his finger at the screen. "Get to the photos of Sierra's personal effects and get a picture on your phone of those bracelets."

While Natalie followed his instructions, Michael took

two long strides to the coat-tree and plucked her jacket and purse from it. "Got it?"

"Give me a few seconds." Once she'd snapped a picture of the bracelets, she logged off her laptop and pushed back from the desk. "Do you know where to find Mrs. Nguyen?"

"I do."

"What's your story going to be?"

"Me?" He tapped his chest. "I'm there for tax advice. You're there to ask her about Alma."

"You're going to make me the bad guy?" She jerked open the door and almost ran into Lou Gray, who was charging down the hallway. "Oops, sorry."

Lou ignored her and tipped his chin at Michael. "Heard you were looking for me."

"It can wait. Find anything in the drug dealer's vehicle yet?"

"Oh, yeah." Lou rubbed his hands together. Then his gaze darted from Michael to Natalie. "We'll catch up later."

Lou saluted as he ambled toward the lunchroom.

As they went downstairs, Natalie asked in a low voice, "You called Lou? What for?"

"About your rental-car brakes."

She tripped on the last step, and Michael caught her arm. "You don't suspect him, do you?"

"I'm not going to come at him like that, but I wanted to judge his response."

"He'll see right through you." Natalie waved to Sam as they breezed out the front door. "Your car or mine?"

"No offense, but I'd rather drive."

She punched him in the arm. "Not my fault."

They drove to Penny Nguyen's house, situated in a neat tract of homes, settled near the town. No two-lane roads, no tunnel of towering trees, no animals darting into the street.

Michael parked on the street in front of a tidy, white picket fence with a wooden sign on the gate. Blue lettering on the sign advertised CPA/Taxes.

Natalie lifted the latch on the gate. "If she has a client, you're out of luck."

"I'll take my chances. We're nowhere near tax season, although the end of the year always puts me in a panic, looking for receipts and looking for investments to lower my taxes." Michael followed her through the gate, their footsteps crunching the dry leaves, and up to the front door.

When she reached the porch, she stood to the side, allowing Michael access to the front door and the doorbell, which was connected to a camera. She murmured, "She might not let you in once she sees you."

"Thanks for the vote of confidence." He pressed the doorbell with his thumb.

Whether or not Mrs. Nguyen checked the camera, she opened the door almost immediately and smiled, the lines crinkling at the corners of her eyes making her look a lot jollier than she had a reason to look. The gray streaks in her hair gleamed beneath the light from the house. "Hello. Can I help you?"

Michael took an audible breath. "Mrs. Nguyen, I'm Dr. Michael Wilder. I work for the Washington State Patrol at the forensics lab here in town."

She dipped her head. "I know who you are, Dr. Wilder. I followed your wife's case, and I'm very sorry for your… troubles."

"Thank you, Mrs. Nguyen, and you can call me Michael."

"I'm Penny." She tilted her head, birdlike, her face tightening over her delicate bone structure. "Something tells me you're not here for tax advice. You'd better come in."

She widened her door, and Michael waved Natalie in first. "I'm sorry. This is FBI Special Agent Natalie Brunetti."

Penny closed the door and locked the dead bolt. "Now, I *know* you're not here for financial advice. I'd actually heard about Agent Brunetti's presence in town and her accident last night."

Natalie whistled. "The rumor mill in Marysville is alive and well, and I'm Natalie."

She stuck out her hand, and Penny took it in a surprisingly firm grip for such a petite woman. "Tea, anyone? I always find it helps for tough conversations."

Natalie exchanged a glance with Michael. This woman was prescient. "Yes, please."

Penny invited them to sit down and went into the kitchen to prepare their tea.

Seated on the couch next to Michael, Natalie leaned over, bumped his shoulder and whispered, "You'd abandoned the tax story as soon as you saw her, didn't you?"

"I couldn't lie to her, not after seeing the pain in her face. It's still there, isn't it? Her clients probably don't see it, but you and I know the look. We've had the look."

Natalie gave his hand a surreptitious squeeze before bounding up from the couch to help Penny with an elaborate tea tray.

Once they were settled, Penny held her cup to her lips, her pinkie finger raised. "Now, what do you want to know about Alma's death?"

Natalie almost choked on her first sip of tea. Did Penny still have hope that they'd find her daughter's killer? This woman made Natalie even more determined to dig in and see this through. She had no intention of leaving Marysville until she got to the bottom of these homicides. She didn't believe she could solve them on her own, or even with Michael's help, but just maybe she could get another investigation started—one that would look at these three cases together.

Natalie daintily dabbed her lips with a napkin. "I'm here to look into evidence for several cold cases. Alma's isn't one of them, but I've seen some similarities between hers and some others."

"Sierra Conchas and that poor girl Katie Fellows, who disappeared."

This time Natalie almost dropped her cup in her lap. She put it down in the saucer with a clink. "How do you know that, Penny?"

Penny smiled sadly. "Call it mother's intuition. I tried telling Detective Morse, who was on my daughter's case, and that Deputy Reynolds, but they wrote me off as a grief-stricken parent, which I was."

Michael glanced around the room. "Is Mr. Nguyen still with you?"

"He's still with someone, but it isn't me." Penny gripped the arms of her chair. "After Alma's murder, my husband, my ex, he went off the rails. I redirected my grief by conducting my own investigation. He redirected his into the bottle. I'd finally had enough of his drinking and kicked him out. He moved to Hawaii. Still drinking, I think."

"I'm sorry, Penny." Michael hunched forward, his elbows on his knees. "A homicide is hell on everyone left behind."

"It is." Her dark eyes bright with unshed tears, Penny asked, "How's your little girl?"

"She's fine."

Michael seemed to handle accusations better than sympathy, so he rose from the couch and studied some photos of Alma on a bookshelf. "Pretty girl. Was she good at the piano?"

"Alma was good at everything…except self-preservation. She trusted everyone." Penny dropped her gaze to her hands folded in her lap.

Natalie gave Michael a glance from the corner of her eye, and he nodded. She took a deep breath through her nose. "Penny, in your interview with the police, you mentioned that Alma was wearing a piece of jewelry at the time of her death, something you'd never seen her with before. What was it?"

Penny's head shot up and she encircled her wrist with her fingers. "A bracelet, one of those circles without a catch. A bangle, you'd call it. Alma never wore those kinds of bracelets. Her wrists were too small, and the bangles wouldn't stay on."

Natalie slipped her phone from her purse and tapped the picture of Sierra's bracelets. Licking her dry lips, she crouched beside Penny's chair and held out the phone. "Did it look like any of these?"

Penny gasped and grabbed the phone, tugging it from Natalie's hand. She held it close to her face, staring at the display from behind her glasses. "Just like this one."

Penny's hand trembled when she handed the phone back to Natalie. "Where did you find it?"

"I-it's not the one you saw on Alma, but how did you know about the bracelet on Alma's arm? It's not listed in her file. There's no other mention of it except in your interview with Deputy Reynolds."

"When that couple found Alma's body on the trail, she'd been missing overnight. My husband and I were out all day looking for her, questioning her friends. My husband had a police scanner in the car. We heard about the discovery of a body, a young woman, and we arrived there almost the same time as the police." Penny removed her glasses and rubbed her eyes. "I saw my baby lying in the dirt, blood soaking the ground around her head like a halo. An angel in life, and an angel in death. They couldn't stop me. They couldn't hold me back. I ran to her. Even in my frantic despair, I knew enough not to touch her, not to interfere with any evidence, but I saw the bracelet then. I noticed it because I thought it was a handcuff, but when I looked close, I could see it was a silver bangle, imprinted with little flowers…like the ones you just showed me."

Michael crossed the room and dropped onto the couch,

as if his legs couldn't support him anymore. He croaked, his voice rough. "You never saw that bracelet again?"

Penny shook her head. "No. I told them about the bracelet, but they acted like they didn't know what I was talking about. I asked them why she had a bracelet that didn't belong to her. They dismissed me, but I knew what I saw. I-is it important?"

"It could be." Michael placed their cups on the tea tray.

"Penny." Natalie sat on the floor at Penny's feet. "You said Alma had a piece of her own jewelry missing. What was that?"

"That was a bracelet, too, but not that type. Alma had bought a bracelet at a Native American fair—a pretty, delicate thing with seed pearls and little sea turtles and beads. She wore it every day since the day she bought it." A shudder rant through Penny's slight frame. "That bracelet wasn't on her body, and I never saw it again. So her killer replaced one bracelet with another."

The silence hung in the room until Michael broke it. "Penny, can I ask you not to say anything to anyone about this?"

She snorted softly. "Whom would I tell? My husband is gone. Alma's brother is a doctor in Boston and hates it here. The friends I have left don't want to hear about my tragedy. I'll keep it to myself."

Natalie patted Penny's knee. "We'll get to the bottom of this. I promise."

As Michael carried the dishes to the kitchen, Natalie collected her coat and purse. "One more thing, Penny. Did Alma ever mention Deputy Reynolds before?"

Penny had risen to her feet a bit unsteadily and kept the back of her knees pressed against the cushion of the chair for support. "Not really. I know he had given some talks at the high school about drugs when Alma had been a student there a few years earlier. The girls at the time had thought he was cute, but that was before Alma's murder. Why?"

Michael emerged from the kitchen and cleared his throat. "We're looking at all the deputies on the cases, the ones who managed the evidence. We may have to talk to them again."

Penny put her hand on her hip, not quite buying it. "I see. I won't say a word, Michael, about any of it."

They thanked her for her time and left the house as Penny stood on the porch and watched them.

Natalie scooped in a big breath of pine-scented air. "Intense."

Penny lifted her hand. "Give your little girl a hug."

Michael waved back, and they got into the car. Michael clenched the steering wheel for several seconds before starting the car. "That poor woman."

"Michael." Natalie tugged on his sleeve. "It seems like this killer had some jewelry exchange going on. This was his MO, and it connects Katie, Sierra and Alma. He took a piece from one girl and left it on his next victim."

They pulled away from Penny's home. "We don't know if he left anything with Katie because she's the one who's never been found."

"Perhaps Katie was his first. Maybe seeing that pendant around Katie's neck is what gave him the idea, but my guess is that if her body is ever found there will be a piece of unfamiliar jewelry with her."

"I hope that happens one day—for her family's sake as well as yours." He gave her knee a quick squeeze and made a turn. Dusk had already settled, painting the horizon with orange streaks. "I'm starving. Are you hungry?"

"I could use a bite to eat before you drop me off at the lab. Don't forget. My car's there, and I left my laptop, too."

She twisted in her seat to face him. "Wait. Can I get into the lab without a key after hours? If not, we'd better go straight back there."

"You don't need a key, just your temp badge. Miles is the nighttime security guard. I'll bring you back and let him know you need to get inside."

He turned off the main road, and she tapped the window. "I thought we were going back to town to get something to eat."

"My house comes first. We can eat something there."

"Oh." She twisted her fingers in her lap. "Are your sister and daughter going to be home? Won't it be an imposition on your sister?"

"They'll be there, and my sister doesn't care about rules of etiquette. I could bring an army home for dinner, and she wouldn't blink an eye. She'd just reach for the phone and my credit card and order in."

"Maybe you should call her, anyway. Give her a heads-up."

"Too late." Michael pulled down a lane with a row of trees on either side, but the road was well-groomed, and other houses, or at least their mailboxes, made an appearance every 200 hundred feet or so. Far enough apart to maintain the woodsy, bucolic atmosphere of the neighborhood but close enough for shouting…in case someone needed help.

Instead of the unrelenting darkness that surrounded Nicole's area, this place had twinkling garden lights and the yellow glow from windows from the house set back from the street.

Natalie exhaled. "It's beautiful here. Spacious but cozy at the same time, if that makes sense."

"You're right. Most of our backyards are connected by

a trail that winds through the woods with gates between the properties. In the summer, we'll leave our gates open to each other's yards and we'll have a barbecue across a couple of lawns." His jaw tightened. "Not much of that this past summer."

Did his own neighbors suspect him of Raine's murder? Penny Nguyen proved that the whole town didn't believe him guilty. His coworkers didn't, either, judging by the way they respected him.

He turned into one of the driveways, where a white mailbox entwined with purple vines sat at the edge. "Circular driveway and everything—not that I've been able to take advantage of that since my sister moved in."

He pulled behind an old VW van, the back painted with curlicue flowers. Michael said, "Molly parks that in the driveway at an angle as if it were an abandoned car. She *should* abandon that car. I won't let her take Ivy out in that van. The thing could break down at any minute."

Michael's house fit into its surroundings seamlessly, with its cedar-shake siding and natural stone accents at the base of the house and around the wide porch. Two large windows looked out onto a garden, which was riotous with color, pinwheels and mermaids. A wooden bench sat on one edge of the garden, with a yellow cushion added for comfort—the perfect spot to read. A shadow passed in front of the window, and a little knot formed in Natalie's stomach.

As they got out of the car, a young woman with long black hair flying behind her tripped down the porch to meet them. She gave Natalie a sweet smile, but her smooth face had a furrow between her eyebrows. "Am I glad to see you. I didn't want to bother you at work, but I was just about to call your cell."

Michael slammed the driver's-side door and strode toward his sister. "Is Ivy okay?"

"Yeah, I'm sorry to scare you. Ivy's fine, but…" Molly craned her head over her shoulder to glance at the house behind her.

"What is it, Molly?"

The edge to Michael's voice only made Molly's smile wider. "It's probably nothing. Is this the FBI person who's making your life hell."

Michael grunted. "Natalie, this is my thoroughly annoying, but indispensable sister, Molly. And I never told her you were making my life hell."

Molly thrust out her hand. "I'm just kidding. Nice to meet you, Natalie. Are you joining us for dinner?"

"I'm sorry we're just dropping in on you like this. Please don't go to any trouble."

"Moi?" Molly's hair was fashioned into a low chignon with a few twists and tucks. "I never do. Ask Michael. If you can handle some leftover spaghetti, I got you covered."

"Whatever is honestly fine with me." Natalie spread her hands. "And I'm sorry I don't have anything to bring. This was totally last-minute. We were out working, and Michael has to take me back to the lab for my car and laptop."

Molly threw up her hands and aimed a broad wink at Michael. "You don't have to explain anything to me."

Poking his sister in the back, Michael said, "Now, can we get inside, and you can tell me why you were so anxious for me to come home."

Natalie hung back, allowing brother and sister to enter the house before her. The scent of warm vanilla permeated the air, and it didn't take long for Natalie to see that a candle, and not the oven, was the source of the aroma.

"Daddy!"

Natalie's gaze traveled to the little girl standing up and holding on to the edge of a playpen, a giant area outfitted with blocks, stuffed animals, dolls and books. Michael's blue eyes stared out from the little round face, but any other resemblance to her father ended there. Soft brown hair framed Ivy's face, glowing with peaches and cream and happiness. She didn't look like a little girl missing her mommy, just one incredibly pleased to see her daddy.

Michael's strides ate up the space between them, and he swooped in and lifted her in the air. Ivy giggled and splayed her arms and legs out, as if trying to fly.

Natalie pressed a hand to her heart. "She's adorable."

Molly stood beside Natalie and bumped her shoulder. "I know. Pretty hard to believe with a moody dad and a nut-job mom."

Molly had lowered her voice on her last words, but Michael shot her a scowl as if he'd heard.

Michael brought Ivy close to his chest and kissed the top of her head. "What have you been doing today?"

Ivy twisted her body and pointed to the large picture window that looked out onto a grassy backyard with a swing set and massive trees that signaled the beginning of the forest. The view must be breathtaking during the light of day.

"Peaches, Daddy. Peaches."

"Peaches went away, my peapod." Michael rubbed Ivy's back as he rolled his eyes at Molly.

"That's what I was going to tell you, Michael. I was sitting on the couch on my laptop looking up my friend's exhibit in Portland while Ivy was playing, and she started yelling Peaches's name and pointing outside." Molly crossed to the window and placed a hand against the glass. "I looked but didn't see anything, or maybe I just saw some bushes shaking. So I went outside and called for Peaches. I even walked into the yard. I did hear noise in the underbrush that sounded like an animal, but I'm not going out in the wild to check—besides, I had Ivy inside."

"Maybe Ivy just saw a small dog and her brain went straight to *her* small dog." He bounced Ivy in his arms. "Did you see a doggy outside?"

Her blue eyes grew round and sparkled with excitement like Michael's did. "Peaches. Peaches outside."

"I hate to give you any more work, Molly, but I think I'm going to have to get another dog." He tapped Ivy on the nose. "Would you like that, Ivy? Another doggy?"

Her face crumpled and grew red. "Peaches."

"Michael." Molly put her hand on his arm and tickled Ivy under the chin at the same time. "Could you just go look outside to be sure? She seemed convinced and would not give it up."

"She's two and a half, Molly. Any small dog is going to look the same to her."

"Then go out there and make sure there's not some other dog wandering around." She gave Michael a shove and held out her arms for Ivy.

Ivy clambered into Molly's arms.

Michael raised an eyebrow at Natalie. "Care to join me in the great dog hunt?"

"Absolutely. I think I can still tell the difference between a fox and a dog."

Michael brushed past Natalie on the way to the kitchen and opened a cupboard. "I have a flashlight. Molly, turn on the outdoor lights."

Natalie hadn't removed her jacket when she'd come inside, so she tugged it around her and followed Michael out to the backyard, now lit up. The smell of roses and rain tempered the sharp scent of the pines, which could be overpowering. Truly a slice of civilization amid the untamed forest.

Michael clicked on the flashlight and the strong beam swept across the edge of the grass and along the tree line. The light picked up the shared community trail that wended through the underbrush before plunging into the woods.

Michael whistled. "Peaches. Oh, P-e-e-eaches. C'mon, girl. You out here?"

He replaced the whistle with kissing sounds that would've definitely had Natalie come running. A smile curving her lip, she crept closer to the trees, their leaves shivering in the light breeze and touched by the icy beam from the flashlight.

She whispered the dog's name. "Peaches."

Something rustled beyond the trail, and Natalie hissed at Michael. "I hear something."

He joined her and aimed his light at the area where she'd heard the noise. "Peaches."

An animal whimpered, and they looked at each other. Natalie said the obvious first. "That sounded like a dog to me."

"Could be a fox." As he scanned the ground with the light, it picked up a pair of gleaming eyes.

Natalie grabbed his arm, her fingers digging in. "Right there."

"Peaches?"

A small dog hurtled out of the bushes, yapping and dancing around Michael's ankles.

Natalie sank to her knees in the wet grass and reached for the wriggling pug. "Is it her? Is it Peaches?"

"My God." Michael's mouth had dropped open. "It's really you. It's really Peaches, after all this time."

He dropped to the grass beside Natalie, handing her the

flashlight, and scooped up Peaches. He buried his nose in the dog's filthy fur. "She's still wearing her collar."

As Natalie illuminated the collar, Michael hooked his finger around it. "Looks like her tag might've come off."

"Are you sure?" Natalie squinted and peered at the collar, which must've been pink at one time. "I see something glittering on the collar. Maybe the tag got bent or something."

Michael stroked Peaches as he tugged on her collar. "There's something caught on it. It's not her tag."

Something jingled as he untangled the object from the collar. When he had it cupped in his hand, he choked. "No."

"What is it, Michael?" She wedged the flashlight between her knees, aiming it at Michael's hand, and hovered over the shiny object in his palm. "Oh, my God. It can't be. It can't be the same."

"It has to be, Natalie." He dangled the pretty bracelet from his fingers. "It's Alma Nguyen's bracelet. The one taken from her dead body."

Chapter Fourteen

Michael sat on the grass, Peaches's emaciated body in his arms and the dew soaking through the seat of his pants. He felt none of it until Natalie shouted in his face.

"Michael! What does this mean? Why does Peaches have Alma's bracelet from twelve years ago?"

Molly called from the house. "Did you two get lost out there or is there some hanky-panky going on?"

Michael closed his fist around the bracelet and held a finger to his lips. "Not a word about this to Molly…or anyone else. Not until we sort it out."

Natalie started to talk, but he gripped her wrist before she could say anything. "I don't understand, either, but we can't discuss it now."

He slipped the bracelet into his pocket, where it burned like a living thing, and he pushed up from the soggy grass with Peaches under one arm.

As he marched back to the house, he felt Natalie slip her finger in his belt loop, as if she needed something to keep her steady. Her touch anchored him, too, and he cleared his throat as he approached the house.

"Ivy was right. Never doubt a toddler." He held up Peaches, and Molly squealed.

"That's Peaches? She came home."

Molly ran to pluck up Ivy from her playpen, and Ivy smiled from ear to ear, repeating Peaches's name and patting the dog on the head. At one point, Ivy looked up at Michael. "Mama?"

The lump in Michael's throat proved too big for words to slip past it, so Molly combed her fingers through Ivy's hair and said, "Mama's not coming home."

Ivy hugged the little pug, smooshing her face into her fur. Michael would worry about fleas later. He could barely think straight, and he had three people eying him for answers.

Molly chewed on the side of her thumb, a habit she'd inherited from Mom. "You're going to have to tell the police, Michael. This is huge."

His sister had no idea how huge.

"I realize that."

"You might even need to tell them before you wash the dog. I mean, you don't want to destroy any evidence, do you?" Molly grabbed her phone from the coffee table and snapped several pictures of Peaches. "Just in case."

He closed his eyes. He'd already removed the biggest piece of evidence from Peaches's collar. "Peaches has been gone for over six months. She's not going to yield any evidence worth having."

Molly tapped her chin. "I get it—rain, dirt, mud. It would've destroyed any evidence from the, uh, thing."

Michael cuddled Ivy in his arms, while she cuddled an exhausted Peaches in hers. He caught Natalie's reflection in the window, her face a while oval. She hadn't recovered from the shock yet, but in all the excitement Molly hadn't noticed Natalie's demeanor.

"I need to get Natalie back to the lab, so she can get her car and her laptop, and we never even fed her."

"Don't worry about me. I'll figure out something. I can order a car on my phone to take me back."

Molly jumped up from the floor. "Michael, don't make her do that. I can take care of everything here. Ivy and I will give Peaches a bath and feed her. Do you have any dog food left?"

"Not any of the dry stuff, but I'm sure there are a few cans in the cupboard in the garage over the washer and dryer." Michael left Ivy on the floor with Peaches and brushed off the knees of his pants. "I don't want to dump all of this on you, Molly. Are you sure?"

"Positive. Just go take Natalie back, and then you can help me when you return. Ivy will be my assistant." Molly ducked down and ruffled the top of Ivy's hair.

After they settled everything with Molly, Michael walked with Natalie back to his car in silence. Neither of them spoke until he'd backed the car out of the driveway and hit the road.

Then Natalie went off like a teakettle. "What the hell just happened? First the dog that was with your wife when she was murdered returns home after six months, and if that weren't astounding in and of itself, the dog has a dead woman's bracelet attached to her collar. Michael, tell me you're thinking what I'm thinking. Or am I losing my mind?"

"If you are, I'm right there with you. The person who murdered Alma thirteen years ago and stole her bracelet is still at large, and he killed my wife. The reason Raine wasn't found with this bracelet is because it somehow got tangled with Peaches's collar, or Peaches somehow got it from Raine's body, or…" He slammed his hands against the steering wheel.

Natalie put her fingers to her lips. "Or the killer attached that bracelet to Peaches's collar."

"Wait. We don't know for sure." Michael clapped a hand on his forehead. "Maybe that's not even Alma's bracelet. We just talked to Penny. We had that bracelet in our heads, and it materialized."

"Yeah, a Native American-style bracelet with seed pearls and sea turtles. That's just so common."

Michael lifted his shoulders, desperate for something to make sense. "Alma bought it at a Native American fair. They could've sold others."

"Those must be some bad-luck bracelets, then." She snorted. "Of course, it's Alma's bracelet, Michael, and Raine's murder is connected to the others."

"That's impossible. It's been too long since his previous murder." His foot had been coming down on the accelerator, and he took the last turn way too fast. He eased off the pedal and loosened his grip on the steering wheel, flexing his fingers.

"We don't know that. He could've been operating in another area. He could've been in prison. You know the score. It's all too coincidental."

"Raine is out of his age demographic. She was thirty, she had a child. She was strangled, for God's sake. The other two were stabbed and shot." Michael's hand shook as he snatched up the water bottle in the cup holder.

Natalie took the bottle from him and unscrewed the cap. "Let's see what Penny has to say about that bracelet. If she verifies that it belonged to Alma, will you believe Raine's murder is connected to Alma's and the others?"

"I guess I'd have to. There's no way Peaches just happened to get tangled up with Alma's bracelet thirteen years after her murder. Peaches didn't even disappear in the same area as Alma was discovered." Michael took the turn toward the lab. "Where was she? How did she survive out there? It doesn't look like someone had found her or was taking care of her."

"Six months is a long time. Someone must've been feeding her. If she could only talk."

Natalie tapped her fingers against her chin. "If this is the same killer, he would've taken a piece of jewelry from Raine. I mean, why change your MO when you're trying to make a comeback. Was Raine missing any jewelry? Wedding ring?"

Michael spit out a breath. "She'd stopped wearing that, months before her death. You'd have to ask her boyfriend, RJ."

Michael pulled into the parking lot of the lab sooner than he would've liked. He and Natalie still had so much to discuss, but he had to go home to his little girl and try to explain why Peaches had returned, but her mother hadn't.

NATALIE HAD TO convince Michael that he didn't have to wait for her to collect her things from the office. She could tell he was anxious to get back to Ivy, and he'd already waved to Miles to let her into the building. Several stray cars remained in the parking lot, so there had to be a few late-night stragglers.

Once inside, she strode toward the security desk and introduced herself to Miles. "Is there a cut-off point when the office closes? I'd like to do a little work while I'm here."

"You can work here all night, if you like. Some do." He tapped the desk. "You need to check out when you're leaving, though, and exit through the front doors. I have to know who's in the building."

"Got it. Thanks, Miles."

She made a detour to the lunchroom on the way back to her office. She never did get that leftover spaghetti at Michael's house, but she did get something much more important. Could Katie's abductor and presumed killer be back in Marysville, determined to pick up where he left off?

Had Raine been missing any jewelry when her body was discovered.=? That seemed like a very important point right now, but she wasn't about to interrupt his family time to ask him. What kind of killer took a thirteen-year break? Like she'd told Michael earlier—an ex-con, someone in the military, someone who'd recently returned to the area.

She inserted her debit card into the vending machine and punched a button for a bag of chips and a bottle of water. She collected her dinner and returned to the conference room. On her way, she didn't see any other employees in their offices or cubicles, but they could be in their labs.

As she let herself into the room, her gaze swept the area, looking for anything out of place. Even though she'd locked up every day since getting the key, something always felt off in this conference room.

She dove back into her databases and added the details about Sierra's bangle, the photo of Alma's body showing a bracelet on her wrist and Penny's assertion that Alma was also missing a bracelet. Then Natalie held her breath and created another file for Raine Wilder.

Michael had the bracelet wrapped around Peaches's collar in his possession, but Molly hadn't been the only one taking pictures tonight. Natalie had a couple of photos of the bracelet on her phone. She could send it to Penny right now and clear up any doubt…not that she had any.

Michael needed to know, too. The truth would bring him

out of his denial that his wife's murder was connected to the other homicides. The link would only benefit him, as it would completely establish his innocence.

Now, they just somehow had to convince the police. Nobody knew the necklace found on Sierra belonged to the missing Katie, and that was her fault because she'd never told the police that Katie was wearing her pendant. Sierra's mother hadn't seen the necklace before, but that didn't mean anything. How many teenage girls hid items of jewelry or clothing from their parents?

Sierra wore so many bangles on her arm, nobody would've known if one were missing, and nobody but Penny could attest to an unknown bracelet around Alma's wrist. The bracelet hadn't even been logged in the evidence. And who was going to believe a mother who'd been grieving for thirteen years that her daughter's missing bracelet was found on the dog of another murder victim?

All she and Michael had was hearsay, supposition, disgruntled parents looking for justice, a suspect in his wife's murder and a lying FBI agent. They also had a cop who'd been too close to the victims and the crime scenes. Maybe Michael could talk to Max Reynolds about Alma's bracelet. Michael would be telling the sheriff's department about the return of Peaches, and he'd have to mention the bracelet. Whether he told him his suspicion about the bracelet was another matter.

She leaned back in her chair and popped open the bag of chips. She stuffed a few in her mouth and cracked open her water, then wiped her greasy fingers on a napkin. She pulled out her phone and tapped on the picture of the seed pearl bracelet. Then she texted the picture to Penny along with the million-dollar question.

She placed the phone on the desk and stared at it while she continued to crunch through the chips. As she tipped the crumbs from the empty bag in her mouth, she heard her phone buzz. Letting the bag drop to the floor, she lunged for her phone. The first two words of Penny's text slammed against her heart.

It's hers.

A million thoughts rushed through her brain at once, causing a severe crossing of wires. She squeezed her eyes shut and forced herself to breathe in and out, slowly. Then she opened her eyes and read through the questions in Penny's text, none of which she could answer right now.

She did her best to placate Penny, and herself, before packing up her laptop. She had to break the news to Michael, but in his heart, he already knew the truth, just as she'd known it.

She gulped down the rest of the water and tossed the chip bag in the trash, and the water bottle in the blue recycling bin. She could always order some room service if she felt hungry when she got back to the hotel, but she didn't think she'd be able to eat the rest of the night. A drink, maybe.

She rubbed her hands together, still feeling the residue from the chips. She'd make a quick trip to the ladies' room to wash her hands before going back to the hotel. She left her stuff in the conference room and headed toward the bathrooms next to the lunchroom.

She pushed on the door, but it wouldn't budge. She bumped it with her hip but got the same result. Maybe the janitorial staff locked up the bathrooms at night, but that didn't make sense if people were working here. Maybe they locked up certain bathrooms.

Natalie leaned over the staircase railing that looked into the lobby to ask Miles, but he must've been on rounds. All the labs were downstairs, and it made sense if the bathrooms in the lobby stayed unlocked. Made sense for Miles to keep track of the people in the building, too.

She jogged downstairs and swung to the right for the hallway leading to the restrooms. The fluorescent lights above flickered but never went on completely. She should've just brought her stuff with her to save a trip back upstairs.

This time when she pushed on the door, it eased open with a creak. A tiled wall separated the door from the rest of the bathroom, and she skirted it and parked herself in front of the mirror.

She patted her hair, which had frizzed out from all the moisture in Michael's backyard. There was only so much she could do with her curls in this weather. She even had a smudge of dirt on her chin, which nobody had bothered to tell her about, and the bruises on her arms from the airbag had reached the dark purple stage.

Sighing, she cranked on the faucet and squirted some soap into her palm. She lathered up her hands under the water and rinsed them clean, even rubbing the dirt spot on her chin.

When she removed her hands from beneath the faucet, the water stopped, and she turned to yank a paper towel from the dispenser. She reached for a second and froze, as she heard a creak from the door.

Holding the paper towel from her fingertips, she looked at her reflection in the mirror, her wide eyes staring back at her. A shuffling noise and another creak had her spinning around, but she couldn't see the door due to the privacy wall.

If someone wanted to use the bathroom, why didn't she

just come in? Maybe it was Miles or the cleaning crew. She crumpled the paper in her hands and called out. "Hello?"

A hooded figure appeared at the corner of the wall, and Natalie screamed.

Chapter Fifteen

The man at the door flicked his hood back from a head of silver hair and growled. "Who the hell are you?"

Natalie put a hand to her throat where her pulse fluttered wildly. "Who are *you*? You're in the ladies' room."

"Yeah, because I heard noises in here."

"Yeah, because it's a bathroom with running water and everything." Natalie's fear was beginning to turn to annoyance.

And then Miles's broad frame appeared behind the silver-haired man. "Oh, hello, Dr. Volosin. Everything okay in here? Thought I heard someone screaming."

Dr. Volosin, the DNA lab manager. Natalie narrowed her eyes.

Volosin jabbed a finger at her. "She screamed. Who the hell is she, and what's she doing near our labs?"

Natalie fired her balled-up paper towel at the trash can and missed. "I'm FBI Special Agent Natalie Brunetti, and I'm in this ladies' room because the one upstairs near my office is locked."

"My bad." Miles patted his chest. "Should've warned you, Natalie. The cleaning crew locks up all the bathrooms at night except the ones down here. Everything okay now?"

"Fine. Thanks for checking, Miles." She bent over and swept the paper towel from the floor.

When Miles left, Volosin leaned his tall, wiry frame against the tile wall. "I thought Nat Brunetti was a man."

Spreading her arms out to her sides, she said, "Clearly not. Why are you dressed like a burglar?"

He tugged on his hooded sweatshirt. "Just came off a cross-country flight. I dress for comfort after wearing suits at the conference all week. What are you doing here at this hour?"

"I could ask you the same thing. You came straight to the lab from the airport?" She crossed her arms. She felt sorry for Rachelle working for this disagreeable person. Why didn't he leave?

"After being away all week, I have a lot of work to finish up." He crossed his arms, mimicking her. "You might've heard. The Feds are doing an audit on this lab."

"Yeah, I had heard. I also heard that you've been working at this lab for almost twenty years."

"That's right. Long enough to have worked on your cold cases—Collette, David, Lizzie, Aaron, Sierra...and Katie." Volosin winked and slipped out of the bathroom, leaving her mouth gaping open like a fish's.

How had he known she was looking into Katie's disappearance? The others had been on the FBI's audit notification to the lab, but not Katie. No wonder Rachelle had wanted to meet with her in the lab before Volosin returned, and now, they'd missed their chance.

Natalie left the bathroom without even glancing in the direction of the labs. When she got to the conference room, she checked that everything was in place. Why had Volosin brought up Katie's case? How had he known?

She'd stayed longer than she'd intended. Ivy would probably be in bed by now. She tapped her phone to call Michael and almost hung up after four rings, but he answered, out of breath. "Are you alright? Did you make it back to the hotel okay?"

"I'm still at the office. How's Ivy doing? Did she settle down?"

"Fast asleep with Peaches on the floor beside her. We did give her a thorough bath—Peaches, not Ivy—and she looks healthy if a little underweight. No wounds or anything like that. She somehow survived out there before making her way home." He let out a long, raspy breath. "I'm not gonna lie. It's been tough on Ivy having Peaches come back and not her mother."

"It must be so confusing for her…and you." Natalie doodled on the pad in front of her. "Look, Michael. I made an executive decision and called Penny Nguyen about the bracelet, sent her a text with a picture I took."

"And." His voice sounded tight, and she hated to add to his distress.

"Penny confirmed that the bracelet is Alma's. There's no doubt now that Raine's murder is linked to the others." She stopped breathing until he replied.

"I guess that's it then. I'll be giving Detective Ibarra an earful tomorrow when I tell him Peaches returned with a dead girl's bracelet wound around her collar."

"I was just thinking about that tonight. We really don't have any proof of anything, do we?"

"We have a photo of Alma's dead body with a bracelet on her wrist that wasn't recorded in evidence. This is exactly what you're looking at, Natalie. Someone dropped the ball." He cleared his throat. "You're going to have to come clean, though. You have to declare your connection to the

Katie Fellows's case because you'll have to explain how you know the pendant on Sierra Conchas belonged to Katie."

"I can't do that, Michael. I'll be removed from this investigation, and we'll never find out what happened. We can work around that bit of information. Sierra's mother insisted she'd never seen the pendant before, so it must've come from the killer."

"That's a big leap. Do you want to come over to my place tomorrow when I call Detective Ibarra? I'm sure he's going to want to come by to look at the dog and ask questions. We can lay things out for him then."

"I was supposed to meet Rachelle in the DNA lab tomorrow, but her boss, Dr. Volosin, came back tonight. Do you know if Rachelle is coming in tomorrow, or is she still sick?"

"I haven't heard from her yet. So you met Phil Volosin."

"He came straight to the lab from the airport."

"He does that a lot."

"He's obnoxious."

Michael chuckled. "He can be abrasive, but he does a good job. He was the keynote speaker at that conference."

"And yet…" Natalie clicked her tongue. "He was at the forensics lab when all these issues occurred."

"I don't believe any of the issues involved DNA testing. There might've been DNA samples missing, but that would've happened before they reached Volosin's lab."

"If you say so." Natalie stood up and stretched. "I'll let you go. You must be exhausted."

"Send me a quick text when you get back to the hotel."

"Why? Are you afraid I'll have another brake failure?"

"You never know."

Natalie ended the call and left the conference room. She sailed through the lobby and waved at Miles on her way out as he clicked the lock open for her. The parking lot had fewer cars than when she'd arrived.

As she made the short drive back to her hotel, the skies opened, and rain spattered against her car. She parked as close as she could to the hotel entrance and made a run for the lobby, holding her bag over her head.

The front desk clerk called to her as she made a beeline to the elevator.

"Ms. Brunetti, you have a message."

A message? She glanced at her phone clutched in her hand. Had Michael tried to reach her on her cell phone? Nope. Battery fully charged, no messages.

She shifted course and veered toward the front desk. "A telephone message?"

"It's actually a written note, or at least something in an envelope. Somebody left it on the counter earlier this evening." He handed her a small white envelope with her name written on it in a childish scrawl.

Something about that handwriting made her skin tingle, and she took the envelope with a trembling hand. Inserting her thumb between the flap and the envelope, she ripped it open.

She plucked out the folded sheet of paper and read the words.

Nat, meet me in our regular spot tonight. Luv ya, Katie.

The *i* in Katie's name had a heart for the dot, just like Katie used to write it. The words blurred together, and she gripped the edge of the counter.

"Is everything okay, Ms. Brunetti?" The front desk clerk's face crumpled with worry.

Pinching the note between two fingers, she held it up. "Who left this?"

"I'm sorry. I don't know. It was sitting on the counter when I started my shift at five. I recognized your name and put it by my computer, so I wouldn't forget it when you walked in." His gaze darted to the envelope. "Is there a problem?"

"No, but I'd really like to know who left this. You must have cameras in here. Can I look at the footage?" Even she could recognize her hysterical tone, and the clerk's eyebrows were climbing higher and higher on his forehead.

"Ma'am, I'm sorry, but we can't allow guests to view our security footage. If there was a crime committed, if someone threatened you, we can get the police involved. They can request the footage."

"N-no crime. Just a note from…an old friend. I wanted to see if it was really her."

"If anything changes, ma'am, I'll be happy to get the police involved." He held up one finger. "And you can ask our day clerk, Daria. I believe she's working tomorrow."

"Thanks—" her gaze dropped to his nametag "—Ben. Maybe I'll talk to Daria."

Ben pasted the smile back on his face. "I'll give her a heads-up."

Natalie nodded and walked to the couch in the lobby on shaky legs. This had to be some kind of cruel joke. Had Zane done this? Did he really blame her for Katie's disappearance? Who else knew her identity? Did Dr. Volosin put two and two together. He was here at the lab when Katie disappeared. Would he have remembered the scared teen who'd narrowly escaped a similar fate that night?

She flattened out the note on her knee. She knew where their regular spot was. She'd been there earlier in the week.

A swing set and slide sat at the entrance to the campsite near Devil's Edge Trail. She and Katie used to meet on the swings or up the stairs at the top of the slide. They'd even scratched their names into the metal of the slide.

Tonight. Someone wanted to meet her there tonight. Who knew about that meeting place? Who knew Katie put a heart over the *i* in her name? Had Katie returned? Maybe she had been a runaway all this time.

She wouldn't go alone. Not this time. Not that place.

She tapped Michael's number, and he picked up after the first ring. "You didn't have to call. Just a text, but I'm happy to hear your voice again."

And she was happy to hear his voice. The low, firm timbre made her feel grounded. "When I got back to the hotel, the clerk had a note for me at the reception desk. It was a note from Katie telling me to meet her in our regular spot tonight. Handwriting looked like hers, including a particular quirk."

"Someone's playing a prank on you, Natalie. Could it be Katie's teenage boyfriend?"

"Zane? I thought about that, but doesn't seem to be his style. He came right to the hotel to talk to me face-to-face. Someone else must know my identity, Michael."

"Where is this meeting spot?"

"Entrance to the Devil's Edge campsite—the playground equipment."

He sucked in a breath. "You're not considering it, are you?"

"I am if you come with me. Even if it's a prankster, I want to know who it is and why he's doing this."

"Okay, I'm closer to Devil's Edge than you are. Drive to my place and we'll go over in my car."

"Whoever wrote that note is not going to be there if I come with backup. You need to stay out of sight."

He growled. "I'll stay out of sight, but you'd better be strapped."

"Don't worry about that." She pushed up from the couch. "Separate cars. We come in the same way as the night we met. I'll park in the lot for the campsite, and you park in the pull-out for the trail and come in that way."

"Give me a head start. I want to be on that trail by the time you reach the parking lot. Hopefully, this rain will let up. That trail is nasty when it's wet."

"You leave now." She strode toward the elevator. "I'll go up and change clothes."

Fifteen minutes later, she'd changed into dark jeans, a black jacket and hiking boots. She texted Michael to make sure he was already on his way, and then she hopped in her car.

Before the turnoff for the campsite parking lot, Michael texted that he was at the trailhead and ready to go. Natalie's shoes scrunched over the soupy gravel of the parking lot, its one light trying valiantly to illuminate every corner. It failed.

Natalie's gaze swept the empty parking lot through the windshield wipers sluicing rain from her windshield in a rhythmic pattern that seemed to say "go back, go back."

But she wasn't a foolish teenager this time. She'd failed Katie before, but she wouldn't allow that to happen again. She flicked up the hood of her jacket and placed one booted foot on the ground, then grabbed a flashlight and patted her weapon in her pocket.

She had no intention of creeping around like a scared rabbit. She called out in a loud voice. "Hello? Who's out there? What kind of game are you playing?"

Drops of rain trickled from the edge of her hood and sprinkled her face. The chain on one of the swings whined, and she jerked her head around. A light breeze ruffled the tips of the leaves and pushed at the swing again, as if there was a phantom person sitting in it.

Katie used to love the swings.

Despite herself, Natalie whispered her friend's name.

Then she stamped her feet and shook the rain off her jacket. This person wanted to get under her skin, wanted her to feel uneasy. They'd succeeded.

"Hello! You wanted this meeting. You got it." Could Michael hear her inane yelling? She sure as hell hoped so.

As she passed the swing set, she grabbed the chain on one swing, pulled it back and released it, sending the seat dancing back and forth. She marched to the slide and grabbed the slippery handrail. The metal steps clanged with each tread to the top of the slide. The familiar covered platform beckoned, and she ducked to take a seat in the space, which was big enough for two to huddle within its confines.

Lowering her body, she leaned her back against one rounded side. She flicked her flashlight over the graffiti and scratches on the inside of the cover until she found the names—Katie and Nat. Only Katie's name was scratched out.

A breath hitched in Natalie's throat and as she reached out to trace the names, flakes of paint came off on her fingertips. As she let out a stifled sob, a loud clang reverberated in the small space, deafening her.

The next pop sounded more familiar. Someone was shooting at her.

Chapter Sixteen

Michael slogged into a puddle and swore. What did Natalie hope to find out here? At least she hadn't run out helter-skelter on her own. She'd called him. She trusted him. It had been a long time since someone trusted him.

He heard a woman yelling, and he froze. Was she in trouble already? Then he made out the words and realized Natalie was just announcing her presence. That was probably the best way to go about this. No sense sneaking up on someone.

An animal crackled in the bushes to his right, and he aimed his flashlight in the direction of the noise. It scurried away, and he continued on the trail. The rain-soaked earth gave off a loamy smell that he tasted in the back of his throat.

A branch cracked ahead of him. Startled, he tripped over a root. As he grumbled and clambered to his feet, the sound of gunfire echoed through the forest—and he knew hunting wasn't allowed in this area.

Before he was even steady, another shot rang out. He yelled, "Natalie."

His legs pumped like pistons as he ran through the woods, wet branches smacking his face, twigs grabbing at his hair. The shooting had stopped, and he hoped that at least one of those bullets had come from Natalie's weapon.

He stumbled into the campsite parking lot, Natalie's car taking up the space beneath the only light. He called her name again as he careened toward the playground equipment. One swing shivered as he blew past it, his flashlight scanning the old metal slide.

His eyes widened as he spotted Natalie flying down the slide on her back, her gun in front of her. She hit the ground and got into a crouch.

Michael called out quickly. "It's me. Michael."

"Get down, Michael. Someone just took a couple of shots at me, and I have no idea from which direction."

He dropped to the ground, but all he wanted was to get to Natalie. He army-crawled toward her, his elbows digging into the mud. When he reached her, she pulled him beneath the slide with her.

"Are you alright? Did you get hit?" He grabbed her shoulders and ran his hands down her arms.

"I'm fine. I was up on the slide's platform. It saved me. The first bullet hit the cover, but it didn't penetrate."

"And the second?" He fumbled for the phone in his jacket pocket.

"Missed the slide completely." She put her hand on his phone. "What are you doing?"

"I'm calling nine-one-one. Someone just shot at you."

"And what were you doing at Devil's Edge campsite in the middle of the night in the rain, Agent Brunetti. Well, you see I got a note from my best friend who went missing, presumed dead, thirteen years ago, and I thought we'd catch up on old times." She shook her head, and droplets from her hood sprinkled his face. "We can't call the sheriffs, Michael, just like I can't tell Detective Ibarra about the pendant found on Sierra's body. I'll blow my cover. If the FBI takes me off this audit, I'll never find out what happened to Katie, and you may never find out what happened to Raine. Nobody wants answers to these questions more than we do. Please."

She'd gripped his wrist in a vise hold, her gaze still turned outward, scanning the parking lot and the trees beyond. How far was she willing to take this? Someone tampered with her brakes and just took a couple of potshots at her. What next? How guilty did she have to feel about Katie's disappearance to risk her own safety?

The raindrops slowed to an intermittent pinging against the metal of the slide, and Michael's heartbeat matched the rhythm. If they called the cops, he'd have his own explaining to do as to why he was on the trail where his wife had been murdered.

He dropped his phone back in his pocket. "Let's get out of here. That bullet that hit the canopy of the slide, do you think we can find the pieces?"

"If it shattered, which is most certainly did, what good will that do us?"

"You work in forensics. If the pieces are big enough or there are enough of them, there's some reconstruction work that can be done. Also, you're lucky." He knocked on the side of the slide. "The slide is metal, but it's not that heavy. A different type of bullet may have even pierced it. A full-metal-jacket bullet probably wouldn't disintegrate at all. It's worth a look."

"Yeah, as long as someone's not shooting at us while we try to find it." She narrowed her eyes as she stared into the darkness.

"You're the one with the gun. Cover me while I take a look."

She dropped her chin to her chest. "Go."

He crawled toward the slide's ladder, leaving his flashlight behind. No sense in giving the shooter a target. When he got to the base of the slide, he cupped his hand around his phone and used the light to illuminate the ground.

He felt along the ground, his fingers becoming accustomed to the feel of the rocks and gravel that pebbled beneath them. He didn't expect the bullet or any fragments to still be hot. They'd been fired long enough ago to have cooled down, and the rain would've done its job, too.

His fingers stumbled across a smooth arc with a jagged edge, and he dragged his phone's light along the ground to highlight the piece. Definitely a bullet fragment.

His next find had his heart thumping—the distorted and flattened point of a bullet. He closed his hand around the bullet fragments and scuffed along the ground back to Natalie, her gun aimed in front of her as she scanned the area.

"I found something that might be useful." He unfurled his hand, the pieces stark against his palm. "This guy just made the biggest mistake of his life."

FOR ABOUT THE one hundredth time that night, Natalie thanked God that she'd had the good sense to call Michael before going on this fool's errand.

Hunched over, they ran back to Natalie's car, and she gunned it out of the parking lot. Michael had to point out his vehicle parked in the outlet, and she eased behind it, both cars hidden by overhanging tree branches and dripping leaves.

She cut the engine and sat with her eyes closed, breathing heavily. "I suppose that means the note wasn't from Katie."

"Unless Katie turned into a psychopath and doesn't want to be found." He rubbed her thigh through her damp and dirty jeans. "Someone wrote that note to lure you out to the campsite. But then you already knew that."

"I knew it, but—" she swung around to face him, tears hanging from her eyelashes "—when I was up on that slide, and I saw our names scratched into the metal, I remembered. And those memories hurt."

She blinked and a tear rolled down her cheek. Michael reached over and caught on his fingertip before it dripped off her chin.

His voice husky, he whispered in her ear. "It's not your fault. None of it is your fault."

Grabbing his hand, she pulled it to her lips and planted a kiss on the center of his palm, where he'd cupped the bullet that almost hit her. "Thank you for being there. Thank you for keeping my confidences when the information we have would probably clear your name in your wife's murder once and for all."

He wedged a finger beneath her chin. "I'm no saint. I have my own reasons for playing this close to the vest."

"Don't do that." She brushed a lock of wet hair from his forehead. "Don't downplay your kindness, your integrity. You're one of the good guys, Michael Wilder."

A short and bitter laugh erupted from his lips. "I haven't been called a good guy in a long time. I tried to prevent a mother from seeing her child. I pushed her away instead of getting help for her. I left her on her own, and someone murdered her."

She placed two fingers against his soft lips. "What did you just tell me? It's not your fault. Stop blaming yourself for what had to be done to protect your daughter."

He puckered his lips against her fingertips. "How do you see me? How do you know me so well?"

"Because when I look at you, I see a reflection of all my

doubts and fears…and my hopes. Because I still have hope, even more now that I've met you."

He reached for her across the seat, and she went willingly, squeezing past the steering wheel to straddle him in the passenger seat. His hand scooped through her curly mop of damp hair as he leveled her head with his for a kiss.

As his tongue probed her mouth, she ran her hands down his body and peeled off his jacket. Despite the cool temperatures, Michael wore a thin, white T-shirt beneath the jacket, and it clung to his muscled framed.

Her fingers danced beneath the hem of his shirt, and she lightly ran her nails across his chest. He shivered beneath her, encircling her waist with his hands. As she rocked against him, he lifted his hips and reached down to fumble with the fly of his jeans.

She shooed away his clumsy hands and deftly undid the button and zipper. He returned the favor. As she rose to her knees, he yanked her jeans and panties down her thighs.

Falling against him, they met, skin on skin, and a deep need pulsed in her core. She trailed her lips across the dark shadow of bristles on his chin and whispered in his ear, "Are we mad?"

"I've ached for you for days. When I heard the gunshots tonight, I felt a dread so pure, I couldn't name it." He smoothed her hair back from her face. "I can't name this."

"We don't need to label it." She shifted against him, feeling his physical need for her, fueling her desire for him.

He cupped her backside with his strong hands and lowered her hips until he entered her tentatively at first, and then his pelvis thrust forward. He slid deep inside her, filling every recess of longing and hurt.

She undulated against him until they found a cadence all their own, where he seemed to anticipate her desires, and she answered his every request. Their passion raged to a fever pitch, and Natalie threw out a hand against the foggy window to try for some leverage against the coming inferno.

When Michael came, he wrapped his arms around her waist and took her along for the ride. Throwing back her head, she pressed against him, gritting her teeth, her muscles taut, until she shattered.

They clasped each other close, arms, legs, clothes, all in a tangle, rocking together, not wanting to let the other go. Her head dropped to his shoulder, and her tongue darted out to lick his neck, salty with his sweat.

As she began to peel herself from his chest, a siren whooped twice, and a red light illuminated their love nest.

Wide-eyed, their gazes locked until Michael broke the spell by cursing. Natalie scrambled back into her seat, pulling at her jeans. Just as she grabbed her zipper, a hard object tapped at her window.

She murmured to Michael. "Are you decent?"

He grunted. "Getting there."

Natalie pulled her hair from her face and powered down the window to reveal Deputy Reynolds's grinning visage. Knots formed in her gut, as she searched his face for signs of recognition. She had darkness on her side.

His gaze jumped from her to Michael, and his mouth turned into an *O* and his eyebrows shot up and disappeared beneath his hat.

"Well, well. Is this a work meeting?"

The sight of his face made Natalie's stomach turn, but he didn't seem to know her beyond her purpose here in town. How could Katie have ever thought this smarmy loser was cute?

Michael's voice, so different from his whispers minutes

before, boomed in the car. "Yeah. Yeah, it is. Are we break-ing any laws, Deputy Reynolds?"

"Excuse me." He lifted his shoulders. "Saw the car, the steamy windows and figured you two were a couple of kids making out."

Tipping up her chin, Natalie huffed. "Clearly, we're not."

"Clearly." Reynolds's gaze dropped to her lap, where her jeans still gaped open. He rapped on the outside of the car with his knuckles. "Can't get enough of this area, hey, Wilder?"

Michael slicked back his hair with one hand. "Actually, Raine's homicide might have something to do with some cold cases—a few you even worked on, Reynolds."

Reynolds's face seemed to blanch in the darkness, but that could've been Natalie's imagination. His Adam's apple did bob. "Is that so?"

"Yep. Just discovered some bombshell evidence to-night…but you'll have to wait until tomorrow when I pres-ent it to Detective Ibarra. Now, if you're all done harassing us, we've got a meeting to finish up."

Reynolds backed away from the car, hands raised. "Carry on."

They sat still until they heard his car pull away. Then Natalie covered her mouth and giggled. Michael slapped his knee and let out a guffaw. They turned to each other at the same time and fell into each other's arms, laughing.

Natalie buried her face against Michael's T-shirt, wiping her tears. Maybe they laughed all the more because they knew tomorrow they'd be unleashing a firestorm.

Chapter Seventeen

The following morning, Natalie climbed into Michael's car, which was parked behind the lab. They'd both shown up for work but had kept their distance. She didn't know if she could look at him in public after what had happened the night before—and and not because of the shooting.

She'd rewound their encounter so many times last night, she'd had trouble sleeping. After Reynolds left and they'd had their giggling fit, they'd kept it all business, discussing the plan forward today. Then he'd given her a chaste kiss, gotten in his car and followed her back to the hotel... but not to continue what they'd started in the car. He just wanted to make sure she got back safely, which was almost as sexy as the sex.

She smoothed her wool skirt against her thighs and pulled the shoulder strap across her body. "I hope Reynolds isn't at the station."

"You said you didn't think he recognized you." Michael started the engine and pulled out of the lab parking lot.

"I don't think he did, but in the light of day with me standing right in front of him instead of cowering in a car, he just might."

He snorted. "Didn't look like you were cowering to me.

Are you ready for this?" He squeezed her knee right above her black boots. "Are you ready for the derision and disbelief as we lay out this story?"

"I'm ready if you are." She flipped down the visor and touched up her lipstick in the mirror. "Did you take care of the bullet fragments?"

"I put a rush on it. My friend at the Seattle lab owes me, so he'll keep quiet about it. We do each other favors sometimes."

She covered her ears. "I didn't hear that. It's exactly the type of thing we're supposed to uncover."

"You're the one who wanted to keep the shooting quiet. I'm just helping you out."

"And I appreciate it. Does your contact in Seattle think he can trace the bullet, even though it's in pieces?"

"He's done more with less. If he can detect the striations on the bullet and if anything matches in the database, we can trace it. Without bullets from the same gun or the firearm itself, we're out of luck." Michael brushed his knuckle across her cheek. "Any regrets about last night?"

Her skin prickled. "Besides getting shot at? No, it was great."

Chuckling, he pinched her chin. "That's not what I was talking about."

"The only regret I have—" she caught his hand and kissed the inside of his wrist "—is that we got interrupted. You?"

"Only that such a momentous event took place in a car. You deserve scented bath water and rose petals and champagne." He made a flourish with his hand.

"All that's nice, but doing it in a car is kinda hot."

And talking about it was even hotter. She changed the subject. "You know, I noticed something last night while

I was on the slide that slipped my mind after…everything else."

"What was it?"

"Katie and I had scratched our names into the metal on the inside of the slide's canopy. Our names were still there, but someone had scratched out Katie's name. When I ran my fingers across the etching of her name, paint flakes came loose. It was as if someone had just scratched out the name recently. Do you think someone was on that platform before I came? Maybe he was waiting for me there first."

"If so, I'm glad he left. He would've had a clear shot at you walking up the ladder. That covering saved your life."

She'd thought the same thing. Actually, she'd thought it was Katie looking out for her, but she didn't want to admit that—not even to Michael.

Michael pulled into the parking lot of the sheriff's station, and the knots in Natalie's stomach tightened. Nothing much had changed about the building since she'd walked through those doors as a teenager with her parents, their faces stoic. She never would've believed she'd be back here as an adult, still with no answers about what happened to Katie that night.

Michael cupped her elbow up as they walked to the front doors, and then dropped it as he ushered her inside, ahead of him.

The deputy at the front desk greeted Michael, said hello to Natalie and then buzzed Detective Ibarra.

Detective Ibarra came out with a swagger to his walk and crinkles around his warm, dark eyes. If he'd been investigating Katie's murder, Natalie would've spilled her guts to him.

"Michael, good to see you again." The men shook hands, and then Ibarra turned his attention to her. "Michael doesn't even need to introduce you. Even if it weren't for the town buzz, I'd have you pegged."

Natalie's eyes widened, and she held her breath.

"Special Agent Natalie Brunetti, the Fed who came to town to straighten us out." Ibarra's broad grin took the irony out of his words, and his warm grasp put a nail in it.

"A bit of an exaggeration, Detective Ibarra, but I'll do my best to clarify some of the evidence in those old cases." She squeezed the large hand that engulfed hers.

He tilted his head. "But you two aren't here about an old case, are you?"

Michael answered. "Yes and no."

Ibarra invited them to his office in the back, and they settled in two comfortable chairs across from his desk. At least he hadn't put them in an interrogation room.

Ibarra flattened his tie against his shirt and folded his hands on his stomach. "What news do you have for me, Michael?"

"The dog came back home last night."

The pleasant smile on Ibarra's face dropped, and he hunched forward. "The dog that was with your wife when she was murdered?"

"That's right. She wandered into the backyard last night, a little worse for wear, but healthy."

"My God. If dogs could talk, huh? I'm assuming the dog didn't have any evidence on her—bloodstains, fibers, hair? After six months, that would've all washed away.

"There *was* evidence, Gil, just not the evidence you'd expect." Michael reached into his jacket pocket and pulled out Alma's bracelet, which he'd placed in a plastic bag. "This jewelry was wrapped around her collar."

Ibarra held out his hand. "Was it Raine's?"

Pulling out her phone, Natalie said, "No. We believe the

bracelet belonged to a young murder victim from twelve years ago—Alma Nguyen, and I have Mrs. Nguyen's verification."

"What are you saying?" Ibarra brought the baggie close to his face, studying the bracelet within. "Alma's killer stole her bracelet and had it with him when he murdered Raine twelve years later?"

"And it's not the first time he's done it, Gil." Michael launched into everything they'd discovered and suspected about the jewelry of the dead women, giving Natalie ample opportunity to contribute, even though she still kept her true identity a secret.

When they'd finished, Ibarra didn't throw them out of his office, which was the good news. The bad? He narrowed his eyes, all warmth vanquished, replaced by cold, hard suspicion. The look he must get when listening to a suspect lying, knowing he has the receipts.

"First—" Ibarra held up one finger, nail bitten down to the quick "—why did a serial killer come out of retirement after twelve years to murder a woman a good ten years' senior to his usual victims?"

Michael interrupted. "Can I answer that before you get to number two?"

"Go ahead." Ibarra sounded bored, as if he knew what was coming.

"The killer could've been in prison, in a different area, been in different social circumstances like a marriage and children. As far as the age, this guy doesn't have a clear MO except for the jewelry. That's what links the victims."

"Michael—" Ibarra chewed on his lip "—if this guy killed Sierra and Alma and maybe Katie, his MO is victims in their late teens and early twenties. That's probably not gonna change for him. Was Raine a victim of opportunity for someone out of practice? Maybe. But you don't even have the jewelry part nailed down. An unfamiliar pendant was found with Sierra's body, but there's no way of knowing if that pendant belonged to Katie Fellows."

Natalie kept her eyes on Ibarra as she felt Michael's gaze hot on her cheek.

Ibarra sat forward in his chair, warming to his subject. "Sierra may or may not have been missing one of her many bangles. One of those bangles may have been on Alma's wrist, but we don't have a clear picture of it, and it's not listed in evidence. That's something for Agent Brunetti to expose in her report, I'm sure. That's sloppy police work. Sloppy forensics."

Natalie hit the desk with the flat of her hand, making both men jump. "And Alma's bracelet on Peaches?"

Picking up the corner of the baggie containing the bracelet and swinging it from his fingertips, Ibarra said, "I'll turn it over to the forensics lab in Seattle. They'll test it for blood, prints, DNA, the works. Of course, it's important, but is it Alma Nguyen's? You have a grieving mother ID'ing it from a texted picture on your phone twelve years after the fact."

"You're not going to reopen these cases or entertain the idea that Raine could've been the victim of a long-acting serial killer?" Michael slumped in his chair.

"I'm going to let Agent Brunetti do her job and let the chips fall where they may, even if it makes this department, and your lab, look bad. I'll support her in any way I can." He dropped the bracelet. "I'm also going to send someone out from Seattle to check on… Peaches, just in case, and as far as I'm concerned Michael, your alibi stands, and you're in no way a suspect in your wife's homicide."

Michael stood up abruptly. "You have to admit, Gil, the connections are interesting."

"If we had all the proof, I'd agree. These are cold cases. They're not closed. Maybe one day the proof will materialize."

As Michael held out his hand to Ibarra, he kicked the leg of Natalie's chair, and she jumped up. "Thanks for your time. Let me know when you want to examine the dog."

Ibarra shook Michael's hand. "I'm glad Peaches is back, Michael—for your little girl. I'm glad the dog is back home."

When they got back to the car, Natalie tipped back her head. "The worst part is that he's not wrong. We just don't have the proof."

"Proof would've been stronger if you'd told him what you know about Katie's pendant. Not pictures on a phone, not hearsay. It was your pendant, you let Katie wear it the night she disappeared, you saw it in the evidence from Sierra's homicide. Proof."

She whipped her head around at the hard edge to his voice. His tight jaw matched the tone. "If everyone knew about my connection to this area and to Katie Fellows, I wouldn't even be here. You never would've known the bracelet attached to Peaches belonged to a past homicide victim."

"But now we know the connections. It doesn't have to be you."

"Doesn't have to be me, what?" She pursed her lips and dug her fingernails into the edge of the seat.

"You don't have to be the one to solve Katie's disappearance. You can help someone else do it. It's still justice."

Tears pricked the back of her eyes, and she swallowed. "Just take me back to the lab. I have work to do."

They finished the ride in silence and when Natalie got out of Michael's car, he stayed put. They'd already agreed they shouldn't be seen leaving together. She slammed the car door, anyway.

On a mission to get back to her office, she almost bumped into Jacob Reynolds moving some computer equipment. He made a grab for a keyboard as it slid from the cart. "Oops. Sorry, Agent Brunetti. Didn't see you."

She glared at his smiling face, so like his father's, and growled. "Watch where you're going."

When she closed the door to the conference room, she immediately felt bad. It wasn't Jacob's fault his father was a jerk. He seemed like a nice kid.

She hadn't seen Rachelle yet today and wondered if she was still sick. Should she go ahead and tour the DNA lab with Dr. Volosin alone? The thought made her skin crawl, and she pulled up the lab's personnel files. She found Rachelle's cell-phone number and called.

A woman answered tentatively after a few rings. "Rachelle? It's Natalie Brunetti. Are you still sick?"

"Not feeling great. I'm sorry I wasn't there for our appointment the other day, Natalie…and I know Dr. Volosin is back. He already called me with a thousand questions about how I ran the lab in his absence."

"I feel for you. I met him last night. Unpleasant." Natalie put her phone on speaker and strolled to the window to see if Michael had made his way back into the office yet. "I still need to tour the DNA lab. I wanted to wait until you're there, even if Dr. Volosin joins us."

"I'm still feeling under the weather, Natalie, and Dr. Volosin doesn't make me feel much better, but…"

"But what?" The quality of Rachelle's voice had changed. It had taken on a quality of urgency, one she'd heard the first time Rachelle suggested Natalie visit the lab before Volosin returned.

"I'd like to talk to you about a few things, and it would be better if we were away from the lab. C-can you come to my place this afternoon, or even after work?"

"I can do that. Are you far from the lab? I can drop by when I'm done at the lab, if that's okay."

"That's fine."

Rachelle gave her the address of her town house on the lake, and Natalie jotted it down on a pad of paper. After the call, Natalie tapped the pen against the pad. Rachelle hadn't even been working at the lab at the time of the cold cases Natalie was investigating. Were things still off here? Or did Rachelle have some information about her boss who was here at the time of the cold cases?

For the next several hours, Natalie put aside the distractions and her own investigative efforts to work on the cold cases assigned to her. The other victims deserved their justice as much as Katie did hers.

She finished up the day by sending her boss another report. He'd be happy with her progress, and she had to keep him happy to stay out here and complete *all* her work, even the stuff he didn't know about.

As she packed up her files and laptop, she glanced at her phone. Michael hadn't dropped by or contacted her the rest of the day. She could understand his frustration, but she had to do this her way, or not at all.

Before she left the office, she entered Rachelle's address in her phone's GPS. Maybe she should tell Michael about her off-site meeting with Rachelle, but if the woman had info about the lab's current state, maybe it would be better to keep this to herself.

The drive to Rachelle's place didn't take long and offered relaxing views of the lake on one side. These developments had gone up since her residence here in Marysville. She'd remembered her father complaining about the proposal to build on this side of the lake, but the tasteful town houses fit in with their surroundings.

Natalie wheeled into the guest parking lot and nabbed an empty spot. She had an easy time finding Rachelle's building as a backlight illuminated the numbers on each one. She'd parked close to Rachelle's building and the walkway that led into the courtyard.

Her boots clicked on the pavers, a harsh contrast to the soothing sounds of a bubbling fountain in the center of the courtyard. She ducked onto a rustic path that led to more town houses around the back.

Spotting Rachelle's address, Natalie took the gravel path next to the lakeside walking trail to the town house. Moving furniture into this place had to be hell, but she'd take the inconvenience for the bucolic beauty.

A row of neat flowers edged the porch, and Rachelle had added more splashes of color with adorable window boxes. Natalie rang the doorbell next to the red door.

She shifted from one foot to the other, giving Rachelle time. If she'd been the one home sick all day, it would take her a while to get to the front door. Several seconds later, Natalie pressed the doorbell again, this time putting her ear to the solid door to listen for the sound of the bell inside. Yep, it worked.

Natalie placed her hand flat against the door. Was she okay in there? Did Rachelle have the flu? Nobody ever said.

Natalie curled her hand into a fist and knocked. "Rachelle? It's Natalie. Are you alright?"

Was that a moan? A rustle? Natalie bit her bottom lip and tried the door. The handle turned beneath her fingers, and she pushed open the door.

She squealed as a cat jumped off a bookshelf and swished its tail with an angry squawk.

"Rachelle?" She closed the door behind her, so the cat wouldn't run outside, and crept into the town house, although she didn't know why she needed to be quiet. In fact, the quiet was unnerving.

She called Rachelle's name again. A lamp lit the living room, along with the muted TV, but most of the light came from the kitchen. The cat had gone that way, so Natalie followed it.

As she peered into the kitchen, she gasped. Rachelle was lying crumpled on the tile floor, a broken bowl beside her and a smear of blood on her face.

Chapter Eighteen

Michael stretched out on the floor and scratched Peaches's head. "You must have a story to tell."

Molly poked her head out of the kitchen. "Do you want any more food? I'm putting it away."

"No, I'm good."

"I thought you might bring Natalie back here for dinner, since we didn't get to feed her last night." She put a hand on her hip.

"Have you turned into Mom? Mind your own business." He lifted Peaches up and placed her on his stomach. "We need to fatten her up."

"Sorry Ivy went to sleep so soon after dinner. She was playing with Peaches all day. Wouldn't let her out of her sight."

"That's fine. She needs her sleep. I'll spend time with her this weekend." Michael's phone rang, and his heart skipped a beat when he saw his friend, Deputy Cole Foster, pop up on his display. Did they want to check out the dog already?

"What's up, Cole?"

"Just got a call on my radio. Thought you might wanna know. One of your lab employees was found dead in her home."

"What? Who?" Michael nudged Peaches from his stomach and staggered to his feet.

"It's Dr. Rachelle Butler. She works in the lab, right?"

"Rachelle? Cause of death? She's been out sick, but I had no idea she was dangerously ill."

"Can't tell you much more than that. The FBI agent you have working for you found her body."

Michael clamped the back of his neck. "In Rachelle's home? She was in Rachelle's home?"

"Dude, I don't have anything more than that. Just happened. I'm on my way."

"Address." Michael grabbed a pair of running shoes. "Do you have Rachelle's address?"

As soon as Cole recited the address to him, Michael ended the call and strode to the closet for his jacket. "Molly, I have to go out."

Before she could answer, he slammed the door. How was Rachelle dead, and what was Natalie doing in the middle of it?

He drove faster than the speed limit to reach Rachelle's place, the new development out by the lake. Rachelle was a doctor. She should've known if she needed medical attention. Hell, she hadn't even looked that sick the day she came to tell him she was leaving early.

Emergency vehicles clogged the parking lot, so Michael pulled onto the street outside the town-house development. He didn't need the address number to find Rachelle's place. As he walked up to the building, he could see a deputy questioning a tearful Natalie off to the side.

Recognizing him, the deputy keeping the lookie-loos at bay allowed Michael to dip beneath the yellow tape. CSIs were already on the scene, but his lab wouldn't be getting the evidence. Were they there out of courtesy for Rachelle, or did they believe her death was something other than natural or accidental?

As Deputy Ellis walked past, Michael grabbed his arm. "What happened in there? How did Rachelle die?"

Ellis shrugged. "We don't know that yet. The only visible injury she sustained was a cut to her cheek, but that was from a broken bowl. Looks like she fell to the floor with the bowl in her hand or on the counter, it broke, and a piece cut her face."

Michael pinched the bridge of his nose. "Did she die from the fall? Head injury?"

"Not that we can tell, unless there's something internal. Uh—" Ellis glanced over his shoulder "—her skin was blueish, and she had a little vomit in her mouth."

"Well, she didn't do drugs. Maybe she took something for her illness. She'd called in sick, but she didn't tell me what was wrong."

Grabbing Michael's shoulder, Ellis said, "We owe it to one of our own to figure out what happened."

"Do you know what Agent Brunetti was doing here?"

"Ask her yourself." Ellis jerked his head to the right at Natalie approaching them, still wearing her knee-high boots from this morning, her hands shoved into her pockets.

Ellis asked, "Are you doing okay?"

Natalie waved him off and grabbed Michael's sleeve. "Did he tell you what happened?"

"Just that you found her on the floor. A piece of glass from a broken bowl cut her face but no other injuries." He wanted to pull her into his arms, but it wasn't the time or the place. "Do you want to tell me what you were doing at Rachelle's place after hours?"

"Not here." She strode back to the deputy who was questioning her earlier and had a brief discussion with him.

Then she made her way back to him, stumbling when the coroner's van pulled up.

When she reached his side, she prodded him in the back. "They're done with me. Let's talk in my car."

He followed her to the rental and slid into the passenger seat. "What the hell is going on, Natalie?"

"I didn't tell you before, but Rachelle wanted to show me around the DNA lab before Dr. Volosin returned."

"Doesn't surprise me. He's a difficult guy to work with." He rapped his knuckle against the window. "Can you drive out of this parking lot? I'm in the street."

Natalie started the car and maneuvered around the emergency vehicles to get to the street in the front. She pulled behind his car and cut the engine. "Anyway, Rachelle got sick, and Volosin returned from his trip, which meant he'd be present during my tour of the lab. So I called Rachelle at home today to ask her if she wanted to be present during my lab review. She got all weird and told me she needed to see me, that she had something to tell me."

Michael rubbed his eyes, suddenly so tired. "Did she give you any hints?"

"None, but she definitely wanted to have this conversation away from the lab."

A pain stabbed him at the base of his neck. "What are you suggesting? She didn't feel safe at the lab? She thought something was going on there?"

"Whoa." Natalie cut her hands through the air. "I'm not suggesting anything. I'm telling you what she said. You're the one who doesn't trust me."

Michael toyed with the scrap of paper in his pocket. "How did she sound on the phone? Ill? Did she ever mention what illness she had?"

"She didn't say, and I didn't ask. But she didn't sound

congested, and she didn't seem worried about being contagious. Maybe she wasn't sick. Maybe she didn't want to be there when Dr. Volosin returned."

"If she wasn't sick, how did she die? Did her fall look serious to you? Could there have been something she hit her head on when she fell?"

Natalie sniffed and dabbed the tip of her nose. "I don't know. I felt for a pulse, tried CPR. Her body felt cool but not cold, which would make sense, as I spoke to her on the phone several hours before I found her body. Michael, I think someone murdered Rachelle."

Pressing the heel of his hand against his forehead, he said, "What could she possibly know about any of this? Did you talk to her about the jewelry we found and the other connections?"

"Of course not." She shifted in her seat impatiently. "But she was about to tell me something about the lab. Something she didn't want anyone else there to hear."

Michael ground his back teeth together, sick of veiled accusations against him and the forensics lab he ran. He pulled the balled-up piece of paper from his pocket and bobbled it on his palm in front of Natalie.

"What's this?" She pinched the paper between her fingers and plucked it from his hand.

"While you were looking for dirt on the lab, I was busy trying to find out who shot at you last night."

"You got a match?" With trembling fingers, she picked open the crumpled piece of paper. "John Westfall, Shady View Rest Home in Everett? This is the shooter?"

"One fragment of the bullet was large enough to contain striations. My friend in Seattle was able to pick them up and run them through his database. Something finally went our way. He was able to match it to an old forty-five-caliber Beretta."

"Used in the commission of a crime? How could it still be on the street?" Natalie flattened the wrinkled scrap of paper to her chest, as if they'd found the Holy Grail.

"Wouldn't exactly call it the crime of the century. Some old guy was causing a nuisance, drunk and shooting at targets in the forest."

"John Westfall."

"Right. Deputies picked him up, checked his gun—the Beretta, registered to him—and let him off with a warning. They did put the bullets in the National Integrated Ballistic Information Network, though."

"NIBIN. Of course, I know it." She blew out a breath that fluttered the edges of the paper. "And the bullets from last night matched the bullets from this Beretta."

"Correct."

"Then what are we waiting for? Let's take a trip to the Shady View Rest Home."

NATALIE SAILED OUT of the hotel with cups of coffee in each hand and placed one on the hood of Michael's car as she opened the passenger door. He'd closed the forensics lab today in honor of Rachelle's death the day before. Nobody would've been able to get anything done, anyway.

"Thought you might want a coffee for the drive to Everett. Black?" She put the paper cup in the cupholder for him.

"Thanks. If you can dump one of those little creamers in there, that'd be great. If not, don't worry about it." He started the car. "It's just a thirty-minute drive, on the outskirts of Everett."

"I can manage the cream if you idle for a second while I pour it in." She peeled back the foil on the creamer and tipped it into Michael's coffee. She swirled the liquid with a stir stick and placed the cup back in the holder. "I didn't tell you. The FBI ordered the rental-car company to do a more thorough examination of the brakes and send them the report."

"Are they concerned that someone may have tampered with the rental car belonging to one of their agents?"

"That's why they're ordering additional tests." She sipped her own coffee. "Did the cops send someone to look at Peaches yet?"

"Nope. I'm getting the feeling that they think I'm some kind of jinx."

"Maybe we can get something on this John Westfall. Were you able to find out anything more about him besides his current residency at Shady View?" Natalie hadn't had any time of her own to check into him after leaving Rachelle's last night. The car accident, the shooting and discovering Rachelle had taken a toll on her body and mind. She'd fallen into bed last night and had slipped into an exhausted sleep. The old nightmare didn't even revisit her.

"Not much. Enlisted in the navy. Worked at Boeing for years, and retired from there when he had his accident."

"The shooting accident?"

Michael shook his head. "No, he almost drowned. Suffered brain damage. That's why he's in the rest home. He's not that old, or at least not as old as you'd expect a resident of Shady View to be."

"Brain damage, huh?" Natalie swirled her coffee and watched the little whirlpool in the cup. "Is he going to be able to talk to us?"

"No clue." Michael lifted his shoulders. "But it probably means he didn't sneak out of the rest home and murder Raine or fix your brakes or shoot at you."

Natalie folded her hands in her lap and tried to squeeze away the disappointment she felt. When Michael had told her about the bullets matching Westfall's gun, she'd figured they'd finally gotten a break. Something going their way for once. Now, the prospect of an interview with Westfall didn't seem so promising.

They arrived at Shady View faster than Natalie had time to regain her previous optimism. She eyed the spruce, the firs, the maples and alders ringing the property, blocking out the daylight. "They weren't kidding about the shady view, were they?"

"Shady and green."

Michael got out of the vehicle, and she followed suit, inhaling the competing smells from the different trees that gradually melded into a fresh scent that slapped the face.

She shivered and zipped up her jacket. "This is pretty, but I wouldn't want to end up in a place like this. Too dark."

"I know." Michael flipped up his collar. "I mean, they have a bay, a river and a sound out here. You'd think they could've given the guests a nice water view."

She jostled Michael's shoulder with her own as they approached the entrance. "They're not guests."

A smiling woman greeted them at the front desk. "Hello, I'm Monica. Welcome to Shady View. Are you looking for a place for your loved one?"

Michael spoke up first. "Uh, no. We came to visit one of your…guests. John Westfall."

Did Natalie imagine it, or did Monica's smile dim just a little?

"Do you have an appointment to see John?" Monica started clicking away on the keyboard in front of her.

"No. John's an old friend of my father's. I was in the area, and thought I'd drop in to say hello from my dad. That's alright, isn't it, Monica?"

Maybe Michael's blue eyes mesmerized her, but Monica was all smiles again. She even had a pink tinge to her cheeks. "Of course. We just need to ask John. What's the name?"

Natalie kicked Michael's foot. What if Westfall refused to see them?

"Tell him it's Jerry Wilder's son—from their old navy days."

"Just a moment, Mr. Wilder. I'll call his nurse."

As Monica got on the phone, Michael wandered to the window to look out on the unrelenting green.

Natalie came up behind him and whispered, "Is your dad's name Jerry?"

"No. Just thought I'd try a common name. Is he going to remember everyone he served with?"

"I don't know. These old guys can surprise you. My grandfather couldn't remember my nephew's name, but he could tell you all about the Battle of the Bulge…in detail."

"Great." Michael spun around when Monica called out.

"Mr. Wilder? John has agreed to your visit. Room one-sixty-five, down your hall, to the right."

"Thank you, Monica," he said sotto voce to Natalie as Monica buzzed the door. "We're in."

They ticked off the room numbers as they walked down the hallway, their shoes squeaking on the linoleum floor. Natalie's nose twitched at the smell of antiseptic that tried to cover the mustiness that seeped through. The denizens of Shady View should open the windows more and let in some of that fresh air.

When they reached 165, the door stood partially open, and Michael tapped on it before walking inside. The balding man facing them in a wheelchair did not look like he was capable of standing, never mind cutting brake lines and shooting a gun.

Undeterred, Michael pulled a chair close to Westfall, his knees almost touching those of the disabled man. "John, can you hear me?"

One side of John's mouth quirked upward in a permanent grin, but he nodded.

Michael got straight to the point. "John, did you own an old Beretta?"

John moved a stiff hand in his lap, the fingers curled inward. Natalie held her breath as she focused on his hand.

A nurse bustled into the room with a board under her arm. "If you expect to have a conversation with John, he needs his bell."

"Bell?" Natalie watched as the nurse put the board on John's lap and set a call bell on top of it, positioning his hand on top of the bell.

"One for yes, two for no. Right, John?" She squeezed John's shoulder and exited the room, leaving the door open.

Michael exchanged a look with Natalie and started again. "Did you own a Beretta, John?"

John's finger went to the ringer, which he tapped once.

"Do you still have that gun?"

Two rings.

"Was it stolen?"

Two rings.

Natalie held up a hand to Michael and asked, "Does a family member have the gun?"

Two rings.

Michael hunched forward, almost in Michael's face. "Do the cops have that gun?"

One ring.

Natalie gasped and drew back. "How could that gun be in police custody? They gave it back to him. It said so in the report, right?"

"Unless the cops gave the gun to a family member, and that relative didn't tell John he still had the gun." Michael rubbed a twitch at the corner of his eye.

"Is that what the report said?"

Michael sighed. "It didn't specify whether it was given back to John or a family member."

"Can I try something else?" Natalie put her hand on Michael's arm, and he drew back from John.

"John, did you know about a girl named Katie Fellows?"

One ring.

Natalie's adrenaline spiked, and she dropped to her knees in front of John. "Did you harm her? Did you, John?"

The other side of John's mouth lifted. His crooked finger hovered over the ringer. Natalie's breath came in short spurts as she watched him lower his finger to the bell.

He pressed down.

She waited, heart pounding.

The finger stayed pinned against the ringer.

She lifted her gaze to his face, noticing for the first time the blackness of his eyes as he stared at her. Fury whipped through her veins. "Ring the bell, John. Yes or no. Ring it."

"Natalie." Michael stroked her back, but she shrugged him off.

"Ring the bell, you bastard. Ring it once. I know it was you."

"Mr. Wilder!" The nurse had come charging back into the room. "What is going on in here? Get out now, or I'll call the police."

Michael gripped her arm and practically dragged her to

her feet. "Let's go Natalie. There was a misunderstanding. We're leaving now. John's fine."

The nurse crouched in front of John's wheelchair and as Michael led her from the room, Natalie craned her neck around the nurse's broad back to meet those black eyes again. Then she heard the bell ring once.

Chapter Nineteen

Natalie pulled out of Michael's grip. "Did you hear it, Michael? Did you hear the bell? He rang it twice. He's responsible for Katie's disappearance. I know it. He knows it."

"Shh." Michael took her by the shoulders and pinned her against the wall. "If that happened, if that's what your heard, we'll figure it out, but not like this."

She sagged, all the fight draining from her body. "*If* that happened? You don't believe me? You didn't hear the two rings?"

"I heard a very angry nurse ready to get us kicked out of here. How is that going to help?" He took her hand and kissed the inside of her wrist. "Let's not give them that opportunity."

Her head throbbed as the anger dissipated. Michael was right, but she knew in her heart that they had their man. He took Katie. He murdered Sierra and Alma. He stopped because he almost drowned and became disabled. Did he have a copycat now? Did the person who killed Raine mimic John Westfall to throw the cops off the scent?

She allowed Michael to lead her outside, and the crisp air hitting her face did its job. Her head cleared. Her brain clicked back into focus.

"It's him, Michael. We have to tell the sheriff's department. They need to investigate him thoroughly."

They sat on a bench outside the facility, and he slung his arm across her shoulders. "They'll have a hard time questioning him."

She twisted her head to face him. "Is that supposed to be a joke?"

"It's not a joke, Natalie. It's the truth." His body stiffened. "Uh-oh."

"What's wrong?" She followed the nod of his head toward a sheriff's car pulling into the parking lot. "Oh. I'll take all the blame. Don't worry."

The patrol vehicle parked, and two deputies got out and walked toward them, their equipment clinking on their duty belts. Michael murmured, "I know both these guys. We got this."

One of the deputies tipped back his hat. "Michael? Did you already tell her?"

"Tell her?" Michael stood, resting his hand on Natalie's shoulder. "Tell who, what?"

Natalie pinned her hands between her knees. If she got arrested out here, she'd be in big trouble with the Bureau.

"Mrs. Butler?"

"Wait, who?" Michael placed a hand across his furrowed brow.

Natalie stood up beside him, swaying a little.

"Mrs. Butler. Rachelle's grandmother."

"Here?" Michael jerked his thumb over his shoulder at the entrance to Shady View.

"Oh, sorry, man. I thought you came here to notify Mrs. Butler about her granddaughter's death. Got my hopes up there for a minute that I wouldn't have to do it."

Natalie squeezed Michael's bicep, her fingernails digging

into the material of his jacket. "Rachelle's grandmother is a resident of Shady View?"

The deputy dipped his head. "She is. She's Rachelle's closest relative in the area. They already called her parents in Atlanta, but her parents wanted someone to come out and tell the grandma."

"Sorry you guys have to deliver the bad news." He pinched Natalie's waist. "Any updates on what happened to Rachelle?"

"I'm hearing suicide, but that's just a rumor. I'm just telling you because...you know, you were her boss, and you're my friend." He put a finger to his lips. "You didn't hear it from me."

"No, no. Of course not. Appreciate it, man. We'll let you get to it."

Natalie walked beside Michael, afraid to talk, afraid to turn around. When they got into the car with the doors closed, Michael whistled. "What are the odds?"

"The odds that the man who owned the gun that shot at me two nights ago is in the same rest home as the grandmother of the woman who just turned up dead in her home after trying to tell me something? The odds of that being a coincidence are zero." She grabbed Michael's hand as he reached for the ignition button. "We have to go back in there and talk to Mrs. Butler. She must know Westfall, know what he is. She told Rachelle, and someone on the outside took care of her for Westfall."

"Stop, Natalie." He brushed aside her fingers and started the engine. "We cannot go back inside and grill an old woman who just lost her granddaughter. Your scenario makes no sense, anyway. I could understand why Mrs. Butler might be too afraid to tell anyone in authority about Westfall, although he doesn't look like much of a physical threat, but why would Rachelle keep that information to herself. If her grandmother told her something about West-fall, Rachelle would've gone straight to the police."

Falling back against the seat, Natalie covered her face with her hands. "I know you're right, but there's something just out of my reach. Some connection between Westfall and Mrs. Butler."

"And the lab." Michael clenched the steering wheel. "If what Rachelle had to tell you concerned only Shady View or John Westfall, why did she have to meet you at her house instead of the lab?"

"I wish I knew. Have there been any crimes at Shady View? Any evidence the lab has processed from there?"

"Not that I know of." Michael shook his cup, and the dregs of his coffee sloshed in the bottom. "Do you want to get something to eat on the way back to your hotel?"

"I'm not very hungry." As Natalie yawned, her phone rang. "It's my boss. He liked my report, but I haven't told him that I discovered a dead body." She answered the call. "Hey, boss."

"Brunetti, I want you on the first plane back to DC."

He must've heard about her involvement with Rachelle. "I can explain. Dr. Butler is the one who called me. I be-lieved she had pertinent information about the lab and my cold cases."

He paused. "Who the hell is Dr. Butler?"

Natalie's mouth went dry, and she peeled her lips apart. "What are you talking about then? You were happy with my work yesterday. Why the sudden turn-around?"

"Yesterday, I didn't realize you were out there in Marys-ville under false pretenses, Nat Cooper. I don't know who you think you are pulling a stunt like that, but I'm sus-pending you as of now. We'll have an investigation when you get back."

"Give me chance to tell my side of the story." Natalie licked her lips and tried to keep her voice steady.

"You'll get your chance—at your disciplinary hearing."

"H-how…?"

"How did I find out?" he growled, which was never a good sign with Jefferson. "That's the kicker. Not only did you humiliate me and the Bureau, I had to find out from an anonymous source and then do the research myself to verify."

"I…" Jefferson had already ended the call before she could formulate an answer. She sat frozen, staring at the passing scenery, a green blur.

"What just happened?" Michael's voice sounded a million miles away.

She cranked her head to the side, and a muscle at the corner of her mouth danced wildly. "My boss found out about my connection to Katie Fellows…from an anonymous source."

"Somebody must've recognized you, but why rat you out to the FBI? Could it have been Reynolds?"

"It could've been Reynolds, but why would he want to remain anonymous? It also could've been someone who wanted all the evidence on the table. Someone who wants to connect Raine's homicide to the others even more than I do."

Michael's eyes widened. "Just a minute. First you accuse me of hiding things at the lab, and now you think I squealed on you to your boss?"

"You know what, Michael? Just take me back to the hotel." She folded her arms and clenched her teeth, more to hold back the sobs than in anger. "I'm done."

MICHAEL YANKED AT the front door of the lab, but it didn't budge. He pulled again in anger, almost wrenching his shoulder, before the lock buzzed and clicked. By the time he stepped foot in the lobby, he'd remembered that he was the one who had closed the lab for the day.

Sam was standing behind the security desk with a worried look on his face. "Sorry about that, Michael. When you ordered the office closed, I figured that meant locking up, even though a few people did come in to work."

"My fault." Michael fumbled for his badge in his pocket and flashed it at Sam. "Habit. Who's here?"

"Dr. Volosin, catching up. Nicole Meloan, cleaning up the evidence room for the inspection, and that kid Jacob is helping her." Sam cleared his throat. "Sorry to hear about Rachelle."

"Yeah, tragic." Michael stomped up the stairs, his feet like blocks of lead.

He left his door open as he collapsed behind his desk. After everything he and Natalie had been through this week, she still didn't believe he wasn't the anonymous source who had reported her.

He didn't want her to leave, ever. He'd wanted to make this right for her, to give her peace. But maybe now that everything was out in the open, that solution could be realized faster.

She could go to Ibarra now and tell him about that pendant. Someone had taken it from Katie and put it on Sierra. Those two cases were linked.

Could that old, wrecked man in the rest home really be responsible for the murders of three young women? And what did any of it have to do with Raine?

Natalie mentioned something outside Shady View. She'd said something about someone on the outside assisting Westfall. He hadn't been able to discover much about Westfall before heading out to the rest home to see him, but he did have two children. They must be adults. Were they still living in the area?

He logged in to his laptop and started checking databases. He wasn't part of the law enforcement branch of the Washington State Patrol and didn't have access to the same information as they did. He could probably circumvent protocol and get some info on the sly.

A shadow passed by the blinds of the windows that looked onto the rest of the office, and Michael glanced up. A door closed quietly down the hall. Volosin wouldn't be upstairs, unless he was going to the lunchroom, but if Jacob Reynolds was still in the office, he could be anywhere. He had access to most areas of the lab.

Michael had hired him as a favor to a friend of Reynolds, and the kid had proved himself to be competent, friendly and helpful. Maybe too helpful. He always seemed to be into everything, offering his services to everyone.

Michael got up from his desk and poked his head out the door. Dead quiet.

When he returned to his computer, he tried to find information about Westfall's two children. Nothing came up under that name in Marysville. He couldn't even find any property listed for Westfall. He needed the help of his buddies in the department. Or maybe once Natalie came clean about her identity and her connection to Katie, the sheriff's department would take this link to Westfall seriously and get some warrants.

In the meantime, Michael snapped his laptop closed and jumped to his feet. He could at least try to find out who had visited Westfall at Shady View. If the man did have outside help, that assistant would have to visit Westfall in person. The man couldn't speak on the phone or send an email without help.

Michael packed up his stuff and jogged down the stairs, raising a hand to Sam as he exited the building. With any luck, Monica would not be working reception at Shady View. After Natalie's outburst this morning, he wouldn't make it two feet past Monica.

He drove back to Everett, barely noticing the scenery, his foot getting heavier on the accelerator. If he could make this right for Natalie maybe she'd trust him again. Maybe she'd stay.

He parked on the edge of the parking lot and slinked along the side of the building to peek in the window before heading through the front doors. He released a long breath when he spotted someone other than Monica sitting behind the reception desk.

Squaring his shoulders, he entered the lobby. Low-burning candles emitted a peachy scent that beat the hell out of the antiseptic burn in the hallways. His gaze darted to the doors that led to the rooms in the back. If that nurse from this morning came through those doors, he'd be toast.

He nodded briskly at the smiling woman behind the computer. She said hello without asking him if he had a loved one he wanted to park here. Good. He had a different image to project.

"Good afternoon, ma'am. I'm with the Washington State Patrol, and I need to have a look at your visitor log for the past few months." He placed a hand on his badge that did, in fact, have Washington State Patrol on it, but it didn't much look like law-enforcement ID, especially as the picture had him in a white lab coat.

Her kind face creased, and her lips turned down. "Oh, this must be in connection to poor Mrs. Butler's granddaughter. The police were out here this morning, I understand."

"Yes, we were here to notify Mrs. Butler. Now, something else has come up, and we need to check the visitor logs."

"Two months, you say?" The woman, Fay, was already clicking keys on her computer, and Michael stood still, his muscles tense.

Fay tapped the guest book on the counter. "We have people sign in here, but then we transfer that information to the computer for easier access. We do keep all the books, though, if you want to see those."

"I think just the names would suffice for now. The computer record includes the resident the visitor signed in to see, correct?"

"Oh, yes, so you'll see all of Mrs. Butler's visitors, although honestly, I think it was just her granddaughter, who was a sweet person and a doctor." Fay tapped a key with a flourish. "I'm printing the pages out for you now."

"Thank you, Fay. We appreciate your help." *More than you'll ever know.*

She whipped the pages from the printer and handed them to Michael. As he reached for them, she playfully pulled them back. "I even highlighted Mrs. Butler's name for you."

"You're so considerate." He turned just as the door to the hallway swung open. He didn't want to move to draw attention to himself, so he ducked his head to scan the pages in his hands.

"Barb isn't eating her meals. I'm going to see if she'll have some nutritional supplement."

Recognizing the nurse's voice from this morning, Michael buried his head even farther in the pages. He ran his finger down the list, searching for John Westfall's name. He found the first instance and dragged his finger to the right under the visitor name column.

He almost dropped the whole sheaf of papers on the floor. How was this possible? He found the Westfall entry, and the next and the next, and the same visitor name met his horrified gaze each time.

He stood with his back turned to the conversation, clutching the edges of the papers, a bead of sweat trailing down his temple to his ear. When the nurse went back through the door, Michael spun around to face Fay.

His finger jabbed at the name of Westfall's visitor. "Do you know John Westfall?"

Fay's mouth grimaced before she managed to turn it into a tight smile. "Yes, I know Mr. Westfall."

"This is his only visitor? Are you sure?"

Tilting her head, she said, "Of course, I'm sure. I thought you were looking at Mrs. Butler's visitors."

With his hands trembling, Michael dug his phone from his pocket and swiped through his photos until he found one from the office Christmas party last year. He used his fingers to zero in on one face in the group. "This? Is this his visitor?"

Fay put on a pair of glasses and leaned in. "Yes. That's Mr. Westfall's daughter, Nicole."

Chapter Twenty

Natalie put her eye to the peephole in her hotel-room door and peered at Nicole standing there with a basket in her hands, a hood over her head. She looked like Little Red Riding Hood, delivering goodies to Grandma.

She opened the door. "Hi, Nicole. C'mon in."

As Nicole stepped through the door, she shook the hood back off her head. "It's starting to sprinkle outside."

"I know. I was going to take a walk and get some fresh air. I feel cooped up in here." Natalie waved her hand behind her at the room. She hadn't started packing yet. Hadn't even booked a flight home. Since she was suspended, she might as well take her time.

She sniffed the air. "Whatever you have in that basket smells great."

"Scones." Nicole lifted the cloth napkin covering the contents of the basket. "I baked some scones and thought I'd bring some to you. I'm so sorry you discovered Rachelle yesterday. So heartbreaking."

"It was devasting. I'm glad Michael closed the office today. Not sure anyone would get any work done." She declined to mention to Nicole that she wouldn't be returning to the lab…ever.

Nicole placed the basket on the credenza next to the TV. "Do you have any tea in here? We can have ourselves some afternoon tea and scones."

Natalie snatched up the tin next to the electric pot. "Earl Grey?"

"Perfect." Nicole held out the basket. "Help yourself."

Natalie's stomach rumbled as she smelled the sweet buttery goodness of the scones, remembering she'd refused Michael's invitation to lunch. She should call him. She spoke out of anger. There's no way Michael would've betrayed her like that.

She picked up a corner of one of the scones with her fingers and bit into the crusty edge, her teeth sinking into the softer center. She brushed the crumbs from her chin. "These are perfect."

"I told you. I can't cook, but baking's my thing." Nicole turned her back on Natalie to rip open the tea bags and drop them into the hotel's paper cups. "Have you heard anything from Michael about the cause of Rachelle's death? I mean, I know she went home sick, but I thought she just had an upset stomach."

"Oh, really? That's what it was?" Natalie broke off another piece of scone and stuffed it in her mouth. "Haven't heard a word from Michael. He and I…"

"You two had a disagreement?" The kettle beeped, and Nicole lifted it from the base to pour the boiling water over the tea bags. "He does have anger-management issues, but you two seemed so…close."

Natalie swallowed one bite and went right in for another to avoid talking about Michael with Nicole. Anger management? She could see it. The man was practically seething when she first met him.

Nicole held out a cup. "Cream or sugar with your tea?"

"I think there's one of those sweeteners in the yellow packets." Natalie wagged her finger at the credenza.

"Got it." Nicole handed her the cup and the packet of sweetener. "I'm ready for you to visit the evidence-receiving room whenever you like next week."

Natalie picked up a blueberry that had fallen out of her scone from the napkin and popped it in her mouth. Should she tell Nicole now that someone else would be handling the audit? If she did, she'd have to explain why. "I'll let you know."

"I heard Michael's dog, Peaches, came back home." Nicole took a sip of tea, her eyes wide over the rim of the cup. "How crazy is that?"

"So crazy." Natalie picked up the last chunk of scone on her napkin and finished it off. Then she dabbed the crumbs with her fingertips and sucked them from her fingers. "The sheriff's department is going to check out the dog, but there won't be any evidence after this much time."

"I heard the dog actually came back with Raine's bracelet on her collar. I'm sure RJ will be happy to get that back." Nicole took another drink of her tea, holding up her pinkie finger.

Natalie shook her head. How did Nicole know this? "Wait, what? Raine's boyfriend? What bracelet?"

The room felt hot all of a sudden, and Natalie pressed a hand against her forehead, surprised to feel it dampened with sweat.

"Yeah, RJ. Raine's boyfriend. He'd given her a diamond tennis bracelet as a gift—probably stolen. RJ was a criminal, and Raine was no better. She was a bad person, Natalie. I don't know why Michael feels so guilty about her death." Nicole shrugged. "Anyway, RJ said that bracelet was missing when Raine's body was found. Most people thought he was just trying to run some insurance scam, but I guess the dog showed up with the bracelet."

"Who told you that?" Natalie winced as a sharp pain lanced her gut. Peaches had Alma's bracelet on her collar, not a diamond tennis bracelet.

"Michael told me." Nicole dabbed her lips primly. "Michael tells me everything, Natalie. We're quite close."

A wave of nausea passed through Natalie's body, making her shudder. She grabbed onto the edge of the table, knocking over her tea.

"Are you okay?" Nicole scooted back from the tea dripping off the table onto the floor. "You look sick."

"I—I feel…" Natalie cried in agony as another cramp twisted her stomach.

"Don't worry, Natalie. I'm not going to let you die alone like Rachelle."

"Are you going to call an ambulance? I think I need an ambulance."

"Ambulance?"

Natalie unfolded her body and met Nicole's eyes. Dread pounded against her temples. Where had she seen that evil dark glare before?

Nicole stood and grabbed Natalie's arm. "I'm not going to call an ambulance, but I am going to take you someplace I'm sure you've been dreaming of for a long time, Nat."

MICHAEL RUSHED FROM Shady View to his car, tapping Natalie's number on his phone. They had some real evidence, along with Natalie's information about the pendant. Rachelle must've seen Nicole here and wondered why she'd never told anyone about having a father in town. As far as he could remember, Nicole never mentioned family and barely mentioned her dead husband.

Natalie's phone rang and flipped over to voice mail. Was she still angry at him? Did she really believe he'd ratted her out?

He tossed his phone into his cupholder, where it promptly rang. He grabbed it without checking. "Natalie?"

"Sorry to disappoint. It's your sister. Where have you been? I've been calling you for about fifteen minutes."

"Is Ivy okay?"

"Ivy's fine. I just wanted to let you know that someone picked up Peaches."

Michael's heart went back to normal beats per minute once Molly had verified Ivy was fine. She really needed to learn to start the conversation that way. "Okay, fine. I didn't realize they'd be taking her. I thought they'd look at her at the house. I mean, what are they going to do to her?"

"Not sure, but I don't trust them."

"Why not?" Michael started the car. He had to get to Natalie's hotel room to tell her about Nicole before she left. An aching gulf opened in Michael's chest at the thought of Natalie already on her way back to DC.

"Because the lady who took Peaches was weird."

"Coming from you, I can't imagine."

"Well, she brought scones. Who brings baked goods to pick up an animal for forensic examination. Was she afraid we'd say no, or something?"

Michael slammed on his brakes. "She brought scones?"

"That's what I said, and she really wanted us to try some before she took the dog. I mean, that's weird, right?"

Michael wiped his mouth with the back of his hand. "Did you eat any? Did Ivy?"

"You must think I'm an idiot. Of course not."

"D-did this woman show you a badge?"

"See, there you go again." Molly huffed out a breath.

"She had a badge like yours from the Washington State Patrol. You ever bring anyone scones?"

Michael's stomach dropped to his knees. "Dark brown, curly hair? Tall?"

"Yeah, you know her? Nicole something. Sorry, I didn't catch the last name."

Stabbing two fingers against his temple, Michael asked, "She took Peaches? Is that all? Did she get near Ivy?"

"What do you mean?"

Michael spluttered, "Did that woman get anywhere near my daughter?"

Molly gasped. "No. What's going on Michael? Should I call the police?"

"For what? Kidnapping a dog? Just lock the doors, Molly, and don't let Ivy out of your sight. Have you heard from Natalie at all today? Did she come by the house?"

"I don't like this, Michael. Should I throw away the scones?"

"She left them there? Dump them in a plastic bag and put them out of Ivy's reach. Don't throw them away."

Michael's mind raced on the way to Natalie's hotel. He'd been hoping she hadn't left for DC yet, but now he was hoping she had. Why had Nicole come to his place with those scones? Had she shown up to harm Molly and Ivy? Had she always been planning to take Peaches, or was that plan B when Molly wouldn't touch the scones?

A half hour later, wheeled into the hotel parking lot and surveyed it for Natalie's rental car. He didn't see it, but that didn't mean she'd left. The hotel had a parking structure, and she may have parked there with this rain coming on... or to load up her suitcases more easily.

He marched into the lobby and hung back as the reception clerk handled a customer. When she was free, Michael approached the counter. "I'm wondering if you can tell me whether a guest checked out today?"

The woman pulled her keyboard toward her. "Name?"

"Natalie Brunetti."

"Ooh." The clerk glanced up, her bottom lip between her teeth. "Ms. Brunetti is still a guest, but she wasn't feeling well."

Michael swallowed. "She's had a few...incidents since coming to town. Is she in her room? I have the number. I'll go up."

As he started to turn away, the clerk stopped him. "She's not here. Her friend took her to urgent care."

Michael felt the blood drain from his face. "Her friend?"

"Yes, so sweet. I just caught them going out the side door. The friend had her arm around Ms. Brunetti and was helping her walk, half carrying her."

For the second time that day, Michael scrolled through his photos. "What was wrong with her? Was she injured?"

"No, she was ill—stomach flu, I think." The woman's face paled when she met Michael's gaze. "I—I offered to call an ambulance, but her friend seemed to have a handle on the situation."

"This friend?" Michael thrust his phone in front of the hotel clerk's face.

"I think so. She had a hood pulled over her head. I told her about the urgent care down the street, so close. You should be able to find them there."

"Thank you." Michael staggered through the lobby. They wouldn't be at the urgent care. What did Nicole plan to do with Natalie? If she just wanted to kill her, why not poison her and leave her in the hotel room? She didn't want anyone to find Natalie before the poison killed her.

He pressed a fist to his mouth. Think. Where would

Nicole take her? The most likely place would be Devil's Edge Trail. That's where she'd lured her before, or at least to the parking lot.

This time he needed a weapon to confront her, especially if Natalie was in a debilitated state. He got on the phone to his sister. "Molly, you still have that gun you brought with you?"

"Why do you need a gun?"

"I think, no, I know, Nicole took Natalie."

"What?" Molly squeaked. "The crazy scone lady? Should I call the police?"

"Yeah, yeah. I'm on my way back. Get that gun loaded and ready for me. Tell the sheriff's patrol that you're concerned about Nicole Meloan and you'd like a wellness check. They'll know her address. At least they can look there while I try the woods."

"I'm on it, Michael."

Ten minutes later, Michael screamed to a stop in front of his house. Before he could even get out of the car, Molly was running down the steps with her gun in her hand.

"I got it from the safe, along with the ammo. I didn't want to load it in the house with Ivy there." She held the gun out to him, barrel down, and pressed a box of ammo into his hand. "Why would Nicole be taking Natalie to the woods? What's going on?"

"I'll tell you about it later. I need to start looking for them."

"You're going to search the whole forest around here? How's that going to work out?"

"I don't have a choice." Michael grabbed his hair as the task at hand overwhelmed him. He'd start in the parking lot, near the playground equipment, and then hike down the trail. It's the only place that made sense. But Nicole didn't make sense. None of it did.

"Michael, Michael." Molly dragged on his arm. "Does Nicole still have Peaches?"

"I have no clue. I'm a little more concerned about Natalie."

Her grip on him tightened. "If that witch still has Peaches, you can find out exactly where she is."

"Peaches is no bloodhound, Molly. She's a pug."

"I bought Peaches a new collar this morning, and I put a GPS tracking tag on her." She tapped on her phone's screen and waved the device in his face. "She's on the move, Michael."

He took the phone from his sister, grabbed her face with his hands and kissed her on the forehead. "You're a genius."

THE CAR JOSTLED along the unpaved road, and Natalie clutched her stomach. The sharp pains seemed to be receding, but every few minutes her gut would cramp, and she'd let out a low moan.

Peaches had climbed from the back seat to the front and huddled in Natalie's lap. Did the dog remember her from the other day? Why did Nicole have Peaches? Where were they going?

The car stopped so abruptly, Natalie lurched forward, pulling against her shoulder strap. She grabbed the little dog to keep her from sliding to the floor.

If she had the strength, she'd take Peaches, escape from the car and start running. But she had very little strength. Whatever Nicole had slipped into those scones had done a number on her stomach. Arsenic, she'd guess. If she hadn't ingested enough to kill her, the symptoms should dissipate. She'd already vomited twice, which helped clear the poison from her body.

Before she had any more time to contemplate her predicament, Nicole yanked open the passenger side, leaned across her and unhitched her seat belt. "Get out."

Natalie held on to Peaches, tucking her beneath one arm, as she lurched out of the car.

Nicole shoved her, and she tripped, almost falling. Peaches squirmed out of her arms but didn't run away.

"Start walking, Nat." Nicole flashed a knife as she gestured to the path.

Natalie knew this path. It led to the abandoned sawmill. The county had thrown a chain-link fence around it, but people over the years had cut through and trampled the fence so that she and Nicole walked across it now.

The dilapidated chip loader and tower stood like old companions, sentries outlined against the gray sky as the sun began to sink. A chill permeated her skin, giving rise to goose bumps, and she sank to her knees and retched. She didn't want to be here.

"Let's go, Natalie. I think you must've been searching for this place for a long time."

Shaking her head, Natalie wiped the hand across her mouth. "What is John Westfall to you?"

"He's my father. I had to do whatever I could to protect my father...up to a point."

"So...you what? Destroyed evidence of his crimes? He was a serial killer. He murdered three young women. How could you protect someone like that?"

"Four, but who's counting, really? Not the King County Sheriff's Department." She brandished the knife. "Keep walking toward the chip tower."

Natalie swayed to her feet and judged the distance between her and the knife, aimed at her chest. "How did you find out?"

"About my father? After the very first killing, which was before Katie's. She was a sex worker, though. Nobody cared much about her. He should've stuck with those. I kept protecting him while I worked as an intern at the forensics lab, but he kept getting sloppier and sloppier. Thought he was so clever with the jewelry. I knew those would connect his victims, so I made them disappear."

"Why did he stop? It must've happened about the time he had his accident." Natalie's trembling legs couldn't carry her much farther, so she plopped down on a rotting log, which creaked beneath her.

"Accident." Nicole let out a nasty laugh. "That was no accident. I pushed him out of the boat. Unfortunately, there was a boat nearby, and some guy saved him…sort of. Well, you saw him. Worthless now."

Bile filled Natalie's mouth, and she spit to the side. "You tried to kill your own father to stop him from murdering people. Why not just turn him in?"

"And pay for lawyers, and have my reputation ruined?" Nicole glanced down. "Where'd that dog go?"

"What happened to your husband, Nicole?" Natalie clenched her teeth. She might as well find out everything now, and Nicole might as well tell her.

"He killed himself with a little help from me. He'd discovered my secrets. He was going to turn me in. Can you believe that?"

"You tried to kill your father and killed your husband to protect yourself." Natalie heard a rustle in the bushes and caught the gleam of Peaches's eyes. She also saw the toe of a boot. She dragged her gaze away quickly. Was there someone out there? She just hoped it wasn't someone helping Nicole.

"No, I was trying to protect my father. I'm always doing things for other people."

"Michael's wife?"

"Protecting Michael." Nicole raised her chin, her nostrils flaring. "She was a slut who didn't deserve him. She was making his life hell with the custody battle over Ivy. I just thought the jewelry would be a nice tribute to dear old dad. He still had that piece-of-junk bracelet he'd taken from that last girl."

Natalie caught her breath. "You're in love with Michael."

"And he's in love with me." She swung the knife at Natalie. "You coming in here trying to destroy his lab, his reputation. I'm not going to allow that."

Natalie laughed until a sharp pain in her side made her gasp. "There you go again. You're not killing me to protect Michael. It's all for yourself. Just like you killed Rachelle, so she wouldn't tell anyone that you were visiting Shady View. Is that the only reason? Had Rachelle discovered something about you at the lab?"

"Shut up, Natalie. I'm tired of this."

As Nicole turned her attention to the wood-chip tower, Natalie glanced toward the opening where she'd seen the boots. If Nicole had someone waiting in the wings to help her, he hadn't made his presence known yet. And if she did have an assistant in the woods, why didn't Peaches bark at him?

Her heart leaped with a shot of optimism but soon sunk. Who would be out here? Who would know where she was? Michael didn't even know about the connection between Nicole and John Westfall. Maybe if she hadn't lashed out at him, they could've stayed together and worked things through—everything.

Nicole narrowed her eyes at her. "Are you feeling well enough to climb to the top of the tower?"

"I'm not climbing up there." Natalie laughed. "If you want to dump my dead body in that wood-chip tower, you're going to have to lug me up there yourself. Good luck with that.

"I would've thought you'd want to go up there after all this time."

"What are you…?" Natalie swallowed as her gaze shifted to the rickety structure. "Wh-why would I want to go there?"

"C'mon, Natalie. You've done such a good job of figuring out everything else. You can't put the last piece of the puzzle in place? You don't see the poetic justice of coming back here to find your missing friend only to join her?"

Natalie dragged herself to her feet, the adrenaline of anger and fear replacing the poison in her body, making her strong. "No!"

"Yes." Nicole held the knife aloft.

Natalie sobbed, tears streaming down her face, her throat thick with them. "No, no, no. Katie's not in there."

Nicole clicked her tongue. "She's been in there for fourteen years while you left and went on with your life."

A scream tore from Natalie's throat as she hurled herself at Nicole, at the blade pointing straight at her broken heart. Before she could tackle Nicole, before the blade made contact with her skin, a loud pop came from behind her, the sound deafening.

Nicole crumpled in front of her, a surprised look on her face, blood pumping from the carotid artery in her neck.

Natalie flattened her body on the ground and twisted her head around as Peaches waddled toward her and licked the tears from her cheek. Pulling Peaches against her chest, Natalie rolled onto her back.

Michael emerged from the tree line, a gun in his hand, now pointing at the prone figure of Nicole on the ground, the blood from her throat no longer pumping.

"She's dead." Natalie clambered to her knees, and Michael dropped beside her, taking her in his arms.

"Scared the hell out of me when you charged her." He buried his face in her curls.

"How did you know where to find us?"

He reached down to Peaches and flicked her collar. "Molly put a GPS tag on her this morning. I was praying all the way here that she hadn't just dumped the dog somewhere."

"Michael." Natalie sniffed as she pointed to the stark, ugly chip tower. "Katie's in there."

He stroked her back. "I know, my love. You found her."

Epilogue

Stretching her toes toward the fire burning in Michael's fireplace, Natalie scratched Peaches under the chin. "You've had too much excitement, pup. You deserve to relax and get belly rubs."

"She looks like she's put on a few pounds, right?" Molly came from the kitchen, carrying a tray with three mugs of hot cocoa and a sippy cup.

"Peaches looks great. Thanks for looking after her, Molly. I know you're more of a cat person." Michael took the sippy cup from the tray and held it for Ivy, snuggled against his side.

"And thanks for getting her that GPS tag. Michael never would've found me without it."

Molly had scattered mini marshmallows on the tray for Ivy, whose cup had a lid on it. Ivy picked one up and shoved it into her mouth.

Natalie smiled as she took a sip of her own cocoa. "Is that good, Ivy?"

Ivy's head dipped shyly to her chest, and she looked up at Natalie through her eyelashes. "Mmm."

Then she seemed to make a decision. Ivy collected a handful of the little marshmallows and slid off the couch. She toddled up to Natalie and crouched beside her. "S'mellows?"

"I'd love some marshmallows." Natalie held out her hand, and Ivy dumped several sticky, smooshed marshmallows into her palm before running back to Michael and burying her head in his lap.

Michael grinned at Natalie. "You don't have to eat those."

"Are you kidding? This is when they're the best." She threw the marshmallows into her mouth and chewed, smacking loudly until Ivy turned her head and peeked at her.

Natalie felt a warm wave wash through her body that had nothing to do with the fire crackling in the grate. For the past few weeks, Ivy had looked at her with some interest but had kept her distance...until now. This progress with Michael's daughter shored up Natalie's belief that she'd made the right decision to give up her job with the FBI and move back to Marysville.

Molly cupped her own mug with both hands. "I still don't understand why Nicole came over here and took Peaches."

"I think Peaches gave her an excuse to show up here and make some kind of assessment." Michael twirled a lock of Ivy's hair around his finger. "If she could've convinced you and Ivy to eat those scones, she may have thought that would've given her some leverage over me or at least distracted me from digging any further into John Westfall. When that didn't happen, she sort of had to take Peaches with her."

"I'm glad she did." Natalie stroked the dog's ears. "Wish I had been able to say no to the scones. Do you think she also poisoned those cookies? Is that why Rachelle went home sick that day?"

Michael shrugged. "Possibly, but nobody else got sick at the office."

"She could've selected some cookies specifically for

Rachelle. Did she—" Molly glanced at Ivy, who seemed alert, her gaze tracking back and forth between each speaker "—use the old scone trick on Rachelle?"

"Soup." Natalie took a sip of cocoa and shivered.

Pointing to Ivy, Molly said, "It's bedtime for my favorite niece."

"I'll get her ready." Michael stood, lifting Ivy in his arms.

"I'll give her a bath." Molly put her mug on the mantel. "You two should have some alone time before Natalie goes back to DC."

Michael handed off Ivy to his sister, giving her a one-armed hug in the process. "You're the best, Molly."

"Hold that thought." Molly held up one finger. "I may be asking for a loan shortly."

Natalie stood also, and kissed Ivy on her soft cheek. "Good night, Ivy."

Ivy waved by opening and closing her hand, as Molly carried her to the back of the house.

Michael patted the cushion next to him. "Molly's right. You're leaving tomorrow, and I feel like I've barely had any time with you—hospital visits, police interviews, TV interviews, meetings with the FBI."

She curled up next to him and rested her head on his shoulder. "It's been a hectic few weeks."

"Have you recovered from your meeting with Katie's parents?"

Natalie stared into the fire. Mr. and Mrs. Fellows had come out to Washington to claim their daughter's remains and had requested a meeting with her. She didn't know what to expect, but they couldn't have been more kind. They didn't hate her. They never blamed her for Katie's disappearance, and they were so grateful that Natalie had never given up on their daughter.

Natalie hadn't suffered from one nightmare since that meeting.

"Talking with them was special. Maybe finding out where Katie's body had been all this time made me feel better, but seeing their relief was a hundred times more important. It should've always been about them, not me."

"But you felt the guilt." He kissed the top of her head. "It was about you."

"And you?" She turned her head and placed a finger on his lips. "You didn't replace one set of guilty feelings with another, did you? You never gave Nicole any encouragement. You had no way of knowing she'd fixated on you."

"I don't feel guilty. Some things are just out of our control." He kissed her fingertips, and then bent his head to kiss her mouth. "That's why when fate does put something, or someone, in your path, you grab it with both hands and never let it go."

"I feel the same way." She cupped his chin with one hand. "Terrible circumstances drew us together, forged something between us that can't break. Fate."

A small hand on Natalie's knee ended her kiss with Michael, and she turned to find Ivy standing next to the couch, fresh bath scent floating from her baby-soft hair.

Molly rushed from the back. "Sorry. Had my back turned, picking out books, and she took off."

Ivy pointed at Natalie. "Nat read."

Sitting forward, Michael asked, "Do you want Nat to read you a bedtime story, Ivy?"

Ivy nodded as she curled her fingers around Natalie's hand.

Natalie brushed Michael's cheek. "Can fate wait another fifteen minutes?"

"What's fifteen minutes when you've promised me a lifetime?"

Natalie stood, hitching Ivy on her hip. She blew Michael a kiss as she waltzed his little girl off to bed. It seemed only right that she'd returned to the place that had stolen her happiness only to replace that emptiness with a new life, overflowing with joy. Fate. Timing. Serendipity. Whatever.

She'd take it.

* * * * *

COLTON'S SECRET
WEAPON

TARA TAYLOR QUINN

For one of my longest-standing friends,
one who knew me then, Cinci Davis. It's no mistake
that as I was writing this Alaska book, you were cruising
her waters! Our paths are forever crossed.

Chapter One

Summertime. Eighteen hours of daylight. Hiking, fishing, flying to do. And Mitchell Colton sat in his cushy law office on Main Street, waiting for noon to arrive so he could take the rest of the day off and get to it all. June and July had already passed him by, and there were so many more adventures he wanted to get to before winter hit.

The lull in business at his Shelby Law Office, while not a problem financially, did not bode well for him. He needed to be busy. Or be outside.

He'd prefer to be busy. In his experience, lulls generally meant an avalanche was coming. As the only corporate law firm in town, he'd have to handle the ramifications for every business, all needing him ASAP, were something to happen that affected the Main Street merchants. An online scam, say, that somehow hacked into Shelby's internet service and stole customer information.

Finishing the revisions on a series of privacy policies for several of his clients with online offerings that mirrored their brick-and-mortar stores, Mitchell shook his head at the dark route his thoughts had taken. While it was his job to foresee possible pitfalls and do all he could to protect his clients from falling prey to them, he most definitely did not need to borrow trouble.

And…there it was.

Trouble.

Glancing up from the email he'd just sent, with the up-dated privacy policy attached, he saw the woman parking her little 1968 Meadowlark yellow Mustang right out in front of his place.

And hoped to God she wasn't headed his way.

Dove St. James. Local yoga queen.

In black leggings covered only by a thin, very thin, see-through-thin veil of what she might think was a purple skirt, a black crop top that ended right below her breasts, and lavender flip-flops that had more glittery junk on their straps than any one pair of shoes should bear, she was head-ing straight for his door.

Every inch of her slim, toned body was on display. Like some kind of billboard advertisement. Take a class with me and you, too, can be exactly who and what you want to be.

He did not relish taking on the completely untraditional woman as a client. Even for the minute it would take to refer her to someone cheaper in Anchorage.

As though staring at a train about to wreck, Mitchell swallowed, unable to not watch her very purposeful prog-ress toward his establishment. The long auburn hair, as wild and free as the woman was, seemed to wave at the world with every step she took.

He hadn't heard of any trouble at Namaste, the Main Street yoga studio the twenty-seven-year-old owned and operated. In a rented second-floor studio above the Repo—a secondhand shop he *did* have as a client. Surely, if there was a problem requiring his legal expertise, he'd have heard about it by now.

Most particularly with the lull and all. Mitchell tended to

overconcern himself with problems that weren't his business when he didn't have enough to keep his brain occupied.

His outer door opened. Stuart, his paralegal who also handled reception, had the day off. A long weekend.

"Hello?" Dove called in that singsong voice of hers that reminded Mitchell of her free-spirited mother. He'd never understood what Whaler—officially known as Bob St. James—had found so enchanting in his now-deceased wife. Free spirits were great for children. But young ones had to grow up. To be equipped to face life realistically.

Thinking of Dove's father, a retired whaleship captain and the current owner of the only boat rental company down on the pier, St. James Boats, and a man Mitchell respected, he called out, "In here."

For Whaler's sake. If the ship lord's daughter was in trouble, Mitchell would do what he could to help.

The woman burst in through the opened door like a swirl of leaves in a storm. Smelling like…he didn't know. A cross between lavender and rose with a bit of peppermint thrown in. Certainly not any perfume with which he was familiar.

Not horrible, though. So thinking, he nodded toward the seat in front of his desk, figuring she'd earned herself a minute of his time. Mostly because of her paternity. And a tad due to the scent she'd brought in.

"You know my father," she said, looking at him square in the face with her wide green eyes.

"I do."

"He speaks highly of you. Respects you."

Sitting back, Mitchell straightened his tie, dropped his arms to his chair, and watched her. He'd seen her around town. With her shop just down the street from his, knowing her identity was pretty much inevitable. But with the five years between them, he'd never had an occasion to actually socialize with the woman. He'd graduated high school before she'd entered.

"He's in a bad way, Mitchell," she said and then followed the statement with, "Mitch. I like Mitch. Sounds much more accessible. Can I call you that?"

Accessible? What the hell? "No," he said, moving nothing but his mouth. "I go by Mitchell."

Her tongue darted out along her lips as she nodded. "He's been drinking more and more since my mom died a couple of years ago. He's pretty much drunk all the time now."

Mitchell was aware. He'd heard, but he'd seen, too. And while he felt real sympathy for the guy, he said, "I'm a lawyer, not a doctor. Or mental health counselor."

She nodded. "I know. I'm here because he's losing his business, Mitchell. I've tried everything I know to do, but nothing is working. One of his longest-standing employees, Oscar Earnhardt—you know him?"

"I thought Whaler fired him."

"He did. He had to. Oscar's got as bad a drinking problem as Dad has. I think he thought that since Dad was drinking, he got a bye on his own situation. His wife left him, which made things worse. He quit showing up to work, or would show up drunk, and tourists would be left with a precious vacation day wasted because there was no one to facilitate the boat rental they'd reserved. Dad cut him slack again and again. Warned him. The last straw, though, was when he wrecked one of Dad's most expensive and sought-after boats. There could easily have been customers in it with him, and as much as Dad hated to, he had to let him go…"

Mitchell figured, with as fast as words were bursting out of her, that she'd rehearsed the whole thing. Figured it was only polite to let her get it out. It wasn't like he was in a huge hurry to find out how she thought he might be of assistance to Whaler. He'd help if he could.

"The other couple of guys working for him don't know nearly as much as Oscar did about the area. You're a Colton, grew up in the field of tourist adventures with RTA, you know how important that kind of knowledge is to someone on vacation up here."

At the mention of Rough Terrain Adventures, the company founded by his father and uncle and currently run by one of his older brothers and his cousin, and the segue from there back to Whaler's business, Mitchell frowned.

Again, lawyer. Not professional adventurer. Though, he knew the area as well as anyone else in his family. And was out in it, on his own solo adventures, every chance he got.

"I've been hoping the loss of his job would help Oscar sober up, which would let Dad hire him back, but so far, not at all. And if Dad loses his business, I'm going to lose him."

She had problems. He'd give her that. "What is it you think I can do?"

"You helped him form his corporation years ago. He said then that you'd talked to him about things you, as a corporate lawyer, could do to help him with parts of running it, too. But Mom was already sick then, and he'd been worried about the money."

Mitchell raised his eyebrows at that one. He was to believe that years later, and with the business failing, Whaler suddenly had more money?

"Dad did well in his career," Dove said. "He'd invested enough to provide for him and Mom into retirement, but we're still paying off her medical bills, so I can't pay you much, but I'll sign over a portion of the company to you. Or you can write up some contract that gives you a portion of the proceeds until your fee is paid. I'll pay you myself, if you can take monthly installments—small ones... I just need your help. Please."

For a second there, unable to miss the woman's sincere distress, Mitchell considered any possibility that he could give her the positive response she was so desperately seeking.

A split second.

While he knew a whole lot about running an adventure company for tourists, his expertise came in preventing disaster before it happened, or cleaning up messes after they'd been made. As a corporate attorney, he could help with investments and suggest various ways to make them, but clearly there wasn't enough cash flow to get started.

Sometimes dealing with employee relations was the key, and again, getting someone sober wasn't in his wheelhouse.

Mitchell gave her the respect of appearing to seriously consider her request before he said, "I sympathize with your situation, but I'm just not seeing where the Shelby Law Office can be of any help here. If your father had come to me sooner..." He let the sentence fall short. Shrugged.

Not sure that, with Whaler's drinking, he'd have been able to help even then.

And, as her shoulders slumped, Mitchell wished that, like Stuart, he'd taken the whole day off, too.

HE WAS TELLING her no. Dove's heart put up roadblocks, which caused a major pileup of emotion. She couldn't just give up. And Mitchell Colton was her last resort.

She'd dreaded coming to him. Had known what a long shot he was.

Holding her lips together by sheer force of will, she lifted her head slowly. Breathing in deeply through her nose as she did so. Tapping into learned resources to calm herself.

And made it right until Mitchell's face came into view. *No* was written all over it. But something in his eyes wasn't…cold.

Maybe not warmth. Or compassion. But her heart, which never lied to her, recognized an understanding that unleashed her desperation.

Tears sprang to her eyes. And spilled over, too. Before she had any conscious sense they'd broken free. "My father needs your help, Mitchell," she said. "You're his last hope. And until you've taken a look at things, how do you even know there's nothing you can do?" She blinked against the tears, talking through them. "How would you ever get new clients if you didn't at least vet them? Maybe there's something you'd know how to capitalize on. Could even be a lawsuit or something that he could bring for something." That last pie-in-the-sky scenario was accompanied by a large, inelegant sniffle. After which she helped herself to a tissue from a box on the corner of his desk.

Blew her nose. Took another and wiped her eyes. And wondered if he kept the box there because he was used to making his clients cry.

Words continued to spew rapidly through her mind, and once they'd started to break free, she couldn't hold them all. She'd bite some back and, while she was busy doing that, others slipped through. "Isn't this some kind of discrimination?"

Cringing inside at the absurdity, she knew she couldn't take it back and so went forward with it. "Refusing to even take a look at a possible case? And isn't your oldest brother a cop? I wonder what he would think of his little brother breaking the law?"

As soon as the words were out, she knew she'd gone too far. And still she couldn't back down. Or completely stop the tears that were filling her eyes. More of a trickle than a flood but still there.

"All I'm asking is that you take a look," she said then. Finding a small piece of zen in the midst of her storm. "Please." She looked him straight in the eye. "I know you and my dad are on good terms. He's on the verge of losing everything," she said. "And that would kill him."

"What is it you expect me to find?"

She'd thought she'd made that obvious. "I don't know. If I did, I'd already be implementing a plan and be on my way to saving the business." Her heart flooded with hope, as her stomach clenched with tension.

He hadn't said no a second time.

Nor had he given any indication that he was changing his mind.

"Does Whaler know you're here? That you're asking me for help?"

There was that. The man had a way of getting right to the challenge. Which was what she needed from him, right? "Do you think I'd be here if he did?" she countered. "Or be here without him right behind me, apologizing to you and telling me to mind my own damned business?" He knew Whaler. He'd get the point.

Still sitting back in his chair, arms lying casually on the rests, he continued to study her. Not all that much of a phenomenon, actually. Dove—who'd been raised almost exclusively by her free-spirited mother while her father had been out at sea—had been getting stares since before kindergarten. Had been taught from birth that her choices were not to be dictated by what society or popularity prescribed. Life wasn't measured in terms of an endeavor's success but rather by how fulfilled something had made her feel. Or how happy.

And pursuant to that standard, she was in the midst of what could end up being her biggest failure of all time.

"How do you propose that I get a look at things without him being aware of my doing so?"

Finally, an answer she had. "My father's going to be taking a charter of tourists out tomorrow. A half-day cruise of photography students from Anchorage who've been assigned to get various types of images of the glaciers. They're leaving at seven in the morning. You could show up after they leave. I can let you into his office." Her chin came up as she said that last bit. Perhaps issuing a challenge.

While she didn't know Mitchell Colton well, he was surprisingly different than she'd expected. Analytical and serious, yes, but there was that hint in his expression of more.

Still waters running deep. The cliché came to her. Along with her mother's reminder that clichés became such due to the fact that they spoke to a universal truth.

There was no hint of anything beneath his surface as he sat up straight and said, "Is seven thirty too early for you?"

Dove's mouth dropped open. Afraid to speak, she slowly closed it. Had she just heard correctly?

The way he was watching her, brow raised, gave her the sense that she should go with a *yes* just to get out of the tension flooding the room before it drowned her.

"No," she said. Just as she'd been taught to follow her heart, she'd also learned how important it was to put on her big-girl panties when life got tough.

"Then, I'll meet you there, tomorrow morning, at seven thirty."

Nodding, silent—for fear of somehow cracking the very thin layer of ice upon which she stood—she rose and turned toward the door.

"Dove?"

His voice, the way he'd said her name, slid through her. Not so much with the fear she'd have anticipated but with something just as forceful. So much so that she stopped in her tracks. Stood frozen, her back still to him.

"No funny stuff," he said then. At which she did fly around.

"What?" Her frown spoke of her genuine perplexity.

"No oil incensing, candles burning or any other means to manipulate an outcome that you might not like."

Had he not sounded so genuinely serious, she would probably have been offended.

"I guess that includes voodoo dolls?" she asked, tongue in cheek. And couldn't quite stop her droll tone. She managed to keep a straight face, though. For which she was immensely proud.

She was kind of taken aback at the slight sideways tip of his head and the possible hint of a smile turning up the corners of his lips, as he said, "Yes."

With a nod, she turned back to the door, eager to make her exit before something happened to change his mind.

"Dove?" he called a second time. Sounding more as if he was calling out to someone he knew. Curious, in spite of herself, she turned back again.

His expression had changed. There was no mistaking the seriousness there as he said, "This is only a cursory glance, out of respect for your father. Don't get your hopes up."

"I understand," she told him and then bugged out before he could call on her a third time. She fully grasped that from his perspective, there was no reason for hope in the matter between them.

But he didn't view life in quite the same way she did. He likely saw the world analytically. With an eye to preventing danger or damage. And that was fine. For him. To her way of thinking, if one gave up hope, one might as well stop breathing, too.

Chapter Two

Suit or cargo pants? Mitchell faced the question Saturday morning as he finished a workout in his home weight room and headed for the shower. Not looking forward to the seven thirty appointment at St. James Boats.

Wearing his lawyer hat, suit every time. But if he wanted to make the most use of his time, he'd take a quick look around St. James Boats, fulfilling his obligation to Dove, and then help Whaler's business by renting a fishing boat and heading out toward the sound. Which meant cargo pants.

Wouldn't be the overnight hiking adventure he'd planned for his weekend, but a way to salvage the day just the same.

Definitely cargo pants... Cargo pants if he was okay with being a self-centered ass. Whether he was wasting his time, professionally speaking, or not, he'd agreed to give the woman a few moments of his expertise. He wasn't going to disrespect her by showing up ready to fish.

Which was why, half an hour later, Mitchell was the only person at St. James Boats in dress clothes, tie, and leather dress shoes—expensive ones—that had already been splashed on twice. They most definitely didn't have the sole necessary to efficiently traverse the dock he was touring.

The area was overrun with the end-of-summer tourist rush. Not the best time for him to be there, but Dove had requested he visit then due to the six-passenger glacier charter Whaler was captaining that morning. Meaning Whaler wouldn't be privy to Dove's request for Mitchell's help.

Dove was thorough. He'd give her that. She might be as flighty as her name implied—as evidenced by the elastic-waisted purple and pink balloon pants she had on with a crop top and tennis shoes—but when it came to her father's livelihood, she'd educated herself impressively.

To the point that, after the tour of the docks—including a listing of every boat's use, power, sleeping capacity, and value—and brief introductions to the two full-time staff members who were busy with customers, he had a sincere interest in following her into the office and getting a look at the inner workings of Whaler's business.

"Unfortunately, it all goes downhill from here," Dove said as she led him into her father's office. "I've tried to make sense of what I could, but when I saw that even if I sorted out the various receipts, reservations, charges—basically I need an accountant for that—the problem is bigger than paperwork and bank accounts." She threw up a hand, and his glance caught on the plethora of rings spanning every one of her fingers.

Most, he was guessing, remnants of her mother's homemade jewelry business. Having spent so much of her childhood exclusively with her Mom, Dove couldn't help being like the woman.

She'd stopped talking and was watching him stand there.

Clearly, she was waiting for him to figure out what to do, to start looking at ways a lawyer might be able to help, rather than thinking about rings and…her slender, soft-looking hands.

Straightening the knot on his tie, reminding himself why he was there, he said, "I've actually got a couple of ideas."

That was the truth and not one he'd planned to share. With twofold reasoning. He'd need Whaler's cooperation, which meant anything he might think to suggest was a moot point until Dove talked to her father. And he didn't want to give the false impression that he could help when he wasn't yet sure that he could.

His gut clenched with tension when Dove's eyes widened and a very definite new light came into them. "You do?" she asked. Her hands clasped together in front of her breasts as she said, "I had such a strong impression that I had to see you, and yet I was still so worried. I should have had more faith."

"I didn't say I could help, Dove," Mitchell was compelled to point out. "Just that I have some thoughts to pursue that will determine if I can. Or can't."

She smiled. Nodded. "I understand," she said but didn't look as though she did at all. "You take your look. Do what you need to do. And then let me know our plan."

What the hell?

"We don't have…" he started then stopped when she shook her head, waving both of her hands in front of her face.

"I know," she said, her tone still light and breezy. "But I've been given all the signs I need. You'll find what you need to know how to help. And I'll be right here, ready to take on any task you have for me. As soon as you have it."

With that, she moved to a small wall space that wasn't cluttered with boxes and papers, boat parts, file cabinets or the desk and chair that took up most of the room. Sliding down the wall, she sat on the floor, legs crossed, hands on her knees, palms up, and closed her eyes.

He could be gone before she knew it. Just quietly head out. Get in a day hike. Far away from any and all doves in the world.

It was the sensible thing to do. Full of logic and good business sense, too.

He took a quiet step toward the door. Stopping, he pictured her opening her eyes to find him gone.

And dropped his dress pants–clad butt in her father's greasy old chair.

BREATHE. IN THROUGH the nose. Out through the mouth. Deep breaths. Relax. One muscle at a time. Toes first. No, better make that neck. Breathe. Cleansing breaths.

Until she could get to her crystals and have a private session of hot yoga.

Losing focus once again, Dove refused to open her eyes. To give up. In spite of the bad karma emanating from the man seated behind her father's desk.

Seriously. The man was filling her aura with his negative energy. She could only imagine what it was doing to his. She should offer him a session.

Imagining the tight layers they'd have to get through to even find his spirit, she figured the long process would be a fair trade for his help at St. James Boats.

Deep breath. Eyes closed. You don't need to look at him. He's there. His tension is suffocating you. No reason to open your eyes. Even if you saw what drawer he was reaching into, you wouldn't know the significance. Breathe. Do. Not. Open. Your. Eyes.

When Dove realized that she was expending far too much precious energy on keeping her eyes closed, she opened them.

Energy was the one thing she absolutely did not have to

waste. Without it, she had nothing to offer her clients. And without them, she couldn't afford to live.

Negativity! Negativity! Negativity!

Deep breaths!

Slower ones.

You hyperventilate and he's really going to think you're a flake. Not worth his time.

Stop.

Blinking, Dove put an end to the destructive self-talk. Reaching into the big pocket on the right leg of her pants, she pulled out her cell phone and the vial of lavender oil she'd also stashed in there with it that morning.

Uncapping the bottle like she'd seen her father do to a bottle of whiskey—with shaky hands and obvious urgency—she didn't even try to hide the small glass bottle held up to her nostril as she inhaled. All the way to her core. And then again.

Recognizing the familiar scent, her body instantly settled. Started to relax. Delivering a shot of zen. Her stomach relaxed.

And her gaze wandered over to Mitchell Colton. A wave of euphoria hit then. A sense that all would be well.

The man really was too gorgeous for the small town of Shelby to handle. At least, unattached as he was. His physical form, features that depicted ruggedness and a sense of dependable astuteness at the same time, was overpowering.

Add to it the deep timbre of a voice that seemed to assure you that it spoke the truth and eyes that held a surprising depth, and a woman could hardly be blamed for having a swoon or two.

He gathered a slew of papers together. Straightened them into one pile.

Was he done?

She didn't want to ask. Didn't want to interrupt.

And desperately needed to know their plan before her father returned. She might only get the one shot to convince Whaler that engaging Mitchell Colton's services was not only a good idea but paramount if his business was to survive.

Someone was bound to tell Bob St. James that the town's only corporate attorney had been taking a tour of his docks. Maybe even ask him if he was thinking about selling the place.

Which meant Dove had to get to him first.

With a positive plan.

It only worked with that plan pre-established and first steps ready to implement…

"I'm missing a couple of boat invoices." The deep timbre broke into her thoughts.

Panic hit her. She knew nothing about her father's bookkeeping other than the drastically bad state she'd found it in.

"*Ladybird* and *Wicked Winnings*. You have any idea where they might be?"

Euphoria hit again. Just a small wave. Reminded her that it was there. That she just had to access it. Trust. Refuse to let fear have any portion of her brain. "*Wicked Winnings* was actually a win," she said, half smiling at the memory. "Dad bought a couple hundred raffle tickets because proceeds went to support the leukemia foundation." Leukemia. The earthborn darkness that had taken her mother back home far too soon for Dove's liking. "A boat maker in Anchorage had put the small trawler up as a prize. A buck for a chance to win a boat? It seemed like everyone in the state bought into that one. The guy ended up buying enough tickets himself to pay for twice what the boat had cost to begin with. He got the write-off for his business. And he gave my dad the boat. He knew about my mom."

She was surprised Mitchell didn't know the story.

He'd turned to face her, his gaze alight with what felt like real interest. "When was this?"

She shrugged, not always that great with earthly time passage. "Ten years, maybe?"

He nodded. "I was in law school."

Right. He'd won a full scholarship to Harvard. She'd still been in high school, and every teacher, the principal, pretty much anyone who was vested in getting students to study and get good grades, had held up the possibility of a Harvard scholarship as potential reward.

She'd forgotten about that. Studied him anew at the memory.

The man, for all his surface living, had more layers than she'd expected.

Interesting. But not pertinent to the moment. Or his purpose in her life.

He was still looking at her. It felt like he was touching her, too. In what seemed to be a kind way. Unless she was self-imposing her own needs onto him.

Seeing herself starting down a path upon which she would only get lost, Dove gave herself a mental shake and forced herself to focus on the more mundane—but vitally important. "*Ladybird* was Mom's boat. She used an inheritance from her grandmother to buy it after she got sick. She used to take me out on the water and…"

No. Stick to the mundane.

"She left it to my father in her will—"

Emotion welled, but anything else Dove might have said was interrupted by the sound of her cell phone alerting her to a call.

A particular call.

From a problem she was tackling by begging Mitchell Colton into helping her father.

Brad Fletcher.

He's looking for a soul to steal. The line from the famous song filled the room. She'd set the ringtone to remind her not to let the man trick her into captivity.

Fear struck her. She let the phone ring twice. She had to answer it. Wouldn't let him think he'd intimidated her. *He's looking for a soul to steal.* The line of the famous song played a third time. Giving her a boost of strength. She needed at least one more.

"Are you going to get that?" Mitchell's voice pulled her out of her haze. Drew her gaze in his direction.

And she didn't need the fourth ring.

Filled with confidence, she said, "Hello?"

MITCHELL DIDN'T MEAN to eavesdrop. The office space Whaler had chosen for himself among the buildings on his little property was about the size of a cubbyhole.

He still couldn't make out all of the words booming from Dove's phone. A *take it or leave it* and *best you're going to get.*

It wasn't so much the words that had him tuning in. It was the tone of voice he heard over the smartphone in Dove's hand.

That, and the way her hand was shaking.

A sign of fear or weakness at odds with her tone as she said, "I've told you, Mr. Fletcher, I'm not interested. Please do not call again."

She was pushing to end the call as she issued the last word.

Timed perfectly. Like a movie scene that had had many takes and film editing to make it so.

Her phone calls were none of his business. Except that she'd asked for his help. Beyond that, he'd heard a threatening tone that had raised the lawyer in him. "What was that about?" he asked, without a hint of apology.

"Brad Fletcher. My dad won't take his calls or open his emails, so he's taken to calling me. He wants to buy St. James Boats. I've told him multiple times that we aren't interested in selling. And the offer he just made was so low, no way I'd accept. He keeps warning me about the business losing equity and that when I'm forced to sell, he'll get it for half of what he just offered."

Mitchell's radar had been up just from the man's tone. He liked the situation even less with Dove's added information.

"There was menace in his tone, Dove. You need to be careful. Block his number. If he shows up here, call the police." His lawyer's brain was going at Mach speed. They could file for a restraining order...

On what grounds? A phone call? A tone of voice? Because the man hadn't actually issued a threat. Except by way of stating the obvious. Whaler's business was failing. The longer he waited to sell it, the less it would be worth.

Unless Mitchell found a way to help St. James Boats succeed.

"I just need to take care of things here," Dove said, glancing around the office. "If Dad can start turning a profit again, we don't need to worry about the business losing value."

Her words so oddly aligned with his own thoughts that the response popping into Mitchell's head seemed perfectly logical.

"I might be able to help with that."

He regretted the words the second he said them. Most

particularly when Dove flew toward him. Threw her arms around his neck and hugged him.

Before stepping back. "Thank you," she said. "What's next?"

"You go do what you normally do in a day and give me time to get that far."

She was already heading toward the door. And Mitchell's gut tightened. "Dove?" he called her back a second time.

She turned. "Yeah?"

"I'm serious. You be careful with that Fletcher guy. Block his number. And if he shows up anywhere near you, err on the side of caution and call the police. Tell them I told you to, if it comes to that."

Sometimes it helped to have a big-brother cop.

With a nod, accompanied by a smile so huge it felt like another hug, the woman finally left Mitchell in peace.

And five seconds later he was on the internet via his phone, looking up every Brad Fletcher within the area code he'd been able to make out on Dove's screen.

He might never come up with a feasible plan to get Whaler's business back to health, but he could damned sure see to it that the old captain's daughter didn't fall prey to its demise, too.

Chapter Three

Freed from chaperoning Mitchell Colton in her father's office, Dove got to work helping out on the docks. While she didn't know anything about general maintenance or fixing the boats—her father had always insisted that was men's work—she'd been helping with tourist check-in on and off since her father had used his savings to buy his own boats and start the business.

She had also adjusted her class schedule at the studio to free up Saturday mornings when her father had been forced to let Oscar go.

The adjusted schedule was temporary. As was, Whaler hoped, the termination. He was ready to rehire Oscar as soon as the man got sober.

Holding the position open was part of what was hurting the business. While most of the revenue came from boat rentals, Whaler used to make good money with the chartered excursions he and Oscar had run on a regular basis. He'd had to take those outings off the St. James Boats offerings at the start of the current tourist season. With Oscar gone, and as much as Whaler was drinking, he'd made the responsible choice, in terms of client safety.

The best choice, of course, would have been to curtail

his own drinking. Something he was managing to do on a case by case basis as special requests came in for excursions. He'd blow completely sober before he went out and when he got back, too. An hour later, no way.

As she headed to her studio before lunch, needing an hour of self-provided therapy before her afternoon classes began, Dove still hadn't heard from Mitchell Colton with any kind of plan. She found herself thinking not about what that silence meant in terms of her hopes but about the fact that the lawyer hadn't pointed out the most obvious solution.

Bob St. James had to sober up.

With a failing business that wasn't going to happen.

If he was sober, the business would bounce back.

Catch-22. Which comes first, the chicken or the egg. She'd been diving headfirst into emotional pools of bad energy with her lack of solutions every time she thought about convincing her father to try and go even a day without getting drunk.

But if Mitchell could find a way to help her save the business in the interim, her father would sober up. She just had to believe that.

On a wave of hope, she climbed the stairs to her studio, key in hand to unlock the door. And stopped just short of reaching to slide it in the slot it matched. The doorknob was tilted at a downward angle. And the quarter-inch gap between the jamb and the front of the door told her that it wasn't latched. Pulled closed, but not tightly.

Curious more than anything else, she pushed a shoulder against the door. Hanging back enough that if someone was inside, she could call out and be heard by Repo customers at the bottom of the stairs.

When no sound came, she cautiously took one step and then another. Could be there'd been a leak from her bathroom and maintenance had had to get in to fix it before it damaged goods in the store below. The plumbing was old. She'd put in requests to have it fixed but hadn't pushed because she couldn't afford to have her rent raised.

She also hadn't delivered a key to the place after she'd had the locks changed shortly after moving in. She trusted her landlords implicitly. Not so much the taxidermist who'd had the space before her.

She'd spent a month ridding her studio of bad energy before she'd moved a single thing in. With salt in a bowl at the door, scrubbing every corner and then applying pinches of salt in each one of them, burning incense and essential oils, leaving windows open when the air outside was fresh, leaving music playing twenty-four seven at frequencies that were proven to relieve tension, she'd finished by changing the locks.

Four steps was what it took to get around the wall that faced the studio's front door and blocked the peace of the classes from those entering. There was also a wall filled with cubbies in which clients stored their personal belongings—suffused with energy from their everyday lives—before entering the studio itself.

Four steps and Dove froze. Gasping for air. Eyes flooding with tears, she found the strength to move her head, allowing her a glimpse from one end of the studio to the other.

The entire space had been trashed. Literally. The expensive sprung wood floors she'd put in were covered in what looked to be an entire garbage truck's worth of everyday items human beings threw away. Piles of it. A crushed empty toilet paper roll. Empty cans. Broken and stained food containers. A ripped egg carton.

And the smell…spoiled food? Used hygiene items?

Covering her nose and mouth, she stood there, tears

streaming down her cheeks. Unable to comprehend what she was seeing.

Feelings always came first. They spoke the loudest within her.

And in that moment, all Dove knew was despair.

MITCHELL'S PLAN WAS half-formed and weak at best. He'd found problems with the leasing agreement Whaler had signed years before, giving him lifetime access to the dock space he used. The fishing captain had been charged illegal fees over a period of years. Enough so that the money would be a boon.

St. James Boats needed employee contracts that better delineated a benefit package that would serve the two men who worked for him but also save the company money.

Mitchell could oversee contract negotiations under which Whaler could use the equity in *Wicked Winnings* to borrow enough money to buy two new smaller boats to be rented out for private fishing charters—currently St. James Boats largest income stream. But without Whaler sober and at the helm of his operation, Mitchell didn't see much hope of any of it making a big enough difference to save the business.

That particular message wasn't first on his list as he climbed the stairs inside Repo to speak with Dove before her afternoon classes started. Assuming she was adhering to the schedule he'd just accessed on the Namaste website.

He'd also spent time that morning doing some research on Brad Fletcher. And did not like what he'd found.

Mitchell was equally displeased as he saw the studio door standing open—allowing anyone to enter as they pleased. He'd just warned Dove to be extra careful. Keeping her studio door closed and locked while she was in there alone was part of that. She could unlock it when it was time for class.

Muscles tensed beneath his shirt, he pushed on the door with one shoulder. And was hit simultaneously with an eerie silence... and dreadful smell.

In two strides he was around the wall blocking the entry from the studio and ran straight into Dove's back. Catching her shoulders between his hands, he held her upright long enough for her to give a backward jab of her elbow straight into his rib cage.

And barely had the wherewithal to protect his area as she spun with a knee already poised to hit. Hard.

"Oh!" Her exclamation was part of a hiccup as she looked up, her gaze—wide-eyed and blank—connecting with his.

Aware of the destruction in his peripheral vision, Mitchell tuned out any specifics as he saw the tears dripping down Dove's face.

Had he been too late? Fletcher had done something to her?

Filled with an anger that was foreign to him, he softened his hold on her arms, though not letting go as he feared she might need his support. "Are you okay?" he asked.

His gaze intent, he brushed by his own mental *Of course she isn't* to get the information he needed first. Had she been physically compromised in any way?

When she just stared up at him, he rephrased the question. "Are you hurt?"

Her eyes cleared some as she frowned. Opened her mouth slowly. And said, "Not physically."

Relief flooded through Mitchell. More than any he'd ever experienced in court when a questionable verdict came back in his favor.

With the confirmation that he wasn't rushing her to emergency care, he took his first good glance over her shoulder and tensed all over again.

"Who did this?"

Dove shrugged. But it was the desolate look in those big green eyes that caught him. "I just got here and found it like this," she said. "I think the lock on the door was broken." Her voice was threadbare. Sounding nothing like the woman who'd spent the past twenty-four hours challenging him to step up.

Strands of that long auburn hair, wet with tears, were sticking to the sides of her face. He pushed them back over her shoulders. Like somehow that was the first task toward making something better.

What, in her life, he could improve, he had no idea.

Only one thing was clear to him.

Pulling out his phone, Mitchell tapped the contact for his older brother. A lieutenant in the state major crimes division, Eli didn't handle break-ins, but he'd get someone over to the studio who did. More than that, he had the means to quickly find out where Brad Fletcher had been all morning.

To look for any evidence there might be of him or someone he hired having been on Main Street.

And to have someone keep an eye on the man in the meantime.

MITCHELL WAS THERE. His phone to his ear, though he hadn't yet spoken. She had no idea who he was calling. Or why. She just stood by him, shaking, until he said, "Come on, we've got to get you out of here."

Still in shock, she wasn't even sure he was talking to her, until his grip on her elbow brought her to an awareness that he wanted her to move toward the door.

She went. At that moment, she knew of no reason not to do so.

Until she was standing out in the hallway, listening as

he said, "Eli." In a tone urgent enough to shake her up and out of the stupor she'd fallen into.

Eli. He'd called his brother, the cop.

He broke into a concise accounting of the past few minutes, detailing the state of her studio, while trying to lead Dove away. With awareness slowly coming back, Dove dug her heals in. She needed to hear Mitchell's conversation, and she wasn't leaving until she could find a way to block off the door of the studio.

No way she could have any of her clients seeing the space in its current condition. The traumatic sight could leave a permanent scar that would block the good energy they came to her seeking.

She had to call them all. Immediately. Prevent them from experiencing the horror still assailing her in waves.

Thoughts tumbled one after another, until she heard, "Bob St. James is a new client…"

He'd officially taken them on? She'd told him his bill would have to come in monthly installments. She'd gladly sign on to paying them for the rest of her life if that's what it took.

Relief and horror mingled inside her.

With a hand still wrapped around her elbow, Mitchell took another step toward the stairs. She held her ground. And he said, "Have them get eyes on Brad Fletcher."

The name tore through her. And she moved with him to the staircase. She could stand guard and prevent any of her students from seeing the degradation in their peaceful place from the bottom of the stairs just as easily as she could the top. Should have already thought of that.

Brad Fletcher?

"I looked into him this morning," Mitchell spoke softly, but with authority into his phone. "He owns boat rental places up and down the sound, with Shelby being a noticeable hole in his monopoly, and, due to our location in relation to the glaciers, a definite drain on his tourist population. He issued a very clear threat to Bob's daughter, Dove, this morning. Cushioned, but clearly there. I heard it myself."

They were halfway down the stairs. And in the next second, Mitchell had hung up. "Eli's on it," he told her. "The police will be here in a minute or two, and then we need to get you out of here until they know more."

She needed to back up a step. "My dad's business is cutting into this Brad Fletcher guy's profits?" she asked, refusing to go down another stair until she had her answer.

Mitchell's gaze met hers. "Most definitely."

She'd searched the man on the internet. Knew he had similar businesses to her father, but every town had similar businesses to those in other towns. How Mitchell had secured actual financial information, she had no idea, but he was good. Far better than she'd expected if the past minutes were anything to go by.

But that wasn't all. Looking him in the eye, she asked, "You're taking us on?"

He held her gaze. Didn't speak. And her tension escalated. "You just told your brother that my father was a new client."

He nodded. "He is at the moment. Because I've taken your authority to seek my assistance at face value. But what's going to happen when Whaler gets back from today's cruise and hears about what you've done?"

Right. His question was valid. But there was no way she was going to lose his help. "You leave my father to me," she said.

She'd call in every single card she had, if that's what it

took, to get Bob St. James to concede on this one. She might not wield enough power over his heart to compel him to stay away from the bottle. But even if she had to remind her father that her mother's last wish had been that the two of them carry on their family unit so that she could smile down on them together from her place in heaven, she'd do so to get him to see that his drinking had left them no other choice but to seek help.

Because she couldn't continue to hold the two of them together without it.

MITCHELL HEARD THE very real determination but also the load of bravado in Dove's assertion that she'd handle her father. As right as she was about Whaler's dire straits, she had to know that part of the reason for the current situation was the man's refusal to admit he needed help.

With anything.

Including his drinking.

Which meant that the only one who could help the old fishing captain at the moment was Bob St. James himself. And Whaler just didn't seem to have what it took to face the truth.

Or to have enough internal strength left to do the work required to fix things.

Two officers were entering the building as Mitchell and Dove hit the bottom of the stairs. They took down Dove's brief statement. Asked a couple of questions. And reminded her that with Shelby's low crime rate and no need for CCTV or alarms, they didn't have a lot to go on. They'd secure the scene. Dust for fingerprints. But without a witness, there was no telling who'd vandalized the property.

When the officers went upstairs, Mitchell stayed close to Dove as she called clients to cancel the day's sessions, determined to give her the assistance he could before getting on with his weekend plans.

It appeared that the biggest challenge facing St. James Boats—and currently the most critical one—was Brad Fletcher. Who was not in Mitchell's lawyerly wheelhouse. Investigative efforts had to run their course first and foremost. Something which Mitchell had just set in motion.

So...he'd helped. Fulfilled whatever prophecy Dove thought she'd envisioned pertaining to him. He just had to make sure that she was safe until the police had eyes on Brad Fletcher, and then he'd be off on a boat. Or hiking some remote neck of the woods that would be treacherous enough to discourage anyone else from seeking him out.

Just until Monday. Then he'd be back in the office and willingly at the beck and call of anyone and everyone who could benefit from the talents and skills he had to offer.

They'd reached their cars—he'd deliberately parked next to hers—in silence. Her proclamation to leave her father to her, still lingered between them.

"I'm going to follow you home," he told her unequivocally. Until she heard back from those processing her studio, she had no way of knowing what kind of danger, if any, she might be in.

Still, he hadn't needed to tell her his plans. The streets were public property. Anyone could use them. He just hadn't wanted her to freak out if she saw him right behind her as she turned into the drive of the small house she rented by the marina. Or saw him parked out front until she got inside.

Stopping as she reached for the handle on the door, she turned to him. "I'm not going home. I'm going to the marina to see my father, and I'd rather you didn't follow me.

It'll go better if I have a chance to talk to him without him seeing you hanging around."

"He'll have heard by now that I was there this morning." They were in Shelby, not Anchorage. There were few secrets in their small town. And word traveled fast.

"Yes, but no one knew why," Dove said, seemingly unfazed by his point. Her confidence impressed him. As did her, "No need to make him feel as though we're ganging up on him before the conversation even begins."

She really believed she had a chance to get Whaler's approval of her plan.

The realization gave Mitchell pause for the second it took him to remember that Dove also thought that sitting on the floor with her eyes closed and taking deep breaths made the bad things that happened in life go away.

Or that cleansing auras could change someone's life. When, clearly, it was actions taken every day from choices made—either deliberately or not—that determined one's course.

He was facing just such a choice. And knew that his course would take a downward spiral if he watched her drive off and then heard that something happened to her on the way to the marina. "I'll follow you long enough to see you make it back safely and then keep driving," he told her. "But only if you allow me to call and make arrangements for someone to check your house and then see that you get home safely tonight." The words came without forethought.

Not a usual occurrence for him. Or one of which he was fond.

Dove's eyes narrowed on him. The way she studied him, as though she could see things others couldn't, made him feel like he did when a fly was buzzing around him. He needed to swat the intrusion away. Keep his space to himself.

And was about to tell her so when her gaze cleared, and she nodded. "I would appreciate you making that call," she told him. Surprising him yet again. "And if you could have someone let me know when I can get back into the studio to start cleanup, I'd be thankful for that, too."

Cocking his head, he watched her, looking for something more ethereal attached to the words, but discerned nothing more than a practical request. And so he nodded and said, "I'm happy to do so." He wasn't just being polite. He felt good about helping the woman.

Brushing the thought aside, Mitchell took a few quick steps to his own vehicle and had the engine started before he pulled the door closed. Not trusting Dove to actually give him a chance to position himself behind her.

She did, though. Waiting to pull out into traffic until she'd had a nod from him, and then stopped at a yellow light when she saw that he wouldn't be able to make it through the intersection without stopping.

The woman might be flighty, what he'd call woo-woo, even, but she appeared to put value in keeping her word. As did he.

A nice note with which to seal the ending of their short acquaintance.

Chapter Four

There was nothing nice, or particularly noteworthy, about the situation in which Dove found herself. Within minutes of watching Mitchell Colton drive away, she was once again in her father's office. Pacing. Which she hated. On the floor in the lotus position would be the better choice.

But anything that reminded Bob St. James of his wife—which Dove did just by existing, so no need to exacerbate that by practicing her teachings in front of him—made the downward spiral worse.

"You like Mitchell," she said, for the third time in as many minutes.

With another tip of his whiskey bottle at his lips, Whaler swallowed. Smacked his lips and nodded. "'S right, I do," he said, the slur already obvious in his diction. "But no reason for him to be in here."

The petulant tone, along with another swig, did not bode well. But Dove had no other option but to take him on. And words came to her.

"Fletcher called again, Dad…" she started, only to have him cut her off with a wave of the hand holding his bottle, on the way to his mouth.

"Call all he wansh. He can't toush ish place," the man said, full of whiskey-induced bravado.

"Mitchell heard the conversation," she said then, raising her voice only a notch and instilling the sternness she'd heard her mother use on Whaler a time or two when he'd been working himself too hard. "Found it to be threatening enough that he called Eli to check into the guy. Apparently, Fletcher is a shady character."

She stopped short of telling her father about the break-in at the studio. Only because, due to his drunken state, she feared what foolish thing the man might do to avenge her.

Whaler's grunt gave her hope. She rode it for the few seconds she needed to breathe and ready herself for battle.

"Mitchell's smart, Dad. And noticed some other things while he was here. Things he can help with. I think we need to take him up on his offer." She chose the words carefully. "Before Fletcher tries anything more than just threats."

Whaler put the bottle on his desk. Hard. "No."

Standing still, she faced him. "Dad—"

Slamming his hand down on the desk, Whaler stood, too. Slurring some very strong words the gist of which she understood.

He had the right to make his own choices. Even if they were the wrong ones.

In any other circumstance, Dove would have looked him in the eye, nodded, told him she loved him and walked out.

She couldn't do that. They'd reached the end of the road.

A brand-new thing between them. With no set protocol to direct her.

So Dove did what she had to do to maintain her own inner harmony. Which would give her the equilibrium to deal with Whaler's lack of any kind of peace. Sliding down to the floor against the wall, she closed her eyes. Took slow, steady breaths. Envisioned the sun shining, bringing warmth to her skin. Chasing away the shivers of anxiety that were fighting to take control of her.

Other than the occasional sloshing of liquid as her father lifted his bottle to his mouth, she sat in silence. To his credit Whaler just let her be.

Respecting her need for a personal time-out?

Or just glad that she'd quit harping at him?

More likely, her decision not to walk out had gotten through to him. At least enough to clue him in that something was more wrong between them than it ever had been before.

And he was leery of waking a beast inside her?

The thought brought another singe of tension. And the threat of tears. The last thing she wanted to do was bring any kind of negative emotion to her father. He was already being eaten alive by the grief life had brought him.

Which was precisely why she had to stay her course. To help him find some joy again. Next to her and her mother, he loved St. James Boats more than anything else. If she could just give him a glimpse of what it would be again with Mitchell's help, then maybe he'd lay off the bottle enough to help them make it happen.

She just had to show him that there was joy left to be had in his life.

If the stars fully aligned for him, maybe he could even get to a point where he'd be open to counseling. And be restored to the healthy man he'd been before her mother had gotten sick.

Peace settled over her, and she inhaled the silence. Taking comfort from knowing that her father was right there, breathing in with her. Breathing out.

In between swigs from his bottle.

And that was okay, too, just for those moments. Because

there was always a point in Whaler's drinking when he hit the mellow stage, as she'd learned to think of it.

It came after aggressive, and before he passed out.

A plan became obvious as she cleared her mind and the cloud of negativity. She had to sit quietly with her dad and wait for the mellow stage.

Sometimes it took longer than others. Depending on how much or how quickly he was drinking. Straight out of the bottle, as rapidly as she was hearing it rise to his mouth, she figured another ten minutes or so ought to do it.

He was checking out for the day. She recognized the signs.

Something on the cruise must have triggered his grief. Anything could do it. The sound of a bird at just the right time could remind him of a picnic he'd had with her mother when they were in high school. A wave might be a replica of one they'd first dunked Dove in when they'd taught her to swim.

"They'uz ha-ha-ving a grand time."

Dove's eyes flew open as her father spoke. Centering on him immediately. "Who was?" she asked, truly wanting to know.

To somehow get inside his pain so she could help lead him out of it. Even as her logical mind made note of the fact that they'd arrived at mellow. Which meant she had about fifteen minutes before his chin dropped to his chest.

"People. I made 'em laffff. Your ma…ma…" His attempt to speak was interrupted by a big belch. And without even seeming to realize it had happened, he continued, "Ma… motherrr…she said I was…good…at thhaaat."

With a sad smile and a nod, Dove said, "Yes, she did. She used to tell everyone what a great time you'd show them if they booked a trip out with you."

Whaler's gaze found her then, his eyes bloodshot and weary-looking. "I missh her sooo mush."

"I know, Dad. I do, too. And that's why we have to get through this together, just like Mom said. You and me, we stick together, so she can look down and see both of us at once." She spoke softly but didn't let herself pause long enough for him to flop to another train of thought. "And that's why I need you to do something for me. I can't just sit here and watch this place fall apart. I want to be here more. Help out more. But I don't know nearly as much as you do. And Mitchell, he's an adventurer just like the rest of his family. Yeah, he's got a law degree and sits in an office during the week, but on weekends, from what I hear, he goes it alone even more than his family does. He does it out of love for the land, the sea, the adventure, just like you do. That's why I need him here for a bit. Helping out. Just until we get through this rough patch, and get Fletcher off our tails." Whaler was still conscious, still watching her, so she pressed on. "I need you to sign a contract that will let me be an equal signer on St. James Boats, Dad. That way, if you're having a bad day or are out at sea, I can make decisions here and help you fight off the Fletchers in the world. Just like Mom would do."

Crawling on her knees, she stopped right in front of her dad, putting her hands on his knees, and looked up at him. "Please?" She wasn't just fighting for his life, but for her own, too. She was half him. He was all the family she had left.

"Not highing law, juss 'venture." His eyes were cloudy, but he was still with her.

She didn't move. Didn't speak. She wouldn't lie to him. When he lifted a hand and put it in her hair, softly cupping her head, she couldn't stop the tears that sprang to her eyes. No matter what, he was her father, and she loved him.

"'Kay."

Eyes widening, she sat encased in stillness. As though a veil of safety had enclosed her. "You'll sign?"

Looking her in the eye, he nodded.

And Dove jumped up, rushing to his computer she searched for a contract, filled in some blanks and within a few minutes had it printed and ready for him to sign. But before she gave him the pen, she made the call for the police escort Mitchell had arranged for her, telling her father that she had to talk to the police about her call with Fletcher—true—just not the reason for her call. And when the officer arrived, she gave Whaler the pen. Dove called in the college boy her father had helping out that summer and, with the cop and the deckhand as witnesses, had her father sign his name.

It was possible that, once sober, Whaler wouldn't recall a whit of what had transpired over the last half hour. And equally possible that he'd wake up in the morning and remember it all.

Either way, with document in hand, she had her chance to save his business. And him.

Against all odds, the stars had led her right again.

It was like her mother had always taught her.

She just had to hold on to hope.

It would show her the way.

MITCHELL'S PHONE BEEPED a text at just after eight Saturday night, the moment he stepped up and onto a cliff face overlooking the sea, eight thousand feet up in the Chugach mountain range. The only place he knew of where he could get service.

Why he'd headed in that direction, he didn't want to contemplate. His family was used to him disappearing without leaving word during his time off. Most particularly during the summer when temperatures were mild and days were long.

But with only another hour plus before sunset, if he was going home that night, he had to start his downward trek so he'd be hiking on more level ground by the time it was fully dark.

The sleeping bag hooked to the bottom of his pack told a different story. The plan was to sleep alone up in the mountains where no one would find him. To rest without everyone's cares on his shoulders.

So why was he checking his phone?

He asked the question silently, not seeking an answer, as his thumb pressed the screen to open his messaging app.

Dove St. James.

A contact he'd added that afternoon. Just in case she needed him to put in another call to Eli. To use his influence with the ABI major crimes office in Shelby regarding the ongoing investigations into Fletcher and the studio break-in. Not that there'd been a major crime.

Yet.

Prevention was Mitchell's job. One he took to heart with utmost dedication.

She'd sent two messages. One a single sentence: Dad's on board. Followed by the second, which was a photo of a rudimentary contract, giving Dove St. James power of attorney rights for St. James Boats. It wasn't notarized but had two witness signatures.

Without the notary, Whaler could argue the validity of the contract in court. But unless the older man could argue convincingly that he'd signed under duress, he'd have a hard time winning.

And with a local cop as one of the signatories, a duress claim was unlikely to fly.

Another text buzzed against his palm. Dove's name flashed on his screen. As though the woman really did have some kind psychic connection and knew he'd been thinking about her.

Stopping that thought before it could settle, he shook his head against illogical intrusions and read.

I've been cleared to get back into my studio. I plan to be there at 7 tomorrow morning. Can you meet me afterward? Say, 9? At your office?

On a Sunday?

Seriously?

He read the missive a second time.

Hesitated to answer.

Then it hit him. Her timeline was good. Best that he get her taken care of and out of his hair before regular office hours on Monday.

In the event that urgent business hit his desk at the start of the week, he'd have his little sidebar done.

Sunrise was scheduled for just after five Sunday morning. He could bed down, get several good hours of rest and make it back to town and shower by nine, easy.

Unless he just met her at her studio at seven. No one should have to face the devastation he'd witnessed there alone. He could talk to her about St. James Boats while they straightened her place up. And then he'd have the rest of the day to head to the glaciers. Strap on his new crampons and head out on the ice.

He should test out the cleats before embarking on a longer solo ice adventure with them.

Decision made through logical choice, Mitchell was in his bed at home by one in the morning and up at six. Was showered, dressed in jeans and a long-sleeved flannel shirt and leaning against the back wall outside of Repo, waiting for Dove when she arrived at five to seven.

He couldn't help but watch as she approached him. In purple leggings with a lighter see-through purple skirt made out of some kind of thin netting and a purple long-sleeved tightly fitting top that ended just above her belly button.

Did she dress purposely to make people stare at her? Her aim every morning when she looked in the closet was to appear as bizarrely as she could?

Had she any idea how sexy she looked?

Her purposeful stride spoke of determination, not a come-on.

She was about three feet away from where he stood in the doorway when she asked, "What's up?"

He shrugged. "I figured we could talk while you clean."

With a raised brow she glanced at his clothes. "You don't look dressed for business."

Looking her straight in the eye, he cocked his head at her and asked, "You want my help or not?"

She nodded, put her key in the door, swung it open, and glanced back at him. "Always. Just trying to figure out if I'm paying by the hour yet, or not."

Couldn't the woman accept some help without making a major event out of it? Let him ease his conscience some before he broke it to her that there was no point in her paying for his legal services until she had her bigger problems resolved. "The clock hasn't started yet" was all he said, as he held the door and followed her inside.

Chapter Five

Dove was fully prepared for cleanup duty. She'd spent an hour meditating that morning, separating self from other as one's aura did not have to take on another's. Blocking herself from the negative energy into which she'd be walking. She had a small lavender sachet tucked into the middle of her bra, between her breasts. And knew what music she was going to cue the second she walked into space that was her own.

In spite of the fact that another had inflicted harm there.

One sight of Mitchell Colton and she was grasping to hold on to her calm. Bending her head, she inhaled like she was taking in the last air left on earth. Focusing on the lavender scent wafting up to her, she walked through the back hallway of Repo and up the stairs to the second floor and her damaged sanctuary. The Repo maintenance guy had installed a brand-new lock for her the day before.

Her thoughts more on the lawyer than awaiting messes or new locks, she went with what was hitting her strongest. The man looked too good in a suit. Put those muscled arms and broad chest in a shirt that delineated them, rather than a jacket that hid them, and you had a whole new set of problems.

Or at least, in that moment, Dove did.

Wow.

All of the adventuring Colton men were fine specimens of the male ideal, but Mitchell... She'd had no idea he was so well endowed.

Turning to say something pithy, to rile him and get herself into a different mode, she stumbled on the step instead. He'd been closer to her than she'd realized. Her gaze had been shooting downward, to meet his gaze steps below. And instead landed on the fly of his jeans.

Which much more clearly hugged what it held than suit pants had done.

Wow.

Endowed indeed.

Infused as she was with the sight and the thoughts it engendered, she nevertheless made it into her studio without gagging over the sights and smells awaiting her. Dipping her head for sniffs of lavender again and again, she proceeded across the room to the counter and cupboards that served as desk, storage and sound system station. And zeroed in on feeling her own strength over the destructive emotions of whoever had violated her space.

"The police wanted me to check to see if anything's missing," she said. "Detective Welding was going to accompany me here last night, but I told him I'd rather look in the morning. I'm supposed to call him with a report. He said they took a look and saw my sound system untouched and laptop still hooked up under here..." She pulled out the keyboard drawer that slid from under the countertop, opened the computer and saw the home screen flash on normally, and continued with, "So they aren't expecting me to find anything gone. And without that, there's really no evidence for them to act upon at this time."

She was talking too fast. Glad to see her electronics

where and how they belonged. She hadn't even noticed them the day before.

But the rapid speech was more a result of the tsunami of sexual desire that had hit her on the stairs.

Mitchell Colton? Really?

Good to know her spirits had a sense of humor. And were using it to help her get through the process that lay immediately ahead.

"You have cleaning supplies around here?"

Even Mitchell's voice was sending pleasant shivers through her. With a grin, and a quick thanks to the loved ones she couldn't see, Dove bent to the cupboard below her laptop and pulled out a bucket filled with environmentally friendly cleansers, sponges and towels.

Pulling out a filled spray bottle and a couple of cloths, she passed the rest to the man who'd come up to the counter beside her. "You okay?" he asked.

"Yeah! Fine!" Her tone was a little on the squeaky side. He didn't know her well enough to know that, though. "Just eager to get this done, for obvious reasons, of course," she said as she sprayed and dropped to her knees to get the smears of what appeared to be ketchup off her cupboard. "Let's get to work. I want to hear your ideas and will do whatever it takes to implement them as soon as possible."

She might not be able prevent some of the things that happened around her or even, in part, to her. But she did have control over her own response to them. And of the thoughts and topics that she allowed to hold her focus. She could refuse to linger on that which brought negative energy into her heart. To replace such things with positive thoughts that were also relevant.

Like the fact that Mitchell Colton had ideas to help her save her father's business. And that nothing within her own minimally lucrative business had been damaged. Cleanup only cost a few dollars in supplies. And some elbow grease.

Her sound system and laptop, which could have imposed prohibitive costs, were fine.

So thinking, she stood, cued up the playlist that had come to her during her pre-cleanup meditation that morning. And focused on the golden glow that shone from the wood of her cupboards as they became cleaner than they'd been since she'd first rented the place.

She should have thought to polish them sooner.

And had just found a reason to be thankful that some unknown entity had spurred her on to getting it done.

SPENDING TIME ALONE with Dove in the quiet of her studio was not an easy thing. Mitchell found himself almost thankful for the smells of rotten food that permeated the areas he was working on—anything to keep his feet, and thoughts, firmly planted rather than flying around among the clouds painted on a back wall. Or falling into the trance the music Dove had playing was trying to suck him into.

Shame on her for that one. Trying to manipulate him into…what?

Helping her? She already believed he was on board to do that.

To…*desiring* her? No music needed for that one. The clothes had it covered.

And she hadn't given any hint of coming on to him. Or even noticing that he was male. He was a lawyer. He was help that she needed to save a business. Not a sexual being.

On his hands and knees, he was halfway across the floor when he heard what sounded like a cow mooing. He glanced over to see Dove standing near the end of the wall of cupboards she'd been cleaning, staring at her phone.

She had a moo as a ringtone? A new thing. He certainly hadn't heard the sound in her father's office the day before.

But then, she'd had a call. It appeared that whoever was currently communicating with her had texted.

Getting back to his work on the floor, Mitchell cut off all thoughts of Dove St. James. Whoever she talked to was no business of his.

Her feet walking on his clean floor, heading toward him, was. He looked up as she reached him, saw her handing her cell out to him.

He took it. Glanced at the screen, and then, recognizing the number, gave it his full attention. Switching immediately into work mode, he stood. "Fletcher dropped his offer by ten thousand overnight," he said aloud what she already knew, while his mind drew the obvious conclusion from the maneuver. The shady businessman was upping the pressure he was putting on Dove. Severely.

A person generally only did that when they believed they had someone over a barrel. When their target was running scared and ready to respond to being squeezed.

Pulling his own phone out of his pocket, Mitchell called Eli. Just like his older brother called him anytime he needed lawyerly advice for a case.

The call was short. Succinct. One sentence from him. And one back. Mitchell had eyes on Dove the entire time. The white lines around her lips, the stark glint replacing the usual warmth in her eyes held him there. As though, by a phone call, he could assure her that she'd have no reason to fear.

And that it was his job to do so.

Neither impression was valid.

"What did he say?" she asked as soon as he lowered his phone from his ear.

Mitchell paused, choosing his words carefully, as was his way, and Dove said, "He said something you didn't like."

She was right about that last part. Which anyone watching him closely could have discerned. That did *not* mean she had any special powers enabling her to read people.

Him in particular.

"Your face got stern," she said, helping him along.

"Brad Fletcher has no alibi during the hours this place was vandalized." He gave her a longer version than Eli had delivered. "He says he was out fishing. Alone. A team has been assigned to keep eyes on him."

Her cheeks paled as her eyes continued to seek something from his that he knew he didn't have to give. For a split second there, he almost wished his did.

Until she said, "We have to get to my dad."

We. Not *I.*

Blockades shot up inside him. Even as warmth oozed between them at the familiarity. At being considered a part of something that meant so much to someone.

He shook the thought away.

Because she was right. Whaler needed to know what was going on, to protect himself if nothing else, and the lawyer he'd thought he'd just hired was the proper man for that job.

Not the daughter with whom he had emotional investment and who might try to soften the blow.

"I'll drive," he told her, dropping his cleaning supplies on the counter and heading toward the door. He waited until she'd collected her purse and joined him and then, with a hand at her back, and eyes taking in everything around them, he escorted her out to his car.

Working. Only working.

Pro bono work, possibly.

But still, one hundred percent work.

His earlier conundrum with an unwelcomed awareness of the auburn-haired woman in her out-there clothes had nothing to do with the very real concern currently flooding through him on her behalf.

"HE'S NOT HERE." Dove's voice sounded…off…as she swept through the small space of her father's office. As though the man could be hiding under the threadbare carpet beneath his desk.

Standing in the doorway, Mitchell put a lid on the tension spreading through him. Logic and planning were his guides in life. Emotions did not dictate his reality. "Where does he go when he's not at home, at the bar or out on one of his boats?"

With it being Sunday morning, they'd already checked all three, as Dove had determined them to be the most likely spots to find him. Home first, passed out. Sleeping off Saturday night at the bar. Then the bar, passed out, either slumped on a table or in his truck, not having made it home. The office was usually only when he was close to being sober. But when he wasn't loaded, his favorite place to be was the water.

"He comes here," she said, turning to face him. Her long hair framed her in what appeared to be fire in that first second. Like she was alight with fear. Maybe because her eyes were alight with it. But the rest of her…all the purple, the netting…he had the most bizarre impression of an angelic part of her, there to pull herself out of the earthly flames.

Or one calling out to him to do so.

That sense of need pushing through him kicked him into gear. Whaler had grown up in Shelby. Knew every inch of the town and most of the people in it. As far as Mitchell had ever known, the man had no enemies. At least not local ones, he amended with a thought to Brad Fletcher. Anyone who'd been in the bar the night before could have taken him home. "So we wait," he told her. "Home, here or the bar?"

Wait for an hour or so, he planned silently. Then he'd call Clint Schumer, owner of the local bar where Whaler had his own stool, to put in a quiet feeler as to the man's behavior the night before. Hopefully find out who he'd left with.

Schumer was a client. And one he could trust to keep their conversation confidential, even in Shelby. The last thing he wanted to do was embarrass Whaler. The older man was already undermining himself with all the drinking.

"Here." Dove's answer was longer than usual in coming. "If he's already out, he'd come here rather than going home during daylight."

She moved a couple of piles of paper materials and lifted herself up to sit on the space she'd cleared on top of a credenza facing the door.

Instead of settling on the floor. The choice bothered him. Left him no choice but to try to fix the problem.

If he slid to the floor and closed his eyes, would she follow suit? He was nixing that one before the idea had even completed itself. Giving himself a strong mental shake, he said, "You're worried."

Great. Stating the obvious when he should be helping her get back to her usual way of taking things on the chin. The woman had a reputation in town, and if everything he'd witnessed in the past forty-eight hours was anything to go by, it was well earned.

She'd nodded and was sitting forward, fingers curled over the edge of the credenza on each side of her, swinging her feet.

"I don't think you need to be just yet," he said, cautiously.

Not wanting to lie to her but… "Law enforcement has had eyes on Brad Fletcher since yesterday—before you and your dad signed that contract." She'd put not only the date but also the time on the signature line.

And a guy like Brad Fletcher likely didn't do all of his own work. He'd pay for the dirty stuff.

"You're concerned," she said. "Even when you just said that you didn't totally believe what you were saying."

What the hell? She thought she was some kind of mind reader?

"I need you to be honest with me, Mitchell."

He needed to go. To tell her he was the wrong guy to help with her problems. To apologize. And try to find a lawyer from a nearby city who might be willing to take on St. James Boats when the Fletcher dust settled. He'd even offer to pay the person himself.

Looking for an out, he went for the obvious. Taking offense. Lifting his chin, he gave her a piercing courtroom look and said, "You calling me a liar, Ms. St. James?"

No lawyer worth his salt—or at least Mitchell—would work for a client who didn't trust him. Or for a client he couldn't trust to act according to societal norms. Dive-bombing others' silent thoughts was not okay, as far as he was concerned. Most particularly not if one was going to believe one's magic knowledge over their victim's own words.

"No, Mitchell, I'm not calling you a liar." Dove's face softened as she issued the answer. A smile even teased at the corners of her mouth. "I'm just paying attention to your posture, your tone of voice. You're uncomfortable, which tells me that you know more than you're saying."

A body-language reader, not a mind one. Some of the tension she'd mentioned seeing in Mitchell eased away.

He'd taken a course in understanding the language himself. It helped him to read others during critical negotiations.

And it didn't hurt in conversations with his siblings and cousins, either. Or their poker games.

"I don't *know* anything," he told her, taking a seat in her father's chair, as she'd had him do the morning before, and turning it to face her. "I just don't like how much lower Fletcher's offer was overnight. In business negotiation terms, he'd only do that if he felt like he had an upper hand to the point of assured victory. It doesn't track that he'd hurt your father, though, if he's believing that he's on the verge of getting what he wants—which is your father's signature on a business deal."

Dove slid down to the floor, her back against the wall, but kept her eyes wide open and trained on Mitchell. "I was more worried that he's hurt himself," she said. "He's usually able to carry on, drive on the right side of the road even, when he's been drinking—not that I ever, *ever* condone him doing so—but he was pretty beaten up yesterday. Missing my mom. And then, with me getting him to sign that contract… Do you think he'd, you know, hurt himself on purpose?"

The meaning behind her question was completely clear to him. As was his answer. "I do not. Your mother's death has hit Whaler hard. He's in a bad spot, I grant you that, but a man like him, he just keeps going until he doesn't. He gets up every day. He comes to work when he's supposed to be here. And I'd bet you a hundred bucks that he's never forgotten to tell you *Happy Birthday.*"

Her gaze widened, and a full smile broke out on her face. "You're good," she said softly.

Relief flooded him, and Mitchell sat back, prepared to

wait the hour out with her and then make his phone call. "You aren't taking my bet?"

"Hell, no. I don't have the hundred to spare."

He did.

And he'd give it willingly—more than once—to see that smile stay on her face.

Unfortunately the fates she was so fond of didn't always provide smiling moments. No matter how rich you were. There were just some things money couldn't fix.

And some things a practical lawyer would never be able to do.

Hooking up with a breezy woman like Dove St. James being top of the list.

Chapter Six

In his jeans and flannel shirt, Mitchell Colton looked a whole lot more like he belonged at St. James Boats. And in her world.

Dove didn't kid herself into thinking that he was there to stay. But she was thankful for the time he was giving her. He had no obligation to give up his Sunday to sit with her while she waited for her father to show himself.

And yet he seemed to sense that she couldn't talk boat business until she knew that Whaler was accounted for. Hoping her dad would join in their business meeting might be too much for her to ask, but Dove was planning to do so. Holding onto hope was how she lived, no matter how illogical she seemed sometimes, nor how unrealistic and foolish.

No matter what Mitchell Colton thought of her.

She'd never let others' opinions of her matter. A gift instilled in her by her mother who'd taught Dove from birth to live authentically. Raising her with an awareness that she'd be far happier listening to her heart—trusting herself—rather than worrying about society's whims, or letting those around her influence what she wore, ate or thought.

She refused to allow her sudden awareness of Mitchell Colton to change that. The feelings she'd had in the studio…and they were still lingering in the aftermath…had been nothing more than a way to ward off negative feelings while cleaning up the results of vandalism.

"Why mooing?" Mitchell's words fell easily between them, pulling her gaze from the doorway back to him. The lawyer seemed to have left the room. A man who was curious sat in his place.

"Mooing?" she asked, frowning.

"Your text notification."

Right. The text with the lowball offer. "Like the devil looking for a soul to steal, the line from the song that's his ringtone, the text notification is set just for Brad Fletcher's number," she clarified. And then told him, "The song reminds me instantly I'm talking to the devil, you know, since it's real time direct contact. Text lingers. Sits there with you. So, in ancient mythology, the divine mother is represented by the cow. She is the giver of life. And it's there to remind me that anytime that man tries to contact me the spirits are there with me, to provide what sustenance I need, while I deal with the devil. Takes away his ability to overpower me."

She didn't expect Mitchell to understand. But she had to assert herself fully into the air between them. She couldn't afford to lose any part of herself to him. Not even for business purposes. If she didn't stay true to herself, she had nothing to offer anyone.

And the attraction she felt for the lawyer…it had to be kept in its place. An anomaly. Nothing more. Unless she could find a man who respected and admired all of her, she was better off alone. Which was why she hadn't had a date in longer than she wanted to contemplate.

"I don't know much about ancient mythology, but setting a ringtone to trigger a mindset is kind of impressive." Mitchell's tone drew her gaze back to him another time.

Her initial thought, that he was mocking her, had already dissipated before her eyes pointed straight toward his. She warmed inside all over again. It wasn't sexual, though that awareness was there every time she looked at him now, but more spirit to spirit.

"Did it help?" he asked.

She nodded slowly, holding his gaze in an attempt to understand more about what was going on between them. Until he looked away and pulled out his phone.

Various ringtones sounded within seconds, and she continued to watch him. Not sure what to think. Experience told her he was playing with her.

Her heart told her he was being sincere.

Could she trust her emotions in the moment? With the vandalism, Fletcher's menacing pressure, her father missing and that odd attack of sexual awareness, she most definitely needed an aura cleanse. And she definitely should not make any potentially momentous decisions until she'd had time to detoxify.

While she sat with her impressions regarding Mitchell Colton, he was engrossed with causing his phone to emit a myriad of sounds. Some soothing, some decidedly not.

She sat in the moment, letting the present happen around her. Until he said, "Preventing disaster before it strikes is half my job. I'm thinking I need separate tones for each of my brothers. For my cousins. And some of my problematic clients, as well."

Soft chills spread through her. Followed by a mellow warmth. And she smiled a little as she asked, "You consider your siblings and cousins problematic?" Since she'd never had either, and he had a plethora with whom he was reputed to be close, she was truly curious.

Without looking up from his phone, or ceasing the sound

bombing, he shook his head. "They just expect me to see potential issues and prevent them if I can, though I don't know if any of them are consciously aware of doing so."

"Then, wouldn't just one tone do it for all of them?"

The next shake of his head snared her attention. She couldn't explain the sudden pull from him to her except that somehow the conversation had become personal. Almost intimate. "Why not?" she asked, sitting forward as she focused entirely on him, needing to hear his answer. He was giving her a private piece of himself. And that mattered.

"Because they're all different. I'm aware of their individual pitfalls, and I think it might be productive to have rings that remind me of them prior to our communications."

Leaning back against the wall again, Dove stared at him. Mitchell Colton was truly taking her seriously.

Learning from *her*?

She wasn't sure anyone had ever done that outside her studio. And at Namaste, all anyone came to her for was cleansing and calm. Things they could do on their own if they'd trust themselves enough to try. And had the discipline to make it happen.

An intrusive beep sounded, interrupting her happy mojo, and she looked over at the phone and then raised her gaze to the man's face in time to see his frown.

Fear speared through her. "What's wrong?" she asked. Deep breath.

He shook his head, then, tapping his phone screen a couple of times, held the cell up to his ear. "I set an alarm for nine. Clint Schumer is a client of mine. I trust him not to mention our conversation to anyone."

Clint Schumer. Owner of the bar that had become her father's second home. "You're calling him about my dad?"

Just like he'd phoned Eli, not once, but twice, without first cluing her in.

Dove needed to have a word with him about that. After she got over being grateful for his help. His initiative. And the contacts he had who took him far more seriously than they'd take her.

Mitchell was nodding, then, tapping his phone screen a couple of times, held the cell up to his ear and said, "Clint? Mitchell Colton here." Dove stood up and walked over to her dad's desk. Stood there. Saw him lower his phone to tap the Speaker icon and set the device on the desk and then say, "I'm calling to make a discreet inquiry," he said.

Dove heard the bar owner reply with, "Of course. Who do you need to know about?"

As though it wasn't the first time Mitchell had made such a call.

Some of those preventative measures he'd just been talking about? The wondering helped distract Dove from the sound of the lawyer's voice mentioning her father's name. Asking when he was last in the bar.

"I haven't seen him since Friday night," the man said. And Dove's good vibes dropped to her toes. Slithering away even as Clint continued with, "Someone said he was in yesterday afternoon but didn't stay long."

"Any word as to who he might have been with? Did he leave with anyone?"

"No, but I can ask around," Clint offered. Asking no questions at all. And Dove understood why Mitchell had called the bartender first.

"I'd appreciate that," Mitchell said. "Call me on my cell if you hear any more."

"Will do," the deeper voice said, and the call ended.

Leaving Dove staring at the man who'd just the day before agreed to take her father on as a client. Would he change his mind?

The question lurked but wasn't the one screaming so loudly in Dove's mind, forcing her to ask, "Where in the hell is my father?"

Just before she burst into tears.

MITCHELL WASN'T GOOD with the crying. Its unpredictability made him uncomfortable. And its lack of problem-solving capabilities interrupted his ability to process concisely.

Dove's tears seemed to multiply the effect on him tenfold.

Disliking the situation in which he found himself, Mitchell stood. "We need to focus," he said aloud. Realizing, even as he spoke, that the words weren't his best effort. "Where else would your father go? Who might he be with? Or have seen or heard from him?"

Blinking a couple of times, Dove sniffled. Wiped her face and said, "Any of his crew. They were still here when I left yesterday. The police had the vandalism report ready for me and had questions to ask as well, so as soon as the contract was signed, I left with Detective Welding..." She paused. Seemed to go inside herself, and he suspected he was losing her again until she said, "Oh! And Oscar Earnhardt. They meet for beers every Saturday afternoon. Always have for as long as I can remember."

Frowning, he stared down at her. "Oscar Earnhardt who he fired for driving a boat while drunk and then crashing it?" He'd gleaned the further information about the incident when going through Whaler's jotted notes in his friend's file. And he and Dove were getting further and further apart from each other with each contribution to the current conversation.

She nodded, and he used his own body-language-reading skills to try to assess her current reliability. Her shoulders were back. She was looking him in the eye. And her voice was stable as she said, "They've been drinking buddies for years. It's how Oscar came to work for Dad in the first place. They'd met at the bar. Back then, the whole time Mom was alive, actually, he only went to the bar on Saturday afternoons because Clint has always had a sailors' happy hour. Oscar enlisted in the navy right out of high school but blew out his knee during his first year at sea and was put on permanent desk duty. He got out as soon as his tour was up, came here, and my dad took him under his wing. Oscar understood that my dad had to fire him or risk losing the business to potential lawsuits..."

Mitchell was leading her out the door by the time she got to that part. He'd heard enough to know that they had to find Oscar Earnhardt. It sounded as though if anyone would know where Whaler might be, it would be his drinking buddy.

It wasn't the first time he'd heard the story of the bottle being a stronger bond than career or money.

"Where does Oscar live?" he asked when Dove shot a questioning glance up at him. It didn't make good business sense for Brad Fletcher to have harmed Whaler, but the way facts were suddenly lining up, Mitchell could see possibility in the theory.

Most particularly if Fletcher somehow got word about the contract Bob St. James had signed the day before, giving his daughter legal right to make decisions for the company. With Whaler out of the way, the uptick in pressure Fletcher had put on Dove that morning made more sense.

The sailors' happy hour—something Whaler had been participating in for years—would have been easy for Fletcher to find out about. A few questions in town or at the docks could easily have provided the information. Everyone knew Whaler. And if someone working for Fletcher posed as an old friend...

"Last I heard, Oscar's got a room at the Shelby Inn," Dove's response to his question interrupted the thought. "But it's up for sale," she continued, "so I'm not sure if he's still there. He's in the process of going through a divorce. His wife and son are still living in their small home not far from the docks."

She'd wrapped her arms around herself as she spoke and slid out the door he held open. A sign that she was holding back? Or just giving herself a much-needed hug?

Activity down at the dock looked much as it had the day before. Customers waiting for boats to be readied for them to climb aboard for a day of fishing. Whaler's two current employees making the work look easy. For a second there, Mitchell envied them both. Spending their days at or on the water. The condition of the boats their main responsibility. But only for a second. He'd be missing his job, his clients, by end of day one. The idea of having a boat waiting for him at the end of the day was a good one, though.

Something to think about as he had Dove climb into the passenger seat of his expensive sedan to head out to the renovated hotel. Better that than give any brain time to the warm soft touch of her skin he'd felt when his hand had brushed her bare side above the waistband of her skirt thing and the bottom edge of the long-sleeved crop top as he'd led her out of the office.

What was he doing? Escorting the flighty woman around town searching for her drunk father when he should be on his way to the glaciers to test out his new footwear.

His current behavior was so out of character, he almost told Dove she'd need to go alone as he climbed behind the wheel and smelled lavender coming from the seat beside him. But how could he just walk away?

Most particularly with her thinking that he was going to be taking on St. James Boats as a client.

The thought calmed him. Going the extra mile for a client was not new to him. On the contrary, it was completely ordinary. Almost predictable.

He'd just never had a client like Dove St. James. It wasn't him that was out of character. It was her lifestyle, requiring him to meet different needs, that had his normal routine in flux. As soon as they found Whaler—and had a business conversation that would go along the lines of letting the police get a handle on Fletcher before contemplating any business moves they could make—he'd be free to get to his own Sunday pursuits.

Down the road, if Whaler was willing to listen to any of Mitchell's suggestions to generate cash flow for his business, the sea captain could meet him at Shelby Law Office.

And Dove St. James would be wholly out of his life.

OSCAR WAS STILL in his room at the inn. And wasn't at all welcoming when he answered the door with his growl of "What?"

But as soon as Mitchell told the man why they were there, his expression changed from sourpuss to open concern. And for the first time in a long time, Dove's heart went out to the navy man.

Oscar's drinking had caused seemingly unending pain for his wife—a client of Namaste—and had endangered Whaler's business as well. But Dove was beginning to understand that while raising a glass to your mouth was a choice, it wasn't always a logical mind that drove a person's choices. Sometimes overwrought emotions were in control. Impulses. Physical addictions.

Something she'd been blind to for too long. Because she wanted to believe that her father could be well by just not raising that glass. Cured from one minute to the next.

But with the thought of losing him taking over her mind, she knew that the only way to save him was to see him as he really was.

Which meant she had to see Oscar in that new light as well. Rather than through the many layers of pain she'd helped his wife clear from her spirit.

Not trusting herself to be as efficient as Mitchell would be in the current situation, she stood outside the doorway with the lawyer, and listened silently to the conversation taking place.

Oscar had seen Whaler the afternoon before, briefly. The former St. James Boats employee had had a job interview in the next town and had had to leave the bar shortly after Whaler had arrived. Whaler had walked out with him to wish him luck, and Oscar had assumed the older man had gone back into the bar. But he hadn't looked back to confirm that. Or couldn't remember having done so, at any rate.

He also hadn't been offered the job he'd applied for. But he had another really good possibility on the table. The news drew out a genuine smile from Dove as she told the man thank-you and followed the expression of gratitude with "And good luck with the next interview. Just be yourself, and you're sure to get it."

As long as he didn't show up drunk. Oscar, sober, was an excellent seaman. Was a walking encyclopedia of southern Alaska and most particularly glacier facts. And was a people person, too. As critical as it had been to get him away from St. James Boats after the accident, the business had also suffered for Oscar's leaving.

Tension filled her space, encased her, as she hurried with Mitchell back to his car. She couldn't move fast enough to escape it.

And had never felt so alone in her life.

She couldn't seem to access the spirits that she knew never left her side or the air around her.

"Can we check Dad's house again?" she asked even before Mitchell had his door shut. "Just in case?"

Nodding, Mitchell looked at her, and she didn't want to hear his words when he opened his mouth to speak. Had to restrain herself from covering her ears.

An action she'd allowed herself many times in her life when she knew something was going to come at her that she didn't deserve and chose not to take in.

"And then I'm going to call my cousin, Kansas," he told her, the hint behind those words ripping through her.

She'd known what was coming. Turning a blind eye to the truth was different from deflecting mean-spirited opinions that bore no merit. Life had to be lived with eyes open. With awareness. Or there'd be no true joy. Or real peace.

Kansas was a cop, too. Just like Mitchell's brother.

"She's search and rescue," she said quietly, stepping into the facts slowly.

Mitchell's long look was speculative. She withstood it. He nodded.

She could be heading straight into hell. He needed to know if she was going to be okay.

She wasn't. Not if they didn't find Whaler.

Was this the time when she lost the ability to believe and her spirits left her?

Would Mitchell stand in the fire with her? Or would

she be there all alone? She couldn't ask the question. Not even of herself.

So she nodded.

And he started the car.

Chapter Seven

Whaler wasn't at home. With a quick look around, Dove determined that he hadn't been there since they'd looked for him there earlier that morning. On the way over, she'd called several people she knew that kept in touch with Whaler. The guy who rented space from him at the marina to sell bait to Whaler's customers. Both of the men who still worked for him. The woman Dove had hired to clean her father's house twice a month. And his doctor of forty years. She reached the man just as he was leaving church.

No one had seen or heard from the business owner since Saturday afternoon.

Mitchell was itching to call Kansas in, had been ready to do so for more than an hour, but Dove insisted on checking out one more place. "He might have stopped for a bite at Roasters," she said, standing in the middle of her father's living room as though she couldn't decide where to put herself. "One of my mom's friends works there, and when he's particularly lonely, he'll go order some pie and chat with her in between customers. Not that he'd be eating pie, as drunk as he was…"

Her voice dropped off, and Mitchell paused on his way to the front door. He looked at her face and felt a rush of the horror he read there, as an almost physical being.

"I never should have left him in that state," she whispered, eyes wide and almost blank as she stared at him. Her long amber waves fell around her as her shoulders closed in on her petite, shapely frame, and Mitchell was directly in front of her before he'd had the thought to go there.

Taking both of her shoulders in his hands on instinct, he straightened them, bending his head until he could see into her eyes and then raised himself, pulling her gaze up with him. "From what I hear, you'd never leave him at all if you didn't leave him in that state," he said clearly. Succinctly.

Staring at him as though through the eyes of a frightened child, she nodded. Nodded again. And he felt her muscles engage beneath his fingers, pulling her together. Upright. Ready to stand on her own.

"Let's go to Roasters," he said then, as though nothing had just happened between them. Needing to convince himself that it hadn't.

He was just out of his comfort zone. Reading far too much into normal, everyday occurrences that were happening in the midst of disruption, coating their time together with uneasiness.

Time that he hoped would be drawing to an end before afternoon hit but held out little hope when no one at Roasters remembered seeing Whaler since Friday.

He'd just pulled out of the parking place on Main Street, not far from the café, and had turned the corner to take them back down toward the marina when he heard Dove gasp and then shout out, "Stop!"

His foot was already pushing hard on the brake by the time she'd finished the command. Shooting forward against his seat restraint, he turned to look over at her.

"That's my dad's truck," she said, her voice breathless-sounding. And hopeful, too.

Mitchell shot forward, turning down the side street he'd been about to pass, and sped toward the truck. Dove was out of the car before he had the vehicle in Park and, leaving his car running in the middle of the road, he followed quickly behind her.

Praying that, if Dove found Whaler slumped over the steering wheel, the older man was still alive.

HER FATHER WASN'T in his truck. Nor was there any sign of when he'd exited the vehicle. Could have been an hour or two, or the day before.

"The engine's cold so it's been here more than a few minutes," Mitchell told her, but she knew he was stretching the time for her benefit.

Something she both appreciated and needed him to not do. Whatever was lying in front of her, it was her job to get through it with as much faith, hope, joy and peace as possible. Not to crumple beneath the weight of it.

"It's been at least an hour," she stipulated, more for her benefit than his and headed up to the house in front of which her father had parked.

"You know who lives here?" she asked, as Mitchell showed up beside her.

"Nope."

"Me, either." But she couldn't let the unknown stop her. With Mitchell standing right behind her, his car still running in the street, she knocked.

A few times. Until an older woman called out to her from behind. "He's a captain, out to sea. Won't be back for another couple of months."

She turned to see a seventyish woman, dressed almost stylishly in linen pants and a blouse and jacket—probably just coming home from church Dove realized—standing on the sidewalk between them and her father's truck. "I live across the street," The woman said, "and saw you through my front window."

Dove wanted to smile at the woman. To thank her. And ask questions. But felt the sting of tears too sharply to do anything more than nod.

"Do you know how long this truck's been parked out front?" Mitchell jumped in, covering her weakness.

"It was here yesterday afternoon when I got home from playing bridge. Hasn't moved since, that I've seen."

Saturday afternoon. Again. Dove's heart took a dive so deep she struggled to stay upright and moving forward.

Except that Whaler needed her. She was all he had left, and she was not going to fail him. Or the spirit of her mother who would be there, guiding her, if she'd let it.

If she could access it.

She had to access it. To find her center and be fully present. No matter what it cost.

Even if it meant finding enough good feeling to supersede the bad by turning to a man she hardly knew and had no business leaning on.

He'd been put in her path for a reason. It wasn't up to her to question why. Not then. Not yet.

And so when she felt Mitchell's hand at her back, his palm against the strip of bare skin between her crop top and skirt, she landed right there with it. Absorbing his touch. Going with the flow of warmth it gave her. And let him lead her back to his running car.

MITCHELL WAS ALREADY on the phone by the time he slid behind his steering wheel. Heading down the street and around the corner, he stopped just a couple of blocks from the local office of the Alaska Bureau of Investigation. As far as he knew, his cousin Kansas, a search and rescue state trooper, didn't have a current case, so probably wasn't at the office.

But he'd bet Eli was. And he didn't want to pull his older brother's attention away from his major crimes duty another time if it wasn't warranted.

"Hey, cousin, what's up?" Kansas answered her cell on the second ring, sounding wide awake and ready to go as always.

"I'm not sure. Maybe nothing," Mitchell said, more in deference to Dove sitting next to him, hearing every word, than his own take on the situation. By his calculation, something was most definitely up. He just wasn't sure it was within Kansas's wheelhouse.

"You wouldn't be calling me on Sunday morning if it was nothing."

Watching Dove he said, "Whaler St. James hasn't been seen since yesterday afternoon. He's not home, at work or at the bar. No one who works for him has seen him. And his daughter's studio was vandalized as well. Welding's working on that. There've been some less than friendly offers to buy Whaler's business issued to his daughter as well as Whaler, from a businessman named Brad Fletcher. Eli has had a team watching him since yesterday. The most recent text from him came before eight this morning."

He paused, sent an apologetic look to Dove, who'd been staring out the front windshield during his entire missive, and said, "We just found Whaler's truck parked outside the house of a deployed sailor. Neighbor said it's been there since yesterday afternoon. Whaler wasn't in a great state the last time he was seen yesterday. I'd even say worse than usual." His opinion. But based on facts. He finished with something they both knew, more for Dove's sake than anything else. "Local police aren't going to do anything about this until more time has passed. He could have just wandered off."

"And, if you mean by he *wasn't in a great state* that he was drunk, then he could have fallen while he was wandering and might need help," Kansas said, stirring up an influx of affection within Mitchell. His family, their closeness, was a pain in the ass at times, but he loved them all. Would die for any one of them.

Sitting there with Dove, who had no one but a failing father who was missing, Mitchell realized how lucky he was. Feeling grateful for the first time in a long while, rather than just accepting life as it came and giving his best to it.

A good man didn't just sit with his wealth. He gave back. And as Kansas told him she'd head out and see what she could find on Whaler, Mitchell hung up the phone and turned to Dove. "This is going to sound like overkill, but my family and I...we don't ever take chances when it comes to someone's safety..." He paused as she turned and looked into his eyes. Tried to read what her gaze was telling him. And got nothing but openness.

"Every Colton home has top-notch security," he said, speaking without carefully choosing his words. And stopped himself as he was about to further expostulate. She didn't need to know why his family lived as they did. Eli and Kansas in law enforcement were reason enough.

He was going to help Dove. He wasn't there to bond with her. To tell her he knew about tragedy. About living with those who'd experienced inexplicable loss.

Eli might be the only one of the siblings and cousins who remembered their aunt Caroline, having been five when he and their father had found Will Colton's seventeen-year-old sister murdered, but every single one of the Coltons lived with the devastating grief that day had wrought.

Will's parents, Mitchell's grandparents, had been found that day as well. Slain in their bed. Years before Mitchell had been born. He'd never had the chance to know them, but the shadow of their deaths had shaped every day of his life.

None of which mattered to Dove or the current situation. It just served as information Mitchell could use to understand and predict his client's current needs.

Pseudo client. There'd been no official business arrangement made as of yet. And wouldn't be until the owner of the company was found.

But he'd said he'd help her. Which, by his own moral code, obligated him to do so.

"I don't think it sounds like overkill to call in your cousin," Dove's words pulled his head out of his ass and back to the car where he'd started to make an offer and had then just stopped.

"She's in search and rescue, right?" Dove continued, her pinched face in contrast with the calm tone. The fact that she was repeating something they'd already discussed was telling.

She had to be worried sick. And there he sat, thinking about himself.

"She is," he confirmed, to give her the moment she'd obviously been seeking. And then said, "I have a guest suite in my home. I want you to move into it until this is resolved."

She sat back, her body rigid, a clear indication of rejection. Reading the response, he didn't give her a chance to express it. Just kept right on talking. "Free of charge," he said, trying to hit every one of her upcoming arguments before they became such. "I'm on the outskirts of town, but just. It'll only be another few minutes' commute to work. A little farther to the marina, maybe. The place is big enough that you wouldn't be encroaching on my space. And most importantly, you'll be safe while we get this thing figured out."

The tension in her face, her shoulders, hadn't eased a

bit. "The suite is there for just this purpose," he said then came up with his closing argument. "Several of my clients have used it over the years."

Truth… Barely. Clients who'd also been friends. Having moved away and come back to visit. Or needed a place to stay while damage to a business had been repaired. Once when a house didn't close as soon as expected and the rooms at the Shelby Inn had been sold out.

None of which mattered. He'd inferred that she was a client. Her shoulders should be relaxing. They were not.

How long could Whaler's truck sit on the street, awaiting his arrival? Weeks? Months? Should he see about having it towed back to the sea captain's home? The marina?

"Of course I'll stay in the suite," Dove said then, her gaze flecked with gratitude but filled with unrest. "Gratefully. And I'll do whatever housework or anything else you need done, I'll cook your meals, whatever to show my gratitude. I just… The fact that you called your cousin, and thinking I might be in danger…you really think something's happened to my dad, don't you?"

Right. He'd hoped they were going to let that lie for a bit. Until Kansas had a chance to do her thing. "I think it's possible," he told Dove.

She nodded then said, "It's more than that. He's in trouble. I can feel it."

And for a second there, until he came to his senses, Mitchell was certain he felt it, too.

DOVE HAD NO idea what kind of a bill she was racking up with her and Whaler's new attorney, but didn't care. Fate had driven her to his door on the longest shot she'd ever taken. Every good thing that had happened since was because she'd let hope guide her.

While she hadn't even dreamed that her circumstances had been about to turn so horrible so quickly, she'd been fully aware that she'd been in need of pursuing her last-ditch effort.

Just as she knew that, until she heard news of her father, she had to stay busy. If one of the boats had been missing, she'd have taken another and sped to all her father's favorite coves. She knew every one of them. Or if his truck hadn't been found, she might have driven every road out of town, for as many miles as it took to find the old vehicle.

As it was, she wanted to knock on the doors of all seventeen hundred homes in Shelby. Instead, she told Mitchell that she had to get back to her studio, finish removing all signs of vandalism, and then give the space a thorough spiritual cleanse. She accepted his offer to help make the studio appear normal for her classes in the morning.

When it became clear that he had no intention of leaving her alone, she opted to forgo the most important work until morning. And even agreed to him waiting outside her small house by the marina as she packed a bag for the next day or so. But when he went to load her things into his car, she finally spoke up, insisting that she take her own car to his place. She might be in need of assistance, but she would not become dependent. No way her spirits would be leading her to *that*.

Though she'd only had oatmeal and fruit for breakfast at six that morning, she wasn't hungry when Mitchell suggested that, before leaving town, they get something for lunch. But because the chance to sit and watch for her father, or anyone she knew who might have seen him, was too good to pass up, she agreed to lunching at The Cove— a place right on the water, not far from the marina or her house—and ordered the fresh salmon salad she always got.

When her mother had been alive, their small family had dined at the somewhat dimly lit, quaint restaurant at least once a week. The water called to all three of them—though in different ways. To her mother, it brought a sense of peace and wellness, of enough space to store all of life's answers. To her father, the sense of adventure that he'd always craved.

Before all he'd craved was the contents of a liquor bottle.

For Dove, it was a combination of the first two. And a reminder of a third. The danger that lurked and could take a life with little warning. As disease had taken her mother.

If she'd been fully present she might have thought it would be awkward, being at The Cove at all that day—with her mother gone, her father's business on the brink of collapse and him missing—let alone sitting at a table for two by the window with the lawyer.

Maybe because she was on and off numb, her comfort wasn't even an issue.

If he was embarrassed to be seen sharing a table alone with a woman in what most would consider unfashionable purple attire, he certainly didn't show it.

"You've been nothing but kind to me," she said, reaching with all the might she could muster to stay focused on that good feeling. "I'll find a way to repay you, Mitchell. It's important that you know that."

Unfolding his napkin and putting it in his lap, he shrugged then said, "I don't charge for kindness."

The statement made her smile. Inside and out. It didn't quell the fear slicing through her. But it helped ease the immediate sense of impending doom enough for her take a couple of bites of her salad when it arrived.

He seemed okay with letting her control the conversation while they sat together. So she asked about his family. He'd been born in town, but she knew his parents and aunt and uncle had moved from California when Eli and Parker had been little. The family was well known for their adventure tours. That had not only helped keep Shelby on the map but had contributed to the success of St. James Boats as well. Unfortunately, it also prompted the interest of outside businessmen like Brad Fletcher.

"I was born here," Mitchell confirmed when she mentioned what little she knew about Colton family history. "So were Spence and Kansas. My cousins. Our fathers are brothers."

She'd known that much. Wanted more. But couldn't clear her mind enough to get there.

"And Lakin, of course," he added. "She's the real gem among us."

Dove's heart caught at the warmth she heard enter Mitchell's voice when he mentioned his adopted sister—a woman who'd been two classes behind Dove in school—and a native Alaskan who exuded love.

"I heard she'd been abandoned at a grocery store," Dove said, and then, with a quick intake of breath, needing to take back the crude words, ended up choking.

Which caused her to miss Mitchell's initial reaction to her rudeness. "I'm so sorry," she said, taking a sip of water as her coughing subsided. "I am most definitely not myself." Which was scaring the crap out of her, and lending strength to the negativity invading her system.

Reaching over the table, Mitchell used his napkin to wipe the tears from her cheeks, caused by the coughing. "No need to apologize," he said. "Lakin would be the first one to tell you about how she came to us. I'm convinced that she considers her story to be her lucky talisman, though she's never admitted that. She was three when she was found alone at the grocery store. Friends of my parents fostered her while authorities searched for her parents, and my parents ended up adopting her. She's been the light in our family ever since."

The way he said that, as though his family had been lacking light, caught at Dove. She wanted to ask him about the darkness she sensed but didn't trust herself enough to know if she was sensing him, or just projecting her own current state onto him.

Before either of them could say more, Mitchell's phone rang. Because he'd placed it on the table when they sat down to eat, Dove saw the name flash on the screen: *Kansas*.

Her stomach clenched around the few bites of food she'd taken. Staring at the phone, she willed herself to take a deep breath. Could barely draw a shallow one.

Mitchell grabbed the phone and went out to the reception area to take his call.

And Dove sat alone, trying to think about her mother, about her family in that restaurant, and picking out the different tables where she had memories of them together. To draw on what she knew rather than accessing any of the emotion that led her through life, certain that doing so in that moment would release the fear waiting to drown her.

When Mitchell appeared in her line of vision, heading her way, she was still breathing, thinking about a birthday she'd celebrated at the table in the corner. She couldn't remember how old she'd been. But she remembered the purple glitter birthday hats she and her mother had worn. Her dad had been out to sea. But he'd radioed in before she went to bed that night.

Mitchell didn't have a radio. He had a cell phone. Still in hand.

Heart pounding, she glanced up as he reached their table. Got nothing from blue eyes staring straight in hers. No warmth. No fear. No strength. Or weak knees, either.

"Tell me," she said.

Wondering what it meant when he sat first, instead. Had they found Whaler? Was he...

"Kansas found drag marks in the back alley, behind the bar."

The last place her father had been seen.

"They end abruptly right next to a pair of tire tracks that left rubber and debris behind. As though a vehicle accelerated rapidly. A truck, most likely, based on the tire tread. But a newer one."

Relief hit for a brief second. She grabbed a breath while she could and said, "Not my father's truck."

He shook his head. Didn't seem to find the news as good as she did.

Because her father wouldn't have hauled himself away. Someone else would have done that. In their own or a stolen vehicle. Made more sense that way.

She didn't want sense. She wanted her father home. Passed out drunk if it had to be that way, but home.

Was that the lesson she was there to learn, then? To be more tolerant of Whaler's drinking? To accept the liquor as part of their lives, rather than constantly trying to get her father to leave it behind?

Fine then. She'd make peace with the bottle.

Did you get that? She wanted to scream the words aloud. Settled for the silent communication that wouldn't get her thrown out of polite society. *I get the message* she added for good measure, just in case someone out there in the spirit world was having as bad a day as she was.

"Kansas is heading up a search and rescue team, and they'll be heading out shortly, starting from the bar. Welding and his partner are going to be canvasing the area, talking to everyone who was in the bar yesterday."

Feeling her face start to tingle from tension, Dove forced herself to relax back in her seat. One muscle at a time. Starting with her neck. Her cheeks. Her fingers. Not in any of the orderly ways she taught. Didn't matter. Toes. Elbows. Any relaxing at all.

Lavender. Remembering that she had it on her, she shoved a hand down her shirt, in between her breasts, and pulled out the sachet, holding it under her nose with both hands. Breathing deeply.

And slowly realized that other than looking like some kind of weirdo, she was just fine. Not passing out. Or losing her life.

It was all right there. Waiting for her to take control and move forward. From a bad moment to what came next. Knowing that if she just kept going, good would be there waiting.

Even if the relief just came from a whiff of lavender.

Mitchell's voice came back to her. "...out of an abundance of caution. There's no evidence to prove that Whaler, or a human being for that matter, was dragged."

Dove took it in, the deep timbre. The warmth. Along with the words. And drew in a full breath, too. "What's next? How can I help?"

"You keep your cell phone charged, and on your person, in case he tries to contact you."

Of course. A given. She nodded anyway. "What else?"

The look in Mitchell's eye brought another flash of fear for a second, but then all she saw was warmth, and she wondered if she'd imagined the fear. Or had projected her own terror onto his glance.

"We go to the grocery store," he told her, as though they'd already had the plan.

She was game. If there was something there, some camera, some person, that could give them information. When he didn't offer more, just counted out cash from his wallet, placing it with the bill on the table, she asked, "What are we doing there?"

"Buying groceries." His tone sounded so normal, she went with it for a second.

Until reality hit again, and with dread she asked, "To feed the search and rescue team?"

Mitchell stood, and so she followed suit. "No," he said. "You said you'd cook for your keep. Dinner's in just a few hours."

Oh. Well. Dove hurried after him out to the car. Thinking about what he'd said. Another few seconds of something to focus on other than what could be happening to Bob St. James.

Or what could already have...

No. It hadn't. She'd know.

The fates had strongly prompted her to seek out Mitchell Colton's help. She had to trust that he knew what he was doing. That whatever it was, and for whatever reason, she was meant to follow along. And so she asked, "Do you prefer your vegetables sautéed, boiled or baked?"

Because at the moment, the thought of planning anything more than the side dish was beyond her.

She'd be in better shape once they were actually at the store. Walking the aisles. She'd find her strength. Come through.

She just had to trust. Trust herself.

Trust her father to stay alive.

And trust Mitchell Colton, too.

Chapter Eight

Mitchell had had no intention of taking Dove up on her offer to cook for him. Didn't want to cross paths with her in his home at all, if he could avoid doing so.

But the whiteness around her lips had been so stark, the blank look in her eyes so acute, he'd seen an emotional break down looming and had felt compelled to distract her.

He'd blurted out shopping plans on the fly.

And had forestalled disaster once again.

Because that's who he was. The prevention guy. His whole life. While his brothers and cousins went brazenly about their lives, to face danger and win, not just against nature, but against odds, too, Mitchell was the one who watched out for them all. Looking for dangers that would beat them, and doing all he could to make sure that that didn't happen. Just as he did before and during every single time out he took for himself.

Maybe if someone had paid a little more attention to the guy Aunt Caroline had said was stalking her…

What the hell?

Pulling into the grocery store parking lot right behind Dove St. James, Mitchell put an immediate halt on his train of thought. He was the prevention guy because he liked the law. Liked facing cerebral dangers, pitting himself against them and winning.

Just as his family did with nature.

Nothing to do with an aunt he'd never met.

Two days with Dove St. James—three really, if you counted their initial meeting in his office—and he was starting to sound as flighty as she did.

It was one thing needing to put himself into a clients' mindset professionally in order to predict what might befall them, but quite another to adopt that mindset personally.

But then, Dove wasn't officially a client yet. And, if Mitchell had his way, she never would be. Whaler might be. Down the road.

They weren't down the road.

He was walking into the grocery store with the man's daughter. Preparing to buy food for her to prepare for him.

To keep her focused and as calm as possible while they waited to hear back from Kansas. And Welding. And Eli, who was reporting in on whoever was heading up the Fletcher part of things.

Because, until they knew the extent of the danger she could be facing, he'd opted to be the one to provide safer housing for her.

Right.

She chose interesting food items as she filled their cart. Other than her earlier query as to how he liked his vegetables cooked, she hadn't deferred to him even once.

About to question and give input, he stood back instead. Literally. Walked a step behind her as she made her way through the store. Curious to see what came next.

And later, after they got home.

If he didn't like dinner, he'd pull something out of the freezer. Order in. Fill up on trail food, for that matter.

Mostly, he didn't want to disturb her mojo. Whatever she had going on in that oddly captivating head of hers, it was working to her benefit. The color had returned to her face. Lines of strain were dissipating from her cheeks. Her shoulders had relaxed. He wasn't going to be the one to mess that up.

Not unless he had to. By way of preventing something worse.

Like the shopping cart that was suddenly flying down the aisle, coming right at the display of cans that… "Dove!" He hollered, and dived forward, catching her around the waist, throwing them both into a ground roll that took them to the end of the aisle.

A woman screamed, cans crashed. Mitchell saw a pair of black boat shoes fly by. Someone running away, not stopping to help.

In the next second Mitchell was only aware of the soft, womanly body clinging to his with both arms and legs wrapped around him.

And for the first time in his life worried about what in the hell he'd gotten himself into.

THE SCREAMING STOPPED.

"Dove! Are you okay?" Hearing the voice from far off, recognizing it but unable to place it, Dove loosened her death grip on the man who'd saved her and rolled off him and up onto her feet.

Recognizing the wide-eyed woman who'd approached, she immediately filled with a semblance of calm. "Cindy, yes! I'm fine," she said, brushing herself off.

Cindy Morrison had lost her husband and young son in a boating accident the year before and had been on the verge of a breakdown when she'd come to Dove's studio just after

Christmas. In the eight months they'd had together, Cindy had finally been able to allow herself to travel through the stages of grief. To begin the healing process. Letting go of the negative energy one breath at a time.

Seeing Dove hurt could set back that process. Not that Dove was some kind of guru protected by her angels, but because she was lending Cindy some of her own strength. Support from one human being to another. She didn't want Cindy to even entertain the idea that anyone else she leaned on or cared about would end up dead.

Store personnel came running up the aisle, darting around rolling cans, and as Mitchell approached one of them, Dove led Cindy around to the next aisle. Away from any hint of danger. To get herself out of the chaos and to tend to Cindy, too.

"That was wild," she said, breathing back a shudder and managing a ragged chuckle. "I'm guessing whoever stacked those cans is going to be getting a demerit today." Making light of the situation helped. Asking Cindy how she was doing helped more. Gave her mind focus while her body's physiological state righted itself.

When Mitchell and the store manager came around the end of the aisle to find her, she felt better equipped to make her statement. And insisted on finishing her shopping, albeit quickly.

"Dove." Mitchell called her gaze to him as the manager left them. "You should have let him call the police."

"I didn't stop him," she pointed out. "I just said I didn't feel a need to report the incident." She started to push their cart that another store employee had brought around to her—still bearing her beans, greens and natural proteins. All foods that enhanced intuitive abilities. She'd roast the raw cacao beans first chance she got.

Her mother's first go-to anytime things were out of whack.

Sticking to her side, Mitchell pulled out his phone. "I'm calling Eli."

"I expected you would," Dove told him, feeling oddly calm as she pushed the cart. "Which is why it made no sense to call in yet another police officer." She stopped and looked at him. "Unless you hurt something when you took the brunt of the fall for both of us?"

He shook his head as he lifted the phone to his ear and gave his brother an account of what had just transpired.

Hearing Mitchell describe the episode, the basket that came forcefully at her, seemingly out of nowhere, set to knock her into a display of cans that would send her into a fall that could easily break bones or inflict other bodily harm, the black boat shoes he'd seen fleeing the scene...

What?

She stopped. Watched a couple of other shoppers pass, who turned to look at her—because of the incident in the canned vegetable aisle, or just because she was her and she'd always been stared at, she didn't know. Didn't much care.

And pinned Mitchell with a stare the second he ended the call. "You think someone deliberately tried to hurt me?"

"I think it's way too much of a coincidence that that cart just happened to come out of nowhere, heading straight toward you, while you were standing directly beside that display."

Fresh fear sluiced through Dove, but she quashed it. Thought of Cindy. Of her mother's roasted cacao beans. And said, "It's called karma, Mitchell. It comes to pay back bad as well as good."

He stared at her. His eyes narrowing. "Which debt did you just pay?"

"Good," she said, needing to believe herself more than she ever had before. "I went to see you even when I so didn't want to. And ever since, you've been like my guardian angel. I don't know what's happening with my dad. But I do know that you were meant to come into our lives. That things are happening to show me that I need to trust you. And to believe that whatever the outcome, it was meant to be."

"You didn't want to come see me?"

"You think I didn't know how much you did not want to agree to help us?"

Mitchell started moving slowly up the deserted aisle in which they'd been standing, and Dove stayed right beside him.

Shoving the tips of his fingers into the front pockets of his jeans, he said, "It's not that I didn't want to help, Dove. It's that I didn't see much likelihood that my skill set would fit your needs."

He'd deftly owned his lack of enthusiasm to come to her aid. She gave him credit for not denying what she'd sensed. And all that mattered was that she'd sought him out against her own best wishes. And in spite of his doubts, he'd been fully present every time she'd needed him since.

Heading straight for the ground beef, and then to the pasta aisle, followed by the dairy, Dove gathered what she needed for dinner, trying not to notice how closely Mitchell stayed beside her. A reminder of the heat and strength of his body as he'd saved her from being scrunched between a runaway basket and the cans of diced tomatoes that, had she fallen into them, could have caused her serious harm.

"What's for dinner?" he asked then.

And she almost smiled as she said, "Lasagna."

He'd paused over the menu item at lunch, before he'd chosen the lighter, more lunchlike club sandwich.

"How do you know I even like lasagna?"

"My spirits told me," she replied, her tone purposefully serious as she kept a grin to herself. Sometimes being perceived as a little odd had its amusing moments.

And sometimes a woman had to grasp at every distraction she could in order to keep her head above water.

While the small bit of earth upon which she stood seemed to be crumbling beneath her.

HE NEEDED HER to change out of the sexiest outfit he'd ever seen. The same one that had just appeared out there to him that morning. Flighty. Not funny how an incident on the tile floor of a public grocery store, with danger-induced adrenaline pounding through him, could completely reframe his perception of clothing choices.

Even less humorous was the way his mind seemed to be playing tricks on him where Dove St. James was concerned. Was she flighty? Or just playing with him?

While he'd have assumed the former two days before, he was leaning more toward the latter as he pulled into his three-car garage and saw her pull into the driveway behind him. He couldn't spend the rest of Saturday afternoon and evening alone with her in his home.

As big and stately as the place was, it afforded far too much privacy. Laying groundwork for things to happen that no one would need to know about.

Activities between consenting adults that happened on a casual basis, leaving both parties able to walk away without looking back.

With her father missing, able to do nothing but wait for news, Dove needed activity. Just not the kind his body was suddenly fixating on.

Almost exclusively as he showed her to the guest suite downstairs, across the hall just inside the garage door.

Didn't seem to matter to his libido that his bedroom was across the three-thousand-square-foot home and up a winding flight of stairs. He could carry her up, no problem. Hell, they could do it on the stairs for all he cared.

Problem was, of course, the rational part of him did care. And that part was boss.

Always.

As he set Dove's suitcase and satchel in the middle of the floor of the room, he did a quick scan of the four-poster bed, nightstand, across to the couch and coffee table beneath the window, checking for security weaknesses.

Found none. Other than that, he'd like it better if the room was on the second floor. That window...there were security cameras, a state-of-the-art alarm system, steel window frames, bolting locks and the same kind of unbreakable glass found in high-rise hotel rooms.

"Do you really think that thing at the grocery store was on purpose?"

Dove's words expressed a sense of vulnerability—at least the way he heard them—and Mitchell immediately turned to her and said, "Logic is telling me that it's possible." Everything else seemed to point to that certainty, but he wasn't a man who allowed himself to dwell in places he couldn't prove existed.

She'd implied that she'd listened to one of her promptings to seek him out in the first place and was taking all of his attempts to help her as proof that her guidance had been spot-on.

But what if, instead, her karma was just playing a bad joke on both of them?

He needed his time-out. The weekend he'd had planned—

the time away he protected diligently—to keep himself lev-elheaded. So that he could serve all of those who relied on him without fail.

Dove wasn't unpacking. She was just standing there, watching him. "To what end?" she asked. "How does some-one benefit from trying to hurt me with a can attack in the grocery store?"

Relieved to finally be certain of a response, Mitchell replied immediately. "First, it's another bout of bad luck in a space in which you feel safe. Which adds pressure to the fear someone is trying to build within you. Second, if you're hurt, you're less likely to get in the way. Right as your father goes missing. All of which could be designed to weaken you. To make you doubt everything you know. Feeling threatened, overcome by fear, you'd be more likely to entertain the idea of convincing your father to sell the business."

"And if something's happened to him, to sell it myself and leave town," she said softly, her gaze clear as she stared at him. "You think my father's dead?"

He couldn't just put that one out there. He told her the less painful truth. "I don't know." He *didn't* know, but he did think the strong possibility was on the table.

Dove shook her head, her long amber waves falling over her shoulders in a confusing array. "It's not like my father's business is worth killing for," she said. "It's not a million-dollar outfit."

"No, but it could be, if expanded upon and run properly." According to what Eli had told him, Brad Fletcher had the funds to invest. He'd built a lodge at one of his marinas. An upscale place that attracted wealthy clientele. The same could be done in Shelby.

A look of fear crossed Dove's face, but it was quickly

gone. Replaced by an almost serene expression that seemed to bear a cloak of steel. "Which is why, as soon as he's home, the three of us are going to get to work implementing your plans for the place," she said and turned to lift her satchel onto the couch. "Which will also then ensure that you get ample compensation for your work."

She had it all figured out. As though, just like that, she sees and it becomes. Shaking his head, Mitchell had no immediate response coming to him. He didn't know what to do with her. How to interact.

With his own internal pressure building, he said, "Do you own jeans and hiking boots? If not, we can go buy some. I've got something to show you."

He just wasn't sure what it was yet.

There were a plethora of places he could take her, sights he could reveal that she never would have seen before, bounty that their homeland had to give that he'd discovered on his own over the years. By the time they headed out, he'd land on one of them.

"I live in Alaska," Dove said, reaching for her suitcase. "Of course I have jeans and hiking boots." He moved to grab her bag, to lift it to the bed for her, but she grabbed it and swung, almost hitting him in the process. "I also brought them with me," she said as she started to unzip the bag. "Just in case my dad…"

She didn't finish the sentence. And Mitchell left it hanging there. For a moment. "Meet me in the garage when you're ready," he said and took the stairs up two at a time so he could change and beat her there.

Patting himself on the back as he did so.

Getting her out of town would be the best way to protect her. And he, with his years of practice of disappearing into the ether, was the best man for the job. If someone thought to hunt for her in the mountains, or along the seashore, they'd follow trails. Shoreline. Even if they went off-trail, no one was as skilled as he was—except, perhaps Parker, Eli, Kansas and Spence, and probably their fathers—at taking on Alaska's challenging terrain.

Mastering it.

Most would more likely get hurt, possibly killed, if they tried.

Ironic, really, how his years of selfish pursuits were suddenly proving to be advantageous to someone in need.

Almost as though fate…

Mitchell stopped the thought before it completed itself.

No way was he going to start thinking that some kind spirits guided all for their own good. If that were the case, his grandparents and Aunt Caroline would still be alive.

Or, at the very least, they wouldn't have suffered such brutal deaths.

Chapter Nine

"Wow, this is…" Leaning back against a tree, Dove couldn't finish the sentence as she slid down to the ground, staring out over the cliff face just feet away, to the Bering Sea beyond. Her gaze landing on the glaciers she'd been acquainted with her entire life, but never seen from that vantage point.

The climb had been hours long. Rigorous. Challenging to her toned muscles, but nothing she couldn't handle.

The bear that had been within yards of them, not so much. Mitchell had taken care of that one all on his own. Other than the noisemaker he'd handed her, something the kids in Shelby learned how to use during grade school. She'd done her part there.

He'd seen the tracks first, had heard the movement when she'd thought he was only listening to the breeze in the trees. He'd been conversational as he'd told her that it was a black bear—not saying how he'd known, and she hadn't asked. She'd been too busy glomming on other bear information she'd learned as a kid in school. Black bears were generally not aggressive.

She'd seen its back as Mitchell stood his ground and the animal had slowly ambled off in the opposite direction.

That had been an hour before. She'd been thinking ever since about the man's appearance in her life.

Leaning her head back against the tree's bark while Mitchell stood gazing at the horizon, Dove closed her eyes and took deep, pure breaths. All the way through her diaphragm and filling her stomach.

Over the course of the past hours, she'd found her way back to herself. To fully trusting. Against her own judgment, she'd followed her heart's missive to seek out her exact opposite, the practical and staid Mitchell Colton. And she'd most definitely been led to the place she'd needed to be in that space and time.

She didn't kid herself that there was any kind of future for them. Dove rarely thought about a future for herself that contained a husband. Or even a permanent male companion.

Most of the men she knew didn't understand her. Or believe in what she knew to be truth. And there was no way she could compromise her heart. Any relationship she attempted to have after that would fail. You couldn't love without heart.

She didn't question why she'd been given a deeper sense of the heart and soul, the spirits within and around her. Didn't ask why she had an understanding that never reached most people. But she knew that, above all else, she had to be true to that which she could feel but not see. Or even explain.

Finishing a litany of thanks, she opened her eyes to see Mitchell pulling out his phone.

"Is this a service point?" she asked, reaching for her own cell. They'd stopped at two others during the hours they'd been out. There'd been no news forthcoming at either of them.

But when she saw Mitchell nod as he tapped his phone

screen, she tapped her own. Saw a new text message, and recognizing the number as one of her father's employees, Hal Billows, she tapped to read it immediately.

Dread flooded her being at the first few words. She finished reading and said, "Mitchell." He reached her in two strides, and she handed him her phone.

Saw the words in her mind's eye as he read them.

Tell your father I'm sorry, Dove, but I'm quitting St. James Boats as of today. I've been offered a position at another marina for a lot more money. And better chances of longevity. Keep my pay for the past week in lieu of my two weeks' notice.

There was no other marina in Shelby. And as Mitchell had pointed out recently, Brad Fletcher owned the marinas in the neighboring towns on both sides of them.

She could no longer turn a blind eye to the facts that were presenting at an alarming rate. Mitchell had been right. Someone was putting the squeeze on her and her father.

Someone with the power to offer a St. James employee a handsome raise at what was surely one of Brad Fletcher's marinas.

At the same time Brad Fletcher was being increasingly aggressive with her in his bids to buy her father's marina.

It didn't take a mathematician to put two and two together on that one.

Nor to see that if she didn't take Fletcher's offer, she and her father would be destitute. St. James Boats was no longer raking in the dough, but it was making enough to cover Whaler's minimal needs and alcohol with enough left over for the monthly installments on her mother's remaining medical bills.

Namaste kept her afloat. But with nothing to spare.

"I might have a solution for this one." Mitchell's words slowly got through the fog taking over her brain.

"For what? We can't offer Hal more money."

"No, but with your permission, I think I might be able to find someone who can take over his duties. The son of a buddy of mine from high school. Dete Littleton. Like your father, Dete's a sea captain, gone most of the time, but his son, Kirk, has been raised on boats since he was born. He's only twenty-one, just back from college graduation…"

A dream come true for St. James Boats. Even temporarily.

That math added up quickly, too. Glancing at Mitchell, accepting without question the good coming from him, through him, she said, "You have my permission" and sat calmly while he made the call.

Bad would come. It was a part of the learning experience. Her job was to trust. To know that, regardless of what happened, her spirit would be fine. She was loved.

To believe that answers would always be there.

And to keep firmly in mind at all times that Mitchell Colton was merely a conduit.

Not intended to be a personal part of her life.

KIRK WAS ECSTATIC at the idea of working at St. James Boats. He'd grown up with the marina in his backyard. Had hung out there as a high schooler, just to learn, to feel like he was closer to his father out at sea.

Unbeknownst to Dove, Whaler had let the kid tag along and help him out when he was working on the boats. And the others had, too.

"It's a blessing of fate," Dove told Mitchell as they

headed back down to civilization to meet the young man at the marina. It would be getting dark by the time they arrived—would be nearly eleven at night—but Kirk wanted to be able to help on the docks in the morning, and Mitchell had to close the deal. Several of the boats had reservations on the books for the next day. Including Whaler's largest, most expensive boat in the fleet—the small trawler, *Wicked Winnings*.

"It's business, Dove. It's what I do. Put together people and products that mesh through fair contracts." It was clear, concise, logical business.

Something he'd done dozens of times during his nearly ten years since he'd opened Shelby Law Office.

Business. Not some kind of guided-by-invisible-powers miracle.

And because he was bothered by her comment, he had to bring the point home strong. "It's what you're paying me for," he said succinctly.

Something that wasn't yet technically true. There was still no official agreement between him and St. James Boats.

Nor was he planning to charge the business for hooking Kirk up with them. More like he was doing a favor for a friend—his high school buddy, not Dove St. James.

He would oversee the employment contract, however. And update the one Whaler had with his one remaining full-time employee, Wes Armstrong. And should get something in writing with Lyle Morris, the college kid who was helping out for the summer. For all he knew, Kirk and Lyle knew each other. Stood to reason since they were only a few years apart in age.

Something to keep in mind, to ask Kirk about when they met up. If there was jealousy or any kind of bad blood between the two, he'd want to see that both men were able to get along at work before he suggested that Dove leave them alone on the dock with Wes. Whaler's senior employee did not need employee-relation problems on his hands.

Energized by the thoughts, back to doing what he did and did well—taking care of his clients' business interests and preventing disasters—Mitchell was almost eager to get off the mountain and back to town. He was back in control of his world, himself again.

Right up until at the marina where, after the grocery incident, they'd decided to store her car that afternoon before leaving on their hike, Dove got in the passenger seat of his vehicle to ride home with him.

"It's like a miracle," she said, beaming in her usual way. Something he hadn't seen since her father had gone missing. The glow hit him in the gut. Hard.

He knew it would fade. Kansas had called in again to let him know there were still no signs of Bob St. James, nor did they have any viable leads. Which meant they were forced to take each road, each trail, each overhang one at a time. Her team would be at it again at first light.

"Kirk is just what St. James Boats needed!" Dove continued to gush. "And the idea you two came up with, him captaining *Wicked Winnings* three times a week to bring in a serious catch to sell, providing fresh halibut and salmon for the grocery store and for The Cove, too, is brilliant. The cash flow from that alone will be a boon. Dad's only been in the boat rental business for others to fish for sport and recreation, but making fish a part of our business is just the step we need, and now with Kirk onboard, we can actually implement the idea."

"We still have to talk to the businesses to see if they'll

buy what *Wicked Winnings* brings in," he warned, trying to let her down easy before he got to the tough stuff.

"Even if they don't go for it, you know locals will come down to the dock to buy fresh catch less expensively, and it's pretty much a given, with the discount you suggested, that the grocery store and The Cove will be on board."

"There will be an initial investment," he warned as he turned to head them out of town. "More insurance, for one thing. And means and protocol for proper handling and storage of the fish. Pricing structures. Packaging."

Nodding, Dove turned to look at him. "What's bothering you?"

It was unsettling how much time the woman spent reading his moods. But in the moment, she helped him get where he had to go. "There's no sign of your father yet."

She nodded. "I figured. You got two calls while we were at the marina. If either of them had been good news, you'd have told me."

So...all her purported happiness about Kirk had just been...fake? Avoidance? A cover-up for what she didn't want to see?

"The second call was from Welding. Someone's been keeping an eye on your place today. Mrs. Bentley called in to report the same car parked down the street, saying she saw an individual wearing a baseball cap in the driver's seat with binoculars pointed toward your house. She didn't get a license plate, and by the time patrol got there, the car was gone."

Mrs. Bentley, the retired English teacher both Mitchell and Dove had had in high school. The longtime widow had been the only upper-class English teacher during the years both of them had been in school.

Dove's response was a little slower in coming. He was prepared for tears again, when he got, "Which explains why I was guided to stay at your place." And then, "Or why you were prompted to invite me to stay."

"Dammit, Dove, this is serious." Mitchell calmed his tone, some, but not the frustration warring with compassion inside him. "Your life could be in danger. Judging from the break-in at Namaste, your property most definitely is. You can't just brush this all off and breeze by it, hoping it will go away."

He'd pulled into his driveway. Slid into the garage in total silence. Wishing he hadn't had to quiet her chatter but encouraged, too. He had to know that she was going to watch her back every second until the police found enough proof to be able to arrest Brad Fletcher.

When he put the car in Park and turned to look at her, she stared right back, saying, "You think that's what I'm doing? Running? Pretending? Avoiding?"

Softening his tone at the obvious disappointment in her eyes, he said, "Your father's missing, I'm telling you your house is a target, and all you want to talk about is spirit guides and their promptings. Where were they when your father either strayed off or was hauled off his path?"

The question seemed kind of cruel. Heartless. And yet, if it got her to take the situation more seriously and saved her life, then he'd appear to be as heartless as it took. No way he was going to stand by and watch the woman fall into more pain.

Her gaze didn't falter. Her hand seemed perfectly steady as she lifted it to push a lock of wavy hair over her shoulder. "I was talking about intuition, Mitchell. As in listening to it. Your brain, in conjunction with your heart, collaborating between what you know, what you believe and what you want, to best guide you."

He'd been put in his place. Succinctly. Firmly. Kindly.

By a petite yoga instructor who'd shown up that morning dressed like a sexy purple daffodil in revealing Lycra and some kind of netted long tutu thing.

A woman who solved her issues by sitting on the floor, closing her eyes and breathing deeply.

Not a solution that would work in court.

Mentally framing his sincere apology, Mitchell was interrupted when Dove said, "As for the rest of it… I can panic, shiver in fear, as I was doing earlier, my initial reaction to a change in my circumstances. And if I continue to do that, I play right into the hands and intentions of whoever is trying to inflict evil on me. My best shot at winning in this showdown is to remain calm. Lucid. And the way to do that is to not let the fear take hold. You prevent that from happening by focusing on good thoughts, which perpetuate good feeling, which lessens fear's ability to take you over. And for the science to back me up, since you seem to respond better to what you can have visible proof of, look up *serotonin*. See where that leads you."

Wow. The woman should be a prosecutor. A defense attorney. Or…just who she was.

"You've got some in your body, in case you didn't know."

His body. The words, coming at him in the dark, from the lips of the oddest and possibly the most fascinating creature he'd ever met, had a wrong effect on him.

Sending him into inappropriate waters.

Clinging to shore with everything he had, Mitchell said, "In the first place, I apologize. In the second, thank you."

She shook her head. "What are you thanking me for?"

"Setting me straight." That wasn't right. Wasn't enough. He revised with, "Reminding me that my perspective is not the only valid one on earth."

"You're more in tune than you think, Mitchell. I've been struggling to get out of the fear. I was failing, in spite of everything I know to do to help myself. But you knew what to do. Head away from the world, from the evil lurking around me, and up into nature."

For a second there, he wanted to be that guy. To live in a world where he could just escape all of the threatening possibilities lurking around the corner. But to do so, he'd have to give up his livelihood and walk away from what he was best at. Looking for the danger. And preventing it from happening to others where he could.

Using the skills he excelled at—analyzing, paying attention to detail, making judgments. Staying focused on the bad that had happened, and could happen, in order to find ways to avoid it whenever possible.

"Are we going in?" she asked, bringing his attention back to her face in the dimly lit garage.

"I wasn't sure you'd still want to stay." Though, he'd have done all he could to talk her out of not doing so, if she had made that choice.

"Of course I want to stay." Her vehemence surprised him. Gave him another stab of the desire he'd been trying so hard to pretend wasn't there. Until she said, "I was prompted to seek you out, and willingly, knowingly, or not, you've been my answer every step of the way. I might appear odd to many in this town, but I am not one to make foolish choices, Mitchell. Nor to turn my back on the opportunity that's been presented at a time when I most need it."

Well, there he had it. She wasn't into him. Personally.

Wasn't maybe starting to trust him. She was relying on her inner guidance. And he just happened to be the means by which she reached her goal.

The thought should have eased much of the bizarre emotional tension that had been building within Mitchell.

Instead, her words left him unusually deflated.

And still tense.

Chapter Ten

Dove went straight to her room. Alone time was critical to her well-being and, other than while using the restroom, she'd had none since early that morning.

More than that, she wanted to get out of Mitchell's hair. If he quit on her, she had no idea what she was going to do.

The answers would come. They always did. She knew that.

But she could also reach her demise in the process of finding them. While she was not one to argue with fate, she also understood that self-will had power of its own. And she wasn't ready to be done with her earthly life.

After a quick shower and then prayer time—focusing fully on her father being alive—her head hit the pillow just before one in the morning. And by four, she was lying there wide awake. With worry bugs starting to creep under her skin.

Throwing off the covers, she tried to meditate but was already too lost in subconscious musings to find her zen. At home, she'd turn up the music and clean.

But she figured Mitchell wouldn't appreciate the chaos at that early hour.

Opening her door slowly, she crept out into the hall

enough to take in the quiet of the house. That's when guidance hit. The kitchen was the room closest to her but the farthest from the staircase that led upstairs to Mitchell's suite.

And she had dinner to make. She'd given her word. Had no idea what the coming day was going to bring in terms of claims on her time.

She loved to cook. Found pleasure in the activity itself, the joining of various ingredients to make something that tasted better together than any of them did alone.

And while the sauce simmered, the ricotta mixture softened enough for spreading, and the noodles cooled, she prepared cacao beans for roasting. And mixed up a bowl of fresh, finely cut cucumber, broccoli, kale spinach, and other mixed greens for breakfast. Her own.

Breakfast casserole was on the menu for Mitchell's.

Even if he liked the idea of salad in the morning, no way she was going to expose the man to her dietary habits. He'd just end up asking questions.

And she'd end up telling him that the foods promoted intuitive abilities…because she *knew* he'd go look up their benefits—and find them, too. Proving her right.

And while she was not going to change who she was or what she did, she didn't have to be in his face with her lifestyle, either. Especially as a guest in his home.

That would be just plain rude.

Adding some cheese to her greens for protein, and then, when they came out of the oven, the chopped beans, Dove moved on to the next project. Roasting salmon in the air fryer on the counter. She'd seen a friend of her mother's use one. Had always wanted to try one out.

With the lasagna in the oven—she'd waited to bake it because it took longer, at a higher temperature than the twenty minutes total for the beans—she pulled out the salmon she'd put in marinade when she'd first come into the kitchen. Reading the instructions on the front of the air fryer, she set the temperature and time before putting the smaller pan in the middle shelf and hitting Start.

From there, she moved immediately to the refrigerator for the sausage for Mitchell's breakfast casserole. Putting that on the stove on low, taking time to crumble it nicely, she was just finding a bowl big enough for the egg mixture when she heard footsteps on the stairs.

At five thirty in the morning.

And was filled with instant dread. An hour and a half of good feeling dried up as she waited for her host to make his far too early appearance.

While she was at his place, and with his family working her father's case, it stood to reason that bad news was going to come from him.

It would also be what would get him up out of bed so early in the morning after having gotten to bed late the night before.

That and the fact that he had an office to open that morning, the thought came to her. With clients that could have early appointments before their own businesses opened.

She'd been selfish. Making the world all about her...

And should have put on more than just the pajama pants and cutoff tie-dyed T-shirt she normally wore to bed—and for cooking. Like a bra.

And panties.

She couldn't very well make a run for it with sausage browning on the stove. Nor was she one to hide from trouble. Most particularly not that which sprang from her own actions.

And if it was bad news coming her way?

Half-frozen in indecision, Dove moved by rote, not

thought. Reaching into the refrigerator for the food she knew would give her abilities an almost immediate boost, she grabbed a fork and was standing by the bowl of eggs, chewing, when Mitchell entered the room.

Not in a suit ready for work.

"Something smells good," he said, seemingly unfazed to walk into his kitchen in a pair of silk drawstring shorts and nothing else to find a woman standing there shoveling salad into her mouth.

"It's salmon," she told him, because the fish was the one project she was least confident about so was most on her mind. The whole air fryer thing being an unknown component.

"And lasagna," she added as he passed the oven on his way to…the coffee maker. She should have made coffee. Hated the stuff. Wasn't sure how to work the machine. But…

"I couldn't sleep," she admitted, as she quickly chewed and swallowed another bite. Nearly choking on a shard of bean.

With a few quick and impressively efficient moves, he had a cup on the plate of the coffee maker, had inserted a pod in the top and was moving over to the stove. "And the sausage?" he asked.

He'd been with her at the store when she'd purchased it—and pretty much everything else she was using that morning—and had tried to pay for it all.

"Breakfast casserole. I planned to have it ready by six. In time for you eat before you have to leave for work." And then, thinking she sounded presumptuous added, "And it keeps well, in the event you didn't need breakfast until seven. Or eight."

The man needed to go. Out of the kitchen. At the very least.

It wasn't like she'd never seen a bare-chested male in the kitchen before, but Mitchell—she'd never been around a guy who...exuded...on overload. Her nipples were hard and, other than putting her arms up over them to cover them—which would just draw attention to her inappropriate reaction to the man sent to help her through a horrible phase in her life—she couldn't do a thing about it.

Except stand there holding her bowl in front of her, take another bite and look at Mitchell's chest again.

To stave off what she knew was coming.

And she'd been so pompous in her self-assertion moments before that she didn't run from trouble.

Kansas had said she'd be back at it by daybreak. Dawn had hit almost an hour before. "Have you heard from Kansas?" she asked then. Ashamed that she'd tried to hide behind the sight of a chest, rather than face whatever the day was going to bring her.

Or was she hiding behind the day so she didn't have to deal with what the sight of that chest had done to her? Way more than what she'd felt in the studio the other day.

She could not be sexually drawn to Mitchell Colton. He was her complete opposite.

And she needed him.

Sex was messy. And after the initial pleasure wore off, relationships usually didn't end well. At least not in her experience.

Every time she'd had to break up with a guy, he'd given her the cold shoulder.

Maybe it was just her. Not knowing how to break up right...

"I'm waiting on a call back from her." Mitchell's words

put an immediate halt to her mental throwing up. And drew her gaze up to his face.

"And you wanted to be down here when the call came in," she said slowly. Because the couple of days they'd spent together had been intense, and his body language was easy for her to read.

Or, more likely, she hadn't lost her ability to tune in and gain understanding, in spite of her extreme mental and emotional flux.

A fact for her thoughts only. As secret and sacred as the sexual ones she'd been having the past couple of days.

Not to be shared with Mitchell Colton.

Ever.

MITCHELL PULLED HIS cell phone out of the pocket of his loosely fitting shorts. Set it on the counter. Wishing, for the dozenth time since he'd come down, that he'd thrown on a T-shirt before leaving his room.

The shorts had seemed sufficient when he'd been thinking that he was pulling them on with the very small chance that he'd see Dove St. James when he went down to make his coffee—a task normally done in the nude, right after he slid out of bed and before he got in the shower.

He'd hoped to be showered, shaved and fully dressed before facing the woman who'd bombarded his life. She'd had a hard few days and had gotten to bed late.

No way he'd expected her to be superwoman in the kitchen, making multiple meals, before six in the morning.

By the time he'd registered the unusual scents wafting through the air, he'd already been detected and could hardly turn tail and run. The explaining that would have required was painful just to think about.

Stirring the sausage that was bordering on being more

than merely browned, he turned down the heat and faced the woman who'd kept him up even after he'd closed his eyes the night before.

Standing up straight, holding her bowl like an iron shield in front of her, she asked, "What are we expecting to hear?"

And he gave it to her straight. "Kansas found Whaler's cap."

Her gaze widening, her mouth dropped open. No words came out.

"I was hoping to know more before I saw you," he told her the truth.

"How much do you know?"

"The cap was found half-buried in some leaves, not far from an overhang about five miles outside town."

"Where? Hanging over what?"

Wishing he was anywhere but where he stood, Mitchell had never felt so underprepared—and underdressed—in his life. "Three miles up the mountain, overhanging the Bering Sea." He gave it to her straight.

Whether she was ready for the truth or not, she'd made it clear the night before that she deserved his full respect. Which, in his world, meant his full disclosure.

"They think he went over."

He couldn't tell her that. Kansas had given facts. Not opinions. "They're thoroughly checking the area." And there was more. "It looks like there was a struggle nearby, like someone was lying down."

Her eyes narrowed, and she took another bite of what looked to be some kind of rabbit food. That needed a load of dressing—for starters. "Were there signs of anyone having been dragged?" she asked.

He shook his head. Knowing full well that the news didn't mean that no one had been hauled to the edge of the cliff. Only that if someone had been pulled across the ground, the dragger had cleaned up after himself.

Dove nodded, then, setting down her container, moved over to the sausage, stirring it, as she said, "If you don't mind, I'd like to hang close until that call comes in." And then added, "Unless you have to go up and get ready for work?"

"I've got my paralegal handling things at the office today."

It wasn't the first time. Or even the fiftieth. He'd always been hands-on when it came to his work. Meeting his clients in their territory, not his. It was the best way to see it all and therefore gave him his best shot at finding ways he could help.

Like the fishing idea he'd come with while talking to Kirk the night before. A way for St. James Boats to make additional revenue.

"Unless something else comes up, I'd like to spend some time at the marina this morning," he told Dove. "To get a better look at everything involved in getting it set up for commercial fishing and additions that will need to be added for the selling process." Standing there naked except for his shorts, he was still a lawyer. Had to stay focused on business, not on the far too sexy woman standing at his stove, giving him full view of the intriguing butt that her thin pants outlined.

Turning suddenly, as though she knew where his gaze had gotten stuck, she looked up at him, her expression eager. "You really think it's going to work, don't you?"

The fishing. Not the sex. "I think it can," he told her, choosing his words as carefully as always. "We can't do anything until Whaler's back to sign off on it."

Unless the older man was found deceased. His pause

seemed to relay the message to Dove, judging by the instant drop in her expression.

Which prompted him to say, "But I'd like to have as much of the logistics ready as possible so that it's something he can run with quickly, if he chooses to do so."

Her eyes filled with tears. Because her father was missing and might not make it back? Because she had new cause to hope that if her father returned, life would be better? Mitchell couldn't read her, which made him uncomfortable in a huge way.

In his own kitchen.

Before breakfast.

He had to stop her before she had a breakdown. Leaked out all over the place.

He had to comfort her before his compassion became more than that and his own heart started to bleed.

Reaching out, he pulled her against him. Just for a quick hug.

Lawyer to aching client.

A business move he'd never made before.

Performed in not-business clothes.

Her untethered breasts pushed against his unclothed chest, with only the thin piece of cotton she wore between them.

Which affected him down below, where he was not appropriately confined.

Made clearly obvious against the thin cotton of her pants.

About to escape from his shorts, Mitchell jerked back abruptly, turned his back and vacated the room.

Leaving his cell phone on the counter behind him.

Chapter Eleven

Turning off the heat on the sausage, Dove sank to the floor.
Back against the cupboard, she crossed her legs in the lotus
position, let her arms fall, palms facing upwards at her
knees, closed her eyes and breathed.

Deeply. Raggedly.

Tears fell.

She didn't try to stop them. She sat with them. Living
through them.

Being.

In the way back of her mind, an image lingered. Mitchell Colton had held her and gotten hard. Just as her breasts
had become over sensitized against his chest.

She didn't dwell there. If sex happened between them,
it did. She wasn't going to fight it. Didn't have the strength
to go up against nature's call.

But only if he knew that sex didn't mean a relationship.
Or commitment.

And she had no idea if he knew that.

Just like he had no idea if her father was alive or dead.

Daddy.

The name of old came to her. Called out of her toward
him. Pulling him out of an abyss and back to her. She was
there. Present. Helping him save the business that he loved.

Hold on, Daddy.

The words came to her, and from her, followed by a flow of conviction, of strength, so powerful that the sorrow left her being. Only for a few seconds. But for that brief time, she'd felt peace.

Grasping hold of the memory, she opened her eyes. Wiped her cheeks. And slowly stood. Holding on to that last impression she'd had, she finished putting together the breakfast casserole. Took the salmon out of the air fryer, wrapping it tightly for future salad use. Washed dishes while she waited for the lasagna to finish baking so the casserole could go in.

And heard Mitchell's phone ring.

Snatching her hands from the soapy water, she grabbed a towel, dried them and grabbed up the phone. Saw Kansas's name on the screen.

Just that. *Kansas.*

She pushed to answer. It wasn't like she had time to run all the way upstairs before the call disconnected.

And he could be in the shower. She had no right to trespass there.

She said the first thing that came to mind. "Mitchell Colton's phone. This is Dove St. James speaking." She shivered, but remained otherwise calm.

"Dove? Where's Mitchell? Is he okay?"

"He's upstairs in the shower," she said. At least that was her summation. She wasn't going looking to find out.

"And he left his phone with you?"

"It's my father you're calling about, right? If not, I'll hang up and have Mitchell call you back." She'd just finished the sentence when she heard footsteps on the stairs. "Oh, hold on, he's coming down now," she said and held out the phone, impatient to give it to Mitchell so that she could hear whatever it was Kansas had called to say.

Life was hanging in the balance, and protocols still mattered. There was something comforting about that.

Expecting to see Mitchell dressed, she stared when he came down wearing a towel with a robe over it. "I heard you talking to someone," he said, his expression containing a question and a bit of alarm.

Warming at his concern—even if it was just because he was a good man caring about humankind in general—she handed him the phone. "It's Kansas."

His instant attention to detail, the way his gaze firmed and he grabbed the phone to his ear, warmed her more. A sensation she clung to as she heard him give a couple of affirmatives but nothing more.

Trying to read anything from him, she failed. The robe, the towel, his bent head, she just couldn't tell what was going through him. Tension, no doubt about that. Having her there at all was causing some of that.

With a "Thank you. Keep in touch," he hung up.

And Dove, while scared and shaky, also felt a bit of a smile start to emerge inside her. They wouldn't be keeping in touch if they'd found a body.

She didn't say a word. Just watched Mitchell. Giving him time to formulate whatever would be forthcoming. Because he needed that. She didn't.

"They found evidence of a skirmish just over the side of the cliff, on a fairly substantial-sized ledge. A couple of footprints, which the forensics team are on now. We'll need your father's shoe size, and as much as you can tell us about the footwear he had on the last time you saw him."

"But no body," she said. No body meant there was still hope.

"No body," he confirmed. Studying her so long she felt a squirm coming on. "A body could have gone over, Dove.

It wasn't visible from the top, but a search and rescue team has been dispatched to coordinates directly below."

She'd already accepted that a body could have gone over. Didn't mean it was her father's. It could be whoever he'd been fighting with. "Signs of a skirmish are a good thing," she said then. "My dad's one hell of a fighter. You might not think so, given the way he hasn't been taking care of himself since Mom died, but prior to that, for his entire life, he's been focused on keeping himself strong and in the best physical shape possible. His freedom to do what he wanted depended on it. He's still stronger than a lot of guys half his age." She might be exaggerating a tad. She hadn't actually seen her dad on a weight machine in over a year. But if she was off, it wasn't by much.

"Then, we'll continue forward with good thoughts for his return," Mitchell said, still standing there, seemingly assessing her. Whether he really believed Whaler was dead or alive didn't much matter to Dove. She needed him, his focus, on her, on St. James Boats, not on her father. She— and she was certain her mother's spirit—had that one covered.

But she was only human. She faltered and fell prey to humanity's greatest evil: fear.

Mitchell's presence was needed to cover her. To keep her afloat while she held her father up. She fully believed that. Had seen proof of why he was there over and over in the past few days.

"Uh, about that…what happened earlier…"

Pulling up an innocent look born of knowing neither of them did anything wrong, she said, "What happened?" He had absolutely nothing to castigate himself for. And she knew she'd done nothing requiring an apology.

At least not in the moment he was speaking about.

"I never should have hugged you. It was inappropriate. Something I've never done before. And I can assure you, it won't happen again."

"Don't make promises you can't possibly keep," her mother's words of old popped out of their own accord.

Frowning, Mitchell wrapped his dark blue robe about him further, tightening the knotted matching dark blue fabric belt holding it in place. "I keep my promises."

"I fully believe you intend to, Mitchell, but how can you possibly see forty years into the future, which could be when you retire, and know that you'll never have occasion to give a client a moment of comfort?"

He stared at her.

And she moved in a little closer. Not physically. But with the softening of her gaze. And the words she let out. "As for the rest...the perfectly normal bodily reactions that occurred when you reached out to offer me comfort...it's not fair to yourself to guarantee that it won't happen again. What if I was falling, and you reached out to catch me, and we ended up in a kiss?"

He scoffed. "You've watched too many Christmas movies."

Aha! That had to mean he'd seen at least one, right? Maybe with his mom or sister?

Could be he even tuned in to one on his own at some point. Or with a girlfriend.

The last thought not as pleasing as the others, she let them go. And grew completely serious.

"Sex has a power of its own, Mitchell. When two consenting adults are both consumed by that force at the same time, there's a good chance they'll come together physically." She was practically quoting her mother then—from her reaching-puberty talks—but with an experience Dove had gained on her own.

He leaned against the counter, suddenly seeming a little more amenable to staying a while, rather than hightailing it back up to his ablutions.

And getting himself all decently covered, tucked in and hidden away.

With a quirk of his head and narrowed blue eyes, he said, "You're telling me that you'd be consenting?"

Delicious flames shot down between her legs. She knew to welcome the release from the dread that had been closing in on her as she pictured her father on a cliff ledge fighting for his life.

"I'm assuming we'll have a talk about it first," she told him.

Was that the time to have it? Right then? Did they schedule a time? She'd never actually done it that way before. Generally she was out socially with the guy and they'd already established that they were just friends.

"What kind of talk?"

"The kind where we establish guidelines. So no one gets hurt."

His eyes narrowed again. Kind of deliciously. And she didn't bother to camouflage her glance down to his crotch. A look that lingered as the robe moved, seeming of its own accord. "Do we make an appointment for this conversation?" he asked.

How the hell did she know? Mitchell Colton had a whole hell of a lot more experience than she did in the mingling-with-the-opposite-sex department. But if he thought that was a good idea… "We can," she said. Then added, "But we better make it soon, just in case. The whole power thing—"

she glanced down at his crotch again "—it seems to be gaining on us rather quickly."

She'd grown wet. Without panties on. It was kind of intoxicating. And a bit uncomfortable, too, considering she'd probably have to wear her pajama pants again before she moved home and could wash them.

The way he was watching her...as though she was a slice of double chocolate cake with rich icing...no man had ever looked at her like that before. "Let's say, over lunch," she blurted. They'd be at the marina. Or she would be, and he'd be on the phone. All classes at Namaste had had to be canceled until the negativity bombarding her life had been resolved. No way she could live with herself if her bad energy spilled over onto those who came to her for help with their inner healing.

She was pretty sure Mitchell was holding back a grin as he nodded. "Over lunch it is," he told her and turned and walked away.

Right as the timer on the lasagna buzzed. "Mitchell?" she called out. Saw him stop, start to turn, and she grabbed the hot pads, pulling open the oven as she said, "Breakfast casserole will be out in forty-five minutes. If that's too long, we can finish it off at the marina. Dad has a toaster oven there." It wouldn't be nearly as delicious that way, but she wasn't the one who would be eating it.

"That's fine," he told her. "It'll give you time to get showered. I can make a couple of calls here in my home office, and we can take it hot to share with Wes and the rest of the crew. It will be a good way to start what will be an unusual day for them."

Bringing good to overshadow the bad. She smiled. Nodded.

And slid the casserole into the oven to the sound of

Mitchell's feet on the creaky stairs. Smiling. Thanking her stars for sending her the helpmate they had.

The man had a deeper understanding of life.

He just didn't know he had it.

And she was okay with that.

THE MORNING KEPT Mitchell busy. Dove, he noticed, not so much. She tried engaging when something came up that could use her attention, or when someone directly approached her. But for the most part, she sat on the floor of her father's office—dressed in a long flowing burgundy, pink and white skirt, and a long-sleeved pink crop top— and made some phone calls.

She didn't go out on the docks at all.

Or interact with customers.

Mitchell didn't blame her. He actually admired her for being there at all. And appreciated her attention to detail when her focus was needed.

But while she didn't go outside, he, on the other hand, spent a good bit of his time on the docks. He'd dressed accordingly, in jeans and a flannel shirt, rather than the suit he'd worn his first day of lawyering at St. James Boats. Hard to believe that only a few days had passed since then.

In some ways he felt like a completely different man. Freer. Which made absolutely no sense, so he pushed the unusual contemplation aside. Disregarding it as woo-woo, a result of the company he'd been keeping, not based in his own reality.

He spent a couple of hours taking a much deeper look at Whaler's books—finding the accounting to be nothing like he'd seen before, but once he figured out the old sea captain's process, he found the entries to be in fairly good order. Consistent.

The business was dying a slow death. But a clearly delineated one. So seeing, he was quickly able to ascertain weaknesses and formulate possible solutions.

If Whaler made it back and got sober, he could have the place running a profit in very little time. Two very big *if*s.

Neither of which were looking to be likely possibilities.

The better bet would be to get the place in shape, to show its profitability and then put it up for sale. With the hope of finding a buyer who wouldn't be intimidated by Brad Fletcher. A conversation he intended to have with Dove over lunch.

Because there was long-term good news in there. And he was particularly eager to give it to her. The woman took on so much. Tried so hard.

And was holding on by a thread—made clear to him by the conversation she'd instigated after his apology in the kitchen that morning. Capitalizing on the change of topic from threats and possible death to a topic that often resulted in extreme pleasure.

Could be she'd been messing with him to cover up her embarrassment.

Or, more likely, she had been using the momentary, very unfortunate lapse of protocol between them as a distraction from the terrifying disappearance of her father.

Either way, it was up to him to make certain that he was never again in a position where he was turned on by her. And absolutely not when he was underdressed enough for her to pick up on that fact. He was the lawyer. The man she was in the process of hiring to help straighten out a very grim situation.

She was the victim.

He'd rather go off the grid and never have contact with

another human being for the rest of his life than take advantage of a woman who'd come to him for help.

To further victimize Dove St. James in any way.

Stepping outside the office just after eleven to take a call from Stuart, his loyal and hardworking paralegal, he walked up to the parking lot in front of the marina so he could discuss other clients without being overheard.

And was just in time to see a man getting out of an expensive-looking sedan and then, glancing in Mitchell's direction, get right back in and pull off the lot. The man had been dressed in fishing gear.

It was possible he'd just forgotten something. Or suddenly taken ill.

Mitchell's mind was heading loudly in another direction. Telling Stuart he'd call him back, Mitchell pressed the contact icon on his screen for his brother and asked for an image of Brad Fletcher to be sent over to him. It arrived almost immediately, with Eli still on the line, and Mitchell was almost certain Brad was the man he'd seen.

The car had been at a wrong angle for him to have gotten a look at the license plate. He hadn't been thinking along those lines at the time, in any case.

"I'll get with Welding, find out what's going on with the team watching Fletcher," Eli said and then, telling Mitchell to stick close to Dove in case Fletcher tried to contact her again, he quickly rang off.

Eli had problems of his own, Mitchell knew. His cousin Spence and Hetty Amos, a sea pilot for the Colton family adventure business, had stumbled over a dead woman in the woods, only partially buried, with her hair and her left hand wearing a large diamond engagement ring still visible. Eli had been assigned the case, and so far, other than being certain the woman's death had been no accident, he had nothing substantial to help him solve the murder.

A mirror to Whaler's disappearance—no viable leads—which Mitchell knew would be eating at his brother. Cases with no solid clues made investigators uneasy. Two of them happening around the same time—especially in their relatively quiet remote town—raised cause for alarm.

Mitchell kept an eye on the marina and watched the road as well while he completed his business with Stuart as expediently as possible, and then he headed straight for the small office not far from the docks.

Lunch in a neighboring town sounded like a good idea to him. Get Dove away from Shelby and all the heartache, intimidation and fear she'd been suffering over the weekend. Yet they'd still be within easy range in the event that Whaler was found alive. In a restaurant, conversation would more easily stay focused on the business he had to discuss with her, even with someone as intent on living through her inner voices as Dove was. So yeah, his reasoning was partly to ward off his own discomfort.

More than that, though, Brad Fletcher, or anyone he hired to keep digging at Dove, would not be looking for her in a dockside restaurant twenty miles down the road.

Calling ahead to the place—one of his regular eateries for business lunches with clients—Mitchell made the reservation. And walked into the office to see…

A card table set with a red-and-white checkered tablecloth, two big bowls from his kitchen, cutlery, napkins and glasses—and Dove on the floor behind it all.

She stood as he came in, saying nothing, and moved to the refrigerator Whaler kept stocked with beer.

No alcohol was his first thought. He'd made a list of guidelines to prevent him from repeating the morning's debacle with his body in the kitchen. Feeling attraction, as he had in the studio the other day was one thing: normal reaction. That morning in the kitchen…he'd made a wrong move and had caused himself to cross a line.

"I'm assuming there's been no word from Kansas?" she asked the same question she'd greeted him with every time he'd entered the small structure that morning.

Shaking his head, more at the table than anything, he said, "No." He wanted to tell her he was sorry but was too focused on the food she was pulling from the refrigerator.

Freshly roasted salmon. Greens. Dressing.

Not beer.

With tension filling him, Mitchell sent a quick text to cancel the lunch reservation he'd just made and went into the small bathroom to wash up. The sink, floors, stool and towels were all clean.

There'd been no cleaning service on the St. James Boat books.

Nor did Whaler seem to deal in cash. All transactions that he'd reviewed, both private and personal, had been completed by card. Even his bar tab.

Which had been astronomical.

Dove. He wasn't going to ask, but he knew the cleaning most likely had been done by her. The bucket of cleaning supplies on the corner bottom shelf—right next to extra toilet paper rolls—looked a lot like the one she'd pulled supplies out of to hand to him Sunday morning in her studio.

It had become pretty clear to Mitchell that Dove had been taking care of her father in all the ways she knew how—and could get away with.

She'd only come to him when she'd done all she could herself.

Some of the things she'd said to him over the past few days lined up in a row, replaying in his mind.

"How do you know I even like lasagna?"

"My spirits told me." The tone of voice she'd used—she'd been playing with him. Letting him know that she knew that he'd branded her as a bit out there, along with much of the rest of the town. Just as they'd done her mother.

And then... *"No, Mitchell, I'm not calling you a liar. I'm just paying attention to your posture, your tone of voice. You're uncomfortable, which tells me that you know more than you're saying."* He could clearly picture the smile that had teased the corners of her mouth on that one. As though she'd known he'd been uncomfortable—because he'd been taken in by the rumors that she and her mother thought they could read minds.

There were others.

In less than four days' time, he'd come to know her better than people he'd been acquainted with for years.

He could almost feel how difficult that had to have been for her. To have to beg for help from someone she hardly knew but was acquainted with enough to understand that he'd judged her without having actually spent time in her presence.

She'd walked into his office, head held high, knowing that he thought her flighty.

The realization held him hostage there in that tiny space, as his mind tried to unravel the implications. Leaving him with the certainty that no matter what happened between them, he couldn't turn his back on her and live with himself.

"Mitchell, you okay in there?"

He jerked as her voice came to him through the thin walls and he was mentally transported back to that morning in his kitchen.

The room was closing in on him.

Pulling the door open he said, "Fine. Just had some boat grease to get out from under my fingernails." True. But a task he'd completed minutes before.

Standing between him and the beyond, she glanced at his hands, while he took in her flat pink leather sandals with laces that climbed up her legs and under the hem of her skirt. When his gaze made it up to her eyes, he found her staring at him.

Without hesitation, she said, "And here I was thinking you were avoiding our prearranged lunchtime conversation."

About to start believing that her fates had it in for him, Mitchell would have bolted then and there, if she hadn't been blocking his way.

Instead, confident that what he had to discuss with her would override their earlier agreement, he said, "I'm eager for the upcoming conversation" and followed her to the table.

He couldn't walk away from her. But he could play her at her own game.

And win.

Chapter Twelve

Dove wasn't surprised when Mitchell took immediate control of their table conversation as he filled his bowl with salad, topping it with the ginger teriyaki dressing she'd made.

From a lawyerly point of view, it was the right thing to do. Keep things on the surface. Avoiding any detours into topics that could be considered inappropriate in the workplace.

She listened to what he had to say. Was somewhat surprised by how quickly an implementation of his ideas could make her father's relatively small boat-rental business into an entity worth a whole lot more money than Brad Fletcher had offered her even when he'd been acting decently. Enough, according to the numbers Mitchell slid in front of her, to pay off all of her mother's medical bills and still have a substantial sum left over.

More money than her family had probably ever had.

It was the stuff her dreams of a week ago had been made of.

"This is all great, Mitchell," she said, forcing herself to swallow bites of the food she knew would not only sustain her but strengthen her intuitive abilities as well. "Exactly what I originally came to see you about, and what we're going to be paying for. As soon as my father is back home, we'll be ready to hit the ground running." She took another bite, swallowed and said, "This should be enough to get his head and heart in gear—enough to motivate sobriety."

She didn't know if the latter was true. But she had to believe it was. And knew for certain that there was a good possibility.

"As for the rest, being able to find a buyer other than Fletcher, someone we could feel good about selling to, is a fine thought, but not one I'm interested in entertaining. You misunderstood if you thought my goal was to absolve financial obligations. I told you about my mother's bills so that you would understand how much of a profit we need to make. And to know that my father wasn't just throwing his current paychecks into the bottle. He pays my mother's bills first and foremost, every month. It's like an honor to him, to do that for her."

And would be for Dove, too, if she was ever required to take over the deed.

When his eyes lost some of their glow, she quickly added, "That's not to say that I'm not overjoyed by the work you've managed to do this morning. I cannot wait to get started on all of this. Just as soon as we find my dad."

Because, hello, that was the only thing on her mind at the moment.

Except thoughts of Mitchell. And possibly having sex with him. Every time she'd started to sink into an abyss of negativity that morning, thoughts of Mitchell and their upcoming conversation had pulled her right back out and into the moment—and task—at hand.

Staying positive long enough for Kansas and the SAR team to work their magic and find her dad.

It would happen in fate's time. Not her own.

The only say she had, the only control, the only choices

she had in the meantime pertained to how she managed herself while she waited.

Did she stay strong? Vital? Present and able to hear the silent promptings within her?

Or did she fall into a hell from which she might never emerge?

Fantastical as it might sound to some, in Dove's mind, the answer lay in having the real conversation that lunch was about. She had no idea what the outcome would be.

Whether or not she'd ever have sex with Mitchell Colton.

The conversation wasn't about whether or not they were actually ever going to do it. Or even wanted to do so.

"So talk to me about your views on sexual activity," she said when he seemed to have no ready response to her replies regarding his business conversation.

They'd made an agreement to talk about it. She hadn't coerced him into doing so and felt strongly that if she didn't hold him to his word on the matter, something not good could result.

No clue what that something was or if it even pertained to her.

"I view all such action to be inappropriate in the workplace."

The response disappointed her, while at the same time she realized she should have expected it. Mitchell was Mitchell. Logical. Living fully in his head. Maybe even a little uptight.

"Well then, it's a good thing that St. James Boats hasn't actually hired you yet. No contracts delivered or signed. While I'm a signer on the business now, I'm not an employee. But I am a guest in your home. Where we ended up in the kitchen, outside of office hours, in less than professional attire."

She could go on. Would go on if he forced her to do so. She could be a whole lot blunter. But she stopped there, giving him a chance to own up to his own culpability in their need for the conversation.

And if he walked away? Told her he'd have her things delivered from his home?

Her guidance had clearly led her to him. Was she on the verge of making a personal choice that ruined the good she'd done by listening in the first place?

"I like sex." He looked her straight in the eye as he delivered the short sentence.

Swallowing, she pursed her lips. Then found enough voice to accept his challenge, maintaining eye contact as she said, "So do I." There were caveats to her proclamation. A lot of them. She wasn't sure why she held them back when he'd given her the perfect opportunity to get them out. She wasn't asking why.

"I don't have it with clients."

She'd figured as much. But just in case he hadn't yet discerned the same about her, she said, "Nor do I."

Forking a healthy bite of salad, he said, "So are we done here?" and filled his mouth with her bounty.

The delicious food she'd provided, she mentally corrected herself.

She took a bite of her own salad, suddenly unable to swallow without discomfort. "No."

He nodded, as though he'd expected the response. Almost as though he was enjoying their repartee.

She kind of was.

Except that she couldn't lose sight of the very real necessity for having the talk to begin with.

"There's a likely chance that what happened in the kitchen this morning will happen again."

"Not if we agree not to be in the kitchen at the same time."

His almost childish response had her gaping at him. It wasn't like they'd planned to be there that morning. Even less likely that they could time Kansas's phone calls to when they were in an office situation.

Chances were greater that the kind of call she was awaiting would come in the middle of the night. It just always seemed to happen that way. Evil at work in the dark.

Except…she pulled herself upright. Evil wouldn't be at work because her dad was going to be found alive.

Giving herself a mental smack for having fallen down the dark hole even while she was consciously working on staying out of it, Dove followed the self-directed negativity with a mental hug. An apology. And encouragement to herself for having seen what was happening and thus could prevent a permanent dive.

She didn't do that by playing around. Putting down her fork, folding her hands on the table in front of her, she said, "I'm not averse to having sex with you, Mitchell. I would never have expected to be attracted to you—business suits aren't my thing—but I am. A lot."

He adjusted his sitting posture, and she pictured him over there growing hard. The image, egged on by their early morning meetup, gave her plenty of impetus to continue.

"However, I cannot engage in the behavior unless you understand that it's strictly a mutual enjoyment of physical activity. No strings attached. No commitment of any kind to any future involvement between us—business or otherwise."

His fork stopped halfway to his mouth. "You're telling me that you no longer want me to work with St. James Boats?" His entire demeanor had turned into one big frown.

"Hell no!" she blurted loudly, as she'd heard her father do.

And then covered her mouth with her hand. Shocked at herself. Embarrassed. And then, half behind her fingers, said, "I'm saying that the sex needs to have no effect on anything outside the physical act. If we work together, that's a separate thing. But…" she lowered her hand, leaned in and looked him straight in the eye "…if us having sex means you won't help my father with his business, then it's off the table."

His gaze lightened. He ate another big bite. Then after he'd swallowed and wiped his mouth, he said, "Then, it's off the table."

Damn. She'd given him a way out. But he had to know…

Staring at him, she held him to the only real fire she knew. The silent kind that couldn't lie.

"I don't want to have sex with you, Dove."

She continued to hold his gaze. Breathing easily.

"Okay, I do. Quite fiercely, apparently. But I can't take advantage of you that way. Or use you—"

"But it's okay if I take advantage of you? Use you?"

He took yet another bite. Chewed. Swallowed. Repeated. Holding her gaze in a way that felt…easy. And that's when she knew she had him. In a place of calm that one reaches through total honesty.

"Do we have a clear understanding that *if* it were to happen, there'd be no strings attached? No expectations? And nothing weird between us after it was over?" She wasn't going to let it go until she knew. Her own future depended on that one.

"We do," he said clearly, succinctly. Confidently. Looking her straight in the eye.

And Dove stood, cleared her things off the table, put the leftovers in her bowl in the trash and the dirty dishes into the bag she'd brought from Mitchell's house. She'd failed to bring dish detergent in with her that morning.

Mitchell emptied his bowl into his stomach. One bite at

a time. Then stood and brought his bowl and fork to her. Holding it out but not letting go of it, he asked, "Are we on for tonight, then?"

And she dropped the bag she was holding.

MITCHELL HADN'T SERIOUSLY been planning to have sex with her. At least, most of him wasn't. But if it did happen, which, given his behavior that morning along with her assertion of wanting him, was a good possibility, he was one hundred percent on board with her terms.

They were way too different to actually sustain a relationship. And he had zero desire to hurt her. But it made sense, her feeling as she did, given what he'd heard about her lifestyle. And had observed from afar himself.

So if they could give each other a little pleasure at some point, he saw no harm in that.

Kind of liking the way his uncharacteristic boldness had knocked her off her game enough for her to drop her bag, Mitchell had his mouth open, ready to tease her a bit more, when the stark fear in her suddenly widened eyes clued him in that she wasn't looking at him.

Swinging around, he turned in the direction she was looking to see his cousin approaching the office. Her head and shoulders were visible through the small window beside Whaler's desk. A window he'd known always to be covered with a drawn blind.

It hadn't even registered that Dove had opened it until that moment.

Kansas was on site at St. James Boats.

She hadn't called.

Dropping his lunch leftovers on the counter, Mitchell moved behind Dove. His hand at her back. Lightly. Professionally.

But most definitely there. They'd found Whaler.

And Kansas had shown up in person.

Without a smile, her step denoting purpose, she approached with tightly pulled back long dark hair behind firm shoulders, and a grim expression.

Clearly like the family notifications his cousin had shared with him over beer more times than either of them would have liked.

They took the wind out of his cousin every single time that Mitchell knew about.

"She was a year behind me in high school." Dove's words came at him out of nowhere. In that first instant, he was worried that he'd lost her. That she knew what was coming and had fallen into some kind of mental paralysis.

"I remember once when Jack Percy was giving me a hard time in the lunchroom. Kansas stepped right up to him and told him to back off."

He hadn't heard that story. But he wasn't surprised to hear that the Percy kid had been a bully. Or that his cousin had come to the aid of one being persecuted.

He also hadn't pegged Dove correctly. Rather than disappearing, she was finding something good to cling to in the face of gloom. How he knew that, he couldn't say. Keen observation over a very intense few days, most likely.

She didn't move toward the door. Didn't move at all, and so neither did he.

When the knock came, firmly and loudly, Dove called, "Come in" in an equally raised tone.

A friendly one.

His hand at her back was stronger then. More the support of a friend than a lawyer. He was briefly aware. Didn't care.

Even if what he suspected was true was about to unfold—Whaler had been found dead—Dove's trials had just begun. There'd be an investigation. Hope to God a quick one. With an equally rapid trial.

And a tie-in to the vandalism at Dove's studio.

Kansas had stepped fully into the room. Her blue eyes steady, and her fit, strong form seemed to dominate the space. "Good, I'm glad you're both here," she said. "We found Whaler." She stopped abruptly. Looked straight at Dove and said, "I'm sorry...*your father.* He's alive, Dove, but unconscious. An ambulance is on the way to the hospital with him, and I came to take you there myself. With sirens on."

Whaler was alive. Mitchell kept the thought firmly at the forefront of his mind as Dove turned to look, wide-eyed, up at him. And when she moved to grab her purse, he allowed the next thought full flight: Kansas didn't expect Whaler to be alive for long.

Following Dove as she ran after Kansas, he locked the door behind him and climbed into the back of Kansas's car just before it sped off.

He wasn't officially on the St. James clock.

But there was no way he was leaving his clients unprotected for a second.

Or so he tried to tell himself.

As though reading his mind, Dove turned then, meeting his gaze over the seat, her gaze filled with trepidation, but something warmer, too.

And he had to admit, at least to himself, that there was only one reason he was in that car.

To be present if and when Dove needed him.

The look in her eye seemed to tell him that she knew it, too.

Mitchell wanted that to be a good thing.

But knew that it wasn't.

Chapter Thirteen

Bob St. James was alive. Dove heard the rest from Kansas during the ten-minute drive to the small hospital, medical and trauma center at the edge of town. And again when the trauma doctor met her in the hallway outside the unit where her father lay unconscious.

He was alive, but barely. They let her in to see him, but only for a few minutes that first time, as they were still tending to him. Doing all she could to fill the small emergency-room cubicle with positive energy, she kissed him on both cheeks, told him she loved him and had good news for him.

She was sobbing when she pushed through the emergency room doors, to the quiet hallway beyond. Releasing the fear that could disrupt her ability to help Whaler pull through.

She dropped down to the first chair along the deserted wall, needing to be right there in case they wanted her. And to know the second her father was being moved to one of the eleven inpatient rooms in the facility so that she could be with him.

Closing her eyes she sat back, lotus position with her skirt secured around her, her head against the wall, and let the tears continue to fall through the cracks in her lids. Drawing on her inner strength in an attempt to have enough to share for as long as it took.

"He's still alive," Mitchell's voice came to her, moving closer with each word, his tone as though he was telling her something new. By the time he'd finished the sentence, he was sitting down beside her.

For a second there, she considered keeping her eyes closed. Blocking him out. Putting up a shield against everyone. But something inside her refused to capitulate to the escapism.

Wiping her tears away, she took a deep breath. Nodded. Then shuddered. "He's in terrible shape, Mitchell. Two days of most likely unintentional detoxing without medical assistance, which is stupefying enough by itself. He has a pretty good lump on the side of his head. A nasty gash in his side. They don't know about broken bones, yet, though there's nothing obvious there..."

"And his vitals?" Mitchell's question was firm. To the point.

"They're stabilizing."

"Good. That's good, Dove. And what you need to be focusing on. If they can keep him stable, the rest will heal. And..." He paused, as he was second-guessing whatever he'd been about to say.

Dove looked over at him, met his gaze and held on. "What were you going to say?"

He shrugged. "Maybe the detoxing...is the good that comes out of this."

Reaching over, Dove slid her hand inside of his, took hold of it and squeezed. He'd gotten her to the point she hadn't been able to see.

The good that was coming.

Which maybe should have surprised her, him being who and what he was. But it didn't. At all.

"I saw Kansas as she was leaving," he said, not pulling his hand from hers. "She said she and a member of her team found him just below a mountain hang outside of town. About half a mile from where they found his cap. She had his clothes in an evidence bag, had already asked Scott Montgomery, one of ABI's forensic scientists at the office here in town, to get on them ASAP. And was leaving here to go directly to him. If we're lucky, we might even get a viable fingerprint."

Heart lifting again, Dove looked over at Mitchell, thanking her lucky stars that they'd led her to him. And got the distinct impression that she needed to lighten up on him a little.

No more sex talk. Or anything else that made him uncomfortable. No challenging him to do better at anything.

The man was already pretty much the best anyone could be. Vastly different from her, but that was okay. To be celebrated, actually. He lived true to himself.

Life's greatest challenge. At least according to her mother. And now…according to her own heart, as well.

Mitchell—just as he was—was exactly what she needed for this period in her life.

So thinking, she smiled at him and as unobtrusively as possible slid her hand from his.

LOCAL POLICE WERE providing protection for Whaler at the hospital. Mitchell stayed with Dove until Whaler was moved to a room, and then, when she went to sit with her father, with the officer just outside the door, Mitchell left to head back to the marina. To make certain that Wes was handling things. And to be there in case of any problems that might develop.

The boat rental business was Brad Fletcher's ultimate goal. With Whaler out of commission, causing Dove to be by his side, Mitchell saw the window of opportunity for the shady businessman to move in. So thinking, he made an executive decision, financed out of his own pocket as he wasn't going to bother Dove with it, and had hidden security cameras installed at the docks. And up by the office, too. The fact that he wasn't, technically, an executive hired to watch out for the business yet was immaterial to him at that point.

Didn't matter to him whether he ever got paid. Nor was he worried that he was opening himself up to potential lawsuits if Dove or Whaler ever decided to come after him for the step he was taking.

Definitely a departure from any other choice he'd ever made—brushing aside potential blowback—but he did it anyway.

Because to leave St. James Boats vulnerable was much more of a risk. And just plain wrong in light of the threats, vandalism and assumed abduction that had all just taken place.

He hadn't forgotten the neighbor's call about someone suspected to have been watching Dove's place, either.

Whoever was out to get Dove and her father had started out tamely enough. But was clearly escalating to dangerous proportions.

A thought that was brought home to Mitchell most clearly when Eli called him midafternoon to suggest that St. James Boats might want to consider getting security cameras installed ASAP.

It was nice validation of Mitchell's decision to have already put that into motion. And good, too, as the least actively aggressive male in his family to be able to tell his older brother "Happening as we speak."

"I'm impressed," Eli said then, sounding tired, but with a note of older brother, egg-him-on punch, too. "It's not like you to get so hands-on involved."

And like the younger brother he was, he let Eli's words rankle. "I'm always hands-on. My job just requires less in-your-face presence."

"From what I hear, you've maybe got more than just your hands on this one." There was no mistaking the quiet humor in that one.

Mitchell tensed, in spite of himself. "You haven't learned by now not to believe everything you hear?"

"I believe Kansas. She tells me that Dove St. James answered your phone just after dawn. You were upstairs in the shower, she told Kansas. And then you came downstairs and took the call."

Damn Kansas.

And... Dove had said *that*?

Making it sound like...

"We are not sleeping together," he said, for the record, while a part of him noted that it was good to get the words out while they were still valid.

Because they most definitely were in question.

"After the break-in and her father's disappearance, it didn't seem prudent to have her in her small place alone. She's staying in my guest room. At the opposite end of the house from me, as you well know. I'd left my phone in the kitchen when I'd headed back upstairs from making coffee. She heard the phone ring and, seeing Kansas's name, knowing it was about her father, she answered it."

"And you're honestly going to tell me you haven't noticed how hot she is?"

He refused to validate the question with an answer.

"I'm just giving you a hard time," Eli said then, all notes of teasing gone from his voice. "Seriously, bro, you're a Colton, doing what any of the rest of us would in the same situation. You think she's going to be okay if Whaler doesn't make it?"

He was doing all he could not to ask himself that question. "She won't have much choice, will she?" he responded in the only way he knew how. Logically. And then asked, "Still nothing solid on Brad Fletcher?"

"Nothing we can pick him up for. Or even sufficient evidence to get a warrant for his phone records. Based on some of his known associations, it's likely that he hired someone to trash Dove's studio. Probably has someone watching her house, too. I know Kansas is looking at him seriously for Whaler's assault. Hope to God some prints show up on the clothes she brought in. In the meantime, I figure him for putting pressure on Dove within the next several hours. Fits the MO. The man is determined to take over Whaler's business."

Mitchell had already come to the same conclusion. "I've told her not to answer if he calls. To leave any text messages and voice mails for me to deal with," he said.

"Be extra diligent, Mitchell. This Fletcher guy…he doesn't need the income from Whaler's business. He's just a number one ass. It's all about him. Him getting what he wants. Anyone tries to tell him no or go against him, he makes them pay. Including the three ex-wives in his past, from what I've heard."

The news tightened the muscles in Mitchell's gut. And

honed his thinking to getting back to Dove—and not letting her out of his sight if he could help it.

Maybe a bit drastic. But there, just the same.

There was an off note in Eli's tone that got through to him, too. Enough so that before he ended the call he said, "You sound tired. Still nothing on the body that Hetty and Spence stumbled upon?"

"It's worse than that," Eli said, gaining Mitchell's full attention. Worse than an unidentified young female corpse half buried with her left hand—bearing a flashy engagement ring—sticking out of the ground?

"Two more bodies have shown up in the past twenty-four hours," Eli said. "Both found along the Muskee Glacier Pass. Both young women, both half-buried, left hands exposed. Haven't been able to identify either one of them. Coroner thinks they've both been dead about a year."

"Dear Lord," Mitchell hissed quietly. Implications quickly piling atop each other.

"It's looking like we've got a serial killer, Eli spoke aloud the conclusion Mitchell was reaching on his own, already grabbing his keys.

To hell with an officer outside Whaler's door. Mitchell was heading straight back to the hospital. A serial killer on the loose with victims getting closer to Shelby?

Dove, a young, gorgeous and sexy woman?

What if there was an explanation far more sinister than Brad Fletcher for the break-in at Dove's studio? And the subsequent possible stalker outside her house? What if her woes, and Whaler's, weren't related at all?

Telling his brother to keep him posted and to let him know if there was anything he could do to help, Mitchell was already in his car, engine started as he hung up.

A serial killer on the loose, and Dove vulnerable and

unprotected? With no family to check in on her? Protocol be damned.

Mitchell wasn't letting the woman out of his sight.

WHALER HADN'T MOVED a muscle, other than to breathe. The fact that he was managing to do that on his own was cause for great thanks. Maybe even miracle level.

As were his vitals. Considering the way he'd abused his body over the past couple of years, sousing it in alcohol and failing to feed it healthy meals often enough, he was actually doing well. His blood pressure was a little high. His oxygen levels were good. Thank God he wasn't a smoker.

The biggest concern was the obvious trauma to his head. The fact that he hadn't shown a single sign of regaining consciousness was a huge concern. He was scheduled for more scanning later in the day or early the following morning. Until then, all anyone could tell Dove was that he was in a coma.

There was no prognosis.

Except to hope, every second, that it would be the one in which he woke up.

Hours of sitting in the chair by his bed, holding his hand, talking to him, while she hoped hard with every breath, was draining Dove of the very strength she needed to help keep her dad alive.

Slowly stealing her positive energy away in the process.

So when her friend and client Hetty Amos texted, saying that she was at the hospital for a checkup on the healing bullet wound she'd sustained in her leg and was available if Dove wanted to talk, Dove agreed to meet her at the coffee shop just down from the hospital.

The second she saw the twenty-eight-year-old pilot, she knew she'd made the right choice to be there. Hetty might still be figuring out how to tune in to her own inner voices, but as far as people went, she was as strong as they came. And, being a year older than Dove, she had been someone Dove had looked up to in high school.

When you lived in a small town your whole life, it always seemed to come down to that. Who was who, who they knew and who they hung with in high school. Hetty's light green eyes were troubled as she gazed into Dove's.

"There's lots of reason to hope," Dove blurted the first thing that came to her mind. And knew she was okay when the words sank in. She'd said what she'd needed to hear. It had just taken someone else needing to hear to get it firmly planted within and without her.

"I heard he's stable," Hetty said, without asking a single question about what had been going on in Dove's most recent past.

Hetty would have gotten the email that Dove had sent to all her clients that morning, letting them know that the studio would be closed for the next few days due to her father's disappearance. There'd been no reason to couch the news. People who knew would hear the truth from her—or the grapevine. She figured it had been better, less alarming, coming straight from her.

Still didn't say how the injured pilot had heard the most recent details.

"Spence told me," Hetty said before Dove had responded. And then the woman gave a somewhat sheepish grin. "Look at us," she said softly, as they sat sipping the coffee they'd ordered from the counter as they'd first come in. "Who'd have thought that I'd actually be dating Spence Colton, and you… I hear you're staying at Mitchell's place?"

She nodded. Met Hetty's gaze. And said, "It's mostly a business relationship," her truth ringing loud and clear.

"I mean, he's sexy and all, but we're so different. I'm sure the gossip is going to have us in a relationship, but I want you to hear it straight from me. Not happening." The words sounded so final, and not exactly accurate, so she added, "I think he might be a friend for life, though."

Warmth flooded her. As though a source higher than herself was confirming the accuracy of her proclamation. She sat back in possession of another huge reason to be thankful and listened while Hetty told her that her doctor had just said that her wound was almost completely healed and Hetty should be able to start back at Namaste as early as the following week.

Assuming classes were back in session.

As far as Dove knew, no one was aware of the vandalism that took place at Namaste other than two people from Repo, the police and her. It wasn't that she had any reason or desire to be duplicitous about the attack: she was just trying to protect her clients from any residual negative energy the mental picture would build to slow down their healing process if they knew the sacred space had been violated. She was about to tell Hetty, though, when Lakin Colton, Mitchell's adored adopted sister appeared, pushing in through the door and, seeing them, headed straight for their table.

While Dove had looked up to Hetty in high school, Lakin and Hetty had actually been close friends. How much of that was because they had crushes on each other's brothers, Dove didn't know. But she'd always wondered.

"I'm so sorry to hear about your father, Dove," Lakin said, her eyes wide with compassion. And warmth. "And I'm praying for him, too."

Kind of uncomfortable with the attention she'd been getting at the hospital…the reaching out to her as though she was a regular person, not just a flighty believer in things unseen... Dove nodded. "Thanks," she said. "He was found alive. The rest will come." She had to state intention.

No matter what others might think of her.

And the fact that she was staying with the woman's older brother? That might have put a bit of a defensive wall up inside Dove where Lakin was concerned. She didn't want to know what Mitchell's close-knit family would be saying to him about having the odd woman in town living with him. Didn't even want to think about them thinking it. Which was why she had to shield herself from Lakin.

Who'd turned to Hetty, anyway, letting Dove off the hook.

"Did you hear?" Lakin asked Hetty. "Troy's due back next week." And Dove had to smile as she heard the words. Troy was Hetty's brother, but Lakin as his girlfriend got the news.

Did that mean that as the one staying with Mitchell, she knew more about what was going on with him than his sister did? She could hope, couldn't she?

What other choice did she have? It wasn't like she'd be asking Lakin what Mitchell might have said about her.

At least she wanted to hope she wouldn't have been that weak, stooped that low, but was saved from finding out as Lakin, hearing the bell at the counter, glanced up and said, "That's my order, gotta go" as she left the table.

But as she collected her take-out drink holder, Lakin stopped back by the table, her glance specifically on Dove. "Seriously, you're in my thoughts. And I want you to know my brothers, my cousin Kansas, they'll get whoever did this. They won't stop until they do."

The promise broke through the defenses Dove had so quickly thrown up when Lakin had first appeared, and she was moved by the woman's sincerity. "Thank you," she said, almost tearing up. "That's just what I needed to hear."

Lakin had just confirmed, heart to heart, what Dove had known but apparently had needed to hear again.

She could lean on Mitchell, just as she'd thought she'd been meant to do. Not just with approval from her spirits but from his family as well.

But more importantly, she could trust him with her life.

She wasn't there. Approaching Whaler's room, seeing in through the opened door before he arrived, he could see part of the man's body in the bed, but no sign of Dove. The chair pulled up to the bed was empty. Blowing right past the officer standing a couple of feet to the right of the door, he burst into the room, his gaze taking in every inch of floorboard around the room, expecting to see her sitting, back up to the wall, eyes closed. He saw nothing but floor. And molding. No Dove.

Two strides took him back to the door, and a young officer he hadn't yet met. "Where's Dove?"

"She left twenty minutes ago, sir. Said she was going next door to meet a friend for coffee and would be back shortly."

"You let her go? You're supposed to be guarding her!" He swallowed as he heard the very clear reprimand in his raised tone. And then, lowering his voice and checking his attitude, he said, "Her life is in danger." A serial killer was on the loose and Dove could already be pegged as his next victim. All the victims were young, and Eli had just said that, so far, they all had long hair. Dove's long wavy amber waves were unforgettable…

The officer's face tensing, he said, "I'm sorry, sir. I didn't know. I just came on. I was told to guard the room. I thought that just meant the patient."

Turning, Mitchell sped off down the hall, hearing the concerned young man's addition, "She left her cell phone number with me in case anything changed with her father's condition…"

If there was more, he missed it. Whaler's was currently the only occupied room in the small unit. No one cared if a Colton on a mission stormed out.

However, he was saved making a further ass of himself when, just outside the unit door, he saw Dove, in that long billowy skirt and crop top, that long fiery hair, walking toward him.

Relief flooded through him washing away the haze of panic that had taken hold. Enough so that he was able to sound at least somewhat like his usual, practical self as he said, "Are you aware that there's a serial killer on the loose? And that his victims are about your age and all have long hair?"

He clenched his teeth shut the second he heard himself. Really heard himself. Looking around, he was immensely glad to see that there was no one else around to have heard the information that was not his to leak out. And took Dove's arm as he led her to a couple of armchairs set in an alcove. "I just talked to Eli," he said softly, slowly, but no less urgently. "This isn't information I should be spreading around town. The ABI will disseminate details as they feel is necessary to best protect the public, but the break-in at Namaste, someone watching your house, it could be him, Dove. Until we know more, I need you to promise me that you go nowhere alone. You've got police protection here at the hospital. And I'll escort you to and from. You've already got safe housing. Everything else we'll work out on a case by case basis."

The deflation, as he reached the end of his litany, almost left him weak. At the very least, strangely unsettled. Like he'd just given everything he had to prevent death and then…faced no immediate danger at all.

Dove was perfectly safe. She'd had coffee. And had returned to her vigil.

"You need to take a breath, Mitchell," the woman said to him, softly, calmly. More like his usual self than he was currently portraying. "Several of them," she added.

She was going to argue with him. He knew the wave was coming. And knew that there was no way he could vacillate on the issue. No matter how much inner truth she brought to the table.

But he would give her what he could. Breathing, his or hers, wasn't a deal-breaker, so he nodded, sat back and prepared to wait for however long it took her to determine he'd completed the task she'd given to him.

A minute passed. At least. Mitchell didn't much mind. Dove was safe. Where she wanted to be—within yards of getting to her father if need be.

Kirk had proven to be a legitimate asset during his first eight hours on the job.

Wes had reported an above-average day with no issues. Stuart, the same.

Pretty much covered Mitchell's responsibilities for a very long Monday. With the night's duties still ahead.

Duty. One duty that night.

Keeping Dove safe while his family members did their jobs. Okay, two duties. He also had to keep his piece in his pants. Which would be most easily accomplished by forgoing his usual sleeping mode—in the nude—for one that included the pants.

Mental note made.

Not sure how much longer they were going to sit there—and pondering best solutions for dinner given the current circumstances—Mitchell leaned his head back against the wall.

Taking a deep breath, he sighed. Settling in.

"Wow, that took a while." Dove's voice, sounding loud to him in the silence, interrupted his reverie.

Straightening, he glanced over at her. "What did?"

"You getting to the point of taking a breath."

Shaking his head, he frowned. Not in the mood for funny stuff. Even as he knew he had to keep her as agreeable as he could. "I've been taking breaths the whole time. One after another. It's what people do to stay alive."

"That's breathing," she told him, quite congenially, but there was no humor that he could see in her expression. "Taking a breath is more. It's pulling air in purposefully, more deeply, than normal breathing. It helps the body to relax."

Mitchell wanted to roll his eyes. To tell her he didn't need her magical cures. Except that…once again…her words contained a certain practical sense.

"Noted," he told her. But had to add, "If you'd explained that ten minutes ago, your mission would have been accomplished that much sooner." Just for future reference—in the event she put him through any more of her life lessons during the time of their acquaintance.

One he'd thought would be miraculously short. He was starting to accept that it could turn out to be much longer than he'd expected.

As in, a regular workload for the time it took to get St. James Boats back on its feet. Whether for Bob to run, or to sell. Either way, Mitchell's part came first.

He had another, much larger challenge facing him before

he moved from the chair. She might think she'd distracted him with her breathing antics. But, "I need your promise, Dove. You go nowhere alone, you continue to stay at my place, until this serial killer is found or the police find proof that Fletcher or someone else vandalized Namaste and was watching your place."

"I promise."

With a sharp turn of his head, he stared into the eyes facing straight at him. "I mean it," he said. "No funny business."

"You mean like saying that an angel was with me so I wasn't alone? Or flew in my window and carried me out into the night?" She looked so innocent as she spoke.

Mitchell wasn't sure if she was being facetious, or if she knew what the town thought of her. He feared the latter.

And hated that he'd made her feel that way.

"I meant no making a promise and then finding a way around keeping it."

She continued to watch him—study him was more like it. Giving him nothing from within herself. "I can't tell if you're saying you don't trust me to keep a promise or just think I'm naive enough to not realize that, under no circumstances, am I to waver from the dictates you laid down."

When she put it like that…

Mitchell took another deep breath. "I'm sorry," he said. "I trust you to keep your promise. And I absolutely do not think you're naive." He meant to leave it there. And started talking again anyway. "But I also know that you're independent, headstrong and smart enough to find a way to manipulate a situation if you feel a need to go outside the boundaries I've set."

She smiled then. An expression that started in her eyes seconds before it landed on her mouth. "You might be right in other, less severe circumstances," she told him and then her expression turning serious in an instant said, "I know that my best chance at making it through this in as successful a way as possible is with you, Mitchell. The things you've already done for me, calling in the best of the best to help when, without you, my father more likely would have died out there before anyone found him. The safe place to sleep you're providing…until this is over, you're the boss. That's just the way it is."

A deluge of sweet relief hit him, wiped away in the next second when she added, "In terms of the guidelines you set out above, and for the stated purposes."

The woman just wasn't going to stop challenging his thinking every step of the way. "Mind expanding on that?" he asked. Not willing to risk another embarrassment by hazarding his own guess.

"Just that," she told him. "Speaking literally here, Mitchell, keep up."

Not hating their repartee as much as he'd have liked, he met her gaze full on. "Go on," he told her. More out of curiosity than anything else.

"I still have autonomy over all of my choices that don't involve keeping me safe from the bad guys."

Here it came. The out he'd been expecting from the beginning. "Such as?"

"Such as a choice I could make to…accept physical activities while in your care." She didn't even blink as she said the words. Her gaze locked on his the entire time. "Were something to arise in that area, I do not want to hear anything about you taking advantage because I'm in your care or beside myself with fear or worry or grief. Nor will I accept that my concurrence with your stipulations put us in a situation that opens the door to concerns about sex in the workplace, or any other possible moral or legal consequence you could see possibly arising in the future as a result of the…activity…while I am under this safety agreement with you."

No smile cracking on that one. Not even a hint.

She was dead serious.

And the only response Mitchell could conjure up was…

A very slow nod.

WHALER HADN'T GIVEN even a hint of waking by nine that evening when the small ward went into lockdown for the night. Two nurses, an orderly and a police officer were all there just to watch over her father, and Dove had to be content with that.

A trauma doctor was on duty in the urgent care portion of the facility and would be checking in on their one inpatient. He assured Dove, just before she left with Mitchell, that he expected her father to rest peacefully through the night.

And that they'd call the second there was any change in his condition or hint of him waking up.

Knowing that she would be no good to her dad if she didn't get some rest—most particularly after her mostly sleepless hours the night before—she gave him kisses on both cheeks. Told him she loved him. That she'd see him in the morning.

And then, with tears in her eyes, walked beside Mitchell out to his car.

"His vitals are good," he said more as a reminder to her, she figured, than anything else.

"I know."

"Tonight is better than last night. We know he's alive. We know where he is. We know that he's safe."

She nodded. Taking in every practical, logical word.

Just as she'd forced herself to eat and swallow most of the salad he'd ordered in and had delivered from The Cove for dinner.

He wasn't her mother. Or a guide. But he was doing a pretty impressive job of reminding her how to keep her head out of the sewer of fear trying to suck the life out of her.

But she was tired.

Had never felt so alone.

And needed to know, "Why are you doing this?"

"Walking you to my car? You know why."

While, in a better state, she might have teased him about focusing so much on the literal, or in a worse one thought he was playing with her, Dove didn't have the energy to engage in light conversation.

"I mean giving up your own schedule, your regularly scheduled life, to babysit me."

They'd reached his car, and when she would have left his side to go to her door, while he opened his he grabbed her elbow lightly, shook his head, and said, "You get in with me."

Without missing a beat, she did so, sliding over on the seat to allow him access behind the wheel, buckled herself in and prepared to sit through the ten-minute drive to his place in silence.

She'd asked a question that wasn't factually based. He wasn't going to answer. And she didn't have the energy to fight him on it.

It wasn't like his reasoning mattered all that much. He'd insisted on his role. She'd agreed to it. Case closed, Counselor.

Keeping her secure between his body and the car door, he'd checked the back seat before nudging her to get in. And gave the same kind of intent concentration on watching all around them as he pulled out of the parking lot and headed down toward Main Street. From there, a short jog west would take them out to his place.

Clint's bar had the door open, with people milling inside. Dove saw Oscar, sitting on his usual stool, and wondered if he'd heard about Whaler yet. Mitchell had told her that the police were keeping things quiet, that the employees at St. James Boats had all been asked not to say anything until the police knew more.

Still, she almost asked Mitchell to stop long enough for her to have a word with her father's young friend. Until she realized that maybe her need to connect with Oscar was more for her sake than his and reconsidered. Oscar had enough problems of his own.

And better that there were answers—and that Whaler was conscious with a good prognosis—before Oscar found out what had happened to him.

No way did she want to be responsible for driving the man to further drink.

Mitchell made the turn toward his place, keeping his eye on the rearview mirror as much as the windshield, and then seemed to relax.

She actually saw him settle back in the seat, his shoulders visibly relaxing.

And she knew. "You were afraid we were going to be followed."

She should have figured that one out for herself.

"*Afraid*, no," he said. "*Aware of the possibility*, absolutely."

Which made her think of something else. "Let me guess, you have a pistol in the glove box." They lived in rugged territory. There were a lot of nonhuman predators that could appear at any moment, making a gun the only difference between life and death.

Her mother had refused to learn to shoot.

As had Dove. She could be struck by lightning or drown in the sea. If nature was going to take her, it would find a way to do so.

"I do," he told her. "And one in the house, too. You get your pick of which one you want to take to bed with you."

She shook her head. "Neither."

"One or the other, Dove..." His tone had grown all boss-like.

"Neither, Mitchell." Suddenly filled with a surge of energy, she sat up straighter. "You're crossing into my autonomy here..." She started in with the fight. And then, just as quickly depleted, told him, "I'm safer without a gun. I've never held one in my life, nor have I ever so much as pulled the trigger on a plastic squirt gun."

When he said nothing, she added, "Or on the handle of an arcade game."

No shooting. None. Period. Her spirit spoke silently inside her, and Dove welcomed the communication. Wanting to hold it within her.

Needing to be hugged.

"You think I'm weird," she said, for no good reason, which meant she should have held her tongue.

"I'm thinking I'd feel a hell of a lot better if you knew how to shoot a gun."

She believed him. The response was so Mitchell. Practical. Logical.

The thought left enough of a positive tail that she asked again what she really wanted to know. "Why have you put your own life on hold to watch over me?"

She didn't really expect an answer. But she deserved the

chance to pose the question. To try to find understanding about something that pertained to her directly.

She knew full well why she was trusting him.

But...what was in it for him?

Sex?

She'd already intimated that he could probably get that just by asking.

It certainly wasn't the money. There wasn't going to be much anytime soon.

"You remind me of someone." His words fell softly into the darkness. Startling her. And ringing with a truth, a depth, she hadn't expected.

"An ex-girlfriend?" He'd never been married that she knew of.

"No," he told her, then, as though making up his mind that telling her was better than not, he sighed and said, "My aunt."

"Spence's mom?" She didn't get the likeness. Not even a little bit.

He shook his head. "My dad's and uncle's younger sister."

The words carried a wealth of grief. It came to her slowly. Heavily. And stifled any question she might have asked. He pulled into his garage. Turned off the engine. Pushed the button for the door to shut behind them and sat there with both hands on the wheel.

"Eli met her. Parker, too, though he probably doesn't remember. I never did. She was killed before I was born."

Her sharp intake of breath had been completely involuntary. She stared through the garage's dim light, wishing for the glorious sunset that had just been beginning to appear outside to infiltrate their midst.

If he opened his car door, she'd follow him inside and

never speak of the topic again. But she'd remember, for the rest of her days, the grief she'd felt emanating from him.

A man who'd always seemed so...emotionally sedentary.

"She was seventeen. My grandparents were upstairs in bed. She was found on the couch with her stalker..."

Suffused with a sudden urge to cover her ears, Dove physically forced herself to remain open by sliding her hands beneath her thighs. Sitting on them.

"Eli was around five at the time. He and our dad came in and found them there, both dead. The killer had never actually met her in person prior to that night, but thought of himself as her boyfriend. He killed her and then himself."

"What about your grandparents?"

"They were murdered, too. Probably before Caroline was."

With tears running down her cheeks, Dove looked over at him through their blur and asked, "Her name was Caroline?"

He nodded.

"My mother's was, too."

He nodded again. "I know."

And she knew, too, right then and there, without a doubt, that she and Mitchell had been meant to connect, for however long either of them needed, and that no matter what happened between them, they'd remain deep, abiding friends for their earthly lifespan—and beyond.

For whatever reason, this uptight man who was nothing at all like her, was a soul mate.

Which meant, to her, he was sacred.

And when the day came that her father got old and passed, she wouldn't be alone on earth.

Chapter Fifteen

What in the hell was this woman doing to him?

Had he pissed off her angels somehow? Failed to see someone in need, to meet their need, and this was their way of getting even with him?

He'd heard Lakin talk about karma once. Some force of nature that supposedly acted as some kind of supernatural adding machine—keeping track of the good and bad you'd done, and dumping your fullest account on you. If you did good, you got good. If not, then watch out.

Not even wanting to get his temporary housemate started on that one, he kept the fact that he knew the term to himself as he led them both into the house.

But was starting to sweat a little as he was running through a tally of his good deeds and bad as he followed her down the hall to the kitchen.

He hadn't made it past the time, in third grade, when he'd accidentally knocked a kid's tooth out with a wildly thrown pitch and then laughed.

He hadn't known yet that the kid was hurt. Hadn't thought he'd thrown it that hard.

Third grade and he was already seeing how his account was going to look.

Dove had emptied the bag from lunch that she'd brought in with her and was rinsing the dirty bowls and silverware.

"I'll get that," he told her. Expecting an argument. Not sure he'd fight her on it, though he deeply needed his space to himself for the few minutes he was going to get that night.

Which was really why he was sweating.

It was going to be a *long* six or eight hours.

"You go do whatever it is you do to get ready for bed, dress in whatever you have that is the most comfortable and nonrevealing, and we can head upstairs."

Spinning so quickly she splashed water all over the floor, Mitchell had the inane thought that maybe the action was going to be a sin she'd need to pay for, too. "Upstairs?" she asked. And before he could explain added, "This is your way of saying you want to have sex?"

"Hell no!" He spoke with such force he almost spit. "You don't know how to shoot. I do. There's a serial killer on the loose. I'm charged with protecting you. You do the math."

He had math on the brain. Karma addition.

Reasoning calculations.

"You want us to sleep in the same room."

At least he knew she was good at adding things up. "Yes."

She turned back to the dishes. Making quick work of them. Not arguing.

He was reassessing his karma situation—only slightly, but the lack of argument was a good thing—when she said, "You have condoms up there, just in case?"

He wanted to tell her no. To put her on the spot and ask her if she'd brought any. Somehow getting to a place where, if she hadn't brought any, there couldn't be any activity that would require a need of them. But couldn't lie to her. "Yes."

She nodded.

He started to get hard. And blurted, "But I'm tired, Dove. And so are you. We have no idea what tomorrow is going to bring, or even if we'll be woken up with an emergency in the night…"

Turning off the water, she turned around, wiping her hands on the kitchen towel she'd pulled from the oven door. "I know," she told him. Then looked him in the eye and said, "But I got your mind on something besides death and grief there for a second."

It wasn't a question.

Didn't require an answer.

And he didn't give her one.

Instead, he stood there with a brand-new awareness of what sex could do…

If someone was in need of relief from the demons that seemed to be hunting them.

Or her.

DOVE DIDN'T LOOK at the room. Much. Enough to get her bearings. To know what would be causing any shadows lurking when darkness fell completely. There were no curtains on the two big windows overlooking—from what she could see—a whole lot of nature and nothing else.

With the quilt from her bed downstairs hanging over her shoulder, and a bottle of lavender clutched in her palm—just in case she needed a quick inhale that wouldn't suffuse the other occupant in the room with the scent—she was ready for bed.

Mitchell had already been up to thoroughly check the second floor. He'd said he'd be a few minutes, giving her time to get settled. He'd had something to do in his office. More like he was avoiding them going to bed together.

He could try to prevent any further closeness from happening between them. She knew they were already as close as any two humans could ever get.

Physical stuff was momentary. Or, in some cases, lifelong, but in one life only. Soul couplings were forever. In the pajamas she'd had on that morning, she quickly arranged her quilt on top of the spread on the left side of Mitchell's king-size bed. Left was farthest from the door, and the nightstand on the right had his phone charger on it. Pulling her own phone out of her pocket, she grabbed the charging cord from the elastic waistband of her pants, plugged it in, connected the device and was…done. Ready for bed.

Except that she wasn't. At all.

She needed to be. She'd only had those few hours of sleep the night before. Fear had much greater opportunity to invade her system when she was tired. And she'd be up at dawn. It was just a thing. Dawn came, she woke up. Nature telling her good morning. A gift she welcomed.

The reminder got her butt to the bed, under the covers. She'd left on the light in Mitchell's adjoining bathroom, having completed her own ablutions downstairs. Turning to face the wall across from her side of the bed, she closed her eyes. And when her mind reacted to the darkness with a vision of her father's lifeless body lying helplessly in a hospital bed, she immediately opened them again.

To reset. Focus. The threes. Three things for which to be grateful. Three things about which she'd been critical replaced by three positive thoughts. Three people other than herself.

Starting with the last, because thinking about others was the best way to stop magnifying her own circumstances and to build her heart cells. Hetty. First, she and Spence had finally been able to see what had been obvious for a long time. They belonged together. Second, her bullet wound was almost completely healed with no permanent damage. She'd be returning to yoga classes soon, but…stop…that was about Dove, too, so probably shouldn't…stop. No criticism of any kind allowed in the sacred moments. Wasn't that criticism? To criticize the thought she'd just had?

And why was self-affirmation wrong? It wasn't. Maybe there should be more than three? Should there be a fourth? Self-affirmation?

Maybe. But not when thinking of others. Stick to the plan. It's there for a reason. It's healthy. Scientifically proven. Not that science had to matter in the larger, non-earthly scheme of things. But they mattered to Mitchell.

Mitchell. He was another. No. Wait. She hadn't done Hetty's third yet. Third. Troy was coming home! That was good for Hetty and Lakin. Double dose of good.

Lakin. Mitchell's sister. His bed. He would be coming up soon. Getting into bed with her. Maybe she shouldn't be thinking about Mitchell.

Back to the threes. Stick to the threes. And no Mitchell. For the moment, anyway. If she said *no Mitchell*, that fostered negativity. And she most definitely did not want… Okay, Mitchell. Three things. He'd been sent to her for her good, but for his own, too. She hadn't quite worked it all out. But she knew. Caroline. Her heart flooded with all-consuming emotion again, just remembering Mitchell saying the word. Second, he'd been able to help his friend's son, Kirk. Which helped his friend, too, which could be a third, but no, she'd lump those two together. Third, he had condoms.

Quick, who else? Her dad. He'd been found alive. Second, with the new initiatives being discussed, his business was going to rebound. Third…

He just missed her mother so much. It was like she was

calling him to her every single day. Or like he thought she was. Love was meant to uplift. To strengthen. Not be a downfall.

Maybe not her father. Okay, who else?

Footsteps on the stairs. No matter how she tried to get herself into an unconscious state, Dove was fully present as she listened to the creaks on the stairs, telling her that Mitchell was entering her space.

His space, too. First. Most. Condoms there.

"Dove?"

His almost-professional tone of voice yanked her back to full reality. Whatever he had to say, she had to hear. Turning onto her back, she looked at him standing in the doorway to his room. Still in jeans and the flannel shirt he'd had on all day.

"Kansas just called," he told her. And the breath she hadn't known she'd been holding released. She let it go. Pulled in a long breath of fresh air. Kansas. Not the hospital.

Sitting up, she prompted, "And?"

"Scott Montgomery was able to pull some evidence off from Whaler's shirt. Saliva."

Heart pounding, she sat up. "Someone bit him?"

Mitchell shook his head, opened his mouth, but before he could say anything else she threw out, "What, kissed him? Someone thought he was dead and kissed him goodbye?"

Who would that possibly have been?

She hadn't yet conjured a single possibility when Mitchell said, "It's spit."

A wave of horror swept through her. "Someone spit on him?" Eyes wide she stared at Mitchell, needing to hold onto him.

He nodded. And before their eye contact could get broken, she asked, "Who?"

Stepping farther into the room, closer to the bed, to her, his words fell over her softly. "They don't know yet. There were no matches in the system. But they have something to test against as soon as a suspect is brought in."

"Brad Fletcher. There's got to be a way to get a DNA sample from him."

"Legally," Mitchell said, just standing there. He'd come close. Then abruptly stopped. As though he'd read a sign that said *no closer.* "It has to be obtained legally or it doesn't stand up in court and he walks free."

Nodding, Dove lay back down. Pulled the quilt up over her tie-dyed T-shirt, the sliver of skin it left atop the elastic waistband of her pajama pants. "Scott Montgomery," she said. He could be her third. Except…he'd found evidence, but she was drawing a complete blank on two other good things…

Because Mitchell wasn't exiting the premises. He was ruffling through a drawer in the dresser farthest away from her. As though looking for something he hadn't seen in a while.

When she saw the black pajama pants he eventually came up with, she turned back to face the wall. Mitchell. He could be her third. Because even in the midst of hell, he could make her smile.

Which made it about her. But about him, too.

He really was a genuinely nice guy.

With a beautiful soul inside that gorgeously masculine body.

DOVE APPEARED TO be asleep when Mitchell came out of the bathroom, freshly showered, and in the brand-new pajama pants and shirt his aunt had purchased for him a decade or so before. Lucky for him, they'd been big at the time, so they fit now.

Whether his bedmate was truly out or not, he was going with a big *yes*. Had no intention of doing anything to find out differently.

Her safety was his business. Her sleeping state, or lack thereof, was not.

Checking to make certain his gun was loaded, safety off, he plugged in his phone, walked back to turn off the bathroom light, pulled down his covers, got into bed and smelled...lavender.

Holy hell. Had she brought the stuff to bed with her? Drifted petals on the sheets? He was too far in to look. Would have to sit up, pull the covers away...

Closing his eyes Mitchell did the only thing he could do—he shut down.

Turned off life's challenges, trials and temptations until morning, and with a last thought about the gun lodged between the bed rail and the mattress, drifted into sleep mode...until he wasn't asleep.

Fully alert suddenly, he lay there, assessing his situation. How long had he been out? Had he heard something? Or was he just so on edge he hadn't fallen fully asleep as he did every single night the minute his head hit the pillow?

Dove hadn't moved. He wasn't looking at her—purposely—but could see the shadow of her quilt-covered shoulder in his peripheral vision. Just as it had been when he'd closed his eyes. Just to be sure, though, he turned his head.

And noticed three things. She was lying on top of his bedspread, the quilt her only source of warmth. She was shivering. And based on the time glowing at him from the phone she'd set up on the nightstand over there, he'd been out for almost five hours.

Her shivering must have awoken him.

Figuring the best, easiest and least obtrusive way to ease her discomfort from the night's chill was to just pull up the spread from his side of the bed and lay it over her, he did so. Slowly. Gently. Careful not to actually touch any part of her with any part of him.

And leaving himself with only a sheet for a cover.

On his back, he checked on the gun, closed his eyes, figuring he could get another three or four hours in and, instead, lay there in the darkness, trying to convince himself that Dove was sound asleep. He'd seen the slight jerk when he'd dropped the last corner of the spread to her shoulder.

And suddenly couldn't clear his mind of images of her. That morning in his kitchen. In those thin pants and ridiculous, half shirt thing. What was it with the woman and leaving a strip of her belly bare? Didn't she get that she lived in Alaska? One of the coldest states in the nation?

Flash-forward. The stark fear in her eyes when she'd first walked into the hospital, seconds away from seeing her father.

The saucy grin she got on her face when she was messing with him.

He heard a sniffle. Tried to pretend that he hadn't. For all she knew he'd fallen back to sleep. Normally he would have done. Should have done. Wished he had.

And might have actually done, if she didn't start to move, turning slowly to a flat position and then scooting toward her edge of the mattress.

Keeping his eyes closed until she was off the mattress, he glanced to see her back as she tiptoed across his carpet. Ready to snap his eyes shut if she started to turn back. Instead, he watched her head not to the adjoining bathroom, as he'd expected but to the bedroom door.

Without moving anything but his mouth he said, "Sorry, that's a breach of protocol."

In the moonlit shadows he could make out her shape. Her nod. He couldn't read her expression as she glanced toward the bed. "I didn't want to bother you with my tears. I'll be right back. Just let me—"

"I'm bothering you by requiring you to remain in my presence. You have a right to bother me back. Please get in the bed. If you go, I have to get up and follow you."

She could ask under whose orders he was working. But what would be the point? They both knew the score. She was free to go at any time.

But she needed his help, and his connections too, probably. And he needed to keep her safe.

Deal or no deal. Up to her.

Spinning on her heel, she faced the bathroom. Then said, "You want to check in there first, to make sure no one's lurking?" He wanted to hear snarkiness in her tone but didn't. He heard compliance.

"No," he told her. He could see the security camera blinking over his bedroom door. And would have had a phone alert if the room had been breached. Same for the alarms on both windows. They were lit, signaling working order.

But he lay alert, staring at the ceiling until he heard the bathroom door open. And then, eyes closed, waited for the dip in the mattress to signal that she was back in bed. Relaxing, he told himself he'd be back to sleep in no time.

"Thank you, Mitchell." The nearly whispered words drifted over him.

"You okay?" he asked then, instead of issuing the *you're welcome* that would have been more his style.

"Yeah. Crying is healthy, you know. Helps release the toxins that build up with stress and grief. You might try it sometime."

He'd take her word for that one. But didn't bother to share the news. "Get some rest," he said instead and, closing his eyes, ordered himself back to sleep.

Chapter Sixteen

Tuesday passed with no new fears hitting Dove in the face. Her father was still showing little sign of waking up, but his vitals were okay. He seemed to be resting peacefully. And most incredible to her was that his brain scans, while showing some swelling beneath the gash to his skull, showed no sign of malfunction or permanent damage.

Mitchell asked about the scans the second he returned to the hospital room where he'd left her under the care of the changing guard outside the door, with a promise from her to order in, not go out.

In the suit and tie he'd donned that morning for a half day in the office, he pulled a chair in from the hallway to sit beside her.

"The doctor said he'll wake up when he's ready," she relayed the prognosis last. Leaving off the last line the woman had issued with clear warning. *Or he won't.*

Leaning forward, his elbows on his knees, Mitchell's gaze was pointed at Whaler. As though he could get answers from the older man. Or somehow telepathically send her father the assurance that he'd be there to help when he woke up.

She was being fanciful on that last bit, she knew but allowed herself the luxury. Hours alone in a mostly deserted facility made it a challenge to keep the demons at bay. Thoughts of Mitchell had helped.

"She said that his continued unconscious state could be a result of the swelling on his brain. Or it could be psychological." That was the part that was getting to her the most. The idea that Bob St. James would actually make the choice to die and join his wife than stay around to be a part of their daughter's life.

She had to be okay with it. To honor whatever choice he made without resentment. She just wasn't ready to let go. Didn't feel as though it was time to do so.

And so she stayed, holding on. To her fortitude, and to him, much of the time, too. Interlocking her fingers through his. Brushing hair back from his forehead. Washing his face. Rubbing his arm. Talking to him of the life they had waiting. The plans for St. James Boats, his lifeblood.

Kirk, the new hire.

But she had no way of knowing if any of it was getting through. Maybe she was just helping herself, maintain her vigil as she was, but if so, then so be it. As long as there was a chance that her father would fully rejoin the living, she had to be ready to be everything he needed as he got back on his feet.

To make life so good he wouldn't reach for the bottle again.

Her job, while Bob finished detoxing and rested, was to keep herself positive. Finding the good. Feeling it all the way to her soul.

So when the time was right, she could share it with him. Like an IV straight from her heart to his.

To that end, she asked Mitchell, "How are things going at the docks?" More to allow her father to listen to the conversation if he cared to than because she had any concerns. Mitchell had said when he'd dropped her off that morning that he'd be checking in with Wes and the others throughout the day.

"A couple of newlyweds, first time to Alaska, stiffed Kirk out of nearly fifty dollars in fuel charges," he said.

And she shook her head. Not the type of conversation she'd been seeking.

Mitchell didn't seem to get the message as he continued with, "Wes rented the boat to them, and they'd said they'd pay for the fuel they used on their return, and when Kirk checked them back in, he told them they were good to go. They didn't tell him that they owed money. He said he'd pay for it himself."

Did her father's finger just twitch?

Dove had been staring for any signs of coming back to life all day. Looking for any movement at all that couldn't just be a process of breathing.

Just in case Whaler had an opinion about the incident involving his newest employee—a young man she'd told him all about, including that his father was out to sea most of the time—she quickly, and more loudly than necessary, said, "Please let him know that won't be necessary. It's our fault for not having a line item on the rental agreement for fuel, just as you already pointed out," she said, watching that finger the whole time. "I'm sure Wes had expected to check the boat back in, and he'd have known about the fuel."

There was no movement. No matter how hard she stared. She glanced over at Mitchell, to see if maybe he'd noticed something she had not.

He was looking at her as though he half suspected she'd spent the afternoon with a bottle herself.

"The doctor said he can most likely hear our conversation. I…thought I saw a finger move when you mentioned Kirk paying for his mistake."

Warmth flashed in the blue eyes gazing back at her. She wanted to believe it was born of admiration. Or comradery, at least.

But feared it had been nothing but a surge of pity.

She didn't need his pity.

She just needed him to believe, as she did, that Whaler was going to wake up.

Or…she just needed him.

MITCHELL DIDN'T STAY long at the hospital. He'd stopped in on his way to the docks. He'd promised Dove he'd keep an eye on things for her, and he intended to do so. Everyone had already left for the day. Their last rental had come in just past two. But he wanted to go over the day's receipts. To take a look at the boats needed for the morning's reservations. And get a start on some of the paperwork he'd said he'd help Dove overhaul. Beginning with the rental agreement.

She opted to remain with her father. And while he didn't think the choice a healthy one—her sitting there all alone, for so many hours, watching a man either sleep or slowly die, he respected that she had to be where she felt the most needed. She clearly felt as though she could have the greatest impact by Whaler's side.

He just didn't like the idea of her being in the room all alone when Whaler took his last breath. *If* he took his last breath, he amended.

In Whaler's office, changing from his suit to the clean jeans and flannel shirt he'd thrown in the car that morning, he kept picturing Dove, sitting there in her spaghetti-strap tie-dyed caftan thing. Draped in darker colors, browns, reds, burgundies with patches of gold, he wondered what her choice of the day's attire stood for.

And, realizing what he was doing, justified the thought by the fact that he knew she chose her clothes for purposes other than looks. Maybe the day's dress had been something her mother made. Or had even been her mother's.

Maybe it was just comfortable.

Maybe if he was a better friend, he'd have stayed at the hospital with her. Or asked why she chose the dress and flip-flops she'd come out to the kitchen wearing not long after dawn that morning.

Her long hair flowing like gentle flames all over her.

His cousin Kansas had hair as long as Dove's. But she kept it tied back most of the time. Dove didn't restrict her locks.

Mitchell liked that about her.

Giving himself a serious shake, he headed out to the docks with purposeful strides, getting himself back to the mindset he'd slipped into the second he walked into his office that morning. His natural self.

Not the mucked-up version that time spent in Dove St. James's company seemed to be bringing out in him.

He'd taken half a dozen steps before he started to run. *What the hell...*

Ladybird wasn't in her usual slip. Jumping into Bob's runabout, he grabbed the keys from the slot in the bottom of the seat where Dove had told him her father kept them and was on the water within a minute. And had Wes and then Kirk on the phone—together, a conference call if ever there was one—seconds later. Both men swore the boat was moored as usual before they left the dock.

While *Ladybird* wasn't their most expensive boat, she

was one of their highest earners with tourists because of how easy she was to take out—even on the sea. And because of the larger number of passengers she could carry.

"I check every single boat myself," Wes said. "Have been doing so since Oscar left. Whaler don't need any more problems."

"I, uh…" Kirk started and then stopped. And Mitchell's heart sank, even as his gaze remained focused intently on every inch of shoreline he was slowly cruising.

"You what?" he asked his buddy's son, knowing without doubt that if he'd made a mistake in recommending Kirk, he'd do what he had to do to make things right.

"I checked them after Wes did," he said. "My dad taught me to use a double bowline, and… I did." The young man paused and then said, "No offense to you, Wes, I just—"

"No offense taken, kid," Wes cut in. "Double bowline it'll be from now on."

Which was fine, except it didn't help him where *Ladybird* was concerned.

"I'm on my way," Wes continued. "About five minutes out."

"I'm seven," Kirk piped in.

The three of them talked about shoreline coordinates and divvying up areas, but Mitchell cut the conversation short. "I've got her," he said. "She's bobbing in the water twenty-five yards out from Bone's Cove."

An inlet that local fishermen had unofficially named.

Both men met him there, in one boat, with Wes jumping aboard *Ladybird* to drive her back to shore.

All three checked her over. Found nothing damaged.

Except the mooring rope.

It was missing altogether.

"IT'S MY MOTHER'S BOAT. And one of our highest, most consistent earners." Dove paced Mitchell's kitchen floor, needing to expend the negative energy that had been building within her all day.

He'd waited until they'd arrived back at his place to tell her about the mishap at the marina. Whether he'd purposely made the choice because he'd known that the tension the news would have brought in Whaler's presence could mean the difference between her father choosing to come back to them or not, she didn't know.

Didn't really care. He'd been led, whether he got it or not.

Believing that gave her the strength she needed to keep looking forward. When all she wanted to do was crawl in a hole, cover her head and wait for the storm to pass.

She wasn't alone. She had her spirits, angels around her and souls up in heaven guiding her. And on earth, she'd been led to a man she'd never in a million years have sought out herself. Just as she knew, without a doubt, he'd never have initiated contact with her.

Her job was to trust. To keep her mind and heart focused and healthy. And to live by the inner promptings that, as long as she was in a good place, would never lead her wrong.

Engulfed in a myriad of emotions that swirled around her in a pool of anxiety, she had no promptings. Just the solid floor beneath her feet. And awareness of the man who leaned against the counter, silently watching her march to no drumbeat at all.

She glanced at him as she passed by. "If you hadn't stopped by after business hours..."

Whaler was the only one who ever did that, and whoever was out to get them would know that her dad was out of commission. They would have lost one of the boats upon which all of their future hopes were based.

"But I did stop by." Mitchell's words were truth. His tone so completely practical that it jolted through the storm raging inside her.

He did stop by. Disaster had been averted.

Halting midstride, she spun to face him. Staring. As her mind slowed and she regained a semblance of her sense of self. Mitchell had said something the night before about having a security system installed at St. James Boats. "Did the security cameras catch anything?" she asked, the question that should have come from her several minutes before. The second he'd told her about the vandalism. No way two ropes, two sailor's knots, tied by an experienced boatman, just unraveled and disappeared on their own.

Missing ropes, no evidence. Except for...

Mitchell was shaking his head. "The camera was angled to cover the entire fleet on that side of the marina. It catches *Ladybird*, all but a couple of feet, including the mooring."

"What about people? Surely whoever did this was seen coming or going."

"Peter Welding has the recordings. They're going over them now. Wes, Kirk and I have already watched them and didn't see anything, or anyone, who looked suspicious. Everyone on tape had cause to be there. And no one is seen after Wes and Kirk left for the day, until I arrived."

"He had to have swum up to the dock!" The answer was obvious to Dove. Maybe because... "I did that once, to trick my dad. There's a cement base under it that forms a platform with a place to stand. Something there from before Shelby was a real town. Anyway, I stood on it, hiding, until he got on his boat. That was back when only his personal boat was tied up there. Before St. James Boats." She stopped, a smile forming but fading before she remembered the rest. "I was banned from reading books for a week." The memory of Whaler's very real anger engulfed her. The danger she'd put herself in, swimming in those waters alone, with no one aware she'd even gone in...

"Banned you from reading for a week?" Mitchell's tone drew her gaze up to his confused looking frown.

"It was the worst punishment they could give me," she said, shrugging. "From prekindergarten, I was always drawn to books. Spent most days after school reading. That was the loneliest, longest week of my life."

Nodding, eyes wide with something...positive, Mitchell asked, "Did it happen often, this punishment?"

Oddly distracted by his interest in a younger her, Dove said, "Just that once." Pursing her lips she nodded. Then seeing his smile, felt a lightening in her heart and said, "I was a quick learner."

"A smart girl who grew into an intelligent woman."

Dove stared at the man who'd just uttered words that changed her world in the space of the second it took him to say them. A minimal change, perhaps, but there.

"Most people just think I'm a kook," she said, knowing that he'd been one of them. And maybe still was.

"I'm guessing you don't give many people the chance to really know you."

Feeling as though she'd always been open to others, she couldn't answer to that. But found his take on the situation curious.

And not nearly as important as, "You want to call Peter Welding, or should I? Someone needs to be checking shoreline, looking for any sign of entry...and do a thorough search of the water around that platform."

The sun had already set. "Best wait until morning," she

revised her thought. Glad to have had it though. To be back in a right mode.

Finding herself.

And saw Mitchell pull out his phone. "It won't hurt to give him a heads-up so he can have someone out there at sunrise."

Before the small St. James Boats marina was open for business.

The dawn of a new day. Shining light on what she'd taken as bad news: *Ladybird* having been left to float until she crashed. When, instead, she should have focused her thoughts on the positive that could come from the way the situation had turned out.

One of her father's biggest assets had been saved—with absolutely no harm done to it—and the police had a chance to find evidence to bring in the man who was hell-bent on ruining the St. Jameses' lives.

A new day, filled with possibility, would be arriving in hours. There was every chance her father would wake up. Their stalker would be caught. And with the start of Whaler's drying out already happening and the new outlook for St. James Boats, she and her father could finally start to live again, to find true happiness—carrying her mother's memory with them into a new future.

Feeling a full-out smile inside her for the first time in many, many hours, Dove looked over at Mitchell. "You ready for bed?" she asked.

When what she'd wanted to do was tell him he was good for her. His practical way of viewing the world, while not her way at all, had a place and a time. And the ability, apparently, to pull her out of negative energy, too.

Something to ponder.

In the new future.

Once they got through the present trials and had returned to their individual and very separate lives.

With differences. They'd say hello when they saw each other out and about. Maybe exchange a *How are you doing?* now and then. And if either one of them was ever in serious need—the other would be there.

He might not get that part.

But she did.

And was content to hold that truth sacred for both of them.

Chapter Seventeen

As he had the night before, Mitchell gave Dove time to get settled in upstairs before taking himself to bed. He'd talked to Peter Welding. But something wasn't sitting right with him. How would Brad Fletcher have known about that underwater platform at the front edge of the dock?

He'd had Dove draw him a rough likeness of the docks, to take a picture of and send to Welding, and he and the local police officer could both see exactly what she meant by someone being able to get to the ropes that moored *Ladybird* from in the water.

Overnight, the sea's constant movement would have taken her from there. She could have crashed into the other boats. Floated for miles. Hit a glacier. Or another boat, potentially taking lives. More likely, she'd have crashed into any of the jutting pieces of land that were an integral part of the landscape in their portion of the world.

What if it wasn't Brad Fletcher they were after?

Could it be Wes? Even as he had the thought, Mitchell shook it away. He'd known the man most of his life. Not closely but he was good people. Happily married, came from a good family, was raising one of his own.

And he was watching his livelihood sink into the sea because of Whaler's inability to get control of his grief and quit drinking.

Hating the heartache such news would bring to Dove— and the potential harm that would come to St. James Boats if they were down their only experienced employee—he decided to keep his suspicions to himself until he knew more. He could be way off base. And didn't want to hurt Wes's reputation, either, simply due to a logical supposition. But he'd keep a closer watch on the docks, until he knew more.

Decision in place, he made quick work of his nightly routine, set his phone where he could see it, checked the gun he'd carried with him that day and lodged it between bed frame and mattress. Dove had covered herself with the same quilt she'd used before. Her choice to not get under the covers had been a wise one, but she needed her sleep. Needed to be comfortable. About to get another blanket to lay over her, he stopped.

She was a grown woman with the right to make her own choices. For all he knew, she'd put on warmer clothes—a wise decision all the way around.

Either way, not his business.

And if she was asleep, he most definitely did not want to risk waking her.

Careful to make as little movement as possible, he slid under the covers and lowered himself to the mattress.

As he had the night before, he closed his eyes, turned off the day and willed himself to a good night's sleep.

Except that there was a woman lying a foot or so away from him, not quite hugging her side of the bed…and he smelled lavender again. A woman who'd suffered enough.

Who had to have some good coming her way. If there was any truth at all to the karma she believed in.

And… Wes had dropped everything to come help secure *Ladybird*. Would a man who'd meant to harm her do that?

He'd come after Mitchell had already found her.

A man trying to avoid suspicion would do that. He'd been around his brother enough to know that perps often insinuated themselves into crime scenes. And investigations, too.

Had he told Wes anything about their suspicions regarding Brad Fletcher? He didn't think so. But couldn't speak for Dove. She'd known the man much more closely than Mitchell had—over a good period of years. It was feasible that she'd said something.

Welding already believed that Fletcher had been instrumental—had instigated, even—Hal Billows's surprise departure that week. It stood to good reason that the businessman had approached Wes as well…

"What's the matter?" Dove's voice, floating softly to him, carried caution. And hit him like a fist to the gut. He was sleeping alone—not with someone.

They were two individuals in the same bed.

They weren't together.

"Nothing," he told her. His train of thought made sense in the dark of the night after a difficult day. He wasn't going to be an alarmist, and possibly irreparably damage relationships, until he'd entertained them in the light of day.

And had done a little preliminary digging.

"Go to sleep," he added, as though talking to a child. Hearing himself, too late, he wished he'd just left it at *nothing*.

Because, other than the current problems in Dove's life, there was nothing. Could be nothing. Between them.

"That's the third big sigh you've made since you got into bed."

He didn't turn his head to see if she was still facing the

wall beside her, but neither had he felt her move. Taking that as a good sign he said, "My mind's on a situation I'm dealing with for a client," he told her in absolute truth. "Nothing I can discuss."

"Attorney–client privilege," she said, helping him out of his mess.

He didn't say yes. Technically, he'd be lying. Because when the client with whom he was speaking was the one whose case he was pondering, privilege was moot.

But he took care to put work out of his mind. Or to put the client who was consuming him on the back burner. To, at the very least, ensure that he kept his breathing even.

And, in doing so, felt himself relax enough to sleep.

SKIN AGAINST SKIN. Brought to a semiconscious state, Dove registered the sensation. Human warmth against her arm. She'd been in a boat on a river in the dark, rowing so she didn't make any sound and bring danger upon her. Her arms were growing weary.

And there was warmth. She wasn't alone.

Lying still, she wavered between sleep and consciousness, relaxed and dropped off again. Until movement woke her completely. Then she froze.

She was lying on her back, not on her side as she'd fallen asleep. And not on the edge of the bed, either. Her arm had most definitely met human flesh. Mitchell's back. A bare portion of it.

And it felt...so incredibly good to be touching him.

Their time together—with no breaks—seemed like weeks, not days, and yet, other than the hug he'd given her the other morning, and the time she'd slid her hand into his at the hospital, they'd never touched.

As though doing so was off-limits.

How could something that brought so much comfort, even just an arm to a back in the night, be wrong?

She wanted to move until her hand was touching him, too. Just to lay her palm against him and go back to sleep, but didn't want to wake him.

Didn't want to spoil the moment.

But the more she lay there, wide awake, the more she wanted. Which led to thoughts of how he'd wanted her, too, the other morning.

And the more she thought, the more consumed she became with knowing how it felt to have her hand flat against his back. To absorb the sense of life emanating from his skin. To feel his essence in a physical sense.

Could her touch help him? Maybe instill some positive energy within him? She'd never practiced touch therapy before, but knew others who had. For healing purposes.

But what about just for…comfort? The word came again. Pushing at her. And Dove capitulated. Because…what if she denied herself and lost an opportunity she'd been given? Keeping her movements as imperceptible as possible, she slowly put her hand where her arm had been.

Just lay it there. And smiled. Never in her life had she taken such a large dose of positive energy from another human being. Maybe she hadn't been as open to doing so.

Or hadn't needed it so urgently.

Closing her eyes, she lay there, not holding Mitchell, just…feeling him…and drifted back to sleep.

MITCHELL AWOKE ABRUPTLY. From an erotic dream that had left him hard as hell, a hand to his penis. A dream that didn't end with consciousness.

He was hard, all right. And holding a feminine hand that

contained the fingers actually covering a part of himself that hadn't known feminine company in months.

He worked to get his mind in gear. Came up with two things. He'd figured out how Dove had handled her getting-cold-in-the-night situation. She was under the covers with him.

And the second was just more of a wondering. Was she conscious?

Followed by a third. Did he want her to be?

Oh, God help him, he did.

He was about to explode, and she wasn't even doing anything. Well, she had her hand…there. With his on top of it.

Knowing that embarrassing himself was imminent, he gave an involuntary push against himself, adding pressure to her hand on him, but managed to hold on long enough for the immediate moment to pass. And breathed a sigh of relief with the victory. Never in his life had he lost control without his own consent.

All that was left was to extricate himself. Preferably without waking her up.

Unless…very softly he whispered, "You awake?"

The clasp of her fingers around him, a very definite sign of consciousness was his response. And made his exit not so clear-cut.

Most particularly when, of its own accord, his body pressed itself into her palm as a reaction to her hold on it.

Rolling to his back, Mitchell turned his head, meeting her wide-open gaze in the darkness. Pinpricks of light to pinpricks of light.

He thought her head started to move toward him. Knew his head started to move toward her. He was going to kiss her. Just fact.

And when he did, other facts hit home as well.

The woman kissed like a temptress.

And there was no option but to accept that they were going to have sex.

DOVE HAD BEEN DREAMING. There'd been clouds. Pleasure.

How her hand had slid from Mitchell's back to his hard-on beneath the waistband of his silky pajama pants, she had no idea. Didn't figure it mattered. His hand over hers, holding her there, was all the impetus she needed to hold on. And to open her lips to his when he turned to her.

Nature had her way of directing her course.

Dove's choice was to follow it.

His pathway was an intoxicating surprise. Precise, as purposeful as he was. But so much more. He took his time to explore her mouth, allowing her to get to know his. Lips soft and gentle, and then more demanding, he took her more deeply into him, somehow, than she'd known a mere kiss could do.

So much so that her hand left his lower region as she had to plant both palms on his cheeks, to be there completely with him.

And when his pelvis pushed against hers, lighting a fire within her that would singe her without him, that was right, too.

She didn't speak. Didn't need words from him.

They'd have been superfluous. Interrupting the communication that mattered.

With her eyes wide open, she drew her palms up his sides as he sat up to remove the shirt that had ridden up on him during the night. And then, lying half on top of him as he rested back against his pillow, she watched as she let her hands get to know every inch of his chest. His shoulders. His stomach.

And squealed when he suddenly rose up and over, lowering her to her back after stripping off her half shirt. Her breasts tight, nipples hard, she lay there a willing and eager captive, delighting in the almost reverent look in his eyes as he cupped and caressed, teasing her nipples with his fingers and then his tongue. Before his mouth suckled in the age-old ways of time.

Just as she was losing herself to that pleasure, liquid seared through her, pooling in her crotch, and as though he'd known the second it happened, he slid on top of her, straight legs to straight legs, teasing her as he moved himself up and down in the crevice between her thighs.

Holding her knees together, she let her clothed thighs caress his hardness, reaching higher and higher as, with each pass, he pressed at the nub of her.

And when she was going to fly off without him, she rolled them to their sides. He reached for her pajama bottoms, got his own bottoms off and, kissing her, showed her another layer of hunger as he taunted and played with her, allowing her to explore him more completely than she'd ever known a man's body.

More than she'd ever before had a curiosity to know one. But, in those moments, couldn't know enough.

And then, somehow timing her need perfectly, he was just there, half on top of her, and she spread her legs wide open, inviting him in.

His initial entry after condom duty was slow, as though he was taking his time to say hello, to know her, in particular, before he danced with her.

She accepted his presence inside her with pure joy, welcoming his size, his strength, his need.

And when it was time to fly, she was there with him,

too. Her body moving as urgently as his did, their need to reach the sky seemingly the same.

Until, in one breath, they cried out, her body convulsing around his as his pulsed within her.

There'd never been a more perfect dance.

A purer joy.

And minutes later, with her naked body beside his under the covers, lightly touching his, she fell back to sleep.

MITCHELL SLEPT, and when consciousness returned, he was wide awake. Forget-falling-back-to-sleep awake.

What in the hell had he done?

Allowed her to do?

Encouraged her to do?

Checking for the blinking lights of the alarm sensors that greeted him every morning, he left his bed in spite of the fact that dawn had not yet made its appearance. Taking his phone into the bathroom with him. A quick look at the downstairs cameras, verifying that there'd been no breaches during the night, he went straight for the shower. A cold one.

And returning five minutes later to his room fully clothed in the blue jeans and shirt he'd put in the hamper the night before, he wasn't at all surprised to find Dove gone.

He had to shave. To grab clean clothes and get into them.

But first, he made a trek down to the kitchen. To get his coffee.

And to make certain that no unseen danger lurked in Dove's midst. Standing outside the bathroom door between her room and the kitchen, he heard the shower running. Took a peek in her room just to assure himself that everything looked normal, and conceded that he was being a little paranoid.

Most particularly when he was relieved to find that she hadn't packed her bags.

The fact that they'd had sex didn't change the circumstances that were keeping them together. He had to make certain that she shared his understanding on that point.

Which was why, fifteen minutes later, when she came out dressed in a gauzy orange flowing skirt with yellow flowers, another long-sleeved cropped shirt in green silk and sandals with ties that ran up to her knees, he was standing barefoot and unshaven in his kitchen, still wearing yesterday's clothes and sipping coffee.

The peaceful expression she'd been wearing as she'd entered the room disappeared the second she saw him. "What's wrong?"

"Nothing," he told her. Except that change, the second she saw him, gave lie to his words.

"Someone called. Who? Kansas? Welding? Your brother?" And then with a deep breath, "The hospital?"

The stiffness in her shoulders propelled him toward her, to reach for her. Except that he had a cup of hot coffee in his hand.

And they weren't…a couple.

"No one called. I just…needed to make certain that things were okay. Between us."

The immediate softening of her features eased his tension immensely. Until she frowned. "Why? Aren't you okay?"

Thinking of the night before, the incredible pleasure they'd made together, he said, "I am."

She nodded then. "You just thought I wouldn't be."

With a nod he shrugged. Guilty as charged.

"No strings attached. No commitment of any kind to any future involvement between us," she said, her gaze clear as she looked straight at him. Repeating what she'd said after the first time the subject had come up right there in his kitchen. "You think I was just kidding about that?"

Another shrug was all he had to give her. He wasn't even sure why. It wasn't like any of the women he'd been with had come after him wanting a wedding ring after one night together.

"Sex is a part of nature, Mitchell," she said then, moving to the refrigerator to pull out the container housing her bizarre grasslike breakfast. "Our bodies are designed to need it. Just like they require—" she held up the container "—food."

He should have been elated by her response. Instead, while he was pleased that she was in a good mood, he felt a little deflated.

Grabbing a fork, she stood there and took a bite of the same unusual meal she'd had the other two mornings they'd spent together. Then, swallowing, she glanced up at him, with an almost otherworldly smile on her face, like she had some kind of great secret. "But we did it in a pretty phenomenal way, huh?"

To which Mitchell said, "We sure did," and hightailed it out of there.

Before he was tempted to throw caution to the wind and ask her for a repeat performance on the kitchen floor.

Chapter Eighteen

She wanted him again. And again. And again.

More so, and much worse, she didn't want him to leave his house. Ever. Didn't want him out there in the world where other women could ogle him. And want him, too.

Which made her the absolute worst human being on earth. A failure on all spiritual levels.

Selfish to the core.

A fraud.

Eating her greens—still holding out hope that their intuitive properties would help her right herself—Dove paced the kitchen, waiting for Mitchell to finish his shower and get her out of there.

Away from infernal temptation.

Him in the shower…water sluicing all over every inch of the body that she hadn't had nearly enough time with… a specimen of nature's ability to create perfection in male form…

She shoved two forkfuls in her mouth at once. Forcing herself to chew with her mouth open. Breaking her mother's heart, she was sure.

"Always chew with your mouth closed, Dove."

"But, Momma, I can do a better job at chewing with my mouth open. Then my cheeks don't get in the way so much."

"But then you take away the appetite of others who are eating with you. Which is the better choice? Chewing for your own comfort? Or making a choice that benefits others?"

Technically, she wasn't hurting anyone else with her current chewing choice.

So...perhaps she was still in her mother's good graces.

With the exception of the whole wanting-to-keep-Mitchell-locked-up-for-the-rest-of-their-lives thing. No, not locked up. It would be a sacrilege to cage the magnificent animal that he was.

Just...just...what?

She wanted the world to know he was hers and respect that choice? To have him tell her that she was the only woman he wanted to be with, would be with, no matter what?

Then she could trust him to go into the world and not be affected by what other women wanted. Like her mother had trusted her father all the months he was out at sea for all those years.

And what about her dad? Had he trusted her mother, too? Had he given any thought to what he was leaving behind?

Or had he taken her mother for granted?

Thoughts she should have had before. Long before. She'd just never looked at her parents from the partner perspective before. How horribly...lacking...of her.

And now? When Whaler looked at all the months, all the years that he'd lost? Thinking that he'd have a lifetime of years with his love when he retired from the sea? Only to have her get sick less than a decade afterward?

An onslaught of regret hit her so hard she slid down to the floor and adopted the lotus position just to get through it. And was hit with another bit of understanding.

The bottle. She didn't condone Whaler's drinking. It was

killing him. But it suddenly made more sense to her. It wasn't just grief sending her father to seek constant oblivion.

It was the sense that his life choices hadn't lived up to expectation. A lesson learned too late to avert the consequence.

How did a powerful man like her father live with the negative impact from a situation he'd created and couldn't fix?

How did Dove help him find a way? When she didn't know the way herself? Her mother had never taught her the lesson—not in words.

And not really in action, either. While she was absolutely certain her parents had adored each other, that her mother had loved her father and Dove, too, with her whole heart, she had no idea if they'd had an open marriage or not. If her mother had taken lovers while her father was away, Dove had certainly never known about it.

Nor could she come up with a single male figure in her mother's life who might have been more than just a casual acquaintance.

The sound of Mitchell's shoes on the creaking stairs had Dove scrambling to her feet. Putting the lid on her greens and shoving the container back into the refrigerator.

Feeling as though she'd had a good morning session, even though she hadn't technically been in a meditative state.

Her incredibly odd reaction to sex with Mitchell hadn't been about her. It had been a way for her to gain understanding of her father's struggles. To be able to find a way to help him, where in the past she'd failed.

A new perspective with which to greet him when he awoke.

She didn't have all the answers yet. But with her new understanding, she was finally on her way to finding them.

And knowing the reason behind her uncharacteristically territorial reaction to the previous night's activities meant that she'd just freed herself up to have sex with Mitchell again.

A thought that brought enough of a flood of good feeling to drown out the pricks of fear as she headed out with him and into her day.

Or would have if he hadn't come into the kitchen with tight lips and lines marring his forehead.

"What?" she asked, when his gaze sought her out and held on.

"There's no sign of *Ladybird*'s mooring ropes, but they found evidence on the cement pad to indicate that someone had been standing on it within the last day. Not a footprint, but a lack of sea debris and algae growth, side by side, in the size of feet."

Picking up the bag she'd packed for the hospital when she'd first come down that morning, she slung it over her shoulder and headed for the door. "So we know that someone tampered with the boat, but we have no way of finding out who."

He was right behind her. Which just plain felt good. "Yep." He didn't sound at all happy about that fact.

"But we know who it is," she reminded him. "It just means we still don't have the proof we need to have him stopped."

"It means he's getting bolder," Mitchell told her as he slid into the car seat beside her. They pulled their doors closed at the same time.

In unison.

As though their sex dance had somehow put them in sync. The thought filled her with pleasure. She clung to it as she asked something that had been toying at the edge of her brain. Something she hadn't wanted to think about. "How would Brad Fletcher know about that cement platform? He's not from Shelby, nor has he ever, that we know of, spent any time at St. James Boats. I didn't even know about it until my dad bought the place and I started fooling around in the water. That was a few years before he'd retired, so before his fleet of boats were in. My folks would let me jump off the dock and swim, as long as one of them—Mom—was around to keep an eye on me."

She was jabbering. Had her parents—their relationship—on her mind. They'd had a good plan for their future together. Her mother had seemed really happy about it. Eager to spend time at the marina. She'd been a huge help in getting the business up and running...

"Same way he got your studio vandalized," Mitchell's words cut into her remunerations. "Hired someone local."

Maybe. Most likely. But... "Why go to all the trouble to swim in to get the job done when he could have just done the job from the docks?" With new horror shuddering through her, she turned to look at him. "Unless he knew about the newly installed cameras."

The way Mitchell's jaw tensed was his giveaway. "You already figured all this out," she said to him. "And you have a suspect. Kirk? You think Fletcher hired him?"

Mitchell's glance over at her as he paused at the end of his driveway held...speculation. Not confirmation. "It's possible Kirk told Fletcher about the platform," sounding... different. Tense, but not as...uptight.

"You suspected someone else."

Pulling out onto the street that would take them into town, he gave her another, easier glance. "Not *suspected*," he told her. "Just wondered about. Not because he's given me any reason to doubt him, personally, at all."

There was only one person left that she knew of that fit the bill. "Wes?" she asked him, incredulous. "Wes would no more sabotage my father's business than cut his own feet off. It's not about the money for him," she said. "It's about family. Loyalty. Keeping businesses local. The man is Shelby golden to the core."

Odd how Mitchell remained silent after her tirade, where normally he'd quietly lay out logical points as he saw them. And, not liking that he hadn't done so—worried that his not doing so had something to do with the sex they'd had, as it was the only thing that had changed between them— she said, "The facts point to him."

When he continued to face straight ahead, not acknowledging that he'd heard her, she pushed harder. "And you didn't want to tell me until you had proof because you knew it would upset me."

Nice. But…she couldn't go there. Most particularly not with him.

But really, not with anyone. She might need his help and physical protection against an attacker at the moment, but that didn't make her any less capable of handling the crappy challenges that life dumped on her. It was all part of the journey. Even if it meant she made mistakes. She had to be allowed to fail.

She'd asked for the help she needed.

He continued to drive. She continued to stare at him. Hard. "You didn't tell me because you're getting all manly on me, thinking I need protecting from emotional pain, rather than seeing me as an equal work mate," she accused.

And Mitchell nodded.

THERE WAS NO point in avoiding the truth. A fact Mitchell had learned probably from birth. And while he did not like, or want, his newfound awareness where Dove was concerned, he knew better than to avoid it.

Most of the problems his clients—and his family members—brought to him were the result of avoidance. Not wanting to deal with something. Hoping it would go away.

Many things did work out as one hoped. There were times when possible problems didn't materialize. But that didn't mean you didn't prepare for them just in case.

And in his case, avoidance wasn't really even a choice. He was in the middle of a huge pile of muck. He wanted a woman he had nothing in common with.

To the point that he'd allowed her to convince him that sex was only body parts. He'd known better than that. A man didn't get a law degree—with a required class in family law—without gaining an understanding of two major truths. Emotions were a huge factor in problems between family members. And emotions were unpredictable. One couldn't see into the future.

Couldn't predict that a young love could turn so deadly.

Or that someone who adored another one year decided five years later that they no longer did. Nor could one predict how one would feel if they found out a spouse had cheated on them.

And how did it all pertain to him?

He'd known the messiest emotions of all stemmed from sex. Often even when one didn't want, or expect, them to do so.

Because sex was the ultimate form of physical expression. And if it was great sex, it often created a new awareness of that person. Which then, due to the way human beings reacted to needs within themselves by seeking to fill that need, created a need for more sex with them. Which led to an emotional bond between them. A bond that—due to a human being's ability to reason, to realize that the other's well-being directly affected their own emotional state—spilled out of the bedroom and into their lives.

He didn't make the rules. He just lived by them.

All of which flew out of his brain when, at Dove's request, he made a stop at the marina before taking her to the hospital to sit with her father. She'd called in. Bob St. James had not yet regained consciousness but had taken no turn for the worse. And she'd wanted to see for herself that *Ladybird* was okay. To look at the area. And check the office, too.

If anything was out of place—if Wes Armstrong had messed with anything Mitchell took that to mean—she'd be the most likely one to be able to tell.

They didn't make it to the office. Though it was only six in the morning when they pulled in, the sun was already shining, and his brain was just registering the sight before him when he heard Dove's sharp intake of breath. Followed by "Oh my God!"

She had her door open before he'd come to a full stop in the drive, but he was right beside her as she ran down to the docks.

He'd been looking at *Ladybird* as he'd first pulled forward, and supposed she had been, too. *Wicked Winnings* had been moored beside her.

The trawler's radar station and pilothouse were intact, but the forward hull, starting with the gunwale, were splintered, bashed in, as though someone had taken a sledgehammer to her. Or had had her out for a joyride and crashed. All of the damage they could see was out of the water, but that didn't mean the immersed portion of the hull wasn't also damaged.

Racing in front of Dove, maybe to get there first, to

somehow protect her from the horror she had to be experiencing, he said, "If she's taking in water, she'll sink."

He was already on the trawler by the time she'd caught up with him. And while he wanted to stop her from climbing aboard—even just to ask her to please let him get a look around first—he didn't do so. She'd made her point quite clear in the car. The fact that they'd had sex gave him no further influence over her. She would not tolerate him trying to take her autonomy from her.

He made a quick check of all at-risk areas, ending up in the pilothouse. She was sitting at the helm, staring out at the trashed hull in front of her. "She was our greatest hope," she said to him. "Our way to make enough money to keep the business going."

"She still can be," he said, words pouring out of him almost faster than he was thinking them. "There's no water coming in, Dove. While the damage is extensive, it's not as bad as it looks."

"Doesn't matter," she said, placing both of her hands on the wheel. "We can't afford the repairs."

His lawyer brain was in full gear. "You might not have to," he told her, placing himself so that she could just as easily see him as the damage in front of her. Wanting her to focus on him.

Not the destruction.

"This is clearly destruction of property," he told her, talking way too fast but feeling as though he couldn't get the words out rapidly enough. "A deliberate destruction. If someone had been joyriding and crashed, then based on the breakage we can see, there'd also have been extensive damage to the keel. The lower hull. There'd be water coming in."

Her face turned slowly, her gaze brushing up against

his. And then connecting. "You think we can prove sabo-tage?" she asked him.

Breathing a tad more easily, Mitchell said, "Yes." And then moved closer to her, taking her hands off the wheel and turning her to face him. Without forethought. Just doing it. Looking her right in the eye, he reminded her, "If this was done without taking her out, we'll have it on video, Dove."

He saw the focus, the strength, the…hope return to her gaze. So quickly the glow coming from her eyes was al-most a physical touch to him. Jumping up, she moved to-ward the dock, stepping around debris as if it wasn't even there. "Should we call the police before we access the cam-eras?" she asked. "I don't want there to be any chance that anyone can say we tampered with evidence."

Mitchell didn't have the heart to tell her the trial, which wouldn't happen for months, was not her first concern by any means. But because he'd used the end in mind to help her fight back, he could hardly point that out. He had her back. For the moment that was all that mattered.

The rest, like the fact that she mattered more than any-thing else going on in his life, was just going to have to wait.

They had him! Standing in her father's office with Peter Welding and Mitchell, Dove wanted to throw her arms around the attorney's neck, hug him and never let go.

She didn't, of course. But she was smiling from ear to ear as Welding took possession of the security-camera memory card that showed Brad Fletcher himself using some kind of gun that shot what looked to be electrical current onto the deck of *Wicked Winnings*. There'd be no fingerprints, no bullets that could be identified by striations. If not for the cameras that Mitchell had had installed, it could have been near to impossible to prove who'd done the damage.

Welding, as an extra precaution, sent a digital copy of the footage to his secure email at the station, and after Mitchell inserted a new memory card into the camera's mainframe, the officer walked with Mitchell and her to Mitchell's car.

Mitchell had an early appointment and needed to drop her off at the hospital first.

"I can take her," Welding offered, looking from Mitchell to Dove. "It's only a mile out of my way." Two for Mitchell, and Welding had no urgent business.

So as disappointed as Dove was not to have those minutes alone with Mitchell, to celebrate the victory in private conversation and ask him the next steps as far as St. James Boats was concerned, she said, "I'm good with that," and before Mitchell could argue, grabbed her bag out of the back seat of his vehicle.

She'd never met Peter in person until that week and enjoyed his conversation as they drove across their small town. She watched as they passed Repo and Namaste, longing for her peaceful space, for her clients, but knew that she carried too much risk of passing her negative energy to them while she still felt…hunted.

Soon, she told herself, feeling as though the universe backed up her silent promise. With Brad Fletcher's arrest imminent, and so clearly, provably guilty, she could be back in her studio as early as that afternoon.

The thought filling her with happiness, she smiled when Peter mentioned that maybe they could get a cup of coffee sometime. And shrugged. Not a *no*. Not a *yes*.

Not an admission that she couldn't stand the stuff.

He didn't push. She didn't reject him. And she gave him an extra warm smile as he pulled up in front of the medical center's main building. "This where you need to be?" he asked, and she nodded.

"Thank you so much," she told him. "You have no idea how much this means to my father and me. We are most certainly in your debt. Maybe, once he's home, we can have you over to dinner. To thank you?"

Let him make what he would of that. He was a nice man. She liked his company.

And had zero desire to lead him on with an acceptance of what could only be considered a predate invite.

"I'd like that," he said, smiling in a nice way as she hopped out and shut the door quickly behind her, turning to wave and watch him drive off.

More because she didn't want him to see her walk from the front of the building over to the inpatient wing that was attached to the separate, urgent care portion of the medical complex, rather than the doctors' and imaging offices where he'd left her.

The man didn't do anything for her in that department. He might have done. If she'd met him at an earlier time. And maybe, at some future point?

She wasn't closing the door on the idea. But wasn't alluding to it, either.

And he wasn't leaving. Reminding her of Mitchell for a second there. Until she reminded herself he was a good cop and doing his job. He needed to see her enter the building.

And so she did. Waiting around for several minutes, before she headed back out to get over to her father. And then, just to be safe, went out the back way, through the playground and park area set up for lunches or kids who had long wait times between procedures. As she walked, her mind filled with the future's possibilities.

The early morning chill seemed to lift her to a higher wakefulness, while the sun filled her with the serotonin that fed her intuitive abilities with its added ability to access good feelings.

She had so much to tell her dad. Now that they had Brad, it would be all systems go with the plans to get the boat rental business back to earning good money. Yes, they'd have a bit of a delay while *Wicked* was fixed, but with Brad Fletcher's money, it shouldn't be hard to at least force the man to pay that bill immediately...

Ugh!

A sudden blow to her back knocked the wind out of Dove, would have thrown her to the ground if she hadn't been honing her body since she was old enough to walk.

She saw the cloth coming around the side of her face, toward her mouth, in the split second before it stunted her breathing abilities, and threw an elbow straight to the side of her face. Knocking the hand behind the cloth just as she kicked one leg straight up behind her. Landing in a squat facing behind her, knees bent, apart, hand on the ground to steady her, preparing for a throw of her palm to a nose with enough of a lunge to knock her attacker to his back.

Except…no face was there. Winded, stunned, Dove looked up to see an average-size figure dressed all in blue, or black…a hood running around the corner of a wing of the building and disappearing out of sight.

She ran then, too. At a pace fast enough to win races on the high school track field, and hurriedly, with shaking fingers, pushed in the code she'd been given to access the private inpatient wing. Fumbling once. Forcing herself to focus and push again.

Once inside, she walked at a rapid pace past the chairs she and Mitchell had occupied the other day, into the waiting area in view of the nurses' station.

Seeing two uniformed women and one man behind the desk, all of whom she recognized, she waved and pulled out her phone.

With her finger on the icon she'd set up for Mitchell, she remembered he was in an appointment and, as reality hit, went straight to the officer standing watch outside her father's door. Someone new, a woman she'd never met before.

Angela Waites her badge read. A first-year officer who called Peter Welding the second she heard about the near attack.

Apparently, Brad Fletcher hadn't been satisfied with damage to the St. James Boats ability to earn an income.

Or threats. He was hiring thugs to make certain that she didn't get in the way of his goal.

"I don't think he was going to hurt me," she told Peter when, in short order, he was sitting with her in the same seats she and Mitchell had used out in the hallway between the trauma and inpatient units. She'd given him all the details, the minimal description she had, and had answered his questions mostly with *I don't know* or *I didn't notice.* "He was definitely planning to knock me out, though," she added after her last useless response. "Probably just to scare me. A warning to sell my father's business since, without *Wicked Winnings*, I can no longer afford to keep the place."

Peter's frown didn't slow her down at all. Not even when he asked, "That doesn't make a lot of sense," he said. "He's going to abduct you, get you to sign, and then think he can just walk away?"

He was right. Didn't make sense. Fear shot through her. A stab at a time. Growing more electrifying with each stab. "He was going to make me sign and then dispose of me, wasn't he? Just like he tried to dispose of my dad?" And then, before giving him a chance to reply, she said, "Or…" eyes wide with horror, she stared at him "…the serial killer…" She swallowed. Hard.

Struggled to draw in air.

The uniformed officer's gaze was kind as he looked at her, shrugged and said, "We can only speculate at this point, but I hope you've taken your last walk alone until this is resolved?"

He didn't call her on letting him drop her off at the wrong spot. He'd only been in town a short while, having applied for and taken the job, leaving a smaller force he'd worked for upstate. But he didn't know she knew that. She wouldn't have, hadn't, until Mitchell had mentioned it when the man had first been assigned to check out Brad Fletcher. One of

Brad's boat rental businesses was located in the small seaside town where Peter had last been employed.

Peter likely knew Brad. Maybe even well.

Filling with horror chills again, Dove wondered if she'd just walked into her own demise—leaving the unit to sit out there alone with Welding. Was he on Fletcher's payroll, too? Like the thug who'd just tried to kidnap her?

And the guy who'd been watching her house?

And had debased the sacredness of her studio?

Glancing at the door into the unit and feeling for her phone in her bag, she was trying to determine her best course of action against an armed and well-trained police officer when Mitchell barged through the door at the opposite end of the hall and came toward her.

Weak with relief, she felt tears fill her eyes.

But didn't take her gaze off him.

Not even when she saw the flare of his nostrils, the anger glaring from those blue eyes.

He'd come.

His anger didn't bother her. It was a natural reaction. What mattered was that he'd somehow known she was still in trouble.

And he'd shown up.

And...was shaking Peter's hand like they were friends.

Mitchell was in on it, then? He was...

The thought hit but only lasted for the split second it took her to slap down the fear that was trying to rob her of her senses.

Mitchell was there to help her. She had to believe that.

And if she was wrong? The insidiousness of negative energy wasn't letting go easily.

But she had an answer for it.

If she couldn't trust Mitchell, she'd just as soon be dead.

MITCHELL SAT WITH Dove after Welding left. Several minutes passed before the glaze left her eyes. The woman was a complete enigma to him. And if he didn't get some kind of protocol for himself where she was concerned, she might just be his downfall, too.

There was no future for the two of them. He saw it clearly. What's more, he was certain that she saw it, too.

So why her circumstances were affecting him so intrinsically he didn't know.

The situation didn't bode well.

Mitchell did not like things going on in his life that he couldn't explain rationally and logically. Which was why he was living the staid life he'd chosen to live. With all adventure happening between him and nature, period. No other humans around.

Until the past week.

He'd excused himself from an important merger meeting between two medical practices—joining two independent DOs into one practice—as soon as he'd seen Welding's name on his phone screen. Expecting to hear that Fletcher was in custody, he'd stepped outside just long enough to get the good news.

And never stepped back in. With a quick call to Stuart and then texts to his clients, he had his paralegal collect preliminary signatures and reschedule the meeting for later that afternoon.

Unprofessional, at best. Something else completely new and inexplicable to him.

Welding had already suggested that Dove get checked out over at the clinic. She'd insisted she was fine. The guy who'd tried to abduct her might not be, however. Welding had all clinics and urgent cares in Shelby and surrounding cities being checked out for any recent nose injuries.

"I wanted to believe there was no chance it was the serial killer after me." Dove's soft words were loud in the deserted hallway. Breaking a silence that had lasted several minutes.

He wasn't going anywhere until he knew that Fletcher was in custody. At the very least.

"We don't know it's him, Dove. To the contrary, there's no indication that women who reported being vandalized or stalked have gone missing."

When her head swung in his direction, mouth open, eyes wide, he quickly added, "I spoke with Eli on my way here from the office." There was more. He didn't want to tell her. To add to her burden. And yet…it wasn't up to him to determine what she could and could not handle. If she were a man, he'd tell her. Or another lawyer.

But because she was so sensitive…was no reason to undermine her.

The woman had taken out a would-be kidnapper with no warning, and it sounded like impressive precision. He'd been picturing the scenario that had been laid out for him over and over in his mind. Just…having a hard time digesting…so much.

"It's also less likely that it was the serial killer because another woman has just gone missing," he told her. Without giving the name, the details, that Eli had given him. Dawn Ellis. From Wasilla.

"Oh my god!" Dove's gaze wide-eyed again but filled with compassion as she looked over at him. "When?"

He shook his head. "I honestly don't know for sure. She was just reported missing." And fit the MO. "Even if I did know more, I'm not at liberty to tell you."

He wasn't free to take her into his arms, either, which was all he'd really wanted to do since he'd seen the look of relief, and what appeared to be gratitude, that had entered her eyes when he'd come walking down the hallway toward her.

Pulling her sandal-strapped lower legs up to her chair, she wrapped her arms around her shins.

Noting, with relief, that she had Lycra shorts on under the skirt, Mitchell resisted the urge to wrap an arm around her and pull her against him. Feeling a bit powerless sitting there.

But equally unwilling to leave. At least until she was ready to go sit in her father's room. She'd said she didn't want to take her negative energy in there. That as long as she was close, in case there was any change, she'd prefer to stay outside his space until she had her breathing, her tension, under control.

The woman was an enigma, to be sure. Soft and needy, and yet, in some ways, he was beginning to think she was stronger than he was.

He controlled his environment. She kept hers wide open.

Thinking of the way she'd put herself in harm's way by walking unescorted, he figured maybe hers was too open.

"I shouldn't have been in the outdoor break area alone," she said, as though she'd read his thoughts. More like the incident that had taken place was replaying itself over and over again in both of their minds.

He didn't bother commenting on the obvious. She'd paid a heavy price for her choice.

"I just thought…within the complex I'd be safe. And mostly, because I felt safe here, my own physical safety wasn't at the forefront of my mind."

He had to bite back the words that came to him first. That her physical safety should always be at the forefront of her mind. But that wasn't his call to make. "We'd just got the proof we've been seeking on Brad Fletcher," he said instead. "It's understandable, with all that's gone on, your father lying in there…that getting the man in custody would be consuming you." Which was why he'd told Welding to make sure he saw her into the building.

Which the detective had.

Mitchell just hadn't imagined that Dove would head in the wrong door.

"Actually," she said, turning her head on her knees to look at him, "Fletcher wasn't the one affecting my thinking right then."

The way she said the words, as though she was telling him something she wasn't sure she should, treading in unsure waters, had him watching her intently.

She'd been thinking about him? Maybe about the fact that, with Fletcher's arrest, and the warrants they could then compel, they might soon be able to prove conclusively that all the destructive things happening to her stemmed from the shady businessman's attempt to pressure her into selling her father's business. Which meant that her time as a guest in his home was at an end.

They'd had their one night together.

And it was done.

"When Detective Welding pulled up to the wrong part of the medical complex, he was asking me out."

Mitchell's gaze swung back to her, more intently than it should have done. He managed to keep his mouth shut, however.

If Dove wanted to date, that was her business. They'd had sex. No commitment. No expectations.

"I didn't want to embarrass him, but at the same time I just had no interest. Except to be noncommittal and get out of the car before he could press for more. I didn't want to risk the chance that he'd hang around for a minute or two, to make sure things were good, and so I went out the back way."

Reeling with the words, he continued to stare at her. The idea that Welding had expressed an interest in Dove wasn't as fantastical as Mitchell's immediate reaction to the man for having done so. He'd have liked to punch the man in the face.

Which was better than the gun he'd have taken to her assailant had he been present during that travesty.

Still, he had no right to any opinion about Dove's love life.

Nor any reason to feel like strutting around like a golden rooster at her response to Welding's invitation.

She'd had no interest.

Which factored in not at all.

It was about the attack she'd endured. And her dealing with it. Getting by it as best she could. That was all that mattered.

About the fact that her would-be abductor was still out there. On the loose. Possibly planning to try again. Unless Welding and his team could get a look at Fletcher's phone records, his finances. Then figure out who was on his payroll and stop them.

Or it was until the door into the ward opened suddenly, with a nurse standing there.

Her expression—not grim—the uniformed woman said, "Your father's awake. The doctor's on her way."

And Dove was gone.

Chapter Twenty

Spirits soaring, Dove practically flew into her father's room, only just realizing, when she heard Mitchell's soft tones behind her speaking to the nurse, that she'd just left him sitting out there.

A part of her was stronger, knowing he was there, but she was fully focused on her father.

And stopped, not far inside his door when she saw the anger glaring at her from his older blue eyes. "What's going on?" he demanded in a tone she hadn't heard directed at her...ever. "Why am I here? Did you have me committed? Because I can tell you..." He started to throw off his covers and sit up.

"Dad, no!" she said, hurrying over to him, both arms reaching out to his chest. Not to push him back but to hold on. He didn't hug her back but had stopped moving forward, and tears burst out of her. "You were hurt," she told him, sobbing. "Please lie back down. At least until the doctor can look in your eyes and make sure you're okay to get up."

The words seemed to placate him. She felt his body relax against her arms, and helped ease him back to the bed.

Sorry to have to let him go, she sat on the edge of the bed beside him, needing to ask him what seemed like a million questions, but completely stupefied and a bit frightened of the uncharacteristic anger he'd spewed at her, she was afraid to say much or do anything until the doctor arrived.

"She's been called," she said then, wiping her tears, but feeling the residual of the storm inside her in the trembling of her lips. "The doctor. She'll be here momentarily, I promise."

With a wary look in her direction, he nodded. Then slid his fingers in between hers on the hand closest to him and held on.

Her daddy, again.

His grip strong enough to feel healthy, but not at all hurtful. And…shaky. His eyes seemed lucid, though he appeared a bit lost. And the vitals she'd been reading for two days on the machine beside his bed were the best they'd been. His pulse ran fast on and off, and she'd been told that was to be expected with the detoxing.

She wasn't a doctor. But she clung tightly to the hope in front of her.

Along with a possible boatload of anger, anxiety or resentment. She hadn't needed the doctor to tell her that part. Just as serotonin was a basis of happiness, the liver was a base for the more negative emotions.

A first-year intern had put a call into Peter Welding as soon as Whaler awoke, and he arrived right alongside the doctor before Dove had a chance for any further conversation with her father. The younger employee shooed her out while the doctor examined him and supervised Welding's questioning.

"It's a good sign that he was angry," Mitchell said the second she stood beside him in the hallway. "He's fighting."

Nodding, she watched the closed door. The anger had bothered her. But not nearly as much as the accusation had done. But she'd read up on detoxification. Hallucinations were sometimes a part of the process. Most particularly when the person was a heavy drinker.

Her father qualified as that. She couldn't take his first reaction to seeing her in a personal way. He was conscious. He wasn't himself.

One step at a time. She knew this stuff. Things were coming to a close. With Fletcher's arrest in the works, and her father awake, life could turn the corner toward the future. One where St. James Boats was fluid again.

Her father healthy.

Her studio thriving.

And her no longer feeling like Mitchell was her life-blood to strength and endurance. No longer needing him. Or anyone but herself.

Standing against the wall, she hardly took her gaze off the door. And jumped when it opened five minutes later. As if by choreographed dance or staging, Welding went straight to Mitchell as the doctor came to her.

"He doesn't remember anything from the time he saw you in his office on Saturday until now," the doctor said softly, her gaze compassionate.

Dove didn't need compassion. Couldn't allow herself the weakness of leaning on yet another human being. "His memories of his time with you are fuzzy, but I understand he was pretty intoxicated then?"

She nodded. Hating hearing her father's situation being discussed so...realistically. Yeah, he'd been pretty drunk. More like totally wasted.

She just hadn't wanted to accept that she was losing him one sip, one bottle at a time.

"His pupil response is good," the doctor continued, talk-ing about running another scan, some more lab work, before she could give Dove any idea as to when Whaler would be able to go home.

Warning that he was already asking for his bottle. Threatening to leave if someone didn't bring it to him. And then telling her that he'd already fallen back to sleep and could be expected to remain that way for a good part of the day. If he was up and alert by nighttime, they could start him on some solid foods. And maybe, depending on test results and his ability to tolerate food, get him off the IV in another twenty-four hours or so.

Dove nodded. Reminded herself that Fletcher was exposed, with or without her father's testimony. And that in spite of the lack of any sign that he was glad to have rejoined the living, her dad had the best chance ahead of him than he'd had since her mother died.

If he'd cooperate. Or even try to.

If he wanted to stick around to share life with her for a few years, a few decades, longer.

If they got through the next few days, she amended the earlier thought a couple of hours later when Mitchell, who'd been in and out, bringing her snacks and conversation in between his appointments, arrived in Whaler's room with a grim look on his face.

"Fletcher was taken into custody," his gaze, his tone, didn't reflect the good news at all, and she braced herself. "He admits to vandalizing the boat, hoping, since you've been completely ignoring him, to get your attention and convince you to agree to sell the place with your dad out of commission. He also admitted to the shady but not illegal way he'd convinced Hal to leave St. James Boats. But he adamantly swears he had nothing to do with your father's disappearance. Or any harm that's come to you. He has solid alibis to back up his claims—he was out deep sea fishing this morning—and his phone and financial records show no evidence at all that he's been hiring anyone else to create havoc in Shelby."

Her stomach a knot of lead, standing at the end of her father's bed in conversation with Mitchell, she stared up at his suit jacket and tie, looking all official and distant from her. "You're telling me no charges are being filed?"

He shook his head. "He'll face property damage charges. Has already agreed to have *Wicked Winnings* fixed, immediately, at his expense." He paused, and then said, "And based on signed statements, and no law allowing them to hold him in custody, his lawyer forced the department to let him go."

"What about the spit on my father's clothes? Did they get a DNA sample from him? Couldn't they hold him until they get those results?"

Mitchell just looked at her. Deeply. And she felt the crush of a hopeful day gone bad. "The ABI forensics lab ran a fast DNA test while he was in custody. It wasn't a match."

Feeling sick, wishing she hadn't eaten the tuna he'd brought her at lunch time, she said, "So he's paying cash and using prepaid phones to hire whoever is helping him."

"It looks that way."

Mitchell pulled a chair in from the hall and moved hers over next to it. Sat down. Clearly intending to sit with her. Seemingly for as long as she needed.

Dove slid down to the floor, with her back to the wall, legs in the lotus position, and closed her eyes.

If ever there was a time she needed an awareness of her spirits, of her inner ability to maintain ownership of herself and give her strength, it was then.

Because all she really wanted to do was crawl onto Mitchell's lap, feel his arms holding her close and cry.

Mitchell had Dove for another night. She'd eaten at the hospital, having ordered in, and he'd had dinner with Eli. Mostly to get his head on straight.

Older brothers had a way of homing in on any nonsense in kid brothers and knocking it right out of them.

They'd met at The Cove, mainly because Mitchell was at St. James Boats after finishing the merger paperwork with his physician clients and intended to return there after dinner as well, until Dove was ready to head home. And The Cove was close.

It was also quiet. Something he needed at the moment. The quiet. A lack of noise in his head so he could find the logic in his current situation.

That's where he'd expected Eli to come in, but the major-case lieutenant had been oddly moot on any mention of Dove St. James other than to mention how impressive her defense against her attacker had been that morning. And to ask how she was doing.

No ribbing Mitchell. And worse, no asking him what in the hell he thought he was doing with Dove St. James. Not even a mention of how out of character it was for Mitchell to be staying so closely involved with the case.

Not that he blamed his brother. With Dawn Ellis now missing, in addition to the three unidentified female bodies on slabs, Eli would be fully engrossed in the case and beating himself up to catch the killer before anyone else got hurt.

Dove had called not long after he'd left Eli and had talked about her father all the way home. Almost as though she couldn't allow a moment for any other conversation to happen between them. Because she was avoiding the possibility of more bad news?

Or didn't want to talk about whether or not they'd have sex again that night?

He studied her face when he stopped at a light, trying to figure out where she was at, but read nothing at all. Her expression was blank.

So he asked questions. Found out that Whaler had woken once before dinner. Had eaten the soft foods given to him, bitching about them the entire time, and then yelled at the game show he'd watched on the television.

Sensing there was so much more, hating that the woman was so used to dealing with every part of life alone—picturing his huge family, all leaning on each other, to the point of irritation sometimes—and wanted to bring Dove in. To let her know that she didn't have to carry the weight on her shoulders by herself.

To that end, as they neared his house, he asked, "How many times did he unload on you?"

He'd heard the abrasive greeting with which Whaler had greeted her the first time that day. Had witnessed the way she'd just taken it and then held his hand, without a single word to let him know that he'd been out of line. And had been wondering ever since if she'd grown up with that kind of verbal abuse.

If so, his respect for and good opinion of Bob St. James had just gone down the toilet.

"I didn't count," she told him, not even sending him a brief glance. Nor was she watching the world passing around them. Just kept staring out the front window. With the sun already set but dusk not fully settled in, there was still a lot to see out there.

Clearly her mind was focused elsewhere.

And he was guessing it wasn't on sex again. Not that he

blamed her for that. To the contrary, he was a little sickened by himself going there, under the current circumstances.

But eased his conscience a little bit with the knowledge that he wasn't just thinking about his own pleasure, or lack thereof. He knew he could bring the woman a good deal of pleasure—with sex. And have a chance to hold her, too, without her feeling as though she was seeking comfort from anyone.

Like doing so was some kind of mortal sin.

Her comments about sex, with her including no commitment and no expectations, were starting to sound loudly in his ears. She hadn't just been talking about sex.

Dove St. James had been talking about a way of life.

In her studio, she helped others deeply but from a distance. And seemed to live all of her life in the same fashion.

And why that should bother him, he couldn't explain. He'd tried. On and off all day. Kept coming up blank.

"He's angry with me for not bringing him a bottle." Her words fell without emotion as he pulled into his driveway.

Stopping to wait while the electric door lifted, he turned to her. "He does know that it's against hospital protocol, right?"

She glanced at him then. Seemed to focus for a moment but then looked away. "He's not in a place where he'd care even if he did know," she told him.

For a second there, as he watched the nearly comatose form sitting next to him, thinking about the way Dove normally effervesced with life, he was pretty pissed off himself.

Not at her. But at all of the forces stealing from her. Including her father.

"It's part of detoxifying," she said. "Rage, anxiety. It's what the liver sends out when it's uncomfortable."

That sounded more like her. In one sentence, she'd eased his concern about her. Some.

There was no teasing, no egging him on, not even any questions about his day or how everyone had done at St. James Boats that day. Or any conversation at all.

She hadn't even asked if Wes had been able to rent a trawler in order to fill the reservations that had already been on the books that day, and over the next month, for *Wicked Winnings*. Wes had arranged to get the boat fixed. Mitchell had paid for it, intending to add the cost to his St. James expense account when they got around to getting him officially on board.

As soon as they were home, she went to her room. He heard the bathroom door close while he was in his office. Five minutes later, heard the stairs creak as she went up. Unlike their previous nights together, he followed her up almost immediately after.

Dove was already in the bed. Her back turned toward him when he entered the room. If not for the very real threat of someone having tried to abduct her that morning, he might have convinced himself to take one of the spare rooms down the hall.

But while the police were thinking that there'd be no more harm coming against her now that Brad Fletcher had been caught—and put on warning—Mitchell wasn't so sure. Just because the man had been able to put on a convincing show for the police—and maybe his own attorney—it just didn't ring true that someone would go so far as to abduct a man, leave him for dead and then go after his daughter, and when he got a slap on the wrist, just walk away.

He wouldn't. He'd get more cunning.

Mitchell made quick work of getting himself ready for bed. And double-checked the gun he'd had strapped at his waist, under his suit coat, all day long before lodging it between the bed frame and mattress. He took one last look at the huddled form beneath the covers on Dove's side of the bed before turning out the bathroom light and heading over to join her.

It was possible that she'd fallen asleep. She'd had an incredibly draining day. He sure wouldn't blame her for wanting to check out and escape from it all. Now that she was safe, lying beside him, he had plans to turn off himself, immediately. To get much-needed rest so that he'd be fully charged to take on whatever the next day or two was going to bring.

Lying on his back, he closed his eyes. Wiped his mind clean. And listened for her breathing. Until he realized what he was doing and stopped that, too. Wondering what he could do to help her. Not financially, or legally, but one human being to another. To give her some of the same sense of support he got from his family.

He'd come up with nothing, except another reminder to himself that he wasn't sleeping, when he felt the mattress move beside him. And a very definitely feminine hand landed on top of his penis, in perfect alignment. Gently holding him while he grew beneath her palm.

He didn't speak. Didn't even turn his head. As he had the night before, he covered her hand with his own. And then found her other one, sliding his hand underneath it, the back of his hand to her palm and lifted them, together, to her breast, his palm first.

It was like a scene from some karate movie, the way their arms were at angles, crossing their bodies top and bottom. It was almost soothing. To be sharing intimacies quietly in the dark.

And it was mesmerizing, too. He didn't stop growing at

merely ready. Her nipple was rock hard, and he moved to the other one, sliding under her half shirt to do so. No longer content just to linger.

As his fingers touched her bare nipple, her hand slid inside the silk of his pajama pants, and Mitchell lost track of all thought.

They joined as they had the night before, and it was all different, too. More. Bolder. Three times instead of twice.

She only looked at him as he entered her, keeping her gaze locked with his as they rode together, and then her gaze was shut off to him.

All three times. She never spoke, so he respected her need for silence and said nothing.

When it was over, he returned to lying on his back, expecting her to turn toward the wall. She leaned over him instead, kissing him softly.

A caress which he answered with more than just his body. He wanted her to know she wasn't alone.

Lifting her lips from his she said, "Thank you, Mitchell," and then turned to her side, facing the wall.

He'd have felt used, except that he didn't.

Instead, he understood. Was glad that he'd been there for her.

And went to sleep.

Chapter Twenty-One

In a complete reversal of how she'd felt when she'd gone to bed the night before, Dove woke up Thursday morning with a sense of hope. She didn't work at accessing it, it was just there as she slid into consciousness. A positive anticipation of what was to come. With opportunities for happiness on the horizon.

Surprised to hear the shower running, she turned her head to see that Mitchell was already up. And when she made it downstairs, saw that he'd been there, too. A fresh coffee pod was in the trash. Figuring he had an early appointment, she got herself ready in record time. Pulling on the last clean outfit she had. A long green flowing skirt, topped with a tie-dyed tank top in all the colors of the rainbow with lace along the collar, and rhinestone-studded pink flip-flops. She was either going to have to go home for more clothes or do some laundry. Not having any idea what she was getting into when she'd packed to leave her home, she'd thrown in a bunch of stuff and left the rest. At the time, she hadn't been in a state of mind to plan.

She'd woken with a mind full of plans that morning, though. Brad Fletcher had been put on notice. Hopefully that bought law enforcement enough time to find their missing pieces. The man was sharp. But so was Peter Welding and his local team. With the experts at the ABI involved, the shady businessman had met his match.

And her father…she asked Mitchell to stop in town so she could grab a six-pack of warm and gooey cinnamon rolls on the way to the hospital. Her father's favorites. The doctor had warned her to expect more anger than not over the next days, but Dove knew that feeling good was a winning adversary over rage, and those rolls always made Whaler smile.

She offered one to Mitchell, a thank-you for stopping, and he smiled, too. Meeting her gaze as he helped himself to a napkin from the box, he said, "You seem better today."

In a knowing way. As though he had the secret behind her healed spirits.

Which, of course, he did. In part. The friend he'd been to her the night before…offering himself up as the source of good feeling, seemingly the only source in the world that would work for her right then, she was never going to forget.

"I am better," she said. And then, once again, said, "Thank you."

His response was a healthy bite into his roll, before heading back out into traffic. He'd dressed in jeans and a blue-checked flannel shirt that morning. "You're not going into the office this morning?" she asked.

He shook his head. "They're coming to work on *Wicked Winnings*, and Wes and Kirk are going to be involved with customers."

For a second, her spirits dimmed. On his behalf. "You don't have to give up your life for us, Mitchell," she told him. "Your work has to come first."

He nodded. "As it has a few times this week. Things are slow for me right now," he added, finishing off his roll and licking his fingers. "Might even be fate, huh?" he asked, smiling over at her.

She knew he was teasing her. Making light of the incredible amount of time he was investing in a new client who hadn't even yet signed a contract.

Her heart open wide and with an intensity she couldn't stop, she said, "I will always be here for you, Mitchell. No matter what or when."

He glanced her way, nodded.

And pulled into the medical center parking lot.

That last look had been brief, but Dove felt it to her core.

It was like he'd just returned the vow. Silently.

But she'd heard loud and clear.

It was as she'd known.

They were soul mates.

"Damn, girl, are you *ever* going to get it in your head that you aren't the boss of me?"

Mitchell paused just outside the door of Whaler's hospital room, just after nine on Thursday night, sharing a concerned glance with the officer outside his door—a young man he'd seen around town but never met.

"I'm just asking you to consider rehab, Dad. And to, maybe, talk to someone who's been through what you have, you know, just talk to them."

"You want me to go to one of those damned groups where everybody sits around and confesses and whines, and there ain't no way..."

Silence fell, and Mitchell was about to go in when he heard "I'm telling you, young woman, if you don't stop... you got no right, and I ain't gonna put up with none of your fairy crap. I've had enough, you hear? Enough!"

Mitchell had to take a moment to calm his own anger,

hearing Dove belittled that way. And by the one person in the world he was certain she loved. "Has it been like this all day?" he shared another glance with the uniformed officer, who nodded.

"She just keeps talking calmly," the man said, "cheerful and upbeat. I don't know how she does it."

Mitchell had nothing to say to that but thought of the police officer's words again a little over an hour later as he readied for bed. Dove had chattered all the way home about how much stronger and more alert her father had been that day. He'd eaten three meals, had been awake for several hours, his scans and blood work had come back better than expected, and the doctor had said that as long as he made it through the night with no trouble he could be released as soon as the next afternoon.

There'd been no further developments in their case. Mitchell had spoken to both Peter and Eli several times that day. Both of them were concerned about Whaler being on his own, prey to whoever had tried to kill him but hadn't finished the job. The man was not only refusing Dove's urgings to enter an abstinence-based program but even to go to rehab for a few days while he got more of his strength back.

She hadn't discussed any of that with Mitchell. Nor had she asked if he'd spoken to anyone. He knew she'd been getting reports, though. Peter Welding had told him that much.

He'd also heard that she'd been submissive, almost to the point of paranoid where her own safety guidelines were concerned.

With good reason. They weren't up against any deadbeat or deranged criminal here. They were dealing with a powerful, moneyed man who had connections. And above-average intelligence. At Peter's invitation, he'd watched the interview with Brad Fletcher from the day before. The man had been properly contrite at appropriate times—like when he'd been shocked to find out that Bob St. James had security cameras—but mostly he'd appeared cocky, sure of himself and not the least bit concerned. Mitchell's take-away had been that in Fletcher's mind, it wasn't a matter of *if* he'd get St. James Boats but *when*.

Glad that he had Dove safely with him one more night—knowing that he had to come up with some kind of plan in the event of Whaler's release the next day, like moving the older man in with him, too—he donned his pajama pants, leaving off the shirt, and headed into his room.

Wondering if Dove would be wearing the same light-weight pants to sleep in that she'd had on every other night in his bed. She'd asked him to stop by her place on the way home that night so she could pick up a few more things.

While he'd only seen the satchel she'd carried out of her room, he'd found himself entertaining thoughts about its potential contents. Mostly pertaining to sexy sleepwear.

The sun had set, dusk had come and gone, leaving the room in darkness broken only by the beam of moonlight coming through the window. One last check that his gun was in place as he'd left it moments before, he checked his phone and climbed into bed.

He wasn't going to reach for her. The call was hers. But he knew it was coming. She hadn't sent any sex signals. There'd been no come-on or tantalizing looks. They weren't Dove's way.

Nor his, either, he realized. He got the looks often enough from women who made it clear they were open to his at-tentions. And found them to be turnoffs.

Wide awake, anticipating, he lay there...for all of twenty seconds. He felt the mattress move. Waited for her touch on his already hard penis—eagerly—and felt her naked leg slide over his silk-clothed one instead.

Dove was the aggressor during that first encounter. Full of confidence that took him to a whole new level of hard with desire, she stripped his pants and played with him, sitting astride him, completely naked. Her exploration took them places he'd never visited. And the culmination was out-of-this-world incredible.

The second time was his turn. He didn't stop until she was writhing, begging and then crying out for release.

After they'd shared a third orgasm, he lay back, replete. For the moment. Heard her sigh, flat on her back next to him, and expected her to turn her face to the wall and go to sleep.

Wondering if he'd get a goodnight kiss as he had the night before.

Wanting it almost as much as he'd wanted the sex.

Neither happened. She didn't kiss him. Neither did she roll away.

Then he heard "We need to talk" come softly from beside him.

And Mitchell's heart sank.

THE FUTURE WAS at hand. Her father was going to be released from the hospital. She'd need to stay with him; that was a given. And, until the situation was resolved with St. James Boats, which somehow meant getting Brad Fletcher permanently away from them, they were going to need some kind of protection.

All of which Mitchell would be sure to have suggestions to deal with, she was sure. And things they could talk about in the morning. Or afternoon. With Whaler present. Or not.

She had something more pressing on her mind. An important something that could help sustain her—and please him—during some potentially challenging days ahead.

"I don't want to be done with our sex, yet."

His head turned sharply, and though she couldn't make out much of his expression, she saw the glints in his eyes pinging on her. Felt them as though he'd touched her, but not with warmth. Or cold. Just…there.

"Unless of course you want to be," she clarified. No way did she want pity. Or any kind of a one-way street.

He didn't turn away. Wasn't saying anything. So she waited. Mitchell had to choose his words. And when he did, he spoke the truth. She wanted that, his truth. No matter what it was.

"What exactly are you proposing?"

A question. With no hint to his truth. Taking a breath, she said, "That we decide, both of us together, whether or not we're done with the sex." And then, in case he needed reassurance, she said, "No commitments, other than that. No expectations. Just…we're not done yet if we both don't want to be done. And if we're together on that, then maybe some kind of arrangement whereby we actually have sex," she said. "Since, after this, we won't be meeting up in your bed at night."

Maybe she'd read him wrong. Their joining that night had been so much more than before, and she hadn't thought that possible. But maybe, what to her had been perfection, a call for more, to him had been…goodbye?

Was that what had made it so powerful? And so sweet, too? He'd been kissing her goodbye?

"No expectation, no commitment." His words, slow in coming, had her heart pounding. "How does monogamy play into that? It definitely speaks commitment. And expectation, too."

So…he wanted to have sex with her and be free to sleep with other women, too? Could she be good with that? "I've never actually considered the point before," she told him honestly. She'd never wanted enough sex repeats for the situation to arise. "So maybe we *are* done." The words sent a sliver of fear through her. But she had to say what was in her heart. What she knew to be true. "I don't think I'd be okay knowing that you're sleeping with other women at the same time we're coming together. I apologize for leading you on. I just… In my mind, sex is sacred to the moment. For however long the moment lasts."

Instead of turning his head back on the pillow to go to sleep as she'd expected, Mitchell raised up on his elbow, hand bracing his head. "I don't know about the sacred part," he said. "Can't say I'm briefed on the matter, but I agree with monogamy. It's smart. Practical. You can't control how others feel, and if another partner outside the twosome has jealousy issues or expectations, they can then become a part of your situation as well."

"The case that was just in the news about the jealous cop who killed her lover after she saw him having dinner with another woman?" It had happened a couple of towns over but had reverberated through their part of the state.

She hadn't seen a discussion of current events being a part of that particular conversation, but the fact that he was still engaged in the topic at all was filling her with joy.

He nodded, so close, his head just above hers. Making her feel, in those seconds, as though she was his whole world.

Giving herself an inner mental shake, Dove smiled up at him. Not her whole world, just a lovely portion of her current one. A gift given to her precisely when she'd needed it.

Life at its best.

"I guess, before I can answer your initial question, I need to know a little bit more about what you're envisioning." Mitchell's words cut into her celebration.

She reached up, touched his cheek. "I'm not good at planning the future in detail," she told him. "Which is why I came to you in the first place, if you remember. A business needs that kind of skill. I'm more day-to-day, going where life takes me."

As soon as she said the words, she felt his withdrawal. Or thought he withdrew. At the moment she wasn't sure which part of herself she was accessing. Mind or senses. A state of affairs that didn't sit well with her.

"Let me ask you this," he said then, his tone more one of curiosity than interview, and relaxing, she nodded.

"Do you ever see yourself getting married?"

Eyes wide she stared at him. Surely he wasn't...no. The easy look on his face, that tone—a getting-to-know-you, not something more personal—relaxed her. "Not really," she told him. "My life, being kind of an outcast in a small town, based on my own choices—choices I'm good with— just didn't lead to me seeing someone wanting to take that on. Nor could I see me giving up what I know, what I believe, how I feel and think, in order to have someone share my life with me."

When he didn't back away or show any sign of disappointment, she said, "I wasn't raised like you were, Mitchell." He was a scholarly man. Looking to understand something he hadn't yet come across. And she was suddenly eager to fill him in.

"I grew up in an essentially single-parent family, with my dad, my mom's husband, sharing time with us whenever he was around. Their marriage was untraditional, my upbringing wasn't like any of my friends'. And certainly nothing like yours. I didn't have two parents, let alone an aunt and uncle, siblings and cousins. I just had me. And I've always, for the most part, been happy. But I don't fit the socially accepted, traditional lifestyle."

He sighed. Kind of smiled. And Dove was left strangely... letdown. "How about you?" she asked then, to let him know that her differences didn't have to change anything between them. His beliefs, goals, life plans were as important as hers. She wanted to know them and would accept them without question.

"I think you already know the answer to that," he told her. "I'm more of a traditional kind of guy."

She nodded. They were opposites. They'd both known that long before they'd formally met. But, "How does that fit with us having more time together?" she asked, the question consuming her.

He leaned down and kissed her. Softly. But with hunger, too. "I'm traditional," he said, "but I'm not a fool. As long as it's working for both of us, we'll be having sex."

With that he lay down, closed his eyes and in less than two minutes was breathing deeply.

A man right with his conscience could fall asleep that easily.

With a smile on her face, Dove closed her eyes and was right behind him.

Chapter Twenty-Two

He didn't have a plan.

Not nearly enough of one, at any rate. Dove was capable of flying in the wind and landing on her feet. Mitchell, not so much. He didn't take off without the flight plan firmly mapped out, recorded and called in with responding verification of receipt.

Aviation laws were in place for good reason. Without them there would be plane crashes, with untold number of deaths, on a regular basis.

He could do the sex part. All day long. And night, too. He just needed the plan.

Pulling up outside the medical center the next afternoon, Mitchell was as tense as he ever got, due to the lack of firmly considered next steps.

Starting with Whaler's homecoming.

He'd offered his home to the old sea captain and had been turned down. Not all that kindly. The man damn well didn't need charity.

So Mitchell had paid for private security—all off-duty law enforcement—at least for the first twenty-four hours. Dove, who'd be staying at Whaler's place, knew the officers would be inconspicuously watching her father's property. Whaler did not.

She also had the head of command's cell phone on speed dial—a phone that would be on-property at all times, held by whoever was in charge any given hour. Had promised to push the speed dial icon every hour if need be. She was to report every single creak she heard in the floorboards. Even if it was because she was walking on it at the time.

Mitchell hadn't yet decided where he'd be staying. Close, he knew that much. Probably sleeping in his car. No way he was going to his place outside of town—too far away.

And there was little likelihood that Whaler was going to stay home. The man was headed straight for a bottle. Probably starting with glasses of amber liquid poured from one for him while he sat on the stool that was as much home to him as his own bed.

Dove didn't think so. She'd been adamant—with Mitchell during a phone call, and, according to her, with her father—that he was not leaving the house.

Nor was she going to let him undo the healing his body had worked so hard to do over the past week. Another couple of days and his liver would be completely detoxed. The rest, the mental and emotional healing, would take a lifetime.

She wasn't looking that far ahead yet.

Which was why she couldn't see what Mitchell already knew. Whaler had no desire to stay sober. Which meant she'd lost the battle before she'd even started to wage the war.

Seeing Whaler's truck already in the parking lot, with Welding just climbing out of it, Mitchell parked and joined the detective. As already laid out, Welding would be catching a ride back to his own car with the officer currently on duty outside Whaler's hospital room. After they led Whaler and Dove home, with Mitchell right behind the truck.

It wasn't a great plan. Or even a good one. But it was the best they could do after Whaler's very loud assertion that he had the right to make his own choices and he was damned well going home in his own truck.

How the man could be so confident that he'd be okay when he'd just spent days in the hospital after having been abducted and left for dead, Mitchell couldn't even begin to understand.

The only thing that made sense was that Whaler just plain didn't care if he lived or died. But he'd allowed the fact—mostly because it was the only way the doctor would release him, which was required in order for insurance to pay his medical bills—that he probably shouldn't drive. Dove would be in the truck with him.

She'd readily agreed to the proposed entourage.

And didn't yet know that Mitchell was financing all of the extra security. When she'd come to his office to hire him, she'd said she'd pay his bill, no matter the cost, on installments. There'd been no stipulations as to getting costs approved first. And it was up to him what line items he chose to include on that bill. As were any discounts he chose to offer.

If she thought the city was financing the locally employed police officers outside her father's home, he could choose to just leave it that way, too.

All smaller aspects of the lack of solid planning that was making him so uneasy.

While Welding waited outside, watching the area, Mitchell went in to let Dove know that her father's old truck was there and ready to go.

He walked up just in time to hear, "This is garbage! You're nothing but a whiner. Always have been. I said I want you to drop me at the bar, and that's exactly what you're going to do."

Dove had told him that the anger was to be expected. As heavy a drinker as Whaler had been, he'd be going through serious withdrawal. But hearing anyone talk to her as her father had just done…he had to make a conscientious effort to unclench his fist.

She'd told him during one of their conversations that her father had never spoken harshly to her growing up—except the time she'd been in the water without permission. And that she'd never heard him speak to her mother that way, either. Didn't mean he hadn't done. Only that he'd never verbally attacked his wife in front of their daughter.

Mitchell took a deep breath, trusting her version—that Whaler was in the throes of a medical situation and couldn't be held accountable for his rage. And put a smile on his face as he played his part in getting all of them out of there.

Whaler followed instructions, keeping himself glued to his daughter, and climbed immediately into the passenger seat of his truck, allowing Welding to help him up.

And then, looking between Welding and Mitchell, who'd seen Dove to the driver's seat, he said, "Thank you both. I'm sorry for being so much trouble."

Mitchell nodded. Glanced at Dove in time to see tears brimming in her eyes, and as he was closing the truck door heard "I'm most sorry to you, my girl. I'm not myself."

As he moved quickly to get into his own car and be ready to follow closely behind when Dove hit the gas, Mitchell was glad he hadn't decked Bob St. James back in the hospital.

Once again, Dove had called the situation better than he had.

Because she was far better at winging through life than he was.

Not a bad thing. Just a fact of life.

She'd made it all so clear the night before. They were night and day. And both were equally necessary and valuable.

They made it through the winding drive and out to the thoroughfare that would lead them to Main Street without issue. Mitchell was on complete alert. Calculating turns, counting down streets, until they got to Whaler's place, where his security detail was already in place.

A few more minutes, five to seven at most and…

Mitchell heard the loud crash before his eyes had even registered what had happened. Heart pounding, he slammed on his brakes in time to see Whaler's truck, with Dove and Whaler belted inside, rolling over an embankment. They'd been hit broadside. By a truck that had come out of a parking lot, plowing through a median and straight into them.

Adrenaline and fear pumping through him, Mitchell was out of his car and running full speed down the embankment before he heard sirens coming from above.

Dove. He had to get to Dove.

The truck lay at an angle, passenger side down. The bed was half-separated from the cab.

"Help!" Dove's scream, unrecognizable to him, but for the fact that it was feminine not masculine, propelling him through the weeds and fallen trees between him and the vehicle. Two feet away, he could see her head clearly enough to know that she was conscious. Rocking forward and backward.

He was there almost instantly, finding the roof so smashed there was no way Mitchell could get the one door accessible to him open. But the window had broken out, and he could reach in to cup Dove's face. "I'm here," he told her. "Help's on the way, and I'm going to stay right here with you until it gets here."

"Daddy," she said, tears streaming down her face. "Get to Daddy, first."

Mitchell had already taken the only glance he needed to toward what had once been the passenger side of Whaler's old truck. Thankfully, the seat was pushed back so far that Dove, trapped by her seat belt, couldn't see. The man's injuries were something that would have haunted her for the rest of her life. Whaler was clearly dead, but Mitchell didn't say so.

Holding her head with one hand, just supporting it, not moving it, he positioned himself so that she could look him in the eye. "Stay with me, baby," he said. "Help is on the way."

"Mitchell? I'm okay, get to my dad."

"It's best that I don't move either one of you," he said, finding words out of nowhere. "Just until the paramedics get here and make sure you're okay."

She nodded. Started to cry but didn't take her eyes away from him. "I can't get my door to open." She hadn't tried since he'd been there. Wasn't sure if she'd already discovered that the door was jammed shut, or was just talking off the top of her head. Heart thrumming through his body, his ears, he focused on her. Her face. Making sure that she got from him whatever she needed most.

Smiling he said, "That's because I'm leaning against it." He was hardly touching the vehicle for fear of dislodging it.

Her eyes seemed well focused. Her words were slow and shaky but clear.

And where in the hell were the…

"I'm glad you're here." Her eyes were still holding his

gaze. And he smiled, blinking back tears. "I'm glad I'm here, too," he said.

And heard voices calling just before multiple sets of boots trampled in the dirt behind him.

"The paramedics are here," he told her, pulling his hand gently away from her head.

A hand splattered with blood came up to grip his arm as panic filled her eyes. "Don't leave me," she cried.

"I'm not going anywhere, Dove. I promise. I'll be right here."

The last was said as first responders, equipped with metal cutters, pushed him aside.

And two minutes later he heard Dove scream his name.

THE LITTLE ROOM was cold. Dove didn't much care. Cold was real.

And all she had left.

As soon as she had the all clear from the trauma doctor, she'd be free to go home. Or…just go. No place felt like home to her.

Not one that existed anymore.

Not in the future.

Her father was dead. She'd known the second she'd been freed from the locked-up seat belt and could turn around.

She'd called for Mitchell. He might have been there. She hadn't seen him. She'd been surrounded by emergency personnel scooting her onto and then strapping her down to a stretcher that had been solid, excruciating wood. A spine board, she'd later found out. In case she'd suffered potentially paralyzing spine or neck damage in the crash. At the time all she'd known was that she'd gone from one hellish situation of being held prisoner into another, worse one.

Daddy was dead.

All the energy…all the hope…all for nothing.

Her bold last-ditch effort to save St. James Boats—to give her father a reason to live—had been a waste. A prompting, she'd believed.

Fantasy cooked up by a desperate mind, more like.

It would have been better for all concerned if she'd just kept out of it. Gone on teaching her little classes, believing that there was actually a way for human beings to have a choice in whether to be happy, ways to get rid of the negative energy if one was willing to work at it.

She'd really believed that the inner spirit could get messages if one could keep one's heart open to accessing them.

Right. That's why she'd just seen her father's mangled body in a vision she was never going to forget. No matter how many times anyone tried to cleanse her aura.

The kids at school, so many of the people in Shelby who'd looked at her askance had been right all along. The joke was on her.

She'd laugh if she had any humor left inside her.

The doctor had proclaimed her a miracle. Other than the obvious soreness she'd be experiencing over the next days, even into a week or two, she was fine. Cuts and scrapes, but nothing that needed stitches. No broken bones.

She'd been incredibly lucky. Escaping from the horrific accident unscathed.

Physically.

In reality, the body the doctor had been concerned about was all she had left. Her father—and the spirit through which she'd believed she lived—had both been fatalities.

At least one good thing had come of it all—she gave a brief, distorted chuckle at the fact that her poor behind-the-times brain was still trying to combat evil with anything that felt positive—at least her future was clear to her.

Something she'd never had before. The ability to look ahead with a set of clear plans from which she wouldn't sway. Within the next hour she'd take the police escort she'd been told was waiting for her to the small house she'd purchased not far from the marina, back when she had the power to make good things come to her. She was going to start packing immediately. Put the house up for sale. Cancel the lease on her studio. And let Brad Fletcher have St. James Boats.

He'd won.

She was leaving. No way she could continue to live in a town where she'd established a life that couldn't possibly sustain her. That was just plain stupid.

Coasting on hope was a pipe dream.

Mitchell had been right all along. Logic, practicality, they were all that mattered in life.

So, lesson learned. A real one, not some make-believe fairy tale.

He was there, at the medical center. Asking to see her.

She'd refused to see him. There was no point. She wasn't who she'd thought she'd been. Wasn't who he'd thought he'd known.

There were others there, too, she'd been told, but she'd waved away the nurse's words before she could tell her more. It was probably Peter Welding.

And maybe a client or two. Hetty Amos.

All of whom believed she was something she was not. They'd find out soon enough it had all been a lie.

She'd do what she could to make it up to them. Find a job and slowly begin to return all the client fees she'd collected over the years. She'd pay Mitchell, too, when she could.

It was the practical thing to do. That or face lawsuits and risk damages being awarded in amounts far greater than those she'd collected. Money to compensate for any pain and suffering she'd caused.

She'd pay that too, if she could…

But she was getting ahead of herself. First release papers. Then ride to the house she owned.

And from there, make short order of cleaning up and finding the quickest way out of town.

It was the only option she could see.

So the only one she believed in.

At least she had that. Something to believe in. Count on. That which she could see.

It wasn't a lot.

But it was going to have to do.

It was all that she had left.

All that she'd ever had.

She just hadn't seen it.

Chapter Twenty-Three

No way was Mitchell going to just walk away to leave Dove to grieve alone. He got why she'd felt like she had to make that choice. In some ways, she'd been alone since the day she was born. Her mother and father had had their bond, before her and through her, too.

And when she'd grown up, been old enough to forge her own relationships, she'd been—due to the way she'd been raised—an outcast in her own society.

The woman had understanding beyond anything Mitchell was ever going to know, but he knew one thing. In order to heal, she needed family. Lots of it.

She also needed the news he had to give her. Maybe more than the rest.

It was that with which he was armed, just before sunset that night. He'd read the note she'd had Welding give to him after she'd insisted on leaving the hospital—through a back door—on her own. The detective had already dropped her off at home before driving back to the hospital to deliver her short missive to Mitchell.

Our time is through, Mitchell. I'm not who I thought I was, nor one who, with eyes opened wide, can continue to pretend. Please believe that while most of what I said wasn't

*real, my gratitude to you was, is and always will be. I wish
you the best life has to offer. Dove.*

Whether Welding had read the note scribbled on that
back of a blank hospital prescription sheet, he didn't know.
Didn't care. Peter was a good man. Had done his job with
professionalism, compassion and seriously impressive skill.

Mitchell could hardly blame the guy for being attracted
to Dove.

In jeans, a button-up long-sleeved shirt and boat shoes,
he presented himself at her front door with her container of
leftover greens in one hand, and her satchel over his shoulder. Her suitcase was in his car, too, if things digressed rapidly to the point of her asking for it.

Neither bag was packed. He hadn't been able to look at
her things, not without tears shed. And he wasn't comfortable yet being that kind of guy. Even knowing he could be
was taking some getting used to.

She looked out the window before opening the door to
him. Applauding her caution—she didn't yet know the security detail that was supposed to have been switched from
her father's house to her own had been dismissed—he was
also patting himself on the back for thinking of the satchel
and greens as a way to get her to give him a second of her
time.

The things themselves wouldn't matter to her. Burden-
ing someone else with her mess would.

She'd taught him more than she'd probably ever know
during her time with him.

Without looking at him directly, she took the bowl from
his hand saying, "I'll wash this and get it back to you" and
then reached for the satchel.

He didn't give that up as easily as he had the container
that he only wanted back if he had her to go with it.

"They found a match for the spit on your father's shirt," he said baldly, completely unlike himself, and yet seemingly right, too. He'd rather have had his speech all thought-out, but with Dove, planning didn't work.

Living authentically did. And while he had no idea how to do that, he at least got that he had to just let it all come out of him as it willed, with no forethought.

The way her hand reaching for the strap of the satchel faltered gave him hope. The first bit he'd had since he'd seen her pulled out of the totaled truck earlier that day and had been told she'd be okay.

"With enough evidence to prove that Fletcher hired him?" she asked, not meeting his gaze, but not shutting the door in his face, either.

"No," Mitchell said and, seeing her shoulders close in, quickly added, "Because Fletcher didn't do it. Not your studio. Not untying *Ladybird*, or watching your house. He wasn't the one who took your father, leaving him out on the embankment, nor was he responsible for your near abduction." He had no idea why he was listing it all out. He just felt a need to do so.

A need driven by her. By her reactions to his words. The more he said, the more she seemed to be listening. To be taking it in.

And if there was one thing he knew about Dove St. James it was that what she took in came out right.

"Who was it?" she asked, when he sensed that he needed to fall silent. "Why?"

He didn't answer. Just watched her. And, eventually, she met his gaze. Holding on long enough to ask again, "Who? Why?"

That's when he knew what he had to say. "Can I come

in, please? It's going to look odd to your neighbor staring at us from her porch down there if I stand here much longer."

Such a Mitchell thing, concerning himself with every aspect of a situation, looking for negative consequences. And yet, fitting that him doing so got him exactly what he needed from Dove in that moment.

"Please," she said, "come in." There was no... Dove in her tone. Just propriety. He took note.

Followed her into the room just off the door. A living space with a couch, a chair. A table with a small television set. And a full wall of bookcases that had books lining it, books on the shelves in front of other books, books sideways on the edges of shelves. Books stacked in rows on both sides of it.

He wanted to smile. But couldn't. Not without Dove sharing the moment with him.

So he sat on the chair, lowering her satchel to the wood floor by his feet. She sat, too. On the end of the couch closest to him. He took that as a good sign.

"It was Oscar Earnhardt, Dove," he told her. And then, as quickly as he could, he got the rest out there for her to access it all when she was ready.

"Once I knew you were okay, I was sitting in the waiting room until I could see you, and Eli started asking me about everything I could remember from the crash."

He stopped, watching to make sure she was up to hearing such details, and saw her watching him with an intentness he hadn't seen from her before. "Eli was at the trauma center?" she asked.

"Of course." The answer rote to him. But to someone like Dove, who didn't know that family came running in times of tragedy... "He was there, first to see how you were and—" he added something he never would have admitted before Dove, or to anyone but her "—to see how I was holding up…then to get all the details he could. The entire local ABI office and of course Shelby police department were working on the accident."

She swallowed. Blinked. And though his mind told him to stop, to give her time, he trusted something deeper and kept on talking. "I remembered the truck, remembered having seen it before, at the bar…the day we saw Oscar. Welding put out an APB on his car and person, found him at the closet clinic to Shelby, compelled a DNA sample and had forensics start running the rapid DNA. Welding called another officer to sit on Earnhardt until he could be booked and headed back here to pull up every description of every crime scene, checked them against Oscar's known whereabouts during each incident, and by the time Oscar was stitched up and his broken leg had been set with a cast, Welding had the warrant for his arrest and the prosecutor standing by to press charges."

He'd skipped some interim stuff. But she had the gist of it.

"But…*why*?" Mouth open, she was staring at him. And for a second there, he had a glimpse of the woman he'd slowly begun to understand had changed him forever.

"First place, he was drunk—partially why he escaped the crash with no internal or head injuries. But after a few minutes with Peter Welding, he confessed to the rest." Mitchell paused before addressing her question. And then, when he meant to state the facts, said, "He was a man not in touch with deeper truths, Dove. He didn't understand that the power to change his life came from within himself."

She blinked. Twice. Hard. Trying not to cry. The conclusion was pretty obvious. What he didn't get was why Dove would hold back tears. It wasn't her way. And he said, "He blamed everything bad that his drinking had brought onto him on you and your dad. Your father for firing him because how could he? He drank right alongside him. And then you because his wife was your client and he says you filled her head with crap. If you hadn't done, she'd never have kicked him out or filed for divorce."

Why he was just putting it right out, almost as though placing blame himself, he had no idea. He just had to get it done. Have her hear it all at once because she was going to find out at trial, anyway.

"His wife… I never gave her any advice at all," Dove said, as though that was the key point in the moment. "She came to the studio for exercise, *quiet exercise*, as she called it. I didn't even know she'd filed for divorce until after Dad told me. I knew she was troubled. I told her I was available if there was anything I could do—more because of Dad's friendship with Oscar than anything else. But she said that Oscar needed our friendship more than she did. And that…" she paused, frowned then said, "…she'd gotten far more from me than she'd paid for." With a blank look, she stared at Mitchell, as though he had answers she couldn't access.

"I'm guessing she learned how to find her inner peace through your example," he told her. And then, for no logical reason whatsoever said, "I know I have, Dove. Before you came barreling into my office I was living a two-dimensional life. You showed me that the way I feel matters as much as how well I think. That trusting one's instincts matters as much or more as facts. That loving is far more than doing. It's living through heart as much as mind."

He was beginning to sound like a damned greeting card.

And had one more thing to say. "You mentioned once that you were led to me so that I could help you. Well, you were only partially right, Dove St. James. You were also led to me so that *you* could help *me*."

She started to sob then. Big, painful, ugly sounds that, strangely enough, sounded a bit like heaven to him. A heaven that acknowledged pain and suffering, that wouldn't stop challenges and couldn't always spare tragedy but that would be there always. With warmth, a steady hand, healing. And more joy than there would ever be sorrow.

And he had Dove to thank for showing him it was there.

SHE'D COME CLOSE to losing her way. Would never have believed there could be a time when she'd be unable to access understanding. Unable to feel. To believe.

And yet…even then…her spirits had been there. She hadn't had to believe in them. They'd been there anyway. In the form of Mitchell Colton.

Lying with him in his bed that night, Dove couldn't find the passion for lovemaking, but she found everything she needed. A safe place to grieve. To be. To breathe.

Her head on his chest, her arm around him, his arms holding her close, was as close to heaven as she was going to get in that lifetime.

"Right before the crash, my father told me that I should have just let him die and be with his wife." The memory stabbed her, but not as deeply as it had when she'd first heard the words. "He got his wish," she said softly. Wishing she understood better, but knowing that, in some space, at some time, she would.

She'd had a dark night of the soul. Her mother had taught her about them. She just hadn't recognized what was happening at the time. Maybe due to the crash. To the shock of losing her father on top of everything else. To an emotional blow out that prevented her from accessing her cortex. And maybe a dark night wasn't really dark without that total separation.

Because within the darkness, light shone the brightest.

"I want more than just sex," she said. It was truth. And she wouldn't deny it its say. She was who she was. Probably more so after all she'd been through. Had yet to get through.

Her father's funeral. Cleaning out his house. Selling his business.

"Yeah, well, you have no idea how relieved I am to hear you say that." Mitchell's response was so unexpected and sincere-sounding she raised herself up to look him in the eye.

"I love you, Dove St. James. I want more than just sex. I want a lifetime. Forever. However we can make it work. Marriage, no marriage. I don't care. Just together. A couple. For the rest of our lives."

She didn't try to stop the tears that fell. The effort would be ludicrous. But she did smile through them. A day ago, she might have struggled with his declaration. Needing to meditate over it. Right then, after suffering the dark night, she just trusted. More deeply, more fervently than she ever had before.

"You don't need to worry about the *forever* part, Mitchell," she told him, meaning far more than the single lifetime he spoke about. "I knew almost from the beginning that we were destined to travel through life together."

"You did not," he said, frowning. "You were the one who said *no commitment, no expectations.*"

"I didn't say I knew we'd be lovers or a couple. Just that we were soul mates."

Shaking his head and grinning, he said, "Soul mates. I can see I have a whole lot more to learn."

He might have. And might not. Mitchell was Mitchell. The world needed him.

But not as much as she did.

And that was as it was meant to be.

"I just figured something out," she told him.

"What's that?"

"The deepest level of truth and learning isn't inside yourself. It's in joining your deepest heart with another's."

"It's called *home*, Dove."

She kissed him then. Needing more than words. More, even, than understanding.

She needed to rest. To heal.

Because finally, she'd come home.

Epilogue

Mitchell woke up to a text message. Long after dawn had arrived. Careful not to disturb the exhausted woman sleeping with her head on the right side of his chest, he reached for his phone with his left hand.

Read the message. And knew he had to wake her up.

There were times when family was a pain in the ass. The thought was quickly quashed with another. There was never a time when family was a bad thing. Not ever.

Then he glanced at the hour and woke her up quickly.

"Dove, it's almost noon." He was texting Wes even as he said the words.

Only to hear back, immediately, that the morning had gone like clockwork. And asking how soon he could get there.

Right. About that.

He hit the bathroom. And found Dove gone from their bed when he came out. As had been their way all week.

Nervous, needing to get a whole lot done in no time at all, he cursed his overemotional, wayward tongue of the day before. And realized he was also going to have to start to accept it. The task would be arduous. Likely slow. But worth the effort.

He was a Colton, an adventurer. He knew more than most that the more effort one put into something, the more benefit that came out of it.

By the time he'd made his coffee, Dove still hadn't come out from her bathroom. Knocking on the door, he received no answer and moved at lightning speed to her room. No Dove there, either.

But he thought he heard a footstep above him.

Climbing the stairs he found her in his room, walking around naked, chomping on...a bunch of what looked to him to be grass.

Seeing him, she said, "I thought it'd be cool to shower together," she told him.

Taking her hand, he led her to the bed, handed her the clothes that she'd obviously brought up with her and laid there, and said, "As much as I want to take you up on that offer, we don't have time." He was already at his dresser, pulling out underwear.

"I have something I have to tell you."

And hurrying into clothes without a shower wasn't the way he'd wanted to go about it.

"I want to buy St. James Boats," he told her, rushing into his explanation even faster than he was getting into a pair of jeans. "You love the place, even if you don't have the interest in or the skills necessary to run it. Living alone as I have all these years and investing well, I can easily afford to give you market value plus a bonus for selling it to me without trying to get other offers. And..."

Still naked, she stood, came over to him and lifted one finger to his lips. "Mitchell, you had me with the first sentence. You can buy it for a penny. Or I'll gift it to you. The fact that you want it is of the greatest value to me."

She had tears in her eyes again. Happy tears. And in

spite of the crowd he knew was waiting for them, he took his time kissing her. Sharing his deepest heart.

Just in case she changed her mind.

And then he went right back to dressing. Hoping she'd get the hint and do the same.

He had no speech. No plan.

He would have had. If he'd woken up at dawn, as he'd done every morning since he was a teenager.

She'd pulled on panties. Was in the process of putting on a frilly purple crop top and stopped. Frowning at him. "What's the big rush?" she asked, as if only then realizing that his talk about buying her father's business had nothing to do with their need to forgo a shower for rushed throwing on of clothes.

"Wes texted," he blurted. Truth. Absolute truth. "He needs us at the marina. Something about a party that is asking for the owner's attention…" The truth. And…so much more than that.

"A customer?" The fact that she translated his perfectly normal sentence into legalese had to be a sign that he was supposed to go with it, right?

He might be aware of an inner knowledge, but he wasn't so great at listening to it yet. Or understanding if he did.

"Right," he told her. And did his best just to get himself downstairs and into his car without giving her a chance for any further conversation about the docks. He asked her how she was feeling.

Listened while she told him what she could do to ease her stiffness, her soreness. She just needed to get her oils. Some bath salts. And a diffuser.

He knew what the words meant. Had no concept of what she was going to do with them all. Asked if she'd taken the muscle relaxants or pain pills the doctor had prescribed.

And was a bit frustrated, but not all that surprised, to hear she hadn't filled the prescription before she'd left the medical center as she'd been told to do.

By then, he was pulling into the marina. Not breathing deeply. And beginning to think that he'd made the biggest mistake of his life.

He'd loved the idea when he'd heard it the day before. From Hetty Amos in the waiting room at the trauma center.

Had forgotten all about it. Until Wes's text.

But after the night he'd just spent, the conversations, the understanding he and Dove had reached…

He never should have told Eli that he wanted to buy St. James Boats before he'd told Dove. Not that Eli would break his confidence, it just hadn't felt right after the previous night's conversations. His brother knowing before she had.

He crested the hill and—holy hell!—the crowd was five times bigger than he'd heard about the day before, and…it was too late to figure out a plan.

And definitely far, far too late to avoid the consequence. For which he had no solution.

"What's going on?" Dove asked, leaning forward to stare at the hundred or more people blocking the docks from view.

For a second he thought about playing dumb. Except that he was not going to lie to her. Ever.

And his family was at the front of the crowd, waiting to show Dove St. James just how much she was cared about. Respected. And even loved.

They'd spent the morning cleaning up the marina, mowing the grass, cleaning all the boats, draping a partially repaired *Wicked Winnings* with a colorful cloth bearing angels' wings.

And loading *Ladybird* with the food they'd prepared for a family day on the water.

The rest of the crowd, he'd known nothing about.

He came up with no words to answer Dove's question. Just got out of the car, hoping she'd join him. And, taking it as a sign when she did, took her hand, linking his fingers through hers and walking with purpose toward his mom and dad. His brothers and sister. His aunt and uncle. His cousins.

All of whom walked out to meet them, wrapping their arms, their mass around them, each hugging Dove in turn.

Showing her what there were no words to say.

What apparently so much of the town had felt, based on the numbers that weren't going to fit on the boat that day but were there just the same.

Dove let go of Mitchell's hand. She cried some. Okay, a lot. She returned hugs. And she seemed to glow with a sense of something Mitchell couldn't put a name to.

Something he might not ever understand.

But when she looked at him, as she did often over the next hour before they finally made it to *Ladybird*'s deck, he fully understood the message she was sending him.

The townspeople meant the world to her.

His family's welcome even more.

But he was her soul mate.

And together, they'd always find their safe place.

Their peace.

And a love that didn't die.

* * * * *

COMING
SOON!

We really hope you enjoyed reading this book.
If you're looking for more romance
be sure to head to the shops when
new books are available on

Thursday 25th
September

To see which titles are coming soon, please visit
millsandboon.co.uk/nextmonth

MILLS & BOON TRUE LOVE IS
HAVING A MAKEOVER!

Introducing
Love Always

Swoon-worthy romances, where love takes center stage. Same heartwarming stories, stylish new look!

LET'S TALK

Romance

For exclusive extracts, competitions and special offers, find us online:

f MillsandBoon

X @MillsandBoon

◉ @MillsandBoonUK

♪ @MillsandBoonUK

Get in touch on 01413 063 232